# ADVANCE PRAISE

This tale of friendship, adventure, and self-actualization beautifully weaves elements of spirituality, Eastern religion, and vividly painted landscape. Reading this immersive story was not only highly entertaining but also very educational, illuminating the culture and way of life in India.

-Grace Mattioli, librarian and author

In *The Hand of Ganesh*, Elaine Pinkerton writes with insight and sensitivity about friendship, identity and the idea of "mother," which is not always what we expect. When Clara and Arundati, both adopted, travel to India to explore their roots, the reader is transported by Pinkerton's deep cultural knowledge and vivid details. I'm grateful for sharing the journey with these authentic, complex characters and would (happily) follow them anywhere.

– Jessica O'Dwyer, author of *Mother Mother* and
*Mamalita: An Adoption Memoir*

Elaine has a flair for writing non-harrowing adventure stories. The relationships of her characters are insightful and interesting. If you want to know about the traditions and landscapes of Santa Fe, NM and India, here they are, between the covers of one book.

—Desirée Mays, M.A. Author of
*Opera Unveiled* book series,
and lecturer to University and Opera groups

# The Hand of Ganesh

## Elaine Pinkerton

*Elaine Pinkerton*

**Pocol Press**
**Punxsutawney, PA**

POCOL PRESS
Published in the United States of America
by Pocol Press
320 Sutton Street
Punxsutawney, PA 15767
www.pocolpress.com

Publisher's Cataloguing-in-Publication
Names: Pinkerton, Elaine, author.
Title: The hand of Ganesh / Elaine Pinkerton.
Description: Punxsutawney, PA: Pocol Press, 2022.
Identifiers: LCCN: 2022935162 | ISBN: 979-8-9852820-3-0
Subjects: LCSH India--Fiction. | India--Description and travel--
Fiction. | India--Social life and customs--Fiction. | East Indians--
United States--Fiction. | Adoption--Fiction. | Family--Fiction. |
Friendship--Fiction. | BISAC FICTION / Family Life / General |
FICTION / World Literature / Southeast Asia
Classification: LCC PS3616.I572 H36 2022 | DDC 813.6--dc23

Library of Congress Control Number: 2022935162

Front Cover: **Photo by Nehaniks**, statue of Ganesh.
Rear Cover: Photo by Naushil Ansari.

# ACKNOWLEDGEMENTS

This work of fiction would not have happened without the support of friends.

Thank you, Deborah Marinelli. Ann Hosfeld, Emily Shirley, Sara Eyestone, Desirée Mays, and others for reviewing *The Hand of Ganesh* in its early stages. More than words can say, I appreciate your editorial eyes. Your suggestions helped shape the novel into its final form. Deep gratitude to Alice McSweeney, who was editor extraordinaire as *The Hand of Ganesh* made its way into the world. If a book could have a midwife, she would be it. Her careful reviews and appreciation for the characters and story helped the book along the way to publication. I deeply appreciate the support and encouragement of friends in Glow Club, a women's walking group founded in 1980 and fellow writers in the New Mexico Book Association. And above all, I am grateful to my parents, Richard and Reva Beard.

I am much obliged to friends who helped me with unwavering support and enthusiasm for this novel. Thanks to Wendi Schuller, Carly Newfeld, Kathy Shapiro, Karla Dillon, Kay Dorko and many others (you know who you are!).

*Dedicated to the world's adoptees*

It is not more surprising to be born twice than once; everything in nature is resurrection.

-Voltaire

Pinkerton has been compelled to write all her life. Much of her inspiration springs from daily journaling, a practice which she began at age 10 and continues to this day. Place in foster care toward the end of WWII, she was five years old when she was adopted by a college professor and his wife.

Ever since her teenage years, Pinkerton believes, the Indian Subcontinent influenced her in mysterious and powerful ways. She may have inherited the India fascination, she maintains, from her father, Richard Beard. Stationed in Calcutta for 18 months during World War Two, Beard sent his wife Reva presents: ivory carvings, silk scarves, intricately beaded purses, inlaid boxes, ornaments of marble. As an adopted daughter, she was very close to the Dad who'd acquired these exotic artifacts.

Beard was a college professor, teaching guidance and counseling at the graduate level, and a number of his students were Indian Americans. He would host parties for his classes at the end of every semester. Indian women students would grace the 'Beards' living room dressed in brilliant silk *saris*. To my adopted daughter, these garments were the height of elegance.

As an adult, Pinkerton traveled to India several times. The first trip was to Delhi, where she recalls seeing a magnificent white tiger in the Delhi Zoo. Carrying her infant son in a baby sling, she walked around Agra and the Taj Mahal. A decade after that initial trip, she went on a tour of the "Golden Triangle." — Delhi, Jaipur, and Fatepur Siri. In 2013, during a journey to Southern India and the shore temple at Mahabalipuram, she was inspired to write *The Hand of Ganesh*.

To learn more about Elaine Pinkerton, visit her website: *www.elainepinkerton.wordpress.com.*

# PART ONE

# THE PAST

# Chapter One
## Mahabalipuram, India

*Rocking her back and forth several times on its journey, the incoming tide delivered a child to the beach. Finally, the waves receded, their human burden laid next to gray boulders, clumps of seaweed, shells, and driftwood. The child's body was not far from a village inn, a popular venue for travelers wishing to visit the ruins of Mahabalipuram.*

*The girl struggled to rise to her feet, collapsed, and then lay, breathing with effort, in a sodden heap. In the midst of beach pebbles, she might—from a distance—have been taken for a piece of ocean detritus. Tiny and delicate, she was clad in the shreds of a coarse muslin gown. She looked to be about five years old. It was hard to tell. Waves lapped gently around the girl's splayed arms and legs, revealing dark, ugly bruises and dried blood from knife slashes. Apparently, her light brown skin had served as the canvas for a madman's rage.*

*The child regained consciousness, mentally floating, as if in the middle of a dream. She had traveled a long way and would need many hours to regain her strength. Though she had been thrown into the ocean and assumed dead, Arundati lived. Night was falling and she needed warmth. She breathed in hungrily, filling her lungs with the damp, humid atmosphere of southern India, exhaling in raspy bursts. It would be a long night.*

Chapter Two
Mahabalipuram
1815

British traveler Jonathan Dinegar Goldingham strolled along the beach south of Chennai, where he was spending his winter holiday. His cousin Elizabeth, a descendant of George Earl of Cumberland, had invited him to Calcutta, from whence Jonathan would travel to outlying areas.

He'd found the India of his dreams. Dinegar, as he was known, was happy to breathe in the cold, salty air of the sea. Southern India was a fortuitous discovery. Mahabalipuram was one of those gifts of travel that came to those with the money and leisure time for indulging the spirit of wanderlust.

As he walked, he pondered the ancient civilization that was said to have existed here 5,000 years earlier. Strains of the Bhagavad Gita came to Dinegar, and he recited aloud.

*He who neither likes nor dislikes, neither bemoans nor desires, who has renounced both the auspicious and inauspicious and who is full of devotion to me - he is dear to me.*

In his travel diary that night, Dinegar would write about the lost city under the sea, an Atlantis of Asia, the splendor of which surpassed mankind's wildest dreams. After all, Mahabalipuram's beauty was allegedly so great that jealous gods wreaked punishment on the people, their temples and all that lived in this place. Using a colossal storm, the gods covered Mahabalipuram with water to keep it forever hidden from man's admiration.

Children's voices interrupted Dinegar's musing. Native urchins scampered along the shore looking for what god only knew. Skinny little boys (were there no girls in this village?) wearing only their dark brown skin or perhaps a loincloth. They were survivors, the perennial small boys to be found in impoverished countries anywhere in the world. Young as they were, they knew that a foreigner visitor might mean a few *rupees* for them.

With innate cleverness born of necessity, the children sized up this white man. Far taller than men in their native villages. Skin a strange paleness, hair a shade not seen on any

2

head in Chennai: blond. The visitor wore a white linen suit, a vest and pocket watch. Even his shoes were white. He walked, stiff and upright, with a cane.

Rani, the tallest of the urchins and the best clothed, if loincloths could be considered dress, greeted Dinegar in accented English.

"Ah-low." He held his hands in the universal greeting of Namaste. When Rani smiled, his young face was quite handsome. What might this child want of him? What might he be offering?

Rani thrust his hand into a black pouch hanging from his waist. He held out a gray fragment of rock. Was it a pebble? A shell?

Dinegar took the bit of stone from Rani. He inspected, to learn it was a hand severed at the wrist, pocked by who knew how many eons of erosion. "Ah, I see you have a relic, my boy." It must have come from the lost city that allegedly existed on the ocean floor skirting Mahabalipuram. The more Dinegar thought about it, the more confident he felt. The relic had been presented by the sea at high tide, and this enterprising little fellow was harvesting the ocean's gift to sell.

Sensing the interest of this prospective customer, Rani began speaking English with astonishing proficiency. "*Sahib*, as you may have guessed, this is indeed the hand of Ganesh, the son of Shiva. It is I am certain arising from the ruins beneath the sea."

"Yes," said Dinegar. "I know of the lost city of Mahabalipuram. It is what brought me to your part of the world. That and the poetry of Samuel Coleridge."

Rani waved the stone hand, broken at the wrist from its Ganesh statue, in front of Dinegar. He held it delicately between his thumb and index finger. "*Sahib*, the hand of Ganesh will bring you good luck. It is rare and valuable. You will not find another. Most of the relics from Indian waters are in museums."

"But if it belongs to India," said Dinegar, "you should not have it. Surely it must be turned in to the authorities. And wouldn't I be breaking the law if I bought it from you?"

"No, no. I am allowed to keep what I find. Name your price and it will be yours."

"Well...I don't know," began Dinegar. Even as he spoke, he extended his hand.

Rani pressed the small object into Dinegar's palm.

It was such a small thing. Surely no one would miss it. With all the statuary buried under the ocean's surface, Dinegar told himself, this stone fragment was no more important than a grain of sand. After all, he mused, it would make a fine addition to his collection of shells, stones, and mysterious objects from his world travels. He relented.

"Only English money. I do not have *rupees*."

"No problem, English money. Please *Sahib*, buy." Rani tapped his mouth and patted his stomach, which looked as though it hadn't been full for a long time. This foreigner could not mistake the message. Rani would do whatever it took to make his sale. Dinegar rummaged in a pocket. He took a few shillings from his pocket and handed them to the boy.

"Good," said Rani. "Relic brings luck. Good luck."

"Ah, I understand. This hand of Ganesh may change my fate for the better. Well, I need that." By now, Rani and Dinegar were surrounded by young boys, all of whom held bits of stone or brass, all of whom wanted a sale.

Dinegar pushed them gently away. "No. Money finished, done. No."

The gaggle of children engulfed him, and Dinegar was forced to use his cane as a prod. He walked briskly away from the shore, encouraged by the fact that a strolling couple, other British tourists, were nearing them. They would serve as a distraction while he made his escape.

Chapter Three
Findlay, Ohio
April 1948

Wind blew dry leaves upwards from the earth in miniature tornados. Nurses in crisp white uniforms turned on electric lights to ward off the growing dusk, the windows of Hancock County Hospital rattled as if bursting from their frames.

The two men in Room Six of the intensive care unit were oblivious to nature's turmoil. Another battle occupied them. Richard Benet, sitting next to the hospital bed of Professor Hendrick Goldingham, was trying to converse.

"Goldie, it's Richard Benet here. I just wanted you to know how much I've learned from you. We all have. Rita sends her respects as well ... " Richard trailed off. What else could he say?

Goldingham, eyes closed and face swollen with edema, breathed weakly. Each breath might be his last.

"He doesn't have more than a few hours left," a doctor whispered into Richard Benet's ear. "He keeps talking about finding a lost city, something like "Mahabali'... we can't make it out."

"May I have a few moments alone with the professor?" Richard strained to interpret the dying man's rasping words. God knows he owed that to him. After Ph.D. Lieutenant Benet returned from his World War II assignment in India, he discovered that his instructorship at Ohio State would not be available until early '49. His beloved mentor had presented his star student with a wonderful surprise. Goldingham had arranged for Richard to spend a semester at Calcutta University as a consultant. Not only that, he'd purchased tickets for a ship passage to India. "To travel, to take a year off to relax," Goldingham suggested. "To take some time to live a little."

That's how the old man put it. He washed away Richard's arguments, insisting: "You can take a Buckeye out of Ohio, but you'll never take Ohio out of the Buckeye. Might as well wait until there's an academic opening here at the University, lad, as you and the missus wouldn't want to end up in Kansas or some unfriendly place like New York."

Outside the hospital, all hell was breaking loose. Rain pummeled the windows and thunder reverberated from every direction. Goldie opened his eyes and spoke what would be his final words.

"There's just one thing," he rasped. "The hand of Ganesh … in my desk. You must return it to the sea....to the Bay of Bengal."

A week later, the mail brought a certified letter from Goldingham's attorney granting the Benet's a generous cash gift. Thousands of dollars had been deposited in their savings account. Richard thought that there must be a mistake. However, after a trip to the bank to verify the bequest, he embraced Rita's philosophy. "Why look a gift horse in the mouth?"

Richard and Rita Benet checked into the Vajra Hotel just before tea time. The hand-carved pillars, intricate wooden arches, inlaid screens, and gleaming marble floors reminded Rita of the India she'd imagined while Richard was stationed in Calcutta: elegant settings with mysterious sitar music wafting through dim interiors. This vision reigned in her imagination even though it clashed with the word pictures Richard sent in daily letters. During their wartime correspondence, he wrote of mundane barracks and sparse army furnishings. She half listened as their "service *wallah*," a man who introduced himself as Prakesh Gupta, rambled on in excellent, crisp English.

Gupta assured them that the Vajra's schedule allowed for a rest before they were invited to come to the lobby to mingle with other guests. Hot tea, scones, and sandwiches would be laid out at four p.m.

"Of course, *Sahib*," Gupta told the Benet's in a solemn tone, as if saddened by the possibility that they might not want to partake. "It is not absolutely necessary that you socialize. Some of our visitors never enter the lounge. They stick to themselves and seem to have no desire to meet anyone else."

"But we're not like the English," Rita said. "We want to meet the other guests. My husband was an American soldier stationed in Calcutta. He lived there for two years. You might say that India was his home away from home … "

"Well, not exactly," Richard interrupted. "I was a psychologist in a military hospital. I thought India was the end of the Earth. The only home I thought of was in Ohio, a state in the U.S., and of being with my wife."

"But why are you back here if home was so much better?" Gupta asked. "It sounds as if you could hardly wait to leave Mother India." His tone was melancholy. "I suspect you do not want to be here at all."

Rita worried that the vacation was getting off on a sour note. In an effort to patch things over, she said, "Mr. Gupta, you seem to be taking offense. My husband found India fascinating, and now that he has a teaching sabbatical for the semester, we are trying to see as much as possible."

"But we have no university here," said Gupta. "We are far from the universities such as those in Calcutta."

"The University of Calcutta," said Rita, "is exactly where we are headed after our stay at your hotel. That's where Dr. Benet will introduce guidance and counseling as a new academic specialty. We came here because we wanted to see more than just the north."

"Yes, right," Richard added. "I'm particularly interested in the ruins of Mahabalipuram. I understand they're within walking distance of your hotel."

"Just a five-minute walk," said Gupta. "In fact, the tide is going out now and you could walk out after you settle into your room. That is, if you are not too tired."

"I think I just might," Richard said.

Rita yawned and stretched. "Me? I need a nap."

"As you wish." Gupta folded his palms in a gesture of *Namaste*, bowed slightly and backed out of the room. He closed the door noiselessly behind him.

"Please be careful, sweetheart," Rita told her husband. "I'll go to the room and make sure our bags are there. It's getting dark and windy, as though it might rain. I have to lie down and close my eyes for a few minutes."

Richard kissed his wife. "I can't wait till morning to see the shore. We've come all this way...Rest, dear, and don't worry. I'll be back before you know it."

The temperature had dropped and raindrops splattered Richard's face as he walked, then ran, toward the pounding ocean. Dust swirled up from the beach and made visibility nearly impossible. Making his way along the narrow beach that led to Chennai's famous temple ruins, Richard had his eyes fixed ahead, toward a lump on the sand. He ran toward it and nearly tripped over the child's body. A girl, barely breathing. He had to get her inside soon. Energized, he swooped her into his arms and began to run. It began raining harder, coming down in heavy torrents. After a dash up sandy dunes, Richard, the child in his arms, staggered into the hotel foyer.

"Help!" he called, hoping to summon the proprietor. No hotel employees in sight. Rita, however, was there, and she cried out when she saw him.

"Oh no, oh no, oh no." She stared in horror at the body. "Why did you have to go to the beach ? Why didn't you wait until tomorrow? Now look what's happened."

8

"We've got to get someone in here," Richard said. "Now!" Rita spied a bell on the reception desk and began ringing it frantically.

Richard lay the limp child on a couch and continued calling. "Help! Somebody, help!" He kneaded the girl's tiny chest and performed CPR, a skill he remembered only vaguely from a long-ago first aid class. She was breathing, but just barely.

"Mr. Gupta! There's a little girl dying! Help! Come help me."

The girl whimpered. She coughed up blood and continued to shake. Despite her cafe au lait skin, her face seemed pale. Richard grabbed a decorative shawl from a chair and used it to cover her shoulders.

Rita's bell ringing finally roused Gupta. He rushed in, wringing his hands. "Oh no, oh my god, what happened?"

"I was just out on a walk and nearly stumbled over this child and ... " Richard began. Before he could finish his sentence, they were joined by a battalion of hotel workers. One man wrapped the girl in a blanket and the entire group headed back to the room behind the registration desk.

"Come along," Gupta barked at Richard and Rita. "We must not upset the other guests." He waved his arm toward the curtain that served as a door. "You." He directed a hard look at Richard. "You must explain to the police exactly what happened. This is not good for my business. I expect you to say nothing to the other guests."

Barefoot hotel *wallahs* lifted the couch and its human cargo out of the lobby and through a curtained door behind the reception desk. The others followed. One of the bearers, much lighter-skinned than his companions, cast a mean look toward Richard. Something about that look seemed very familiar.

Rita clasped Richard's hand. "What's wrong, sweetheart? You look like you've just seen a ghost." When he didn't reply, she added "You just saved a little girl. Gupta should be glad instead of angry."

Gupta shot them an anguished look. "Shush, oh please shush. We must not alarm the other guests. This is most unfortunate and just as we are trying to get established..." He was interrupted by his eleven-year-old son Badal. The boy was always lurking nearby, Gupta realized, and craved attention that his father could or would not give. Most of the time, the father didn't mind, but now it was infuriating.

9

"Papa, can you come outside? There's something wrong with our rooster. You have to come right away." He grabbed his father's sleeve and continued his pleas.

"No, Badal, I can't do anything. Can't you see that Papa is busy? Run to your uncle's house and ask him to have a look. Please. I have a serious matter here. Go to the village. Run."

Badal left quickly and began sprinting to the tiny village outlying Chennai. As he sought his uncle, crowds of people gathered. Like a miniature town crier, he broadcast news about the curious situation at the hotel. His hearers decided they would go see for themselves and flocked to the hotel grounds to see what these foreign visitors were doing. Meanwhile, Badal continued searching unsuccessfully for his uncle.

By now Richard and Rita were in a large, messy back room with a concrete floor, shelves of office supplies and cleaning equipment all jumbled together, sleeping mats on the floor and a small hibachi for cooking. Evidently this is where the hotel staff and the Benet's would hold a vigil until the local police arrived.

News had traveled to Chennai, the southern Indian town nearest the ruins of Mahabalipuram. Mr. Gupta ordered his underlings to quell a mob of curious onlookers who'd gathered on the hotel grounds. When that proved inadequate, he arranged for armed guards to stand at the windows and doors to deter the most determined and curious bystanders. The back room filled with the "authorities," including the chief of police, all of Mr. Gupta's relatives, and Sister Mary Bernadette from the nearby British-run orphanage.

Big band music, skillfully played by Indian musicians sounded from the dining hall. Rita tiptoed to the door and peeked through the curtains. She listened as a young woman in a *sari* directed everyone to the "lovely surprise." Hotel guests were being treated to a feast and entertainment on the house, it seemed. Everyone, that is, except Richard and Rita.

"Mother was right," Rita whispered to her husband. "We really should have stayed home. The adoption we'd been waiting for was about to happen. I just know..."

"Please, Rita. Don't say anything. Some of these Indians understand English. We're strangers in a strange land. We need to just sit here silently until whatever they're doing is finished." Rita straightened her spine, pushed her back against the cement wall and tried to make herself comfortable on the bare wooden bench.

Gupta looked their way with a harsh expression, quite the opposite of his usual pleasant demeanor. A turbaned policeman, talking rapidly in Hindi, pointed a finger toward Richard and rocked his arms as though they were a baby cradle. Rita stared at him in horror.

"Oh my God," Rita whispered to her husband. "They think you had something to do with the child who nearly drowned. They're all looking at you, at us."

"Dammit, Rita. Just keep quiet." Richard was losing patience, and in spite of himself, he began to feel worried. "Of course they don't think I had anything to do with the drowning, Please. Not a word more."

Rita pressed her lips together and stared grimly ahead. Tears were forming in her eyes, but she blinked to hold them back. Richard was right, of course. Anything they said would most likely be used against them. After she regained control of her emotions, she directed her gaze toward the child.

A white-clad nun was tending the girl, getting her to take small sips of water, taking her pulse, bathing her face with a damp cloth. Two other nuns came forth from the crowd, one with a wooden cart. After much discussion with the turbaned police crew, the sisters gently placed the girl in the cart and wheeled her out.

Mr. Gupta walked over to Richard and Rita. "In just another short while, you will be able to leave. I've told Lt. Singh of the Chennai police force that you just arrived at Hotel Vajra and that you, Dr. Benet, merely rescued the child. He thought that you had something to do with her drowning."

"But that's ridiculous," Richard said. "I could have left her for dead. I did what any decent human being would have done. I don't see any reason to put up with these insults." He took Rita's hand and rose to his feet. "We are going to our room right now. Enough is enough."

"*Sahib*, you cannot go. Lt. Singh needs to question you. I will act as interpreter."

"The child, where are they taking her?" Rita asked.

Before Richard could answer, Lt. Singh walked over and introduced himself. They were ordered to follow him to the police station to answer questions. Rita tripped several times in the sandy ground before finally giving up and taking off her spectator

11

pumps. Richard held her arm for stability as they scrambled to keep up with Singh.

After twenty minutes of traversing rough terrain, they reached a white stucco building in the middle of a dirt field, apparently the police headquarters. In the style of many Indian buildings, there were no panes in the windows. Looking oddly oversized was a heavy metal door. A small man whose desktop nameplate announced Mr. Bish Chatterjee stood up as they entered.

"I'm sorry that we must interrogate you," he said. "We have had several of these grisly murders lately and the villagers are in an uproar about it. Someone is kidnapping, beating and then drowning young children."

"But this child wasn't dead," Rita said. "She was weak but still alive when that nun, Sister, sister..."

"Mary Bernadette," filled in Lt. Singh. "She runs the Chennai orphanage a few miles from our hotel. She'll keep the child there, see that she gets proper medical attention, and then she will try to find the family."

"Is she the only victim that survived the ocean?" Richard asked.

"Yes," said Mr. Chatterjee sadly. "The four before her were dead by the time anyone found them."

Richard and Rita were still standing and Lt. Singh suddenly appeared to notice.

"Sit down, sit down," he said, waving a hand toward the offices spindly furniture. Richard and Rita gratefully accepted the offer. Rita leaned over, brushed the dirt off her feet and slipped her high heels back on her bare feet.

"What a hideous situation," Richard said. "We just arrived, and I walked out to the beach for some fresh air. All I did was carry the child inside. Surely you don't think I had anything to do with..."

"You must be quiet," said Singh. "Mr. Chatterjee is in charge of this investigation and anything you say that is out of order could be used against you. We suspect that American tourists may be involved in these abductions, and you are an American who had direct contact with one of these victims."

"We are visitors," blurted Rita. "We don't even know anyone here, and actually my husband is a professor at Calcutta University. We just wanted to see the ruins."

12

A look from Richard put an end to her explanation. It was clear that anything she said would only make matters worse. She looked ahead stonily, trying not to cry but nonetheless feeling her eyes burn from unshed tears. Richard squeezed her hand and leaned gently against her, a silent communication. She knew how much it hurt his pride to have her so worried.

Chatterjee walked out from behind his desk and stood in front of Richard and Rita, who sat uncomfortably in two rickety wooden chairs. He fingered his handlebar mustache and then placed the fingertips of both hands together in a professorial manner. Richard thought of how much he resembled someone at Ohio State, one of his advisers whose name escaped him. Like the advisor, Chatterjee was pompous, obviously taking himself very seriously.

"What brings you to India, Mr. Benet?" began Chatterjee. "And more importantly, what brings you to Chennai and Mahabalipuram? Most visitors from America visit northern India. It is very unusual to have tourists in Tamil Nadu. People want to see the Taj Mahal and Fatepuhr Sikri, Jaipur, and maybe Benares, but nothing south of those sites."

"I'm a visiting professor at Calcutta University," Richard answered. "My classes do not begin for one month. Once they do, it will not be possible for me to get away long enough to see other parts of India. I'd read about Mahabalipuram and wanted to see what little can be observed above the water."

Chatterjee looked startled. "You know about Mahabalipuram? How did you find the information? It's off the tourist map and of interest only to scholars of ancient India."

"Actually," Richard said, "it was of great interest to a British traveler named J. Goldingham in the early 1800s. He wrote about the six temples submerged under the ocean and a seventh standing on the shore. The possible existence of an entire underwater city fascinated him."

Rita sighed wearily and seemed to be having trouble staying awake. Richard turned, bringing her into the conversation, to keep her from falling off her chair.

"Remember, dear, when we read the myth about the ruins?"

"Yes," Rita said. "It was said that the city was so beautiful that the gods were jealous."

Chatterjee forgot for a moment that Richard and Rita were the enemy. He warmed to the subject. "The gods were so

13

jealous they sent a flood. It swallowed the city up entirely in a single day."

"The reason I got so interested in Mahabalipuram is that one of my professors talked with me about the ancient seaport and the mystery surrounding it. He always longed to see it, he told me. When his health failed suddenly and it was clear that he would never realize this dream, he gave me the means to do it for him. It was his dying wish."

Richard did not add the real reason Goldie had enabled him to visit Mahabalipuram. The old man desperately wanted a relic, the hand of Ganesh, returned to the waters of India. Not even Rita knew about the artifact. So far the statue fragment had brought him only bad luck. Even before he had a chance to unpack it, it led him to stumble upon an abandoned child and now he was being held suspect in a possible abduction. Ironically, he did not have the fragment with him. He wondered if his suitcases were being searched as he sat here being interrogated.

"And...?" Singh directed a piercing gaze at Richard. "*Sahib*, you are not telling me the whole story. It does not make sense that a dying man would give away a fortune so a friend could see a historic site after he's dead and gone."

"But it's not just any historic site," Richard said. "Mahabalipuram is the stuff of legends, like the Lost Atlantis in our culture. The myths say that its beauty was so great that the gods, in their jealousy, covered it with the ocean, and so it was lost and forgotten for centuries. A tsunami recently uncovered it. Unfortunately, no sooner was this 'Lost Atlantis' revealed than it was lost again, many leagues under the sea."

Rita, sensing Richard's anxiety, reached over for his hand and held it gently. She moved closer, as much as she could without scraping chair legs along the cement floor. She willed Richard to tell them everything, anything -- just so they could get out of this terrible place, out of Chennai and back to the safety of Calcutta. What a strange thing, to think of Calcutta as a "safe haven." It was all relative.

Singh persisted. "You are not telling me everything. What was the real reason you came here? We have reason to think the heinous kidnappings are being run by an illegal adoption ring. Do you and your wife have children?"

"Well," Rita answered. "Not yet. We have registered with an adoption agency back home in the United States." Richard's glare told her that once again she'd said too much.

14

Chapter Five
Chennai
Orphanage


Stomp.
Stomp.
Stomp.

Arundati was dreaming of her village when the sound awakened her. She opened her eyes to a dark room. She was on a hard bed covered with scratchy material. The smell of sweaty, unwashed bodies of other children filled her nostrils. She heard breathing. A whimper, snoring, some muffled cries. The creaking of a door.

More heavy treading. She shivered. Her stomach growled. She couldn't remember when she'd last eaten. The footsteps grew closer. It was probably the big person who ran this place. Probably he or — or was it she —was not going to hurt her, but just to be safe, the girl kept her eyes tightly closed. If Arundati couldn't see them, maybe whoever it was wouldn't notice her.

Uneasily, she drifted back to sleep. The dream resumed. She was back in the village. Auntie Parvati brought the bad news that both of her parents were not coming home. She was ordered, none too gently, to collect whatever she wanted to take with her. They had to leave before the tide came in and took away the cottage.

"The whole village will be underwater by nightfall," Auntie lamented. "The gods are angry and the ocean wants to swallow us. Hurry, child, we do not have a moment to waste." When Arundati asked what had become of her parents, Auntie told her the harsh truth.

"The tide capsized their boat and they were too far out to swim to safety. My brother was fishing nearby and tried everything to rescue them, but it was impossible. I'm sorry, but they are no longer living." At the time, Arundati heard the words but they were just sounds. It was impossible that she would never again see the gentle mother who sang to her and braided her hair, who told her to smile and stand up tall. Nor would she ever hear her Babu, the fisherman who put food on the table and a roof over their heads.

The scene of her dream shifted. She and her cousins were playing from the roosters' first crowing until the sun painted the

15

sky scarlet and gold. They played hopping and skipping games. They sang and danced. Arundati made a drum from a tin can she found in the rubble that lay in piles around the *basha*.

One morning Auntie's brother Apu came to her before *cockadoodledoo* sounded. "Arundati, wake up. Wake up. Your husband is dead. You are a widow."

"A widow? What's that?"

"I'll explain, but we have to go now."

"Where, Babu? I like it here. You and Auntie are my parents now."

"No, Dati, we are not your parents. Don't you remember getting married?"

As they talked, uncle hurried her to the waiting cart. Two workhorses stomped and snuffled, eager to be moving. Auntie gave her a white bundle with a clean *sari*, her ball, some beads, and a small statue of the Hindu god Ganesh. She was weeping as she hugged the girl and kissed the top of her head.

"We are doing what we must," Auntie sobbed. "You must go live with other widows. We cannot feed you, dear. It is God's will..." She broke off, weeping.

"But I don't remember getting married," protested Arundati. "How can I be a widow? I don't want to go live with the widows. I want to be here with you and my cousins. I want my puppy." She began to wail.

Uncle put a firm arm around her tiny frame as she struggled to get off the cart. With the other hand, he led the horses along the dirt road leading out of the village. Auntie Parvati ran after the cart with Tara, the soft hand-stitched toy she'd sewn for her niece. It was half baby doll, half puppy and Arundati never went anywhere without it. She ran faster, as the horses were picking up speed.

"Here, my sister's daughter. Here, Arundati, is your little Tara doll. May you keep each other safe."

Men on bicycles, camels with decorated saddles and their noses held high, taxis, trucks with gigantic loads that wobbled from side to side: all jostled around the cart holding Arundati and her uncle. He had to worry about not getting hit by the traffic, no time to talk to the girl. She started to tell Tara a story.

"Take a nap," uncle said sternly. "The *ashram* is very far away and you should rest. I must try to cover many miles today, as I promised to take the cart back to the mayor in just two days."

Curled up on the cart's rough wooden floor, she held the rag doll toward her, whispering. "...and Tara, your new home will be so nice. There are only ladies living there, women whose husbands have died. I think you must have had a husband once, a doll husband and he drowned one day when he was out fishing. Don''t cry Tara, I will take care of you." Before she could say another word, Arundati drifted off to sleep. The next thing she knew, the cart had stopped and her uncle was shaking her shoulder.

"Are we at the new home, Babu?" she asked. It didn't seem like anything, as darkness was all around them and there was no sign of a building anywhere. They were at the side of the deserted road.

"No, *Datiji*, we have to stop and let the horses rest. We will find a place to camp for a few hours and then start up before dawn. If you're sore from sleeping on the wagon, I have some quilts and I can make a bed for you on the ground. That will be safer, anyway. Uncle has to rest as well. I'll be very near, near enough to make sure you're safe."

Arundati sat up and felt on the wagon bed for her doll. She nearly panicked, but finally found the ragged scrap of material by feeling for its round stuffed head. "Uncle, I'm hungry and I'm cold." She started to cry but when she saw how sad and beaten her uncle looked, she rubbed her eyes and willed herself to be brave. That's what Auntie told her, to have courage. "Whatever happens, remember how proud I am of you, and be a big girl."

It wasn't so bad sleeping on the ground, and she did feel safe under the wagon. She could hear the horses snorting and nickering, and before long, uncle's snoring blended in with the songs of crickets and frogs. She was back in the village next to the stream where they washed their clothes and themselves. Her friend Chitra sat next to her as they beat the dirty clothes against rocks to clean them. The laundry was their assigned duty and it also gave them a chance to laugh and joke about the tailor who had just moved into their village. He was short and ugly, like a toad. He walked with a limp, as one leg was malformed and dragged after him. They would walk behind him, imitating his gait and making faces. One time the tailor turned around and accosted them.

"I'll cut out your tongues if I catch you following me ever again," he growled. "Don't you dare make fun of me. I'll report you to the elders and your families will suffer." To emphasize his threat, he reached his hands out like claws -- as if he intended to strangle them. The girls ran away crying and laughing.

The tailor had followed her home and was pulling her by one arm. "I'm taking you to your mother. We'll see what she says." Arundati escaped from his grasp, but in seconds he reclaimed her. She kicked and screamed, but he dragged her roughly behind him.

When she awakened from the dream, it was not the tailor who had her arm, but a rough, dirty stranger. He was taking her from under the wagon.

"Help, Babu, help," she called to her uncle.

"He can't help you," the stranger said. "He is dead."

Chapter Six
Chennai

Three a.m. found Richard and Rita still seated in the concrete floored hut, captives of the Chennai police. For the past hour, Richard had been explaining that his deceased college professor gave him an artifact, a stone hand of Ganesh, to throw back into the ocean, that he and his wife had no other reason for being here in Chennai except to sightsee.

"And what about this stone hand," asked Singh? "Where is it? Do you have it? If you would just hand it over to me, I will give it to the proper authorities."

Richard hesitated to answer but finally admitted. "It is somewhere in our luggage but I can't locate it. With finding the child and all the commotion that followed, there hasn't been time to look thoroughly enough and..."

The Indian interrogator cut him off with a clap of his hands, as though he wished to be rid of the whole matter. "I am not sure that there ever was a hand of Ganesh," he said, "and I will be late for my next appointment unless we conclude immediately. There will be more questions and you are not to leave the area until further investigation by my office.

"However, this is enough for tonight. Go back to your hotel. Get some sleep, enjoy the sites, but be prepared to come back in two days," he said. "To repeat, I find this hand of Ganesh story a bit fantastic. Before you throw it into the sea, I or another authority will need to see it. It may be valuable. I will check with the Department of Antiquities and if they wish to have it, you have no legal right to keep the relic."

Richard started to protest, but one pleading look from Rita, and he stopped. She was pale and slouched. Tears glazed her eyes. "Fine, Mr. Singh. We will not perform the relic mission until you grant your OK. My wife and I will stay here for another few days until your investigation is complete."

"But Richard, what about Calcutta University?" Rita asked. "The semester starts in a week. We can't be here too long."

"*Memsab*," said Singh. "I think that you should not have come here in the first place. Southern India is not a good place for visitors. The people here are not used to tourists, especially tourists who might want to adopt Indian orphans."

"But Dr. Benet rescued the girl," Rita protested. "He kept her from dying on the beach. Your insinuation is outrageous! How can you think..."

"We will see," said Singh. "And now I will have my servant see you back to your hotel."

He summoned a skinny black man dressed in a white *dhoti* and handed him a lantern. Speaking to the man in Hindi, he waved the entourage out the door into a humid night. As if remembering that the Benet's were, after all, guests of the local hotel, he softened his tone. "Please do not worry. This is not a hostile country, and you will probably have no problem with leaving in a few days. It is just that we have had too many children captured and dying, and it is my job to get to the bottom of this. No one is above suspicion until proven innocent."

After what seemed like an eternity, Richard and Rita were back in their room at the Vajra. The beds, two singles though they'd requested a double, had been turned down, and a single lamp on the night stand had been left on in a gesture of hospitality. "Surreal," Richard murmured, just before sleep took him.

Noonday sun poured through cracks in the wooden window shutters. A DO NOT DISTURB sign that Richard carefully hung from their doorknob had apparently been ignored. After a soft rapping sounded from the hall for several minutes, the two Americans opened their tired eyes.

"What? Who's there?" Richard called out. He pulled on his trousers and stumbled to the door. He patted Rita's shoulder as she turned to her side and put a pillow over her ear. When Rita got exhausted, she got sick. He wasn't feeling too well himself. His throat was raw and sore, and he felt feverish. "Dammit," he hissed. "I'm coming, I'm coming."

The knocking continued, louder and more insistent. Rita raised her head from the pillow and leaned on one elbow. "I'd better help you. They ignored the sign on the door. It seems like they're not going to give up."

"Go back to sleep, Rita sweetheart. They probably just want to make up our room. I'll take care of this." He was relieved to see Rita turn on her side and pull the cotton sheet over her head. She knew how much she needed to avoid exhaustion. Teaching in an elementary school, the job from which she'd just retired, had taught her that exhaustion led to illness. She did not have time to be ill.

20

Richard opened the door and stepped out in the hall to deal with the overzealous cleaning staff. Instead of a uniformed sweeper or cleaner, however, the man who'd awakened them was a bureaucrat of some sort, dressed in a worn navy suit and starched white shirt. The outfit looked impossibly hot for the southern India climate. People in this part of India seemed oblivious to the heat.

The Indian handed Richard a small white card that read "Dr. Kajol Ghosal, Ph.D. Dept. of Antiquities, Chennai, Tamil Nadu, India."

"My wife is not feeling well," Richard volunteered, looking at the card. "What can I do for you Mr. Ghosal? We just arrived yesterday, when I rescued an Indian child from possible drowning, and we were kept up all night by a ridiculous interrogation. We are here on vacation and I was hoping that today we could be left in peace."

The Chennai official frowned. "It's Doctor. Doctor Ghosal. I've been informed that you have one of our ancient relics and it is my job to see that it is examined and possibly added to our museum collection."

"Oh. It's just a fragment. We were cleaning out drawers from a colleague's attic and came across a hand-shaped rock."

"What do you mean, cleaning out?" Ghosal asked. "And who are the we to whom you refer?"

"I am a university professor. A faculty member died and there were no next of kin. We were preparing the house for an estate sale."

Ghosal frowned. "Please get to the point."

"Yes," Richard said with a calm he did not feel. "One member of the faculty, my Indian American friend, said that the stone fragment looked like a hand of the elephant god and should be returned to the waters of India. As I was planning to teach for a semester in your country, I volunteered."

Ghosal's brow wrinkled. Obviously, Richard's explanation left him baffled.

"Too much, Sahib, to explain. But trust me, it's of utmost importance that it be thrown back in to the ocean from which it washed ashore. That's why I came here, to accomplish a mission."

Rita awakened, pulled on a long silk robe, and walked up behind Richard. She'd evidently heard the conversation for some

21

time now. "A relic?" she asked. "What's this about returning to the sea?"

Ghosal looked at Richard with raised eyebrows. "I thought you said the relic has been in your family for many years. Your wife doesn't seem to know anything about it. I have to wonder if you are making this whole thing up. Why not just let me see this so-called hand of Ganesh and we can then decide about ownership?"

Rita pushed out from behind Richard. "Dr. Ghosal, please just go away. My husband has done nothing wrong and we are here on vacation. After last night we are exhausted. Can't we meet about this tomorrow?"

Ghosal regarded the tousled American woman, her brown wavy hair rumpled, her cheeks flushed, and was convinced of her honesty. About the husband, he was not so sure. He did want these foreigners to think well of him and of his country, so he relented.

"Since you put it that way, *Memsab*, I can let it go for today. But I must ask the local police to put a restraining order on you until we get to the bottom of this matter. Please try to have a pleasant day, and report to the Tamil Nadu district building at 0900 hours tomorrow morning. I will be there to meet you."

At last the officious Indian left. After Richard closed the door, he turned around to find Rita sitting in the corner armchair with tears streaming down her cheeks. He rushed over, sat on the arm of the chair and put his arm around her.

"Sweetheart, don't cry. I'll explain everything. We'll take care of this, go back to Calcutta University, and never mention Mahabalipuram again."

Rita sobbed louder, then finally found her voice. "What relic was that dreadful man talking about? Why did you lie about it? Why didn't you tell me? I can't believe you'd..."

"Keep something this important from you?" Richard finished her sentence. He took her hand, as though she were a child, and looked deeply into her brown eyes. "OK, Sweetheart, prepare yourself for a long story." And so Richard explained the "gift" from Professor Goldingham and its accompanying caveat.

# Chapter Seven

The next morning, mysteriously, Lt. Ghoyal announced to the Benet's that the case against them had been dismissed. The two Americans would not be held for questioning. Someone from the Ministry of Archeology might contact them, but even that was unlikely.

"You see, my darling Rita, my professor's gift of this trip had strings attached. Yes, we'd have the money to travel to India but in return I am supposed to return the relic to the sea. For some reason, it doesn't seem to be in my luggage, but I imagine it will turn up. But for now, let's celebrate with a walk along the shore."

The blazing Indian sun beat down on them as they walked barefooted on fine golden sand. Ahead, to the south, loomed Mahabalipuram, the stone temple they'd read so much about. Rising up out of the green-gray ocean, it looked like a cross between a pyramid and a petrified skyscraper.

"So this hand of Ganesh was cursed?" Rita asked. "Was, or still is?"

Richard paused to dig his toe into the sand. He bent over to pick up the shell he'd unearthed. Seeing that it was just a jagged half, he tossed it back into the water. "We're here to end what my professor called a curse by returning it to the source. Somewhere in the depths, according to Professor Goldingham, there's a statue of Ganesh that's missing the hand from one of its arms."

"You mean that the professor wanted to set things right," asked Rita, "even after his death? Why would he care? Would the curse be passed down to his descendants?"

"Well, I guess so," Richard said. "All I know is the this was very important."

They were only ones on the beach. Despite efforts by a few local business men, the Tamil Nadu region had no real tourist industry. Visitors to India from America and Europe went to Delhi, Agra and Fatepur Sikri. Who would think of traveling to the southern tip of the subcontinent?

"Whew," exclaimed Rita. "We've been walking for half an hour, and the temple looks as far away as when we started. I think it's receding as we advance."

"I have to take pictures," Richard said. "I want to prove that we were, in fact here. I promised Goldie I -- we -- would fulfill his dying wish. We've talked about this..."

23

Seagulls circled overhead, dove into the ocean for food, and quickly regained altitude for better fishing. A single cloud passed over the sun, making the air temporarily cooler. "OK, dear. I'm sorry to keep harping on this. I thought you said that the curse needed to be removed so the professor's progeny wouldn't be punished forever. He seemed to be a lonely figure, a man without children or family."

"Goldie didn't have any direct descendants, but he did have family," said Richard. "He told me of a niece in Columbus who was going to have an estate sale and give the profits to Findlay College. He asked her to start a scholarship in his name. He told me that we could have anything of his we liked, but he wanted me to be sure to get the hand of Ganesh, which was in his top dresser drawer, and to deliver it back to India."

"So is that what you were searching for the day you said you had to go through the professor's home office? I thought it was to find his papers about what he was leaving to the college." Rita shook her head. "You never mentioned an Indian relic. If I'd been along, I would have told you to leave it there, not to get involved."

"Sweetheart, don't you remember how I asked you to please come with me...

" ...and look through a dying man's belongings?" Rita finished her husband's question, trying not to sound annoyed. "It just seemed too morbid, and I felt that Goldie's relatives were really the ones who should have been doing that."

"You know, Rita, we've been over and over this, and I've apologized about keeping you in the dark about the inheritance. You know how I feel about your parents' dislike of me. They've never once felt that I'm good enough for their daughter. I wanted to be the provider, to prove them wrong."

You're right, Honey," Rita said. "We're here to enjoy the shore. I'll change the subject."

A sudden wind churned the ocean into whitecaps. Rita scampered inland to avoid being splashed. She wasn't quick enough, however, and her slacks were wet from the knees down. "It's refreshing," she laughed. "Maybe we should have planned to go swimming."

Richard took her arm and led her away from the surf. "There might be sharks in the water, and I didn't bring you all the way here to lose you. I think the hotel has a swimming pool. We can try it out when we get back."

24

Rita said nothing as they trudged on toward the ancient stone temple. Richard held her hand and gave her a worried look. "Isn't that OK, Darling? It just wouldn't be safe to go into these waters, and not just because a little girl washed up from the sea. We'll look around the temple and then head back in time for lunch."

"The hotel gives me a bad feeling," Rita said. "Even if they have a pool, and we don't really know if they do, I have no desire to go in. Frankly, darling, I'd like to get out of Tamil Nadu as soon as possible. At least in Calcutta, we'll have your academic colleagues to talk with."

They'd reached the towering, pagoda shaped monument that they'd been walking toward for the last hour. They stood, not speaking, craning their heads upward taking in the monument's height. Stone tiers, a golden brown, reached far above anything around them, three times the towering palms. The tide was in, so they would not be able to walk up to the base, a plan that Richard had outlined before they left.

"Rita honey, I feel like I'm standing in the presence of a god," said Richard. He waved Rita to one side of the ancient behemoth. "Stand over there and I'll get your photo with the temple in the background."

Rita obliged, smiling into the sun and trying not to squint. The ocean breezes blew her hair into her face and sand into her eyes. "Hurry, I can't hold this for long," she called out.

Just as Richard was about to snap a photo with his box camera, a dark-haired man in an expensive European suit, walked between Richard and Rita. The suit looked far too hot for the sunny September day. The man held a slender hand out toward the camera. "Here, let me get both of you in the photo," he offered. "I'm Mr. Sathiamoorthy, local journalist, and I'm here doing a story on Chennai and the region's growing tourism business. I couldn't help but see you walk out from the Vajra."

"Why, that's kind of you," said Richard. "We'd love to be together in a photograph." He handed over the camera to Sathiamoorthy and walked across the sand next to Rita. He put his arm around her shoulder.

"Call me Sati. Sathiamoorthy is quite a mouthful unless you speak Hindi." Sathiamoorthy waved his hand toward ocean. His gesture seemed oddly exaggerated to Richard, as though the man was shooing away a swarm of mosquitoes. But during his

25

India time, serving in the war, he learned that he could never trust his interpretations of native expressions or gestures.

"OK, a little further out toward the temple." By now the Benet's had left their shoes and stockings by a small shrub far enough inland not to get washed out to sea. Richard rolled up his trouser legs. They were into the water mid-calf.

"Now we can prove we were both here at the same time," Rita said. "We're ready any time," she told Sati. "Hurry, please, the salt in the air is stinging my eyes."

The Indian snapped three or four pictures, having Richard and Rita move first to the right, then the left. When he was done, he gave them his business card and offered his services as a guide. Richard started to refuse, but a pleading look from Rita stopped him.

"We have to leave for Calcutta, so there's not time to explore," Richard said.

"All the more reason to take advantage of Mr. Sathmurthy's offer," said Rita.

"That's Sathiamoorthy," corrected their new friend. "Sa-thee-uh-moor- thee. There's more to the ruins than just this giant temple. Follow me."

They walked under the shadow of the great monolith to a knobby granite boulder protruding from wet sand.

Their guide stopped and so did they. "Now this may look like an ordinary beach pebble, but it is actually the top of a granite lion. My grandfather was here when a storm washed away so much sand that the coastline receded. He told me about the lion as well as gigantic reliefs hewn from the stone. These merely hint at the seaport city that's been buried by the ocean."

The three of them stood looking down at the top of the lion's head, temporarily speechless. Waves pounded the shore like an ancient drumbeat and they each seemed lost in private thoughts.

"My gosh," exclaimed Richard. "It boggles the mind. We're actually standing above Mahabalipuram, the ancient metropolis that fascinated my professor!"

"So," queried Rita, "before the present city of Chennai, there was an earlier port city here... How old do they think it is?" They were walked briskly as they chatted.

"Actually," said their guide. "They've dated Mahabalipuram back to the seventh century. The architecture is

Dravidian. A travel writer named J. Goldingham visited here in 1798. His journals refer to the town as the Seven Pagodas."

Richard turned around suddenly and faced Sathiamoorthy. "Did you say Goldingham?" he asked. "That's the name of my faculty adviser back in America. Or was, I should say. He recently passed away."

"Maybe they're related," said Rita. "That would explain..."

Richard gripped Rita's hand, as if to say, "what you say." He didn't want to explain their real reason for being here, to return the hand of Ganesh. It was bad enough to have aroused the suspicion of local authorities. Who needed yet another Indian snooping into their private mission? He would redirect the conversation.

"Something really odd happened the first night we were here," said Richard. "I was walking along the shoreline, just before the rainstorm, and came across a little girl nearly drowned. She was on the beach, washed in by the tide. I carried her into the hotel and the manager took her away. I haven't heard anything since."

"The hotel seemed to think Richard had something to do with kidnappings, abductions, something like that," said Rita. "It was horrible. We'd done nothing wrong, but it was almost like we were immediately suspected." She looked at Sati for an explanation.

"Ah, kidnapping. Ah, yes. *Sahib* and *Memsab*, there is a sinister racket going on in Tamil Nadu. Children, orphaned or abandoned, have been taken from Ottery and Pulianthope, labor areas in Chennai."

Photos taken, the Americans and their Indian guide had turned back toward the hotel. Now that the topic had turned to lost children, Sati apparently gave up the idea of being a tour guide. He seemed full of information about this scandal involving Indian children.

Sati continued, warming to the subject. "There is a rash of abductions from mostly poor families."

"Possibly there's a child snatcher on the loose," said Rita, "a heartless brute who's making a profit by preying on those too young to defend themselves."

Sati clicked his tongue in agreement. "Yes, *Memsab*, I'm afraid you are right. We do have such a criminal element in India. They are *goondas*, men gone bad and making a business of illegal

27

activities. It used to be that just Calcutta harbored such unsavory types, but I'm afraid they are now branching out -- even this far south."

"What exactly happens to these children?" asked Richard, although he was afraid to learn the truth. He'd learned more than he'd wanted to, and he knew from official reports that some of the prostitutes had barely reached puberty.

"The authorities maintain that they are adopted by childless couples," said Sathiamoorthy, "through a middle man or an agency. The purveyors of children are paid large amounts of money by people in Australia, the Netherlands, Norway, even the United States."

"So the children at least go to caring homes that want them?" Rita asked. She was particularly interested in this topic, as she and Richard, unhappily childless, hoped to adopt and start a family. Lately they'd talked of little else.

They were within half a mile of the hotel. The sun had gone down quite suddenly and the tide was coming in with huge crashing waves. The color of the sea had gone from olive green to deep gray, almost black. The whitecaps contrasted dramatically with the darkening sky. Sathiamoorthy coughed, then said, "Well, not always. Sometimes the older girls are sold for evil purposes." He broke off, not sure how to state his meaning delicately.

"Oh no, you mean..." Rita began. She couldn't finish.

"But we are at your lodgings," the Indian said. "I'm afraid I haven't told you everything about the lost city hidden in the sea bed. I would be happy to pick you up at your hotel first thing in the morning. We could go into the stoneworker's area of Chennai. The artisans who live here have practiced their craft for centuries, from father to son, on and on. I think you will find it quite fascinating."

"Very kind of you, Mr. Sati," said Richard, "but we have to talk to the archeology office tomorrow about a relic that I brought back to India for a friend of mine. I'm afraid that it will take much of the morning, and after that, that..."

"Interrogation," volunteered Rita.

"After that, we must hire a driver to take us to Calcutta University, where I have a post with the psychology department." Richard held out his hand to the Indian, who did not take it. "We are very grateful for your kindness."

Sati looked crestfallen. He folded his hands in the gesture of *Namaste*. "As you wish," he said dolefully. While speaking, he

28

backed slowly out of the room. Was he really being deferential? Was this a show of respect for the Benets? Was there a touch of irony in his tone? Impossible to tell.

"Wait," Rita called out impulsively. "There is something else you could do for us. Is there any way we can find out what happened to the little girl?"

Sati immediately perked up. "You mean the child on the beach?"

"Yes," said Richard, afraid that Rita would say too much about the suspicion that seemed to accompany his rescue.

"Yes," said Rita. "We -- I -- I'd just like to see how she is. You see, we don't have any children yet, and we like children a lot. I'm a schoolteacher and..."

Richard cut in. "What my wife is trying to say, Mr. Sati, is that she's worried about the child. The hotel director whisked her away quickly and refused to talk about it afterwards."

Sathiamoorthy didn't say anything for a few minutes, but then reconsidered. "Well, *Memsab*, I don't want to get involved in this matter, but I have no doubt that the child was taken to the Chennai children's home run by an order of nuns. They are actually not far from your hotel, down Raja Lane. You'd just go out the back and walk about a quarter of a mile, then the institution will be a brick building sitting back from the road on your left."

"Oh, thank you so much, Mr. Sati," said Rita. "I was going to have to ask the hotel, and they seem cranky and not at all helpful. We really are grateful to you."

Richard reached into his pocket for some *rupees*, but Sathimoorghy saw the gestures and stopped him.

"No, you must not give me a tip. My reward was helping out foreign visitors to my country. If I ever come to the United States, you can repay me then." He turned to leave and the Benet's started up the hotel steps. By now it was dark and chilly.

"Just a final word. I would say nothing to the hotel about what you intend to do. The people who live here are very sensitive to the child abductions, and they are afraid they will lose business if a warning gets out that Chennai is a dangerous place with sinister things going on. Business is already hard enough. Furthermore, I know that your mission of returning the relic to the sea has nothing to do with finding that poor girl, but others might think differently. Do not mention the relic to the orphanage people. It will only make things more difficult. The Indian imagination often runs wild..."

"Don't worry," said Rita with a wave of her hand. "We will be discreet."

Sati gave them a final *Namaste* and disappeared into the night.

"We must leave this place as soon as possible," Richard said. "Unfortunately— hopefully not permanently—I have misplaced the stone hand of Ganesh. It should be in my luggage, but it's staying hidden. The Ministry of Archeology might change its mind about questioning us, and there may not be a chance to throw the relic into the sea."

He gave Rita a tender hug. "Between you and me, my pineapple of perfection, I really don't believe in the professor's superstition."

Rita pulled back from his embrace and looked him in the eyes. "My darling, I'm sure you're right."

Manik Dermotma seldom remembered that he used to be someone else. That self was buried under gritty layers of his life in Calcutta. After he escaped from the American military prison, thanks to Ravi, he reinvented himself. Or rather, he let his rescuer create a new persona. Had it been just three years? It seemed more like an eternity. Better yet, he felt that, Hindu style, he'd died and been reincarnated. Not that Manik had time for reflection. He was sent on missions so vile and exhausting, that what little sleep he could catch was like death. He blacked out abruptly every night. When he awakened, it took time to know where he was.

The effort of remembering was so great, he had no energy left for piecing together his previous life. He had been the commander in charge of a hospital in Alipore, but then he was Mac McDermott. All that had changed when he met Ravi Ghosh and adopted the opium habit. That was long ago, another lifetime. But he must stop thinking, as giving in to random thoughts was a luxury he did not possess. He must focus on getting the job done.

Mac-turned-Manik worked for first one Indian scoundrel and then another, each more brutal than the one before. The black-haired Irishman had grown into his Indian identity, becoming thin and wiry, hunched over in a way that made him look like a man closer to seventy than his actual age of 58. Mac was no longer; he was now Manik, a small-time operator, an employee of those who controlled the streets. Wearing a tan cotton *salwar kameez* and a white turban and sandals, he blended in with Calcutta's throngs.

Manik pushed through a milling crowd of Indians, most of whom carried bundles on their heads or armloads of wares to sell. It was high noon, a good time for the small item trade, and those around the fair-skinned pseudo-Indian were purveyors of food, cigarettes, souvenirs, toys, and trinkets. Manik paused to purchase a single smoke from a nondescript *wallah*. He put the cigarette between his dry, sunburned lips and reached with his right hand into the money belt he kept well hidden beneath his muslin tunic. Manik held a black leather brief case with one hand. In the briefcase were photographs of girl children, homeless or orphaned, who he was to deliver to his new boss-- Rani, Rajeev,

Raul? Then he recalled the name. Antar, a man who collected rents from the poor and was paid in drugs.

Manik scuttled into a tea stall equipped with two spindly tables and three chairs. He had slept only four hours in the last two days, and he would need some tea to keep going. He would also use the time to look at the photos of his latest prey. After the tea arrived in a small glass, Manik added five sugar cubes and then unbuckled his brief case. He took out a file.

*Child: Arundati Chatterjee, somewhere between five and eight —it is hard to tell— widowed and sent to a Calcutta ashram. Nari Kapur intervened as the uncle was transporting Arundati from a village near Chennai to Calcutta. When the police got wind of the transaction and began trailing Nari, she was transferred to a boatman, a cousin.*

Details were fuzzy after this event, the only report being that the child escaped and may have drowned. Or maybe not. It was Manik's job to find out, to retrieve lost goods and deliver Arundati to the Calcutta division of Antar's operations.

Manik held the photo that accompanied the description of Arundati. A young girl's face smiled out from a grainy backdrop - a dung-covered wall behind her, painted with white floral motifs. Red bouganvilla framed one side of the scene. The flowers and the sparkling white teeth of the child offered the only bright spots in the mud-brown setting.

People of the mud, never able to rise above their lowly birth, thought Manik. They were easy prey. At first it made him sick to think of how easy it was, how defenseless these simple folks were and how much profit could be made from this human commerce. Somewhere along the way it ceased to bother him. Now it was just business. Manik slurped down the scalding glass of strong tea. The word irony came to mind. In his former life, he'd envied that arrogant bastard Richard Benet for his frequent contact with the natives. Now, he -- formerly Mac McDermott, now Manik Darmotma -- knew the native people far better than Benet would ever know them.

"More tea, *Sahib*?" asked a skinny boy with a large head and a cleft palate. "Would *Sahib* like something to eat? We have *chapatis*, fish, mangos..."

"No food." Manik slipped a coin to the boy. "I need to talk to the owner of your tea house. Bring him to me."

32

The boy stared at the coin in his hand as if it were a hot burning coal. "Aye, *Sahib*," he said, finally. He nodded his head from side to side in a gesture of assent and then disappeared into the crowd of tables and patrons sipping tea.

Minutes later, the boy was back, accompanied by the proprietor, a huge man wearing an immaculate white *salwar kameez*. His head was small, like a marble atop the mountainous body. "OK , Abu," he snarled, waving his hand at the boy. "Get back to work."

Placing his hands together in a greeting of *Namaste*, the human behemoth turned toward Manik. "How may I help you, *Sahib*?"

"It is a matter of business," said Manik. "May we go somewhere private to talk?"

"Nay," said the proprietor. "My tea house is tiny and the back is crowded with workers preparing tea and meals. I will join you here, at your table."

Manik said nothing, nervously fumbling in his brief case for the photograph. He watched in amazement as the huge man placed his girth on a tiny chair. It looked completely incapable of supporting the human elephant's bulk. When the chair did not collapse, Manek pulled the photo out and put it on the table next to an empty tea glass.

"Have you seen this child?" he asked. "She was kidnapped by gypsies. I promised my brother I would try to find her. My brother is ill and cannot look for himself. We are afraid she might not be alive."

The proprietor took the photo from Manik. "Your niece is a beautiful girl, *Sahib*. I am sorry for your family, but I cannot say that I have seen her." He shook his head. "A terrible business, this abduction of the innocents. Our city has been taken over by *goondas*."

Manik took back the photo and placed it carefully in his briefcase. "I think she is still alive." he said. "My sister-in-law is heartbroken, as this child is their only daughter. Her older sisters both died. I promised the family that I would find her no matter how long it took me."

The proprietor waved away a beggar that came by the table with outstretched arms. "I give alms at the temple. These poor souls are not allowed to come into my shop, but unless I have a guard at the door keeping them out, they come in like flies." Outside in the dirt road, a group of monks in orange robes walked by chanting in a nasal tone. The tea shop was filling up with people and the air filled with cigarette smoke and the smell of perspiration.

Manik stood up and placed his briefcase on the table. "I've taken up far too much of your time, and I can see you have to attend your business." He wrote his name on a slip of paper and handed it to his host. "If you should see or hear of my brother's daughter, please find me. My brother is offering a reward. I will be in Calcutta on Babar Lane near the University."

"Certainly," said the proprietor. "I will ask my neighbors. In the meantime, you should look in the area north of Alipore. I've heard of some children being taken there and sold."

"Sold?" asked Manik.

"Aye," the other said. "It is a filthy business, but these innocents are forced into prostitution. They have no way to escape and they will do anything rather than starve. We have police, but they are easily bought off."

"You mean they just look the other way?" asked Manik. He clucked his tongue in mock disapproval, quickly followed with a gesture of *namaste*. The proprietor responded in kind, and Manik slipped out into the dusty, teeming street.

Hoping to hire a rickshaw, Manik scanned the side lanes. The main boulevard was glutted with taxis, cattle, busses, and automobiles whose drivers slammed on their horns in a nonstop cacophony. In the midst of the maelstrom of traffic, there were also camels pulling carts, elephants carrying humans, men running along in bare feet pulling wagons and otherwise attached loads.

The rush was not peculiar to this hour, four in the afternoon, but typical of the streets morning, noon and into the night. Manik brushed aside beggars as he peered into one side street after another. His hand waved so hard against a small gypsy girl that she fell over and began to cry. Manik looked around to make sure no angry adult would come rushing at him and, seeing that he was alone, walked quickly to the next side street.

The last thing in the world he needed was a run-in with the gypsies who worked the streets of Calcutta. Like him, they traded in children. They used them for begging and pilfering. He, on the other hand was a sort of harvester. He went after his "assignments" to feed the never-ending demand for young prostitutes. He looked at his watch, an army issued timepiece, the

34

only remnant that survived his long journey from American army officer to Calcutta gang member.

It was now 5 p.m. He'd quit using military time when he was in a U.S. prison awaiting trial. He'd have rotted there if it hadn't been for Ravi. But now Ravi had moved on to bigger stakes, and Antar was Manik's boss. Not that Ravi had treated him well, but those days seemed halcyon compared to the degradation of slaving for Altar. He must report to the monster in three hours. He feared the reaction if he'd found nothing. He had already been punished for losing his last assignment, a child born out of wedlock and working at a factory until some relatives could be found who would keep her. He hadn't eaten in two days. Rickshaws were practically free, and he could make it to Alipore with his meagre stash of *rupees*.

"Ride, *Sahib*?" The rickshaw driver, who looked ancient but might be only 30 or 35, leaned over and rang his bike bell. He was the thinnest man Manik had ever seen. Even though Manik could speak a very basic Hindi, he was relieved that this man spoke English. Since the war ended, more and more Indians spoke English.

"How much to get to Alipore District?" he asked.

The driver asked, "How much do you have?"

Controlling his temper, Manik spoke slowly and distinctly. "It is not a question of how much I have. I will pay you one *rupee* and maybe a tip if you earn it. I need to arrive before dark. Are you fast?"

"There's no one faster in all of Calcutta," the driver said with a toothy grin. He opened the door on the rickshaw's side and indicated that Manik should climb aboard. "Would you prefer the south side or the east?" he asked as he began to peddle his bicycle and weave a path through the human and vehicular river.

How could Manik ask the driver where he would be likely to find illegal activities? Instead, he continued the story that he'd begun at the tea house. "I need the most remote section of Alipore. I'm looking for my niece, who was kidnapped and may be somewhere in the chaos."

Peddling madly, the driver said nothing. They careened to the left and right in order to avoid other passenger-laden rickshaws. Manik had to keep his hands inside the small passenger seat, as even a protruding knuckle might be subject to a crippling side swipe. They whizzed past a woman sweeping a small pile of garbage away from her front stoop. It made little sense to Manik, as garbage was never collected and the workers who tried to clean it up just swept it from place to place. A ragged woman next to the sweeper, holding a dead puppy, wept as though it were a child. Manik wondered grimly if her religious beliefs would allow her to eat a former pet.

They seemed to be moving rapidly but getting nowhere near the so-called nicer district of Alipore. That, Manik remembered, was where he had first met Ravi. That was when his name was James McDermott. Colonel Mac to the men. That's when that bastard Richard Benet caused his life to go bad. That's when he got involved with Calcutta's "bad business" community.

"Hey," he yelled to the rickshaw driver. "Do you know where we're going?" The driver didn't answer but just peddled more furiously. No matter how much Manik explored Calcutta, most of the time he had no idea where he was.

Suddenly they stopped. "What's wrong?" he shouted. He looked at the buildings ahead. A sign written in both Hindi and English announced "Calcutta University," south campus. "This isn't a residential area. I need to go to a residential area, near the military hospital, the one that was used by Americans during the war."

The driver got off his bicycle and stood by the rickshaw carriage, indicating that Manik should step down. "*Sahib*, I cannot take you further. As you can see, my tire is flat. You will have to find another driver."

Manik didn't budge. It was growing darker and many of the rickshaws did not operate during the nighttime hours. "Well, fix it goddam you. Surely you have a spare tube. Who ever heard of riding a bike without having a spare tube."

"Sorry, *Sahib* American, but I gave my spare to my brother this morning. I have nothing. You will not have to pay me, but I cannot take you further. I'm sure another driver will come along." The man was walking in the other direction, pulling his disabled equipment along behind him.

Manik wanted to strangle this scarecrow or even better, shoot him in the back. But he didn't have the luxury of giving in to his fury. Antar, the man who never slept, would be waiting for him at headquarters, and he would want results. Manik had learned that he was good at puffing up the truth, at making things sound better than they were. A trick no doubt acquired in the army and perfected as he worked in Ravi's illegal pursuits.

36

Evening cooled the air. Manik walked purposefully toward the broad steps of the university. He thought that with his brief case, he might be mistaken for a professor of some sort. He had no idea what he would do once he entered the huge building, but at the very least he could go inside and try to meet someone who might send him in the right direction. He plotted his cover story: doing a study of homeless children in Calcutta and working for an American charitable firm. His Indian clothing, he would glibly explain, gave him an entrance into places otherwise off limits.

The halls were deserted, but here and there some lights had been left burning. Was this a holiday or some kind of break? It was Saturday night, Manik remembered. Or the Hindu version of Saturday night. He was unlikely to find either professors or students at this hour. The first room he checked must have been a chemistry lab, as there were sinks, vials and counters all around. Maybe a mad scientist would still be at work. Manik heard a scuttling sound and looked behind him to see a black rat run into a corner and disappear.

For a moment he was back at the 142nd General Hospital in the cellar, the place where things had gone so terribly wrong. He forced himself to focus on the present task: to find a person who could tell him where to look for street children in Alipore. Homeless and lost, the urchins would be easy lure. Antar would demand results. Manik had to come back with something.

Other than the rat, not a sign of life anywhere. Manik walked the entire first floor, moving softly down the gray stone halls, stopping now and then to call out "Hello, anyone there?" The latter made him feel like a fool, but by now he was growing desperate.

He walked up a dimly lit staircase to a second floor whose open balcony overlooked the first floor's interior courtyard. Stacks of papers lay beside what Manik assumed were professor's offices. Maybe they'd just had midterm exams and were out on break because of the test-produced stress. Indians, he had noticed, were very good at inventing reasons for a holiday. Unlike himself, they lacked a decent work ethic.

As Manik reached the end of the secondfloor hall and was about to descend the massive stone stairs, he halted and sniffed the air. Cigarette smoke, unmistakable. Not a cheap Indian brand. Something like Lucky Strikes, from somewhere nearby. He made out a light coming from underneath one of the doors just beyond where he stood. Funny, he hadn't noticed before. Instinctively, he slipped behind a pillar and listened. As an imposter and intruder, he had to be cautious. Thinking ahead, he knew what he would say about his purpose in being here if it were a faculty member. But what if it were a security guard or someone who might not understand his rudimentary Hindi?

A faint scratching was all he could hear and it was barely louder than his breathing. The smoke came from the same room as the scratching, and Manik imagined a professor writing on the blackboard. He'd composed himself so that his story would come out flawlessly, so there was nothing to do but go ahead and knock on the door.

As Manik approached the only occupied room in the entire hall, he noted that the door had a small window at the top. He could peer through and get an inkling of who he was about to speak with. As he got closer, however, he saw that the window was covered with papers on the opposite side. All he could make out was a shadow.

Rapping cautiously on the wooden door, Manik stood up taller. He pulled his shoulders back into an erect "at attention" position. There was no answer, so he cleared his throat and knocked again.

"Yes?" said a deep baritone voice. Despite its depth, the voice sounded like that of a young man. As a former military officer, Manik knew the sound of young voices. No matter what type of voice -- baritone, tenor, alto -- the years added a quaver and an apologetic tone. This was definitely a young voice. Or at least not elderly. Maybe someone about his age.

It's Manik Dermotma," he said. "I'm from the Institute of International Child Protection and I'm in Calcutta to do some research. I wonder if I might trouble you with a few questions?"

"It's late, but come in," said the voice.

Manik opened the door and saw the back of someone he'd known in another life.

38

Richard Benet was writing a list on the blackboard titled "Principles of Guidance and Counseling." When Manik entered the dimly lit classroom, he immediately realized that this was not where he wanted to be, not where he belonged. Could he possibly escape being recognized by his former rival, his mortal enemy, his nemesis?

"May I help you?" the clinical psychologist turned college professor asked. "It's after hours and I don't know how you gained admittance to the building. I'm preparing for my first class of the semester early tomorrow morning and actually, I'm very pressed for time."

Manik, used to pretending, stepped into part of the room that was hidden in shadows. He cleared his throat and used his most sing-song fake Indian accent. World War Two had ended years earlier. After the downfall of 142nd General Hospital, his crimes caught up with him and he was court marshaled. Benet had served as witness at the military hearing, affirming the fact that Manik - who was then "Mac" McDermott - was guilty of trading hospital supplies to support his opium habit. Criminal neglect of the hospital and its patients was just one of the charges.

That seemed an eternity ago. Mac was imprisoned in an Indian jail, in a sort of holding pattern, as he awaited trial. Richard Benet went back to the states, where he became a college professor. With the help of his underworld connections, Mac-soon-to-become-Manik managed to escape from jail in exchange for enslavement to the criminal Ravi Ghosh.

"I am looking for an Indian girl who's been kidnapped. Her parents have paid me as a private detective to search the grounds of Calcutta University, which is where they last saw her. It was here that she was taken from them."

Richard Benet's hand trembled as he continued to write on the chalkboard. He and Rita had adopted an Indian girl in a small village near Chennai, but of course it couldn't be the same child. The adoption was unconventional. They paid Sister Mary Bernadette five-hundred dollars to buy supplies for the orphanage in exchange for the small child Richard had rescued from drowning. It was not strictly legal, but there had been no one to declare it illegal.

Ignoring his feeling that this intruder was someone he might once have known, Benet deliberately put his chalk down

39

and swung around to face Manik. "I know nothing about a child like the one you're talking about. I suggest that you contact the police tomorrow morning. It's late and the building superintendent will be coming around to lock up. Before you barged in, I was about to leave."

This was a lie. The college professor had another hour of class preparation to do, and there was no building superintendent. Whoever this shady character was, he needed to go.

To his amazement, the Indian was backing away toward the classroom door. He seemed a bit servile. Who, exactly was he? Benet almost expected him to bow.

"It is not a problem," said the Indian. "Obviously I have been misled. May I show you the girl's photograph? In case you meet anyone who might have seen her. You might even ask your students tomorrow if they've come across her. The family said her name is Arundati."

Richard took a long look at the photograph. Inwardly, he gasped. The child looked exactly like the girl he and Rita had adopted and now planned to take to the states. He went back to writing on the blackboard, shielding his face from the unwelcome visitor. "This country has so many orphans, I'd think your quest would be fruitless. I have a deadline, however, and don't really have time for this." Silently, he added, "Now get the hell out and leave me alone."

The adoption of their girl, a child they called Dottie, had been a very private affair, an arrangement actually, in which they gave Sister Mary Bernadette five hundred dollars to help the orphanage. In return, they now had a daughter to call their own. It was the five-year-old that Richard had saved from washing out to sea. He and Rita decided that fate intended for them to parent her. It had all gone smoothly until now. A very informal arrangement, but in their minds it was fair. Legitimate. Even praiseworthy. Not being able to have their own child, they needed one. The girl obviously wouldn't have any chance in life without a family. Done, finished, accomplished. No loose ends...until now. Calcutta seemed worlds away from Mahabalipuram and he'd never dreamed of anyone coming to claim the girl. Or of even knowing anything about her.

How could he get rid of this busybody before he gleaned that he and the girl were connected. To protect himself, he would not reveal anything. Could the inquirer sense his unease? He cursed himself for staying late to work on the sprawling campus of the University. It was too late to be here. If only he'd gone back to Rita and Dottie hours ago. Maybe he could slip away and manage to get rid of this pest. At first he'd appeared a total stranger, but now he seemed oddly familiar.

"I bid you a good night," Richard said. "I'm leaving now. I have nothing to tell you. Please leave so I can lock up the classroom." He swept books and papers into a briefcase, laid a stack of syllabi on his desk and walked about the classroom putting desks in order. The stranger lurked, standing in one corner of the dimly-lit room.

Suddenly they were plunged in darkness. Electricity at the University was erratic and electrical outages were a frequent occurrence. "What the..." Richard exclaimed. He walked toward the light switch, bumping into Manik, who'd emerged from his corner.

"I will walk you to wherever you're staying," Manik said. "This whole part of the city is plunged into darkness and you will become hopelessly lost unless you let me be your guide. You cannot help me find the lost girl but I can help you find your way home. These streets are not at all safe, *goondas* everywhere. And it is very easy to get lost even in broad daylight."

Richard sensed that Manik might have traced the rescued, adopted girl to him and was going to reclaim her. At the same time, and with a shock, he saw through the Indian disguise to his former enemy McDermott. They'd served together at the 142nd General Hospital in Calcutta. McDermott had been envious of Richard. He'd become "Indianized" and was now in a position to wreak revenge. He couldn't let Manik come to the hotel where Rita and their girl awaited. Then again, he couldn't very well plunge himself into a darkness that was likely to bring death...

Maybe honesty was the best policy. He could ask "Manik" if he used to be someone else. After all, the war was over and he was trying, like everyone, to reclaim a life he'd known before being drafted. The life he'd left behind during his months of serving as clinical psychologist in a military hospital. Right now, he had to get back to Rita and their child, the girl they'd adopted in Tamil Nadu.

As if reading Richard's mind, Manik - or whoever he was - said, "I happen to have a powerful flashlight and will be glad to escort you back to your hotel. As you should know, it is not wise to wander the streets of Calcutta in complete darkness. I believe the power outage covers the entire district, and knowing how

41

these things go, it could be many hours before electricity is restored."

The darkness seemed to deepen. Richard felt something scuttle across his ankles and remembered the rat population that roamed about at night. He cleared his throat. An insincere politeness crept into his voice. "Well *Sahib* Manik - or whoever you are - I really have no choice but to accept your kind offer of an escort."

As soon as the words were out of his mouth, Richard regretted them. Why give this person the power over him? He could take him anywhere. He could rob him. Worse, when then they reached the hotel...

But really, what choice did he have?

Manik was prepared for the inky darkness that had befallen them. He produced a flashlight from his shoulder bag and turned it on. Odd, Richard thought, that his visitor would be so prepared. On the other hand, power outages were a frequent occurrence in this part of Calcutta. He ignored the far-fetched idea that somehow Manik had brought it about on purpose. Preposterous. He couldn't have. And yet...

"Allright, Dr. Benet," said Manik, "we first need to make our way out of the Siksha Prangan campus of the University. You did say your hotel was The Hindustan on Acharya Prafulla Road? We need to make our way to College Row, about half a mile from here. You have your wife and family there, I assume?"

"Yes," Richard said. It's the "Grand Hindustan." Even as he spoke the words, he realized that he'd never told this man the name of where he was lodging. Of course, it was the commonly used hotel for the University's visiting faculty, but how would this "Manik" know that? Worse still, why did Manik assume that he had a family? Had he researched Richard before seeking out the classroom? Maybe he could find a way to get rid of this pest.

"You know, my colleague Dina Pavri works late as well, and I'm sure she will give me a ride home. She's on the next floor, and I can just go check with her. You are free to go."

"No one is at work on the next floor up," said Manik. "When I was looking for you, I checked every room."

Richard felt his face grow hot, as he tried to control his anger. "I thought you were looking for a lost child and discovered me by accident. Who are you, anyway? Please just go. I will manage on my own."

The two men walked uneasily to the classroom door and headed down the steps. Manik, who held the flashlight aloft, was in the lead. Richard felt the knife's outline in his jacket pocket. It was a present from Rita, who insisted that he carry it for self-defense. "I know a pistol might be better protection," she had said, "but since we both hate guns, this seemed like the next best thing. Not that you will ever need to use it. But just in case..."

They were descending the wide cement steps leading from the Birla Building, called "BB" by the students. Richard walked reluctantly after Manik, whose flashlight had gone out. His guide said he had no new batteries, but because of a nearly full moon, it wasn't difficult to see the all-white *salwar kameez* ahead. Richard fumbled in his pocket for his own flashlight, only to realize he'd left it in the classroom. He reminded himself to appear calm. The last thing Richard wanted was for "Manik" to know where Rita and their child were staying. They were probably an hour's walk from The Hindustan. He must discover a way to escape before then.

Amazingly, Manik lit a candle, which kept burning even when they stepped off campus and into Calcutta's fetid night air. Maneuvering carefully down the stone steps of Kasyapa Hill, Richard followed the leader. Not by choice but necessity. The heavy air seemed moist, and sure enough, raindrops began splattering as soon as they reached Vishnu Circle. Without candlelight, it was even more difficult to follow. Now would be the perfect time to make a getaway. But where? They seemed to be among sleeping ghosts, as the poor who lived their lives on the streets were breathing around them. Richard sensed them and imagined the ragged figures lying along buildings, curled up in doorways.

Manik kept up a desultory chatter, asking questions about the professor's family. Richard sensed rather than saw the piles of filth all around them. A lone voice was singing a mournful chant. Richard recognized it as Hindi. Now and then a horse and buggy went clip-clopping by. The rain settled into a steady drizzle. When Manik raised an oversized umbrella and invited Richard to share the dryness it provided, he reluctantly accepted.

"I think you might know who I used to be," said the umbrella holder. "I was then an American hospital commander. Now an Indian businessman. Clever, no?"

The memory of Mac McDermott came flooding back to Richard. He'd been horrified but not surprised to learn that

43

McDermott was accused of strangling a low-ranking soldier. Hadn't he been imprisoned? Suddenly his heart started beating fast and it was all he could do not to bolt in the opposite direction. That, however, would be worse than keeping company with this murderous fake Indian, a man who may or may not be taking him to The Hindustan.

After Manik revealed his true identity, Richard said nothing. He was afraid that his voice would reveal a sense of panic. "You might also be interested to know," McDermott/Manik said, "that I know you stole the child that you and your wife think you've adopted. I tracked you down so I can return her to her family in Tamil Nadu. Did you think I wanted to lead you back to the hotel out of kindness?" His voice was harsh, filled with scorn.

"You're totally mistaken. We did not steal a child. I'm here to teach for a semester, and my wife wanted to see India. Besides, it's none of your business."

The mismatched pair of men plodded on through the drizzle. Richard decided that anything would be better than keeping company with this thug, even facing the dark streets of Calcutta alone. He was taller and probably stronger than Manik, but the former hospital commander could possibly be armed. If only he hadn't listened to Rita, he would have packed a pistol in his briefcase. Too late now.

"Be careful what you say. I will not be insulted by a pompous ass. You pretended to be a hero, the oh so brave lieutenant who saved the 142nd hospital while I was wrongly imprisoned for just doing my job and exercising discipline. You're the real fraud."

By now they'd been walking for what seemed like hours. It felt like it might be four in the morning, and the streets - which had never really gone to sleep - came to life. A double-decker bus rumbled by them. Workers climbed down into manholes. Richard had no idea of direction, but he felt they'd wandered far afield of the hotel. If he could just escape Manik and hop aboard a bus. Once on and safely away from Manik, he could use the card he'd picked up from the receptionist's desk. It had the hotel name and directions in Hindi. Even if the bus driver couldn't read, someone on the bus would surely be able to help. He might even try making an plea for help. It seemed that Calcutta had a good share of English speakers.

44

Unfortunately, the roads were devoid of traffic. The rain temporarily over, clouds had parted and a bright moon illuminated boulevards stretching in every direction. A pale light gave the roads an unearthly sheen. Where was mad Mac/Manik taking him? Surely they would have reached The Hindustan by now. If he asked, however, his "guide" would gain more control. Richard felt a tightness in his throat, a wave of nausea in his stomach, weakness in the knees. An alarm went off in his mind, as he recalled the crimes that landed Mac in a military prison. Strangling soldiers, first during a march through the jungles of Burma, then in a latrine located at the 142nd Hospital.

As though reading Richard's mind, Mac turned savagely. "I know these mean streets and you don't, you ass. Unless you let me take the child who's not even yours and return her to the family, you may never get back to your precious wife. So, you bastard, admit that you stole Arundati and promise to hand her over to me so I can complete my mission." By now, Mac had dropped his fake Indian accent. His voice became a snarl and he hissed, "Admit it: that girl was bought. You bribed the orphanage Sisters. It wasn't even a legal adoption."

The two men now stood face to face on the filthy sidewalk. Mac crouched as though ready to attack. Richard groped in his pocket for the knife that he always carried with him. To his horror, it wasn't there. He and Rita had gone out to dinner with their new little girl and when he changed jackets he'd forgotten to transfer his knife. How was he going to defend himself?

Mac laughed contemptuously. "Once a strangler, always a strangler," he hissed. He glared menacingly at Richard.

"Good God, man. What do you want from me?"

Richard glanced around to see if there was any way to escape. Mac turned Manik was advancing toward him.

"I think you know. I want that girl you stole from the nuns at Chennai Holy Family orphanage. If you will admit that you have her and agree to hand her over to me, your worries will be over and this will end well for both of us. Otherwise, we'll see if I've lost my touch..."

Richard felt the cold hands of his adversary around his neck. By now the rain had resumed, this time in earnest. A steady downpour, making visibility nearly impossible. He kicked out one leg and threw Mac off balance. In the back of his mind, he remembered passing nearby an alleged sinkhole in one of the

Alipore district's roads. His only hope of losing Mac might be to shove him into the earth.

Driven by imagination and a determination to survive, Richard kicked Mac away and began to run. He and Rita had been walking along Acharya Prafulla Chandra Road just yesterday. Wasn't that where a sinkhole was supposedly lurking? Chances were one in a million that he could stumble upon it, but why not try? Desperation was a strong motivator.

Relying on a sixth sense, Richard raced back toward Calcutta University campus. He heard the pounding of Mac's feet behind him. He passed a *sari* shop on the corner of Archarya Prafulla Chandra. Rita told him that before they left Calcutta, she wanted to get mother daughter garments made for her and their daughter.

The thought of Rita made him run faster. Manik might be strong, but he was faster. There was always the possibility that Manik could overpower him if and when they came to the sinkhole. Suddenly the road became uneven. They were here - the point of no return. One of them would die.

## Chapter Ten

The Alipore District of Calcutta briefly lit up. Shop windows illuminated, street lights came on, windows in office buildings turned light. As suddenly as the lights went on, they flickered and went dark again. The sudden electricity allowed Richard and Manik to see more than just the rain-slick road. For five minutes they'd been racing in the dark, Richard in the lead. A narrow side street turned off Acharya Prafully Chandra. Intuition guided Richard to run toward the shopfronts that lined the intersection. He slipped, fell and righted himself. This had to be it: the sinkhole he'd been hoping for. He stationed himself in the doorway of a spice shop and called out to Manik.

"If you'll walk a straight line from where you are to where I'm standing, I will let you meet my daughter and then you will find out that she is not the child you are looking for."

This offer stopped Manik, but just for a moment. "You lying bastard. I don't believe you for a minute. I will find your wife and daughter, but first I need to finish what I started. I will take Arundati back to her village. And your wife? Well..."

By now the light had once again dimmed, then flickered out entirely. Richard stood against a storefront and prepared to fight. Mac was desperate, but he was determined. If he had to, he would outrun this monster.

"You were always a worthless sot," yelled Richard. "The army would have done well to hang you rather than throwing you in prison. I guess your *goonda* connections got you out and now you're their slave. I dare you to walk across the road to meet me face to face. Once you're here, I will take you to meet the girl you're calling Arundati. She is not who you think she is."

The rain started back up, this time in huge, sweeping gales. The two men were yelling across the sinkhole. Mac lunged forward toward Richard. He screamed into the pitchdark sky as he slid into the earth. Miracle of miracles, the earth's cavity was taking care of the killing that Richard had been prepared to carry out. The screams grew fainter as the sand and slush swallowed Mac. Gone. Forever.

Richard shook with cold and breathed deeply to restore his equilibrium. What to do next? Somehow he had to get back to Rita and Arundati, and then they should probably arrange passage back to Ohio. Mac no doubt had underworld connections who might be able to connect his disappearance with Richard.

Steam rose from the asphalted streets. A camel drawn wooden cart clopped by. This looked like the parliamentary area of Calcutta, and it could be that he was going in the wrong direction. Exhausted, the psychologist ran toward what he hoped was hotel row. Rita would be sick with worry, as he should have returned to her hours ago. As he ran, he formulated plans. Leaving Calcutta as quickly as possible seemed advisable. He would pack up everything and order a taxi to take them to the airport. Getting as far from here as possible was his goal.

Though it was dark, Richard's eyes adjusted and he could just barely make out the surroundings. Beggars lining the sidewalk slept in bundled rags. Were they sleeping, or were they dead? In the streets of Calcutta, one could not always distinguish the corpses from the living. Monkeys chattered at Richard as he raced on. It must be close to dawn. To his amazement, a city bus rumbled past. He ran toward it and waved his arms in the air, but it was too late. Surely there would be another one soon. Richard slowed to a walk, looked up and down the street. He removed the hotel's card from his briefcase and put it carefully in his breast pocket.

He was parched. A dry mouth and aching lungs reminded him that he needed to find a way back to Rita, the sooner the better. As the sky grew lighter and his breathing slowed, he allowed himself to remember Mac's screams. The sinkhole method of eradication. In a way, it was too good to be true. Even if Manik the fake Indian was part of a network, it would probably take someone a bit of time before they thought to trace his steps to Calcutta University. The psychology department might have records of Richard's hotel, but he had to be gone before they could be questioned.

Just as he felt unable to walk another step, he heard rumbling and bolted to the curb. A bus, at last. Frantic arm-waving caught the driver's attention, and the bus lurched to a stop. Richard climbed aboard and fumbled in his pocket for a *rupee*. Too much money, but he was too exhausted to rummage further.

"*Sahib*, do you speak English," he asked the driver.

"A little. Where are you wanting to go?"

"The Hindustan Hotel in Alipore." The psychologist showed the driver a card from the hotel.

"Ah, you are in luck. We are going on the proper route. However, there are many stops and some side streets before we arrive. It may take you almost an hour to arrive there."

"That is not a problem, and thank you." The people behind Richard were pushing forward and he realized he'd better find a seat. Light-headed with relief, he walked hesitantly toward the back. *Sari*-clad women were sitting tightly wedged into the worn vinyl seats. Many men were standing. All eyes were upon Richard as he searched. Glancing his way, not unfriendly, but intensely curious. Finally, at the very back, Richard spotted a small, narrow vacancy. He carefully placed himself in it and breathed a sigh of relief.

His seat mate, a teenage boy, looked at him and smiled.

"You are English?" he asked.

"Actually, I am American. A visiting professor at the University of Calcutta. I have been here for the semester and will be returning to the states very soon."

Until he said it, Richard had not admitted that he must do exactly that. The Mac situation made it imperative. He closed his eyes and fell asleep for a few minutes. This wouldn't do, however. He could sleep right through his stop. Fortunately, the young man next to him seemed inclined to talk.

"I get very few chances to practice my English. So you must excuse me for being a noisy chatterbox. What brings you out at this time of night, *Sahib*?"

It was a routine question, but Richard felt a vague sense of alarm. What if he got so engrossed in a conversation that he missed his stop at Ganesh Chandra Crossing? "Sure, I'll be happy to give you some English practice, but in return, I have to ask you a favor. I'm going to the Hindustan Hotel and I need to be warned one stop ahead. Can you do that for me?"

"Ah yes, most certainly, *Sahib*. So, back to what I was wondering. What would bring a professor such as yourself out at this almost morning time of night? As well, I was wondering why you would come to Calcutta. It is not such a tourist attraction as Delhi or Agra."

Outside, through the grimy windows, the sky gradually lightened. A weak sunshine lit up the buildings. Dozens of small sidewalk shops were coming to life. The bus lurched, sped up, screeched, slowed. Droves of Indians disembarked and were replaced by others. Men in *salwar kamizes*, women in brilliantly hued *saris*, children and babies. Here was a man carrying a bleating goat under one arm, a woman with a puppy. Everyone was talking loudly and Richard understood not a word.

"I will answer your questions in reverse order. First of all, I served in the Army Airforce as chief psychologist at the 142nd General Hospital during World War Two, so I wanted to see your city from a different perspective. My favorite college professor, when he passed away, left me a small legacy, enough money to come back for a visit. That was years after the war ended."

"About the time of night," continued Richard, "to make a long story short, I was working a bit late, putting examination questions on the blackboard when the electricity in that part of the University went out completely. A passerby with a flashlight offered to escort me to my hotel but somehow I lost him." As Richard said this, he relived the surreal events of less than an hour ago. Mac/Manik swallowed into the earth. How ghastly and how appropriate.

The young man was looking at him curiously, and Richard quickly swept the horror scene from his imagination. "Sorry, I was just thinking of how glad I'll be to see my wife. I'm sure she's been worried about me. Back to what happened...Then, not speaking Hindi, I had no way of getting to my hotel. Thank God this bus came along..."

"*Sahib*, this is one stop ahead of yours. I recommend that you walk toward the door on the lefthand side of the bus. New passengers will be cramming in on the right. Would you like for me to get off the bus with you to ensure that you safely reach your destination? It is not so good to be walking alone in this part of Calcutta. Or for that matter, in any part of Calcutta. I mean...because you are clearly an outsider."

Before he could say another word, the bus screeched to a halt and, as promised, a stream of Indians started crowding through the newly-opened accordion doors. Relieved of the need to talk further with the young man, Richard thanked him for the offer of help and let the stream of departing passengers nudge him down the bus's metal stairs and onto the sidewalk.

"Best of luck, *Sahib*," called his would-be benefactor. "Thank you," shouted Richard before being swallowed by the outgoing crowd. He realized how much he did not like Indians and how glad he would be to leave the subcontinent forever behind him. This whole academic sojourn had been a bad idea.

While he felt relieved that Mac-turned-Manik was now gone forever, he feared repercussions from the *goondas*. Everyone knew that they controlled the local crime scene. Once they missed Mac, he might somehow end up on their hit list.

50

Explaining all this to Rita would be impossible. Even if he tried to whitewash the grisly truth, she would be fearful. Perhaps he'd make up a story about being called back by the Guidance and Counseling Department at Ohio State.

The Hindustan Hotel loomed hugely just a block from the bus stop. Tall and made of stone, it stood proudly above the humbler buildings surrounding it. Richard bounded up the outside steps and nodded to the doorman who let him in. Ah yes, here was the front desk. He would have to talk convincingly and insist on getting a flight home as soon as possible. Maybe even tomorrow. So tired he could hardly stand, Richard walked to the reception area.

"You are checking out so suddenly?" The handsome, turbaned desk clerk gave Richard a sorrowful look. "Were you not pleased with accommodations here at the Hindustan?"

"Oh no, that is not it at all," Richard said. "I have an emergency back at home in the United States, and I must return to take care of matters." It amazed him how easy it was to lie about the situation. The emergency was right here, right now, with a human life having been extinguished in one of Calcutta's urban sinkholes. He read the desk clerk's nametag and took a deep breath. It would not do to reveal his sense of panic. "You can help me, Mr. Mukerjee, by booking a flight for us to leave as soon as possible to fly to the U.S. If it can be this week, the earlier the better, I will pay you handsomely for all your trouble."

The adrenalin of the evening's misadventures was gone, and Richard felt lightheaded. His temples throbbed, his stomach growled, and he could hardly stand up. And yet another challenge still faced him. Without causing her alarm, he would have to tell Rita about their imminent departure. And then there was their adopted child, Arundati. It was hard enough for her to adapt to her new life without being relocated yet again.

Too weary to climb stairs to the third floor, Richard took the lift up to room 301 and knocked. The door opened, and there, in a rose-colored chenille bathrobe, was his beautiful Rita. He fell into her arms after closing the door behind him.

"My darling, where have you been? I've been sick with worry, and there was no way to reach you. The university switchboard was closed for the night. But - you're here, you're safely back. That's all that matters. Dottie was very upset; she kept asking 'Where Baba?' and 'Me wan Baba.' I had to rock her for an hour before she cried herself to sleep."

51

Together, Richard and Rita walked to the youth bed and looked over the rails at their sleeping daughter. Her olive skin radiated health, her silky black hair splayed beside her face. Richard was reminded that he and his small family could no longer be safe in Calcutta. He resisted the urge to tell Rita everything right away.

"Dear, I'm exhausted. So exhausted that I will not be coherent. I know it's morning, but this will have to be our night. Let's just pretend day and night have been reversed. I promise to explain everything during our trip home. We'll be leaving in the next couple days, maybe even sooner. Everything will be fine, dear heart. Please don't worry." Sweetheart that she was, Rita let it go at that. She trusted Richard to decide wisely on their course of action.

Their room was spacious and, for India, quite comfortable. The dark wood walls and carved wooden furniture added to its restful ambience. After kissing Arundati good night, they slipped into the clean, silky sheets. Rita fell asleep in her husband's arms even before they could make love. Richard supposed that his fatigue would lead him to drop off immediately, but he was wrong. He lay awake for what seemed like hours. When at last, he floated into sleep, a loud drilling noise from the street outside awakened him.

He awakened with a start. He'd been dreaming of Mac disappearing into the sinkhole. Had his nemesis come back to haunt him? No, it was not Mac but the hand of Ganesh. The stone artifact was somewhere deep within his luggage. With the urgent need to leave India as soon as possible, there would be no time to throw it back into the ocean. That, after all, had been the professor's last request.

But now it was too late. Richard couldn't remember exactly where it was, possibly in the depths of his foot locker? Even if he retrieved it, there was little chance he could fulfill his professor's last wishes. Hopefully, he wouldn't be cursed. Maybe he could throw it in the Ohio River when he and Rita and their daughter were safely back in Ohio. He went through a mental list of possible solutions, but nothing made sense. He'd just have to hope the curse had worn off. Did curses fade with time? Or did they live forever?

With that thought, the psychologist professor Richard Benet fell into deep slumber. It was the kind of sleep the Hindus called a little death.

# PART TWO


# DOTTIE MEETS CLARA

Chapter Eleven
Charlottesville, Virginia
1970s


     After their India sojourn, Richard and Rita Benet returned to the United States. With them, they brought a new daughter, Arundati. They'd found the five-year-old child in an orphanage, a struggling organization to which they donated money. The Catholic sisters in charge seemed happy for "Dottie" to have a new life. The arrangement, the Benet reasoned, was not exactly official but neither was it illegal. Besides, they were soon to be located 6,000 miles away. On the other side of the world.

     They settled in northern Virginia. As Dr. Richard Benet focused on his academic career, all thoughts of possibly revisiting India faded. Dr. Benet ascended the faculty ladder at the University of Virginia, being elevated from associate professor to department head. Although his field was Guidance and Counseling, he was staunchly resistant to questions from his young daughter about her adoption. Rita, also unwilling to talk with Arundati about her pre-adoption life, worked mightily to turn the child into an All-American Girl.

     Of course, they loved their olive-skinned daughter and were secretly proud of having adopted her. And she, in her quiet way, loved them. But there were too many secrets.

     "What about my real parents?" she queried "What do you know about them?"

     "My darling," answered Rita. "Your Dad and I *are* your real parents. As far as those who bore you, we don't even know who they were, just that they couldn't keep you."

     Years flew by. Dottie graduated from high school at the top of her class. It was time to plan the future. Things came to a head when the nineteen-year-old opted to attend St. John's College in Santa Fe, New Mexico. Though Richard had gone to great lengths to speed her acceptance to the University of Virginia, she would have none of it. Acting independently, she applied, was accepted and made plans to move to the Southwest. Reluctantly, her parents went along with this new direction.

Chapter Twelve
Northern New Mexico
1980

It was a long way to San Ildefonso Pueblo.

Driving her second-hand Toyota through the rolling piñon-covered hills of northern New Mexico gave Clara time to think. The American Indian Academy was now history. She'd resigned after an exhausting and often terrifying year and had moved to Santa Fe to start what she hoped was a new life. Was it the right decision? How could she ever be sure?

The late May sky was filling with clouds. In a typical New Mexico horizon, the Sangre de Cristo mountains looked purple as the sky darkened. Clara hadn't counted on the possibility of rain. The weather was wildly unpredictable in these parts. She pressed the accelerator as she mused over the recent past. At first it seemed that moving to Santa Fe was a great idea. Clara had barely survived her last year of teaching at the American Indian Academy. She needed a fresh start. She was still in shock because of the death of the school's headmaster. It wasn't just that. She'd fallen for a man who turned out to be a murderous thug, and she'd lost her best friend in a mysterious car accident. The school closed down, maybe for good, and she had to decide what to do with the rest of her life.

The dirt road twisted wildly. She turned on Cañonicito, then on Ridge Road, then left at the adobe church. Just when she felt hopelessly lost, there was the modest stucco home of Mabel Dorame, a cousin of her birthmother Greta. Or more accurately, a cousin of the woman she hoped was her birthmother. Clara parked the Toyota to the right of Mabel's house in a dirt lot. She felt like an imposter. Heart pounding, she knocked on the front door. A frenzy of barking was followed by the door opening a crack.

"Hi, are you Mabel?"

"Yes. Hello, Clara Jordan, and welcome. Come in. My daughters have been excited to meet you ever since the phone call. You're just in time for lunch." The small, black-haired woman had a beautiful, warm smile and several gold teeth. She held out her hand in greeting.

Not knowing if she should shake the hand or clasp it gently, Clara chose the latter. In unfamiliar territory, she did not

55

want to appear either too forward or reserved. As she greeted Mabel, she took in the house's interior. Not luxurious, but scrubbed to gleaming shininess. The walls were lined with photos of relatives. If only any of them were hers.

"If you don't mind, we will sit here in the kitchen, at the table. My brother's dogs have been sleeping on the living room furniture, and it's all hairy." She sat down in one of several wicker-bottomed chairs and gestured for Clara to do the same. Even though the flowered linoleum tablecloth was spotless, she brushed away imaginary crumbs. Clara wondered if she had bad news to share. She knew from students she'd taught that tidying up gestures could be a way of stalling.

"Come here, girls," Mabel beckoned. "This is Maria, my oldest. And here's her little sister Janie. Maria is nine and Janie is six. Their little brother is in day camp and doesn't get home until three."

Solemnly, Maria held out her hand. Where would she have learned to shake hands, Clara wondered. She took the small brown right hand of Mabel's eldest daughter and squeezed gently. Janie, suddenly shy, peeked out from behind her sister and presented both her hands. Clara clasped both. "Thank you. Your Mama has taught you very good manners."

"Are you the lady who's looking for a mother?" asked Maria.

Mabel frowned. "Honey, that's rude. Clara has a mother. Remember what I told you. She was adopted and raised by that mother—her adoptive mom."

"Well, you see," Clara said, "I have two mothers. When I was very young, even younger than Janie, my mother couldn't keep me. She found another home for me, and then I lost track of her for many, many years. In fact, I never found her. It was OK because I had a very nice adoptive mom. But I always wondered about that first one, the one I started with."

Mabel interrupted. "That's OK, Clara. They know about adoption because their cousin lost his mother to cancer and was adopted by an aunt." She fell silent, once again using her open palm to sweep the table clean. "Girls, you need to go feed the chickens before we have lunch. The enchiladas will be ready in 15 minutes. I'll call you when it's time."

Janie and Maria scampered out into the backyard, chattering excitedly. Apparently, feeding the chickens was a big deal. Clara couldn't help feeling that Mabel had something unwelcome to confess. An awkward silence. Mabel sighed before walking to the kitchen sink to pour glasses of water. She put one in front of Clara and sat down heavily, drinking deeply from her own glass.

"I'm not sure how to say this." She looked directly into Clara's eyes, a look filled with sadness. "Your mother died last spring. She was killed in a motorcycle accident. She would have loved seeing the beautiful young woman that her birth daughter has become, but it was not meant to be."

"Are...are you sure it was my mother?" Clara felt nauseous and suddenly exhausted. "She wouldn't have been a motorcyclist, would she? I thought she was a famous potter." Tears streamed down her cheeks and she felt like she was going to pass out. All these years she'd waited, all the distance she'd traveled. She'd based her whole life on finding a blood relative. Everything.

"Yes, my lost bird, dear lost daughter." Mabel handed Clara a box of tissues, got up and refilled her glass of water. Clara hadn't touched hers. "I am so sorry to tell you this, but it is better to know the truth."

Really? Clara thought to herself. Why couldn't she go on believing that out there a mother awaited her? She should have never moved to New Mexico, never have met horrible Henry, never have feared for her life when things went wrong at the school, never have lost her friend Annie.

Mabel sat, hovering and concerned. Her brown eyes seemed full of compassion. Janie and Maria had come in from outside and were setting the table. "Yes, it is easy to feel that way. I can tell that your life feels like it will never be right again. But things do happen for a reason." She held Clara's slender white hand in her plump brown one and gently squeezed. "Things happen, they happen. Time will heal the hurt inside you. Allow yourself to mend. You'll see."

Lunch was on the table. Clara forced herself to eat even though her appetite had left when she heard of her mother's death. And these people she was with—Mabel, Janie, Maria—they had one another. She had no one. Now the waiting was over, the search ended, questions never to be answered. It was clear that her birthmother would always be a myth, someone she would never know.

The luncheon with Mabel went on forever. Dazed, numb with disappointment, she was there but not there. Getting up to

57

leave as soon as politeness allowed, she headed toward the door. She dreaded the drive back to Santa Fe and Miller Street. In the past, the thought of seeing her boyfriend Jerome would have cheered her up, but now she felt nothing but self-pity and anger. He would try, but he couldn't possibly understand her profound grief.

Mabel looked worried. "Are you well enough to drive, Clara? My lost bird, do you want to stay here, and leave in the morning?"

"No, thank you so much, but I'll be fine. You are very kind, and I appreciated having lunch with you and meeting your beautiful daughters. But right now I just need to be in my own *casita*. It will take me a long time to absorb this bitter news. I promise to drive very carefully."

The Toyota was at last on the road from San Ildefonso to Santa Fe, and Clara realized she was not driving carefully. Instead, she speeded. The sky grew dark and large raindrops splattered on the windshield. At times, she couldn't see through her tears. She kept reminding herself to concentrate on driving. By the time she pulled into the driveway on Miller Street, the rain stopped.

Clara realized that she did not have a plan for the future.

Her search for a birthmother had come to a crashing halt. The dreams she'd long harbored about meeting her own flesh and blood had been dashed, a loss nearly as painful as the death of her closest friend Annie Archuleta. She was tired of sad endings. She longed for something to look forward to. How could she ever be at peace now that her mother could never be known?

The last day of September found Clara Jordan perched in the tiny kitchen of her *casita* on Miller Street, writing in a leather-bound journal. She would take Annie's ashes to the top of Sun Mountain. Today's goal was to start out by noon, but she felt a strong need to write about Annie before scattering her to the wind. She brewed another cup of tea and kept writing, recounting events of her last year. She'd loved much about teaching ninth graders at the American Indian Academy. That was the good part, but much of her life in Red Mesa had been traumatic. The boyfriend who was duplicitous and no longer in her life, the loss of a friend; together, these events left a painful void. And, there was the mysterious death of the school headmaster. A wave of sadness and loss caused her to pause her journaling.

But write she must. She urged herself to ramble. It was best to describe the highs and lows of teaching, something she was good at and a career she loved. Visualizing her students one by one, she wrote about the diversity and surprises of her ninth grade class. American Indian Academy was now closed "until further notice." She had a feeling that the school was actually defunct. "Defunct." That pretty well described how she felt.

MEOOWWW... Oscar Segundo, her gray and white feline companion, rubbed against her blue-jeaned legs. Whenever Clara started feeling sadness or regret, Oscar was there, demanding attention. He made it impossible to wallow in self-pity. "Feed me, scratch my chin, massage my velvety ears...It's all about me."

Like her, he was a foundling. Like her, he was five when he was adopted. He was far and above the best cat she'd ever owned. Clara pampered him. She would make up for his rough beginnings.

Oscar had Clara well-trained. First she gave him a thorough head to tail gentle massage, feeling every bone in the large cat's spine. Not once but ten times her skillful fingers traveled carefully down the length and top of him. He purred his approval but then remembered that he was hungry and continued meowing.

"Calm down, Oskie. I know you expect instant service, but I have to open a new can of Kitty's Choice. This is chicken, even though you like tuna better. You can pretend it's tuna. We do the best we can at this restaurant." She emptied half of the small tin of cat food into Oscar's newly cleaned dish and chopped it vigorously with a fork. Oscar dove into it as though he hadn't eaten for days.

"The words you're looking for are 'Thank You'," Clara quipped. Talking to Oscar? Was she becoming a crazy cat lady?

Clara sighed, stretched, and put on her hiking shoes. It would take more than journal-writing to get over the worst year of her life, the first and maybe last year of her teaching career. She needed a new direction. One thing at a time, however. Today she would go to her favorite in-town hiking spot and the dead tree she'd named "Melanie." She would place a heart-shaped rock, in memory of Annie, in one of Melanie's branches and then she would scatter the precious ashes in all four directions. They were not all of Annie's ashes, but a portion that the Archuleta family had given her to scatter. After all, Clara and Annie had been like deeply bonded sisters. The loss had hit Clara hard.

So much had gone from her former life. She missed running. In many ways, it had helped her survive last year at the American Indian Academy. These days, a sore knee kept her from running more than a couple days a week. It was more walking than running since she'd taken up urban hiking. If one wanted to get to know Santa Fe, walking everywhere was a good teacher. Locking the *casita* behind her, Clara stepped out onto the dirt road that stretched between Arroyo Tenorio and Camino de los Animas. She loved learning Santa Fe's Spanish place names, and reminded herself to look up "*tenorio*" and "*animas*." It seemed that half the streets of her newly adopted city were "*camino*" or "*calle*" or "*placita*." The Spanish names were far easier to learn and pronounce than the Indian names she'd encountered at American Indian Academy.

Miller Street was an anomaly. Barely a block long, it was hidden from view to most pedestrians. Few people even knew about it. Lined with towering sycamore and aspen trees, it abounded with honeysuckle, roses, Russian sage, and Jupiter's Beard. The Arroyo Tenorio end was accessible from a narrow path next to a coyote fence. Stone steps led down to Tenorio and Camino del Monte Sol. Looking behind her as she walked from the Miller Street hidden entrance to the well-travelled "Monte Sol," Clara realized that unless one knew it was there, the street was invisible.

As she walked briskly up Monte Sol, Clara thought about the friend she'd lost during the maelstrom of last year at American Indian Academy. Annie was the bright light in that whole sinister environment. Outwardly, it appeared to be an ambitious school for Native America's best and brightest youth. Inwardly, Clara had come to think, it had been a tragic network of pottery contraband, deceit and betrayal.

Worst was the bad boyfriend, the pretender. After Henry learned that she knew about his secret life, she'd lived in constant fear that she'd become a victim of his anger. It was never proved, but she suspected that Henry was the person who rigged her car, the car that became a death trap for her best friend. Though Annie's death had cut her to the core, she'd not allowed herself time to grieve.

Cars roared by, reminding Clara to edge over to the left side of the Camino. Always run facing traffic: that was one helpful adage she'd learned during her many years of marathon training. She missed running, but when she'd had the meniscus of her left knee mostly removed, the doctor told her, "Do not run," and she listened. Now she was reduced to walking and hiking. How she would have loved to have been walking with Annie at her side. The two of them had talked about living in Santa Fe together one day. That was before the Henry debacle and Annie's death.

Uphill, walking briskly. The more Clara thought about Annie, the faster she moved. To keep from overheating, she unzipped her windbreaker. In less than ten minutes from leaving Miller Street, she'd already passed Camino Santander. It was another short half mile to the top of Camino Del Monte Sol. In a way, Clara thought, the death had been her fault. If Annie hadn't met Clara, she would still be alive today. The memory of Annie was hard to bear.

Not yet ten o'clock. She would be at the summit of Sun Mountain before noon. Clara paused at the intersection of Camino del Monte Sol and Old Santa Fe Trail to drink from her canteen. Always important to stay hydrated, she told herself. That and watching for traffic. Santa Fe was the kind of tourist town in which visitors often got lost. They wove around the confusing network of narrow, winding streets and, unlike Clara, they seemed completely oblivious to pedestrians. When Clara ran through the forests and high mesas around the American Indian

Academy, she had to watch for rocks and roots on the trail. Now her vigilance focused on cars.

At the top of Camino del Monte Sol, she reached Santa Fe Trail and turned left. Just half a mile to go before starting her Monte Sol pilgrimage for Annie. The road crossed a bridge over the dry riverbed better known as an *arroyo*. When Clara reached the Sun Mountain trailhead, she was amazed to see so few cars. Usually by ten a.m., hikers had started up, many with dogs or children in tow. She crossed through the wooden fence announcing "Sun Mountain Trail," only recently declared an official trailhead by the city of Santa Fe. Local citizens had gained pedestrian right-of-way to Sun Mountain. It had taken months of working with homeowners who lived near the foot of the mountain. Rumor had it that money greased palms to sway the homeowners. Money talked, a universal truth.

Soon the homes were behind and below her, and she started hiking the slow curves up the face of Monte Sol. Annie would have loved doing this with her. Before AIA unraveled, they talked about doing some hikes together. That was forgotten after the death of her former boss, headmaster of the school where she'd taught. It turned out to have been murder, and his body was found on her classroom floor. Stop revisiting the horror, she told herself, but that was easier said than done. The murder had happened the same school year when Annie, driving Clara's car, had died in an explosion.

Was it possible to leave all this behind, to get a new start here in Santa Fe? Clara pondered the question as she climbed up the first batch of rocks on the Sun Mountain route. Looking out at sweeping vistas below, she felt that anything was possible. Huge, white, puffy clouds drifted slowly across the bright blue sky. In the distance loomed the Sandia Mountains, a place she'd hiked with Jerome.

Quit thinking about the past, Clara told herself. Pay closer attention to the steep, gravelly footpath. It was not healthy to indulge in another painful memory. She was now on the part of the trail where curves turned into sharp switchbacks. Rocky areas were giant stair steps that had to be navigated by hoisting. That was what she loved about hiking. The trail was a strict taskmaster. One should learn to ignore to random thoughts. Her adoptive Dad used to call those random thoughts "woolgathering." Here, inattentiveness could cause a fall. No, she reminded herself, don't let thoughts intrude. *Concentrate on your footing. Move slowly and carefully.*

Several switchbacks and boulder outcroppings later, she reached the top of Sun Mountain. From the distance, hundreds of feet below, the top looked like a peak. When one actually reached it, however, it was a large flat field. Clara retrieved the plastic bag of ashes from her backpack. From the chill of morning, the day had turned hot. She removed her windbreaker and tied it around her waist.

At the far end of the flat area was Clara's "Melanie" a gray, skeletal tree that looked more dead than alive. During her summer in Santa Fe, she'd often visited Melanie to make supplications to what she thought of as the god of her understanding. She also used the dead tree as a repository of heart-shaped rocks she'd collected. When she wanted to remember someone she'd loved and lost, she placed a heart for them in one of the tree's crooks.

She reached into her pocket for the heart rock saved from a previous hike. She took handfuls of the dusty gray ashes and spread them in four directions. She placed the heart on a crook of the tree. Impossible to think that she'd never see her friend again. She walked further away from the Melanie tree and spread another trail of ashes in a wide circle around the tree's base. She did this three times, until the ashes were gone. Tears streaming down her cheeks, she felt drained and relieved, sad, yet lightened. She sat on large, sun-warmed boulders near her tree. Somehow, she couldn't just turn around and walk back down the mountain. Not right away.

Meditation. She'd tried it at various times in her adult life but failed to stick with it. With Annie as the topic, there would be no problem. She'd never been able to do a proper lotus position, so she simply made herself comfortable leaning against a big, smooth rock, feet flat on the ground. She slowed her breath, closed her eyes and thought about her late friend. If she could have had a sister, it would have been Annie. She remembered the bountiful Thanksgiving dinner at Annie's home. The Archuleta *hacienda* was amazingly warm and welcoming. She envied Annie's large, extended family. The aunts and uncles, brothers and sisters seemed genuinely interested in her. Any friend of Annie's was a friend of theirs.

She would enjoy life for her friend. She sat, eyes closed, sun beating down upon her head, for a long time. The grief had

63

gone and was replaced with gratitude and love. How fortunate she'd been to have known and loved Annie. She would always cherish her. And maybe Annie's spirit would help her find her way through this slough of despondency.

"You're at peace, my dear Annie, and you made my life better. Every dawn, every sunset, I'll enjoy doubly. For me, but also for you." The ritual completed, Clara sat, eyes closed, on a muffin-shaped boulder. She breathed slowly, feeling exhausted and grateful at an homage accomplished. A sudden rustling near the Melanie tree broke through her reverie.

# Chapter Fourteen

"Oh, I didn't mean to interrupt your meditation." The speaker, a dark-skinned young man, passed by her and headed toward the path going down the mountain toward Santa Fe Trail. He seemed shy, almost embarrassed, but nice enough.

"Wait," Clara called out. "I'll hike down the mountain with you. Normally I don't talk to men I don't know, but you look like a St. John's College student, and I'm interested in learning more about the college. By now, she was standing up and had brushed the dust and leaves off her jeans.

"Sanjay Jabvala," he announced, holding out a hand to shake. Clara was pleasantly surprised, as no one shook hands anymore and practically no one had such good manners. As if answering her unspoken questions, Sanjay continued.

"You may have guessed. I am from India. Chennai, in Tamil Nadu to be exact. My good friend Arundati and I are here on scholarships. We are both in the Graduate Institute for Western Studies. I think it is amusing that you American students turn to Eastern Studies to be enlightened, whereas we Indians go the West....But I am talking too much about me. Tell me about you."

They had reached a boulder field that extended for several hundred feet. Unlike other rock outcroppings on Sun Mountain, these large stones were smooth and rounded. Some areas contained ripples, evidence of the ocean floor they'd been millennia ago. Walking across this area was tricky. Clara moved slowly and carefully. "Let's get through this part without talking," Clara said. "I'm always slightly afraid of slipping on rocks. I'll follow your lead." Sanjay held out his hand at the end of the boulder field, helping Clara with a very deep step back down to the dirt path. There was nothing forward about the offered hand. It was simply an act of kindness, a sign of solicitude.

When the terrain became less daunting, she proceeded to give a summary of how she'd ended up in Santa Fe, leaving out her disastrous affair with Henry DiMarco and the murder of Joseph Speckled Horse. She wanted to leave that part of her American Indian Academy history behind. Annie, however, was safe conversational territory.

They picked their way down the steep, rocky hillside, Sanjay in the lead and always offering a hand when the incline sharpened. It was a glorious, mellow afternoon. Impossible to stay in a low mood in such a beautiful setting.

"You may have noticed the ashes spread around at the top?" Clara wondered.

"Did someone you love die?"

"Well, yes, and I guess in your religion, people are cremated when their time is up. I guess I shouldn't be surprised that you knew what the ashes were about."

"Yes, I came up from St. John's, above the water tower, and I was amazed to see a trail of ashes. When I saw you, I rather connected you to that, but I thought that asking would be inappropriate, even rude. You see, I am Hindu, and we burn our beloved deceased ones and scatter their ashes in sacred Mother Ganges. Here in the high mountainous country, you do not have water. It dries up.

"Except in monsoon season," Clara said. "Then, I've learned, we can have rain in great torrents, drowning the land and turning the arroyos into raging rivers. Of course, it dries up very quickly. Never hike in an arroyo, I've been told, if there's a storm about."

"Yes, it can turn from bright sunshine to a raging storm in no time at all. People caught in an arroyo in a rainstorm have died. Not too long ago."

"Well, of course you are wondering." Clara found it hard to go on. She hadn't shared Annie's death with anybody except people at the school, and now school was behind her. Disappearing in a metaphorical rearview mirror. She stifled the urge to burst into a sob and instead brought herself back to the present.

"Those were the ashes of one of my dearest friends ever, Annie Archuleta. She was like the sister I never had. We were confidantes, always there for one another. She died in a car accident that in a weird way was my fault."

Sanjay seemed to listen attentively. At the same time, he paid close attention, as the trail down Monte Sol was slippery in places. He navigated some boulders on the trail and held out his hand to Clara. "Your fault?" he asked. "Were you driving?"

"No, it's just that the car was rigged to explode, and whoever did it had been hoping to do away with me. The wrong person was the victim. It would take hours to explain and actually, I'm trying to put everything that happened last year behind me. I want to remember just the good parts. I guess you might say, I'm trying to heal."

"I didn't mean to pry," Sanjay said. "I am just trying to be a good listener."

"Hey, I appreciate that, and you are a good listener. I'm about to break off a relationship and feeling touchy and vulnerable. I guess it's all been too much."

They'd reached the flat part of the Monte Sol trail, the section that bordered residential properties, winding through piñon trees. Signs instructed hikers to walk quietly and keep dogs leashed. Before the grassroots effort that allowed public access, Sanjay explained to Clara, hikers had to bushwhack their way from behind St. John's College.

They'd reached the road by now. Clara was going to miss talking with Sanjay. Nothing but the empty *casita* awaited her unless she relented and called Jerome. She'd promised herself she'd never do that, as their relationship, as far as she was concerned, had grown toxic.

Sanjay started to head up the arroyo that led to St. John College's campus. "Hey, I've got an idea. I have to finish a paper this week, but maybe in the near future, you could come to the coffee shop and I'll bring my friend Arundati. I think you two would have a lot in common. Maybe around three on Monday? I'll call and remind you.

"Sure. That sounds good." They exchanged phone numbers and parted ways. As she headed down Camino del Monte Sol to Miller Street, Clara realized she felt happier than she'd been in weeks.

## Chapter Fifteen

When her latest boyfriend, Jerome, suggested hiking to Nambe Lake, Clara wanted to say no. But because he'd been gone for a month and she wanted to see him, she agreed. Before he came over, she kept checking various weather reports. If it looked like rain, they'd do nearby Atalaya rather than be caught up in the higher mountains. But to her disappointment, it was supposed to be a clear, beautiful day.

As she filled her three-liter Camelback at the sink, Clara realized that she'd rather be doing almost anything else than spending a day with Jerome. He seemed oblivious to her interests and hell-bent on pursuing his own. She felt at times like an ornament or accessory. Maybe today's expedition would somehow help their relationship. Then again, did she even want it to?

Just as she finished filling the rubber water dispenser that went inside her new backpack, she felt a pair of strong arms hugging her from behind. She hadn't heard Jerome slip in, and at first she felt annoyed. Her resentment quickly melted, however, as he leaned down and kissed the back of her neck.

"Good morning, beautiful. I'm glad you're bringing plenty of water. It's supposed to get pretty hot today. Are you almost ready? We need to hit the trail as early as possible. Just got a report that a front might be moving in by afternoon. Late afternoon."

In an unusual move, Jerome had volunteered to bring the sandwiches today. Clara had baked her famous chocolate chip cookies and gotten some organic apples and grapes from Whole Foods. Her attitude about the hike was beginning to lighten up. Jerome really was trying to make up for recent snide remarks about the slowness of her hiking. She would never be the super athlete that he was, but maybe they could reach a happy medium, somewhere in between the two of them.

An hour later, they were on the Winsor Trail, wending their way to the cut-off to Nambe Lake. Clara found herself out of breath and tried to think of ways to ask Jerome to slow down. She didn't want to be a wimp, however, so she tried to breathe more deeply and to lengthen her stride. Why did she feel short of oxygen? Jerome was so far ahead that she'd lost sight of him. Finally, she reached the sign to Wilderness Gate, and there he was, leaning against the fence and munching an apple.

"Whew, I must be out of shape," she said, hoping that Jerome would disagree. When he took another bite of his apple and said nothing, she added, "Have you been waiting here a long time?"

"No, not really. I didn't mean to get so far ahead, but with these long legs, I find it hard to slow down. Remember to drink lots of water, and here's an apple." He tossed a Granny Smith through the air and she caught it.

"I know what the weather report said, but if you look up, it seems that a few clouds are drifting in. We'd better go the shorter way so we get down from higher ground before a storm breaks out."

Clara choked on the water she was drinking and hurled away a half-eaten apple. "Maybe we should just go to the Raven's Ridge lookout instead? I'm not familiar with the shortcut and I really don't want to climb up the Rio Nambe route. Is that what you mean by a 'shortcut'?"

"Come on, Clara, you're underestimating your abilities. You're the woman who's taken an hour off your marathon time. You're the tamer of unruly ninth graders, a fearless Wonder Woman who loves a challenge..."

"Gee, thanks for the praise, but I just don't have a good feeling about climbing up the river. I'd be so slow that we might do just as well with the dry land route."

"I'm psyched to go up the river route. I'll meet you at the lake."

Clara wasn't at all sure of the trail that paralleled the river. The last thing in the world she needed was to get lost. Between that possibility and having to scale the slippery river bank, she decided on the latter. Lesser of two evils. A voice inside was screaming "No," but she told it to shut up.

"Just promise me you'll stay within sight. I'm not really very good on river banks, and I'm hopeless when it comes to stream crossings. Remember how many times you had to help me when we hiked to San Leandro Lake? It must have been at least nine."

"Yes, but remember how richly rewarded we felt when we arrived. That lake was so mellow, so serene...worth every bit of slogging it took to get there."

Jerome had already started off in the direction of the river, and Clara had to scramble to catch up with him. She realized that she didn't actually know the other way, even if she could have mustered the courage to take it on her own.

"So be it, then," she called out to the tall figure ahead, "my fate's in your hands."

They trudged in silence alongside a series of rushing waterfalls and the gurgling stream. The riverbank grew narrower the further up they hiked, until Clara found her feet getting cold and wet. The only alternative was to walk at such an angle that it was hard not to slip right into the stream. She tried using her trekking poles to balance herself, but despite everything, she felt increasingly precarious. She looked upstream and spotted Jerome's quickly disappearing hiking boots. Obviously, he'd forgotten that he was supposed to wait for her. But wait a minute, did he ever agree to do that? She'd meant to ask him but in the past, it hadn't seemed to make the slightest bit of difference.

She was completely out of her comfort zone. The steep grade, combined with gnarled tree roots and slippery rocks, many of them more boulders than just rocks, made the upward climb scarier by the moment. She'd lost sight of Jerome and tried to hurry.

"Honey, wait up. I'm having trouble here."

No answer but the rushing water of Rio Nambe to her left. She tried to scramble up the next impossible clump of riverbank, and that's when she blacked out.

Opening her eyes, she looked at towering trees and the sky overhead. How had she gotten here? On her back in the icy stream, wrenched with pain in her lower back, out of breath, cold and shocked. Apparently, she'd tripped on one of those blasted roots and somehow flipped over. She heard loud, terrified shouting and realized it was coming from her.

"Oh god, what happened?" Jerome had come running.

"No, don't get up. Just sit there for a few minutes and catch your breath."

After a short time, he put out both hands and pulled her gently to the dry trail next to the river. By now, Clara was crying uncontrollably. Her side ached and her lower back felt as though daggers were punching through to her bones. Jerome gave her an aspirin and offered her water from his canteen. She was cold and wet and there was no way out except to walk back down the Winsor Trail to the parking lot.

Jerome took her back pack and slung it to his front, carrying it like a papoose. He took Clara's arm and gently guided her down the rocky dirt path. "Ouch," Clara said. "Don't we have about three miles? At the rate I'm going, it will take three years. Instead of seeing Nambe Lake..." She couldn't finish the sentence. Who knew this would turn into a painful ordeal?

"I'm sorry, darling," Jerome said. "I'm empathizing. It's painful for me too. I should have been watching out for you. Can you ever forgive me?"

She wanted to shout "No!" but instead she started blaming herself. "Well, you didn't know I was over-terrained. It was too steep and rocky. I should have spoken up instead of getting into the fear mode. The one I can't forgive is myself." Clara forced herself to keep going even though she felt that each step would be her last. Later she would replay this scene and she would react quite differently. What she should have said was "No, I can't forgive you and furthermore I never want to see you again!" It was a reflex, she realized, to disguise her true sentiments and to make excuses for someone who was inexcusable.

Finally, the two made their way down the last half mile to the ski area parking lot. With Jerome's help, Clara hoisted herself into the car. She fell asleep as Jerome raced down the hairpin turns to Santa Fe and the Emergency Room of Christus St. Vincent's. After an hour's wait, the doctor on duty could see Clara. He probed her back and rib cage and announced, "You're lucky. Nothing broken." But the doctor was wrong. Clara had lied to herself. Her heart was broken.

# Chapter Sixteen

Weeks passed before Sanjay called Clara to meet for coffee at the St. John's College coffee shop. In her agonizing about Jerome and the failed relationship, she'd forgotten all about the encounter at the top of Monte Sol. Details of the ash scattering came back to her. Even though she'd felt liberated at the time, having honored Annie's memory, she now felt let down, drained, and lonely. After all, Jerome had seemed a welcome relief after horrible Henry. With the river accident and his determination to turn her into the super-athlete she wasn't, she found the relationship a drain. Let Jerome meet an ultra-marathon runner, someone who loved extreme adventures.

She'd nearly forgotten the planned coffee date when the phone pierced her reverie. "Are you still able to meet me this afternoon at three?" Sanjay asked.

"Oh sure," Clara responded. "Where did you say we'd meet?"

"Just as I explained. At the St. John's College coffee shop. I've invited Arundati to join us. So glad you're available. Want me to pick you up?"

"That would be great. Ordinarily, I would walk but I had a bad hiking accident, so I've turned into a wimp."

At 2:30 Sanjay pulled into Clara's driveway. She made sure there was food in Oscar's bowl, grabbed her purse and a windbreaker, and met him before he had time to knock on the door. She did not invite him in. Sanjay seemed perfectly fine, but, after all, she didn't really know him. Was it wise to go off with a strange man?

Sanjay's wide smile melted away her doubts. "I'm a bit early, but it will give you time to see the campus. It's beautiful. I hope you don't mind that I told Arundati a little about your birthmother search. She's adopted also. She's pretty sure her original parents live in Tamil Nadu, somewhere around Chennai, but she's never figured out a way to go search for them. Don't bring it up, though. Once you get to know each other, she probably will."

Clara had forgotten all about the birthmother part of their conversation. "I can't believe I'm about to meet another adoptee! What are the chances of that?"

They sat in silence the rest of the way to St. John's campus. Up Garcia Street, a left on Old Santa Fe Trail, a left on

Camino del Monte Sol, a right on Cruz Blanca and then another right on the drive up to campus. Clara marveled at how convoluted Santa Fe's streets were. Because she walked so much she was learning them pretty well.

The college buildings were nestled on the piñon-covered foothills of Sun Mountain. Designed in the territorial style by John Gaw Meem, famous architect of the last century, they were elegantly arranged. In this city of very little green grass, the campus abounded in verdant patches of lawn. A cascading waterfall and fish pond greeted them at the top of wide brick staircases.

"Wow!" Clara exclaimed. "I can't believe how beautiful this place is. You know, I really haven't been here before." She stopped to look at the fish pond, marveling at the orange carp swimming around in the water. "These fish are great, but what happens to them during the winter. Does someone take them in. What happens when the water freezes?" She knew from the snowy winter she'd spent in Red Mesa how fierce winter could be in this part of the world.

Sanjay laughed. "That would be something...students with giant aquariums in their dorm rooms, adopting the fish as pets! No, the carp stay in the pond, kind of hibernating. At least I think that's what happens. We can ask one of the security guards. You'll notice that the campus is swarming with guards. You'd think there was a huge student population, but really, St. John's in Santa Fe has just a few hundred students."

Clara looked at her watch. "Hey, weren't we supposed to meet your friend at the coffee shop now? I mean, it's great to learn about the campus, but I can see there's a lot more of it, and we could come back another time just to look around."

"Arundati isn't just a friend, she's like the sister I never had. Or maybe like a cousin. She just told the college that she's planning to take a semester off, so she's a bit scattered. Don't tell her I told you that. Anyway, my friend Dottie always runs late. But you're right. It's time."

The coffee shop was full of students. Wooden tables and wicker-backed chairs occupied with students reading scholarly works, others tapping away at laptops, a few eating a late lunch or early dinner. Still others were deep into a game of GO or chess.

To the right, a collection of armchairs and couches were occupied by students having a heated discussion. Clara took it all in, noticing the somewhat disheveled attire of both men and women. It bordered on a Goth look, or in some cases, a definite sixties air. The place was a cross between a study hall and a recreation room.

"Hmmm. Guess she's not here yet. Let me buy you a cup of coffee?"

"Well, sure. That's nice of you." Clara wondered if this younger man thought they were on a date, but told herself to just accept the offer as a friendly gesture. "A small mocha with soy milk would be perfect."

The cafe counter was on the left side of the coffee shop, and it was on the order of an old-fashioned diner. While Clara and Sanjay were placing their order, Arundati walked up behind them. She put her hands over Sanjay's eyes and said "Boo!"

"Here you are at last." Sanjay seemed overjoyed, and gave her a hug. "I'm treating. What can I get you?"

"How about a large black coffee? I have 100 pages of *The Odyssey* to read tonight and a paper to finish."

"Dottie." He turned to Clara in an aside, "We use her childhood nickname rather than Arundati. Sometimes she's even Dot. Let me introduce a new friend. This is Clara Jordan. We met on the top of Sun Mountain and I thought you two might enjoy getting to know each other. One can't have too many friends these days."

Clara held out her hand and Dottie took it. This was so civilized, shaking hands. It was the first time Clara had felt truly welcome in Santa Fe. It seemed to be a place where people were too busy and preoccupied to spend much time with a newcomer. The rowdy bunch had vacated chairs and couches across from the food counter, so the three grabbed them while they were still available.

They settled in the cushiony leather look chairs and sipped their coffee. Not in an unfriendly way, Sanjay and Dottie were both looking at her. Clara felt that she needed to explain why she was in Santa Fe. After all, it's not as though she had a job or even a boyfriend who lived here. Jerome, she was pretty sure, was soon to be history.

"Well," she began, "you probably wonder what brought me to Santa Fe. It has to do with looking for family roots. My parents adopted me when I was really young. I was discouraged from asking questions. Long story short, you might say I came here to recover… You might say I came here to recover from my year of teaching at American Indian Academy. I moved to New

Mexico to look for a possible relative. My adoptive Mom and Dad weren't exactly crazy about the idea, and I didn't want to ask them for money. So, I looked online and saw that American Indian Academy wanted an English teacher. Red Mesa sounded like a middle-of-nowhere kind of place but beautiful in a rugged sort of way. I was ready for adventure. Everything fell into place, and I moved to an off-campus log cabin just before the school year began."

"Wow," said Dottie, "that was a leap. I can imagine how different New Mexico must have seemed from anything on the East Coast. And teaching Native Americans...had you ever done that before?"

"No, not at all. In fact, I hadn't headed up a classroom except for student teaching. But I loved what I read about the school's mission. The founder...I've forgotten his name...wanted an exclusive boarding school for the cream of the crop from the whole Indian nation, but especially from the eight northern pueblos in New Mexico. The goal was to educate them so well that they could get in the best colleges, to inspire them to aim high."

"That's awesome," Sanjay said. "Do you think it's working?"

"It's a really great idea. So much positive energy. Lofty goals. But the year I was there, things were falling apart. In fact, the school nearly did me in. I couldn't leave soon enough."

"What do you mean?" Arundati asked.

Clara sighed. Should she really tell these people everything? Why not? Nothing to lose, and since Jerome was being such a jerk she really missed having someone to talk with. Both her new friends were looking at her.

"OK. It's a long, convoluted story, so you might want to get some coffee refills."

"Sure, I'll do that," Sanjay offered. He grabbed a tray and took all three of their cups to the pump-operated coffee thermoses. Returning, adopting a courtly air, he served Clara and Dottie, bowing before each. "Service with a smile."

"Here we go," Clara began. She proceeded to recount all that happened a year ago, including the murder of Joseph Speckled Horse, dealing with the traumatic aftermath and quelling the anxiety of her students. She mentioned Henry DiMarco as the international pottery dealer who talked headmaster Speckled Horse to part with precious pottery heirlooms that were property of the school." She deliberately left out the fact that Henry DiMarco was her lover. She was hoping to avoid that part of the story.

"And exactly why was he doing this?" asked Dottie.

"Good question. Speckled Horse wanted to leave a legacy for improving the school. The buildings needed a lot, the roofs were leaking, the gym floor was downright dangerous. Times were tight, and there was no obvious way to raise funds. Being that he was headmaster, Speckled Horse held the purse strings as well as keys to the most precious pottery made by anyone in the pueblos. Di Marco apparently talked him into offering the most valuable pieces to international collectors. No one knew anything about this."

"Were these pots kept in an open viewing spot?" Sanjay asked. "Where anyone could view them? Surely it would be noticed if they were missing."

"No," Clara said. "They were in a vault for safekeeping. It was what you might call a 'secret collection,' and it was held as part of the equity of the school. As far as I could tell, not that many people even knew about the collection. It contained not only pottery but precious beadwork and basketry.

"Speckled Horse, without consulting anyone, apparently decided that to keep the school from going into debt, he would let Henry DiMarco sell some San Ildefonso pieces, made by Maria Martinez, abroad. Highly illegal, but very profitable. By doing this, he kept the school in the black and also made all kinds of improvements...a new floor for the gymnasium, uniforms for the 'Fleet Feet Braves,' the school's champion track team. And more."

"Who is Henry DiMarco?" both of Clara's listeners asked at once.

Clara wavered for a moment, wondering how much she should reveal to Sanjay and Dottie. She didn't really know them that well, and what would they think of her when she admitted that she'd once claimed Henry as her boyfriend. Maybe she could omit that part?

"DiMarco?" asked Sanjay. "Doesn't sound like an Indian name to me. Maybe Italian?"

"Yes, it's an Italian surname," Clara said. "I'll try to give you the short version. The DiMarco family founded the school. They were from Italy originally, really wealthy, and in addition they'd collected all the pottery and artifacts that were kept in the

76

vault that only Speckled Horse knew about. Henry, their spoiled rotten son, had been ousted from job after job, so they made him the Information Technology director of AIA to give him a job he couldn't lose."

"What's AIA?" Dottie asked

"It stands for American Indian Academy," Clara explained. "Anyway, Henry was more interested in making money illegally through illicit pottery sales than in working for the school. He convinced Speckled Horse to use the collection to make major improvements. Since no one oversaw the books and everyone had complete faith in the headmaster, people didn't question the situation."

"Wow," exclaimed Dottie, "this sounds like the plot of a murder mystery."

"Strange you should mention that," Clara said. "Speckled Horse was in fact murdered." She held back tears at the grisly memory. "He was found on my classroom floor. By me."

"How horrible," Dottie groaned. "So did you just go to school one day, unlock your classroom and there was the dead body?"

"No, and here's a short version. The headmaster was scheduled to give a talk to my students after the last class. The students, thank God, were out for a short recess before the talk. I'd left to get audiovisual equipment. Speckled Horse was going to show some slides of ancestral native sites. It was to be a lead-up to AIA 'Pride Week.' When I got back to my classroom with the VCR, the door was locked. I got help in getting it unlocked, and there was Speckled Horse in a pool of blood."

"Good grief! How did you cope with that?"

"I nearly threw up, but I had to stay strong for the students who'd soon be coming in for the talk. A janitor called the police. I stood at the door and directed my boys and girls to go to the outdoor basketball court and wait for me. I was on automatic pilot. All hell broke loose after that...the students traumatized, the school turned upside down. I did my best to calm my class, but the damage was done. As you can imagine, we were given another room for the rest of the school year."

"Did anyone find out who did it?" Sanjay asked. "Were you a suspect?"

"Well, I got caught up in another drama right about the same time." Clara wanted to change the subject, but her listeners kept asking questions. She did not want to reveal that her duplicitous boyfriend Henry was suspected of hiring a hitman. He had to keep Speckled Horse from leaking information about the pottery smuggling that he, Henry, was masterminding. He had to get rid of the man.

Clara excused herself to go to the restroom. When she returned to the coffee shop, she brought up the Indian school again, hoping to end the interrogation. "Well," she said. "I really wanted things to work. I'll never forget some of those ninth graders. Story-tellers, artists, amazing runners and athletes. There was potential, but let's just say things fell apart. I had to leave."

"Hey," Sanjay interrupted, "The ultimate bad year. I can tell it's painful for you to recollect. Let's get out of here. Dottie and I can show you around the campus. There's still an hour or two of daylight."

"Yeah," Dottie agreed. "I think one of Stephen King's characters put it best: *What's done is done and can't be undone.*" She gave Clara a sisterly hug. "We'll help you move on. Sanjay has very good taste in people and a friend of his is a friend of mine."

The threesome walked out to St. John's bricked open plaza and up the steps to more academic buildings. Beautifully landscaped, the upper area revealed the Evans Science Building and what Dottie called "the bell tower building."

"I can't believe how East Coast all of this looks," Clara said. "My adoptive dad was a college professor at the University of Virginia. The buildings and grounds here would fit right in with UVa.. It's amazing. Kind of an anomaly?"

"I see what you're saying," Dottie said, "but just look beyond the campus buildings. What you'll see is like nothing at UVa. Behold, the Rocky Mountain foothills; our campus is nestled right at their foot."

Sanjay joined in. "Right beyond where we're standing, we have Sun Mountain, beyond that Moon Mountain, Atalaya Mountain and to the left of Atalaya, Picacho Peak. If you like to hike, I can take you up all of them. Dottie has worked up to everything except Moon. We try to go hiking every Sunday. If you feel like it, join us sometime."

"That sounds great, but I'd need to work up to it."

"Let's show her the new gym," Dottie said. "I could take you as my guest. It's really got everything. Weights, stationary bikes, yoga classes. You could get fit in no time at all."

Sanjay had other ideas. "Why don't we go to the trailhead for Atalaya? It's too late in the day to get to the top but we can do a partial. It's a favorite hike with students and the locals. Beautiful ponderosa forest, quartz formations along the way, great views."

"What's the rise in elevation?" Clara wanted to know.

"I'm not sure, but Atalaya is about 5 1/2 miles. It's fairly steep at the end. There are nine switchbacks. I counted them. When you get to the top, there are some massive boulders, a great place to sit and take in the views."

"Yeah," Dottie added, "and there's a place we call 'the throne.' It's shaped like a miniature amphitheater and it's made of pink, white and gray quartz. You have to sit in it and feel the majesty. It's really awesome!"

They'd walked from the coffee shop to the main parking lot, at the end of which was an official trail map set between wooden posts. It showed a network of routes, many of which were labelled as part of the Dale Ball system. Clara wondered who Dale Ball was, but it was growing cold and the sun was sinking. Better to find out another time, as every time they started to chat, it slowed them down.

They walked briskly along a winding dirt path bordered by scruffy piñon trees till they came to a wide, sandy arroyo. A brown wooden sign told Clara that the trail resumed on the other side.

"Wow! This looks just like a river bed, sort of carved out of the landscape. Does water ever flow through here?"

"Funny you should ask," Sanjay said. "When we have heavy monsoon rains, usually in August, this arroyo might become a raging river. It can happen quite suddenly. People have drowned right where you're standing. We're safe for now. Monsoon season is over."

"There's hardly any warning," Dottie added. "It's just that if you hear thunder, even distant thunder, don't be in an arroyo. Get out in a hurry. One time I hiked Atalaya during late July, monsoon season can come that early in the summer, and when I came down from the top, this whole stretch was full of water. Deep water, roiling along with a current. We had to walk a mile or two out of the river's path to get back to the parking lot."

Clara and Dottie followed Sanjay through a scrub forest to Wilderness Gate Road. They crossed over to a wooden staircase that led to the Atalaya trailhead. "That was the only boring part of this hike," Sanjay said. "When we do tackle the summit, we'll want to drive up to the parking spaces. There are only a few spots available, so you have to get here early or have good parking karma."

Going through a turnstile onto a dirt path, the three hikers set out at a brisk pace. However, daylight was going fast, fading into night. "OK gang," Sanjay announced. "We don't want to be hiking in the dark. Let's turn around here and walk down the Cruz Blanca path. It's too easy to trip in the arroyo we used to climb up. The Cruz Blanca path goes the same way, just a little longer, and it will give us a good view of the sunset."

As if in response to Sanjay's logistics, the sky presented a magnificent pallet of rose, pink and gold. Puffy layers, a celestial flock of pink sheep. By the time they reached the parking lot, night had fallen and an almost full moon peeked over Sun Mountain.

# Chapter Seventeen
## Santa Fe, New Mexico

Naked, Clara stood under the water for a long time. The shower was either too hot or too cold, no matter how much she adjusted the spigots. Finally, she settled for too hot. Why was she showering before going on a hike? The hot water eased her sore torso. Ever since the Nambe Lake debacle with Jerome, she felt the pain of her body bruises. "Soft tissue damage" was what the doctor called it. Any heat helped ease tightness. That, combined with lots of time on the heating pad, was helping her heal. Was she healed enough for hiking? Maybe not, but nonetheless, she was meeting Dottie for their long-awaited trek to the top of Atalaya.

Sanjay, who'd planned to go with them, was called at the last minute to help one of the St. John College tutors. He'd signed on as an adjunct graduate tutor's assistant and this, he'd been told, was an emergency.

As she stepped out of the steaming shower and into an oversized fluffy towel and wrap-around terrycloth bathrobe, Clara chuckled to herself. What on earth would comprise an academic tutoring emergency? St. John's was a school that focused exclusively on the great books of the Western World, philosophy and ideas. As she got into her hiking jeans and several layers of shirts, Clara mused to herself...*Can't understand Kant...Stumped by Socrates...Angry at Aristotle...Nervous about Nietzsche.* But then she remembered Sanjay telling them last week about the girl, a freshman from China, who took her life. The suicide was a combination of academic pressures, anxiety about her parents' pending divorce, and a breakup with her boyfriend.

Yes, compassion, even in the form of a caring tutor and academic support, could make the difference between life and death. She was impressed with Dottie and Sanjay, her new best friends, and especially with their devotion to what they called "the St. John's way." She had a burning desire to know them both better, to spend time with them, to learn about India through these two students. Because of lingering pain from her hiking injury, she'd almost told Dottie that it was too soon for her to undertake such an ambitious hike as Atalaya. However, when they'd made plans, Dottie assured her that they could turn around at any time.

Twenty minutes later found the two friends starting out on the Atalaya trailhead, up the dirt path that would twist and turn several miles to the mountain's summit. They were in ponderosa pine country and already seeing panoramic views of the southeastern part of Santa Fe. Dottie, who'd done the hike countless times, enjoyed Clara's amazement.

"Look at the sky through all the trees! We can see rooftops of Saint John's College. I can't believe these towering pines."

"They're ponderosa," Dottie said. "Used to be huge forests of them but during the old days, they were chopped down for fuel and for building cabins. In town, we have piñons and junipers: that's all that's left."

"I thought ponderosa only grew at higher elevations. The town's lower, right? They wouldn't have been in the town anyway, would they?" Clara found it increasingly difficult to hike and talk.

"Well, the climate is changing, getting warmer they say. I'm not sure about where the ponderosa used to be. All I know is that there were a lot more, say a hundred years ago. You know, it doesn't really matter and I need my breath for hiking. Let's just enjoy where we are." With that, she picked up the pace. The two friends continued their ascent in comfortable silence.

Twenty minutes later, the going became more challenging. "Ah," exclaimed Dottie. "This is the beginning of the nine switchbacks. Not tight, narrow switchbacks. Large, broad ones. Now the fun begins! Watch for the ball bearing effect on some of this loose gravelly terrain. Also, watch for hidden rocks and roots. They can catch you by surprise."

While Clara hadn't planned to bring up the disastrous fall on her hike with Jerome, she felt she knew Dottie well enough to confide in her. Between catching her breath and drinking from her water bottle, she related the Nambe Lake debacle with Jerome. "I'm glad you reminded me about the footing. A moment of inattentiveness can spell disaster. It's been a month and I'm still sore. It's a fine balance, don't you think? It's important to take in the scenery but it's even more important to focus on the trail and placing your feet correctly."

"That's such a perfect motto," Dottie said. "I'd say trail first, scenery second. You're brave to be back out here so soon after your injury. But what about Jerome, what about his responsibility? Shouldn't he have been aware of your being over-terrained? Never met the guy, but he seems like a jerk. I'd say with friends like that, who needs enemies."

"If nothing else, it taught me that I don't need Jerome in my life. He's more trouble than he's worth and..."

Dottie finished the sentence, "you don't feel safe with him anymore. I had a relationship like that once. Tried and tried to make it work, made excuses for the guy- his name was Narendra -I had to call it quits. It was too much of a one-way street. We loved each other but he wanted me to be something that just wasn't me."

They'd been following a narrow, rocky dirt path for the last mile, and now the trail fanned out into a gravelly slope with no discernible boundaries. Leery of skidding, Clara followed Dottie's method of ascending. Zig-zagging up this tricky bit of terrain, the women temporarily ceased their conversation.

"This is my tried and tested method," said Dottie. "A little left zig, a short right zag. It's kept me from losing it more than once. Ah, there's the path up ahead. There are some boulder areas where it will be helpful to grab trees as you hoist yourself up."

"I've got a confession," Clara said. "I've started out on Atalaya a couple times on my own, but - if I make it - this will be my first time getting to the top. Guess I was afraid of wandering off the trail and getting lost. It's great of you to be the pathfinder."

"Last summer," said Dottie, "I hiked Atalaya every weekend. A friend was training to get into shape for the Camino de Santiago pilgrimage. We'd time our Sunday hikes, trying each time to carve minutes from our finishing time. We got it down to under two hours."

"Wow! Impressive. You might not want to hike with me," Clara said. "I'm a slug compared to that. I didn't even note the time when we started. I'm sure it will take me twice that long. I'm strong but slow. Hey, we finished the scaly slope and now we're back to the good old dirt path. Makes it a lot easier to breathe. And to talk."

"And I've noticed that we both like to talk. Frankly, all that timing made it less fun for me. Between paying attention to the trail and the clock, we hardly had time to appreciate our surroundings." Dottie bent over and picked up a rock from the ground. She held it in her palm. "Like this heart-shaped piece of quartz. It's almost perfect, don't you think?"

"It is. You've given me an idea. I'll start looking for hearts and save them for the top. I'd like to start a small shrine and dedicate it to Annie. The heart will go in it as my first tribute to her."

"Oh, you mean the friend who was driving the car that exploded? It was your car, you said, and you were the one who was supposed to die. I don't think you should blame yourself for a quirk of fate. On the other hand, I can't imagine how I'd feel if I had something like that weighing on me."

Rather than continuing with the uncomfortable topic, Clara, who was in the lead, picked up the pace. At the top of the ascent was a sign with two brown wooden slats facing two different directions. On the right was "170," on the left, "174." Taking a deep swig of water from her canteen, she called down the trail to Dottie. "I can see how one could get lost at this juncture. Guess we'll have to remember when we're coming back down whether we take 174 or 170."

By now, Dottie was at Clara's side. "Yes, you're right. We came up 174, so that's what we should hike down. I only made the mistake of going down 170 once. You end up getting off the mountain, but it's a long way to the parking lot, and you have to spend a lot of time on the road. Definitely."

Refreshed by their brief stop, the two forged ahead. Their paces, it turned out, were evenly matched and subconsciously, they took turns being in the lead. It had turned warm on this Autumn day. Without comment and at different times, they removed their windbreakers. Dottie tied hers around her waist and Clara stuffed hers in her backpack.

This part of the trail was relatively flat, and they made good time. A grove of young ponderosa ahead of them looked as though they'd been carefully planted to form a colonnade.
Five or six on either side of a wide path.

"Look at that," exclaimed Clara. "I can just see a phantom horse and buggy clip-clopping and wheeling through. Of course, that would be when no one is here to see them."

"Except the fairies," said Dottie. "I've always imagined that they come out at night and frolic in the branches of these healthy young trees. Especially around May Day, when there's a grand ball."

"Attended by wood sprites, elves, and owls. Creatures of the night. I wonder if anyone's hiked Atalaya at night with headlamps. Maybe it's possible to catch them in the act."

"You mean during their nocturnal festivities? Clara, please don't suggest that we do that, even though it would be fun.

If I were to embark on such an adventure, it would be going to India, to the shore temple at Mahabalipuram."

"Maha-what?" Clara knew that her friend Arundati had not found her parents despite letters, inquiries, and online searches, but she'd never mentioned any locations. "The subcontinent is totally unfamiliar to me. Where exactly is Maha...?"

"...balipuram," finished Dottie. "As you must know, the subcontinent is vast. Think of the shape of India, sort of an upside down triangle. Mahabalipuram is in the southern part, not too far from Chennai. It's a collection of shore temples, ancient and mysterious. The legends go that it was built over another city, a sort of Atlantis, now under the sea."

"Wait a minute, this is all too much to absorb while we're climbing a mountain. Let's take a snack break and maybe you can tell me more when we get to the top. Speaking of which, is it much further?"

"Here," offered Dottie, "have some trail mix. I made it this morning. A combination of granola, almonds, dried chopped up apricots, M&Ms, cashews. I didn't make the granola."

"Ummm, delicious. I'm afraid all I brought besides a sandwich is a couple energy bars. You didn't answer my question. Much further? I'm feeling a little worn out."

"That's because you're not eating and drinking enough." Dottie held up her canteen by way of a toast. "Here's to hydration!"

Clara toasted with her orange REI water bottle. "Cheers, and I promise to quit asking how much further. I'll take more of that trail mix. It hits the spot."

They walked along in silence for another 45 minutes, each lost in thought. Clara reflected on her own search for a birthmother, a failed quest, a colossal letdown. If only she could help Dottie with her mission. That would mean going to India, however, and such a journey seemed as feasible as going to the moon.

"Right now, all I want is to get to the top of this endless mountain." She spoke to herself, but Dottie, who was now in the lead, picked up on it right away.

"Oh, she of little faith, Atalaya is not endless. When we get to the top, you'll know it's all been worth it. After all these slippery switchbacks. And the views will blow you away."

"Hooray! I sense we're on the home stretch." Clara felt energized. "Are we almost at those great boulders with fantastic views that you've been talking about?"

"Yes," Dottie said, "but before we reach them - the boulders with a view - there's a quartz throne that you will love."

"A throne? You mean like for a queen?" Clara quickened her pace and took in the scenery on either side of the path. On her right, piñon-covered hills in the distance. A vast blue sky. On her left, towering ponderosa and huge, craggy rocks that sparkled with bits of quartz and mica. Perusing that side, she realized that Santa Fe lay below. She wandered over to the ledge for a better view.

"Careful," warned Dottie. "I know you're sure-footed as a mountain goat, but there's no way to call 911 up here and I don't want you to lose your footing."

"Um, yes," said Clara. "Especially in light of my recent disastrous hike with Jerome. I don't need to be reminded to be careful. You know, worrying about Jerome may have been why I stumbled. I guess you might call me obsessed."

Dottie walked over to Clara. She put her arm on her friend's shoulder. "Don't beat yourself up. We've all been fools for love. What I'd like to help you do is move on to bigger and better things. Hey! Here we are, at the coronation throne!"

Massive stone boulders to the right of their path formed a semicircle, in the center of which was a sort of natural altar. Behind and above the boulders was a backdrop of pink and gray quartz. A previous hiker had built a small cairn on the altar. Looking more closely, Clara and Dottie discovered that many of the cairn's stones were shaped like hearts.

"I knew it!" exclaimed Clara. "The minute you mentioned a throne, I imagined there would be something sacred about this spot." She emptied her pockets, revealing several stone hearts. "I'm placing one for Annie, in her memory and another as a wish that you'll be able to find your birth family."

Dottie gave Clara a hug. "That means more than you can possibly know. I just have this strong feeling that I'd have to go to India to even begin to search. Right now, I can't figure out how to do it. The expense, the logistics. Also, what if I found her and she rejected me all over again? Did you say you'd met your birthmother and it was disappointing? As long as I don't know my birthmother, I can keep her on a pedestal. And what if she doesn't want to be found?"

As Dottie rambled on, her voice got softer, almost inaudible. Clara realized that her friend was choking back tears. "Come on, let's get to the top of Atalaya and we can talk about it some more. You asked about my reunion with my birth mom. Her name was Greta. Was. I learned that I was too late, so I'll never meet her." Dottie was weeping openly. "I'm sorry. That was the wrong thing to say, but that's what happened."

Dottie regained her composure and forged ahead on the trail. A collection of massive boulders lay before them. Clouds passed over the sun and the air grew cooler. "Here we are," she exclaimed. "Let's have lunch and take in the view. I promise not to get maudlin again."

"You're entitled to feel what you feel, but yes to lunch. I'm famished. Let's put some layers back on and then eat at this exclusive outdoor restaurant."

"I secretly made a reservation," joked Dottie. "You never know when they might be crowded."

It felt cooler now that they'd stopped hiking. After taking jackets out of their packs and layering up, they sat on a wide, flat rock and faced out toward Santa Fe far below in the distance. The space between them served as a picnic table and they spread out their offerings. Almonds, apple wedges, slices of white cheddar, hardboiled eggs, grapes, peanut butter and jelly sandwiches. As they ate, silence reigned. They both were lost in private thoughts.

"I can hardly believe it," exclaimed Clara. "Here we are having lunch at the top of the world. This place is amazing. Thank you for bringing me here. I would never have discovered it on my own."

"Yes, amazing," agreed Dottie. "I think sooner or later you would have discovered it on your own, but I'm glad to have been the first person to introduce you to the total Atalaya experience. It's definitely my go-to place. Sometimes I do it on my own, but it's much more fun hiking it with you."

The picnic consumed, the two hikers packed up and headed down the mountain. The clouds moving in threatened possible rain, so the women moved quickly. Mostly silent, they made good time. When they'd gotten down the nine switchbacks to less tricky footwork, they resumed their conversation.

"You know, Dottie, I think you should pursue finding your mother. I mean, look at me. I waited too late and now I'll never know mine. Even if you have to go to India to search, why not just do it?"

"I don't want to hurt my adoptive mom's feelings. She's a perfectly good mother. She might feel betrayed if I suddenly came up with another parent. I think it would just about do her in."

"I know exactly how you feel," said Clara. "But you don't know for sure. Have you asked her about it? Or are you just assuming?"

"Hmmm...I can't really think about that right now. I'm a little tired and our trail has gotten really narrow. Seems like there are more rocks than when we made our way up. Or maybe I'm just imagining it."

"No worries," said Clara. "You're right. Let's just be here now rather than trying to solve impossible problems. I didn't mean to probe."

The two entered into an undulating stretch, ups and downs, mild rather than steep. For a long time, no one said anything. By silent agreement, they were not going to talk about adoption, birthparents, or Dottie's possible reunion. By the time they reached the St. John's College parking lot, the air had cleared and both women felt more at ease. Their friendship was in its infancy and neither one wanted to threaten it.

## Chapter Eighteen

Clara, who had not told her friends that she'd just turned twenty-seven, felt like she was drifting. She'd always downplayed her birthday, but this year it seemed more important than ever. Pleasant as it was being with Sanjay and Dottie, it wasn't really enough. Jerome was past tense, and she was pretty sure, for now at least, she didn't want to meet anyone else. Santa Fe was lovely and she was glad she'd landed here, but really, what was she going to do with the rest of her life? While she was musing, the phone rang. It had to be Dottie.

"Would you like to hike Picacho Peak today? It's shorter and steeper than Atalaya, but I think you'd love it. I want to go in about an hour. Sanjay might join us."

"I'm really tempted, but I promised myself to do something about finding a job." Clara half hoped that Dottie would convince her to put the search off till tomorrow. What difference would one day make? But before she could express her ambivalence, Dottie bounced back into the conversation.

"Sure, you have to stick to your plan. Working for the New Mexico Legislature, right?"

"Well, yes, it's only seasonal, but the experience would look good on my resume. And this is a short session. When it's over in March, I can resume my search for a teaching job. If that's what I want to do, which I'm not at all sure about." She let out a loud sigh. "I'm a bundle of indecision."

"Hey, friend, no problem. We all do what we have to do. Good luck at the Roundhouse. Let's check in at the end of the day. I'll tell you about Picacho and we can schedule another hike when it works for both of us. And you can tell me about life in the job-hunting lane."

Clara looked through the closet. She'd been wearing what Annie would have called "lumberjack clothes" for months; she'd nearly forgotten what it was like to dress up. Nothing flashy would do. Better to be conservative. Ah, here...this plaid jumper and jacket would be perfect. She would also have to wear heels, something she rarely did. In fact, she couldn't remember the last time. Would she even know how to walk in them?

Time to swing into action, she told herself. Forty-five minutes later - showered, dressed, her long black hair pulled back into a stylish bun - she pulled on panty hose and stepped into a pair of navy pumps. Her black watch plaid sheath was the perfect look for an interview. What to do about a purse? She was accustomed to throwing everything into a backpack. Did she even have a dressy purse?

Rummaging through a catch-all basket in her closet, she found a black messenger bag. Maybe not perfect, but it would do. She put a copy of her resume and xeroxed copies of her college transcripts in a folder, and headed toward the door. Oscar walked across her path, meowing loudly. How did other people, friends Clara had talked with, manage to feed their cats once a day? Oscar demanded breakfast, lunch, and dinner, and she was his attentive servant.

"OK, kiddo, this has to hold you till I get back."

All of a sudden, she remembered earrings. No one should go out with naked earlobes - and then, at last, walked out the front door, locking it behind her. She checked her earlobes to make sure she was wearing both gold hoops, as she'd been known to put in just one earring and forget the other.

Ten minutes later. She'd never been to the New Mexico State Capital, the "Roundhouse," and wasn't sure where she could park. Instead of taking a chance on parking, she drove into the Kaune's Grocery Store lot, diagonally across from the large, impressive building. She'd done a little homework before her visit, discovering that the building was erected in 1966. The style was Territorial, cream colored with white trim. In a town full of adobe and fake adobe, it called attention to itself.

The day was turning cold, and low dark clouds were closing in. Were rain or snow forecast? Weather in Santa Fe had a habit of changing suddenly and dramatically. Pulling her jacket around her and looking both directions, she crossed Paseo de Peralta and Santa Fe Trail. Men in suits and women in heels, carrying briefcases, scurried by. Appropriately, she was wearing heels and carrying a portfolio. How would she feel being one of their league?

Once inside the round marble entrance hall, Clara walked to the security guard's desk for directions.

"Hi, I'm here to see about being hired to work during the session. My friend Maggie Fletcher said I should just go visit legislators in their offices. I have my resumes with me."

The guard, a large man stuffed into a black uniform, gave her a once-over. "Oh, Ms. Fletcher. She works for Senator Farmer. Go up to the second floor, and if you walk to the right in a circle, you'll come to the Senate. Look for the floor-to-ceiling glass doors."

The Roundhouse lived up to its name in roundness. It was also rather grand, all marble and polished surfaces, wood and faux brass. Clara looked above to the Rotunda-style dome. She remembered the Rotunda in Charlottesville, Virginia, part of "Mr. Jefferson's academic village." The University of Virginia was where her adoptive father had been a professor for many years. She remembered that Monticello itself was borrowed from the French, a country whose architecture Thomas Jefferson had so admired.

"Ma'am, need me to escort you?"

Clara flushed. She'd been daydreaming, maybe because working for state government wasn't exactly what she'd planned to do. "Oh, no thanks. I see the elevator right behind us. But I'd rather walk up the stairs. Same directions apply?"

"Yes ma'am. The person you'll want to talk with is Sally. Ms. Sharer. She knows everything there is to know about how this place works. After your interview, she'll probably take you downstairs to Louise Anaya's office. Personnel. I'd advise you to go pretty quickly. Some people take an early lunch."

Clara thanked the guard and scrambled up the stairs. Like everything else in this massive edifice, the stairwell went upward in a circle. At the top, there were no signs announcing "Senate." Instead, there were corridors, one after another, with office numbers. On they ranged...200-210, 211-220, 221-230. There seemed to be no end to offices, and not a sign of the glass doors the guard had described.

Just when she was about to give up and go downstairs to once again question the security guard, there she was, in front of the glass doors. She entered a large room full of people looking at their computers or on the phone. It was silent as a library. She walked up to the first desk on the right. A bewhiskered man looked up from his work. "Hi, may I help you?"

She noticed the neatness of his salt and pepper mustache and goatee. He wore a v-neck sweater vest. In fact, the whole place was very orderly. Cabinets and file cases in tidy manner, like a Rubik's Cube, were spaced between, around and adjacent to the workers' desks. Apparently, this was a bureaucracy at its finest. After the benign chaos of American Indian Academy, quite the opposite of the scene before her, working here would take some adjustments.

"Hi, I'm Clara Jordan, and I'm inquiring about job openings for the 1986 Legislative session. I was advised to start by talking with a Ms. Sharer. Am I in the right place?"

"Bob here. Bob Green. Welcome to the Senate Chambers." He held out his right and she shook it. "Yes indeed, Ms. Clara Jordan. You're in exactly the right place. Sally is delivering a bill update but she'll be right back. Can I get you some coffee or tea?" He walked around his desk and pulled a chair next to it. "Here, have a seat while you wait."

"Well, yes, thanks. That would be nice," Clara said. "No sugar please, just cream." Before she was halfway through her coffee, Sally appeared.

"Ms. Sharer." The tall, blond woman held out her hand for Clara to shake.

A bit taken aback by the formality, Clara rose and shook Sally Sharer's manicured hand. This was a different world. Not that she didn't like it, but she wondered how could she fit in? The school and environs, AIA, had been rustic, casual, maybe even scruffy. This was like stepping back into the fifties, or like being in the country club settings of Charlottesville, Virginia, where she'd grown up.

"It's so kind of you to take me under your wing," she told Sally. "And thank you, Mr. Green, for the coffee. If I am assigned to work in the Senate, maybe I'll be seeing you again." She smiled inwardly. "Mr." was the prefix used by University of Virginia students, and they mentioned one another in third person during classroom discussions. Two could play at this game.

"Let's take the elevator." Sally gestured behind her and walked toward the hall. Clara looked at Sally's very high heels. No wonder the elevator was preferable. Her guide clicked her way to the closest elevator and pressed the down button. The small, close space was full of suited men and women, but they squeezed in and rode up before going down.

In the depths of the Roundhouse, they walked - Sally ahead, Clara following, to Louise Anaya's office. Down here, they were in a windowless world. Louise, a solidly-built middle-aged woman, took Clara's paperwork and scanned it. "Everything looks in order, and I just learned that Senator Riley's office needs a receptionist. Their usual person broke her leg and can't work the session. You see, we have seasonal employees who come back year after year, so the spots available are somewhat rare. Looks like you're well-qualified though, so your chances should be good." Louise jotted down a name and room number and handed a card to Clara.

She picked up the phone and talked with a Senator Riley.

"This is just an initial interview." she told Clara, handing back Clara's resume. "A meet and greet sort of impromptu interview. Sally will take you to the right office. Good luck." She turned back to her computer and started typing.

"Excuse me," Clara said. "Does this mean that I'm hired? Or that I'm being seriously considered?"

Louise Anaya sighed and twisted away from her computer screen. With a forced smile, she answered, "It's just an initial interview, Ms. Jordan. They'll have to check your references. Furthermore, if their former receptionist can possibly come back, they may still keep the door open for her. Remember that the Session doesn't start until January. We're still a few months away. They will call you back if they need you. Good luck." The phone rang and she plunged back into what was apparently more important business.

This was turning into the day from hell, Clara thought to herself. Sally took her to yet another office, where she met Rosanne, Senator Riley's receptionist. Roseanne flashed her a smile that didn't match the suspicious look in her eyes. "You stay here," she ordered Clara. "I'll go get the Senator. He's in a meeting but he'll want to meet you."

Five minutes later, Roseanne was back with not one man (was he the senator?) but two. The taller one, a rangy blond-haired guy who looked like he belonged on a ranch, and another short, fat man with a crew cut.

"Bert Riley," said the taller.

"And I'm Ernie, head of the Roundhouse print shop," offered the short guy.

Clara could hardly keep from laughing at the ridiculous sound of it: "Bert and Ernie." She'd grown up watching Sesame Street and she imagined this Bert and Ernie pair as Muppets. They sat in chairs, facing her and began the questioning.

"Well, my last job, as I said in my resume..."

"We haven't seen the resume," said Ernie. "We just want to get an impression. So, did you work around here? Are you a longtime resident or did you recently move here from somewhere else?"

"Well originally, I'm from Virginia. I came to the Southwest to teach at a Native American school. I'm part Native

93

American and I was hoping to find my original relatives. As it turned out, I was too late. My birthmother had died. But I did teach high school for a year. The school ran into some difficulties. In fact, I think they closed down. Instead of staying in Red Mesa, where the school was located, I decided there would be more opportunities in Santa Fe."

She tried to read her listeners' faces. Had she said too much? Why did she have to mention "difficulties" at the school? She wanted to avoid retelling the complete AIA disaster, but it seemed she hadn't stopped soon enough.

"Oh," said Ernie. "You mean the murder of their headmaster? And all that talk about pottery smuggling. I heard that someone within the school was responsible for illegally exporting precious pots to buyers in Europe. An inside job. I remember the scandal. No wonder you wanted to leave."

Clara's heart sank. The last thing in the world she wanted was for the school to become their topic. She was supposed to be presenting herself as the perfect candidate for this legislative job. Maybe she could steer the conversation away from the American Indian Academy. It was worth a try.

"Actually, I don't know exactly what happened," she said. "I was really an outsider, a newcomer. I focused on keeping my students from being stressed out. The jobs I've had before are related to the kind of work you need done here."

"Oh?" Bert leaned forward and looked directly at Clara. His manner was friendly, as though he was just as glad to leave the school topic alone. "Could you give us an example?"

"Yes, sir. I grew up in a University town. My dad was a professor. From the time I was a teenager, he helped me find summer jobs as a receptionist, a secretary or an administrative assistant. I even worked part time during the school year. One of my best jobs was helping with student registration. I put nervous incoming freshmen at their ease. My organizational and people skills have been praised. If you'll look in my portfolio, you'll see the accolades." She held out a swath of papers.

"No," Ernie chimed in. "We don't need more paperwork. It's clear from talking with you that you are a people person. How about working in a team environment? Do you consider yourself to be a team player?"

"Yes," Clara said. "Before I taught at American Indian Academy, I worked in a temporary position for the state of New Mexico as a writer/editor. It was also my job to head up the

94

employee of the month program. I had to meet with division heads and get them all to agree on a candidate. It was sometimes like herding cats."

"So," asked Bert, "you're comfortable working in proximity with a lot of people?"

"Sure. With the state, we were in cubicles with no privacy. It never bothered me except when I was next to a co-worker who couldn't stop talking on the phone. She was a regular 'Chatty Kathy'."

Rosanne spoke up and Clara realized that she'd been listening closely to everything. "Kathy. My sister was named Kathy. She died last year in a car accident."

"Um...it's just a saying. What I mean is that I work well in a group environment, even if there are distractions." That didn't sound quite right either and Clara realized that the more she said, the worse it sounded. Why did she have to use that particular phrase?

It seemed that Roseanne had opened the door to a more critical look at Clara. Senator Bert began questioning her about political leanings. She, a Democrat, was pretty sure she was in Republican territory, so she kept her answers vague, hoping to steer the questioning in another direction. New Mexico was ruled by a Republican, and she remembered talking with colleagues at AIA about what a terrible non-leader the governor was, vetoing every bill that helped everyday people and passing measures destructive to New Mexico's fragile environment.

Ernie came right out with it. "Are you Republican or Democrat? We need to know."

"Well, I'm pretty much bipartisan," Clara offered.

"Have you registered to vote in New Mexico as a Democrat or Republican?" The Senator joined the drilling.

"Um, like I said, I'm bipartisan," Clara answered. She added "I'm registered with the Democratic party, but really I'm more of an Independent."

Shortly after she claimed to be "an Independent," the meeting ended. She knew as she walked to the first floor and out the grand entrance of the Rotunda that the interview with Senator Riley had been a miserable experience. Not just that, it would never get her a job.

## Chapter Nineteen

It was a joy returning to the Miller Street *casita* after a weary day of job hunting. Clara brewed a pot of Assam tea, changed into slippers and her fluffy chenille robe. She sank into her one comfortable chair and warmed her hands around an oversized mug. Instead of picking up this morning's New Mexican to check the classified ads, she reached for India Treasures, a novel Dottie had loaned her last week. It was a sweeping fictional account of Indian history, not the sort of book she would have chosen for herself. But because she wanted her friendship with Dottie to flourish, she committed to sticking with it.

She read for five minutes, but when Oscar jumped into her lap and began purring loudly, she drifted off. The strain of breaking up with Jerome was taking its toll, and maybe sleep was the only escape. She awakened an hour later, her book on the floor, and Oscar having wandered to his food dish in the kitchen.

"It's just not like me to waste an afternoon," she told her cat as she dished out a generous helping of his favorite canned food. "Maybe I'll spend twenty minutes looking for new job ads and then spend the rest of the evening reading." Then there was dinner, which lately she'd been skipping. "I've got to eat something," she told herself. First, a salad, then job searching, then reading.

Mechanically she sliced tomatoes and cucumbers, all the while musing on her current dilemma. When she and Jerome moved to Santa Fe, where he'd been hired as a dorm supervisor at Santa Fe Indian School, no mention had been made of finances. Clara knew she should find a job. When she and Jerome were dating, the need did not feel urgent. Most of the time, he insisted on paying for their nights out. She never worried about finances. But now that there was no future together, she felt that she couldn't stay in Santa Fe unless she worked, even if it was part time.

Listlessly, she watched the evening news on her small TV. Oscar perched on the arm of her recliner. She thought of what she should be doing and was overcome with lethargy and doubt. She remembered that today was Tuesday and tuned in WSFR on the radio. "Tuesday Night at the Opera" was just beginning. Puccini's "La Boheme," with its achingly beautiful arias and tragic love story.

Putting aside her book and the newspaper job ads, Clara tackled a closet cleanup. When all else failed, it was good to do something practical, a task that would yield visible results. As the music soared, she arranged her turtlenecks, plaid shirts, skirts, dresses and slacks into different sections. She collected shoes she no longer wore and placed them in the "Charity" box. The radio broadcast of "La Boheme" made it easy to stay on task. By the time Mimi knocked on Rodolfo's garret door, she'd finished the closet and started on dresser drawers. The opera was sung in Italian, but it wasn't necessary for Clara to have a translation. Will and Louise, her late parents, had played the opera CDs constantly, and she knew the story by heart.

As the ill-fated love affair between Mimi and Rodolfo unfolded, Clara emptied the contents of a small chest of drawers next to her closet. Belts she never wore filled the bottom two drawers. She dumped half of them into the Charity box and vowed to wear the rest. "Use it or lose it," she said to Oscar, who was very curious about the purge-a-thon. At times, he would bat around the garments and accessories that had been dumped on the floor. Bored with the fact that the clothes didn't move or fight back, he lost interest and jumped back into one of his observation points, usually the bed or dresser top.

Day faded into night, and to the strains of Puccini, Clara delved further into the purging. Having finished the closet and one chest of drawers, she went to what she called her "master dresser." In the top drawer, she kept checks, cash, warranties, her passport and important papers. At the very back, she discovered letters from Henry.

She should burn them, but first why not read these epistles one more time? It might help her understand why that romance didn't work out. It might give her clarity as to why Jerome, though not a deceiver like Henry, was also no good for her. The pull of old love letters was irresistible. She picked out a sheaf of folded stationery and smoothed it out, face up. Henry's style of writing was to print. She'd never thought about it, but now she wondered, "Why print and not cursive?" At the time, she was so thrilled to hear from her lover that she thought printing was cute and endearing. But until she saw Henry's dark side, she'd thought everything about him was cute and endearing. She focused on a page spread on her lap. The letter was written the day after their first night together.

*Dearest Clara,*

*You are the one I've been looking for, longing for, hoping to find. Last night was the happiest I've been in years. I admire you so much. Your skill as a teacher and inspiration to your students, your grace and strength, your wit. I hope in the weeks ahead, we can get to know each other better. Our time together has made my life a lot more about joy. The more I know you, the more I love you. I've found my soulmate at last!- Your devoted Henry*

Remembering how happy she'd felt when reading the letter for the first time, Clara didn't know whether to laugh or weep. "Older but wiser," she told herself. Henry swept her away with words, and she was so ready to believe him that she ignored the signs. He was not who he seemed to be. She'd realized that too late.

Tearing the letter into small pieces, Clara sprinkled it over some dry logs in the corner fireplace. She lit a match and tossed it in. Good idea to burn that useless bit of the past. She pulled out more letters and pitched them, unread, into the flames. Oscar, her gray feline companion came out from his favorite spot on her bed and curled up on a rug in front of the fire. The logs were now burning.

"It's a healing ritual," Clara told Oscar. "Goodbye to all the time I wasted with someone who didn't deserve my love. Goodbye to sorrow and heartbreak. Goodbye to traitorous lovers. From now on, Mr. Cat, you're the number one man in my life."

For the first time in months, Clara went to sleep thinking not about Henry, her old flame or Jerome, the less-than-satisfactory new love. Instead, she tried to imagine that mystical place that Dottie had been describing to her: Mahabalipuram.

Arundati was the sister that Clara never had. In the year since the two had been friends, Clara's first year of living in Santa Fe, the two women were inseparable. Dottie, as she was known to friends, eased Clara's pain and regret at breaking up with Jerome. She was there, unconditionally.

98

## Chapter Twenty

*Six months later*

When Dottie needed someone to go with her to help settle the estate of a deceased aunt who lived back east, a wealthy relative, Clara volunteered. She'd grown up in Virginia but had never been any further north than Washington D.C.. In fact, she'd never been out of the country. Her friend's Aunt Miriam lived a spinster-like life in the outskirts of Philadelphia, on Conshohawken State Road. To Dottie's astonishment, she'd left everything to her. She, the adopted daughter of Miriam's brother, was, it turned out, the only heir.

After a seemingly endless plane trip from New Mexico to Philadelphia, the two friends taxied to the three-story Victorian style mansion that stood atop a grassy hill. The Korean houseboy let them in and showed them to the third floor, a place that Dottie remembered from her teenage years. Unfailingly, Aunt Miriam had invited her for school vacations and summers. Dottie always accepted.

"I can't believe people still have servants," Clara said to Dottie. The third floor, attached to the attic storeroom, had two twin beds and a minimum of very expensive antique furniture.

"Well, Len is more like a family retainer. I'm sure that Aunt Miriam left him something in the will and even provided for him to work awhile after her death. Thank goodness, there's a lawyer who will arrange most of the business aspect of all this. Our job is to see if there's anything worth keeping in the attic." She gestured to the wooden door that separated their bedroom from the rest of the third floor.

"Wow, aren't you relieved that we don't have to go through the whole house and decide what to keep and what to put in the estate sale?" Clara asked her friend. "I'm afraid to even look around until tomorrow morning."

They ordered pizza and, feeling as though they were reliving college dormitory days, went to bed early in the narrow twin beds. Clara slept like the dead, but Dottie was troubled by a dream, one that she'd had before...

*Rocking her back and forth several times on its journey, the incoming tide delivered a child to the beach. Finally, the waves receded, their human burden laid next to gray boulders, clumps of seaweed, shells and driftwood. The child's body was not far from a large resort in southern India. The girl struggled to rise to her feet, collapsed and then lay, breathing with effort, in a sodden heap. Tiny and delicate, she was clad in the shreds of a coarse muslin gown. She was no more than five years old. Waves lapped gently around the girl's splayed arms and legs, revealing ugly bruises and dried blood from knife slashes. Apparently, her light brown skin had served as the canvas for a madman's rage...The child regained consciousness, and she mentally floated, as if in the middle of a dream. She had traveled a long way and would need many hours to regain her strength. Night was falling and she needed warmth. Breathing in hungrily, the child filled her lungs with the damp, humid atmosphere of India, exhaling in raspy bursts. It would be a long night.*

She must have screamed...Clara was sitting on the side of her bed gently shaking her arm. "Dottie, Dottie. Wake up. You were having a nightmare. Everything's going to be alright. I'm here and whatever scared you, it was your imagination."

Clara gently wrapped a shawl over her friend's shoulders, went to the bathroom to get a glass of water, then sat back down on the bedside. "Would you like to talk about the dream? Maybe it will help. I used to write all my dreams in a journal and often they'd give me clues about what was happening in the real world. You know, it's said that the waking and sleeping worlds are closely related." She stopped talking when she realized that Dottie was crying.

"I keep dreaming about a girl who's been slashed with a knife and thrown in the ocean. She's washed up to shore and is having trouble breathing. I'm not sure she's going to live, and I think that the girl is me. It's in India, but I don't know where. I was afraid the girl would die."

By now Dottie had fallen back into the pillow and closed her eyes. She drifted in and out of sleep. She sniffed and turned over on her stomach. Clara pulled up the covers and stroked her back.

"Who did this to the girl? And where did it take place?"

"Some kidnappers. Well, not just kidnappers. Human traffickers. I read an article about all these children who were being taken from Chennai, snatched from homes and orphanages, then sold. A brutal business. I can't remember my early childhood very well. That's a disadvantage to being one of the adopted ones.

100

It could have happened to me. The dream makes me think I need to go to Chennai.

"I told you this, but I'll repeat myself. There's a shore temple at Mahabalipuram. I've read about a lost city in the Bay of Bengal, at the bottom of the ocean. You of all people can understand why I keep dreaming of this part of the world. Do you think I'm losing it?"

"No, I'm sure you're not losing it," Clara said. In my own life, I couldn't stop thinking about the Southwest. That's why I moved there, hoping to find out more about me. Just calm down, It's not even four a.m. Let's try to go back to sleep. We can talk more about your dream and Mahabalipuram when we're going through the trunks and papers. Now that you've brought up the dream, I'm really curious."

Morning in Philadelphia. At 8 a.m., pale sunlight filtered through Aunt Miriam's tall, narrow Victorian windows. The kitchen was two floors down from where Clara and Dottie slept. Clara was the first one downstairs and happy to learn that the invisible Korean houseboy had made a pot of coffee and put out boxes of cereal. She was just about to climb up the narrow flights of stairs to rouse Dottie when her friend, wrapped in a fluffy pink robe, came padding softly into the room.

"Good morning. Are we ready for this?" Dottie poured herself a mug of coffee and added milk.

"You mean the excavation?"

"Yes, it will be a matter of digging. We need to go through decades of books and papers. Aunt Miriam always hinted that one of her ancestors spent most of his life in India, in fact that someone in the family had written a book about it, apparently never published. Probably never even completed. Maybe I've just imagined all this? Maybe I dreamed it?"

"Wouldn't it be incredible to find a manuscript," Clara blurted, immediately sorry. Why set up expectations or give her friend false hope?

"Well, you never know," Dottie said. "But one thing I do know is that we better get started. You won't believe the volume of books, papers, files, notebooks, boxes of letters, generations of stuff. I guess nobody wanted to help Aunt Miriam dredge through it, and she became too ill before she died to do much. She pretty much couldn't do anything but just lie in bed waiting to die."

Within an hour, the two women were ready to delve into the mess. Dressed in jeans, scarves around their heads, Rosie the

Riveter style, they climbed a ladder up to the attic, a floor above where they'd slept the night before. It took several trips to carry up all the empty boxes, labelling pens and large trash bags they'd assembled.

Clara was seeing everything for the first time. Dark and full of cobwebs, the attic looked like a set for a horror movie. One window at the far end of the attic room let in a wan light. Heavy clouds moved in and cloaked the winter sun. "Wow, this is really creepy. No wonder your Aunt Miriam didn't want to come up here and dig around. I wouldn't want to be doing this at night."

Dottie was already delving into boxes and trunks, opening drawers in cabinets, bringing out file folders bulging with papers. The containers lining walls were two or three deep, covered with layers of dust. Obviously, no one had been through this vast collection for years.

"Hold on," Clara said. "If we just start taking everything out at once, we'll never know what to keep and what to pitch. We won't have any idea of what we're dealing with. Let's look at the lay of the land and treat this like an archeological dig. We'll start at one corner of the room...let's say by the window...and work our way down methodically across to the other end. Here are some garbage bags and here's a box for stuff we'll keep."

"Really, I don't know that there will be anything much to keep," Dottie said. "Mainly, we just need to purge. It's a little like looking for a needle in a haystack, and there may not even be a needle. You have a good idea of how to go about this. You make the first move. I'll follow your lead."

Clara opened a large wooden chest and lifted out a rectangle wrapped in tissue paper. She unwrapped it to discover a pen and ink drawing of men on snowshoes traipsing down a snowy path in the forest. Another drawing was of a man in a kayak. Another drawing was of men working out in a gymnasium- doing chin-ups, lifting barbells, wearing boxing gloves and pummeling a punching bag.

"Don't unwrap all of them or we'll be here for years. Our main job is to decide what to keep and what to pitch. If we look through everything, we'll never get the job done."

"You mean we have to make snap decisions?" Clara looked disappointed. "I'm not good at deciding."

"The drawings could be put in an estate sale. They're amusing and the frames look good. A close friend of Aunt Miriam is going to manage the sale. Apparently, the proceeds will be left to me. Along with whatever happens with the house. When we finish our work and the estate sale happens, it will be put on the market."

The day wore on. Clara went back to opening boxes and making decisions. Discard or put in the estate sale pile? When she came across anything she thought Dottie would want, she questioned. Every now and then, she found brass bowls or cups, ivory artifacts, or inlaid boxes. "These are definitely Arundati material," she announced. "I think they'll help you move toward finding out more about your hidden heritage."

Clara was on a roll. She discarded notebooks, receipts, yellowed tablets, photograph negatives, empty three-ring binders. An entire correspondence filled one upright cabinet, from an Army Air Force lieutenant named Don Sturke to his wife Leona, all written on thin onion skin, dated from 1943 to 1945, and apparently from Calcutta, India. Many of the letterheads had the WWII China-Burma-India theater emblem at the top. There were files and files of epistles. A few folders contained letters from Leona to Don. The occasional envelope in the Leona files were postmarked "Findlay Ohio."

Arundati, at the other end of the attic, was deeply involved in going through boxes of photographs and old-fashioned metal framed slides. "They don't even make these anymore," she called out to Clara. "I doubt if you could even find a slide projector very easily. Because I can't identify any of these, they're all going to be pitched."

"We can't just pitch this stuff," Clara said. "There must be World War Two history museums, somewhere all this stuff could be archived. I don't know who Sturke might have been, but maybe we should keep his correspondence. I do know the India thread you're following is more the southern part of the Subcontinent. I have a feeling that may be part of the puzzle of your origins."

"Nobody can project these slides, so out they go. I guess there's a way to translate them into something usable, but I don't see that as part of our mission." Dottie was fond of referring to their task as a mission rather than work.

"You're probably right," Clara agreed. "On second thought, maybe all these Sturke letters should be pitched. What do you think?"

"It's better if we donate them to a military archive," Dottie mused. "I can ask Aunt Miriam's attorney to do that. She

103

left him a small fund for this kind of situation." Dottie had just opened a carton of yellowed newspaper clippings and after a glance at each, was throwing them into a garbage bag. "I think they might be related to Aunt Miriam's side of the family. They were fascinated by India. Sturke might have served there during WWII. But I'm not interested in war history. I'm trying to discover my personal history."

"That makes sense. Why don't I put them in the action pile? We can ask Miriam's executor to donate them to a library or archive. I'm sure someone would be interested. A history buff."

"Yeah, that's a great idea." As she half-listened to Clara, Dottie was moving foot lockers across the attic floor. Clouds of dust arose and a mouse skittered by. "Oh my god, I'm the original mouse-a-phobe."

"Calm down, friend. He's not going to bite you. Or maybe She. The poor thing's probably just going home to put the children to bed."

Dottie looked skeptical. "Well, if it's just one mouse I won't freak out, but if a bunch of them start skittering around me, I'm outta here. That's just the way I am. Always have been, always will be."

"Brace yourself. I'm looking in all the corners for evidence of more. You know, uh, droppings. Could be that we just rustled up one critter and the rest will stay inside the walls. Or wherever they're headquartered."

"Yeah, sounds right. I'll concentrate on getting a lot done while you continue the mouse scan."

"Never let it be said that your friend isn't prepared." Clara slid a stack of banker boxes from a wall, then another and another. "Nope, nope, and nope. Looks as though our mouse was traveling solo."

Clara's remark met with silence, then the sound of pages turning.

"You won't believe this!" Dottie waved a small booklet in the air. "It looks like we may finally have something to go on. This is a tourist writeup about Mahabalipuram. The subtitle is 'where waves dance to the symphony of stones.' I remember my tutor at St. John's, Mr. Vadke, telling us about this historic site near Chennai in Tamil Nadu. I think he has relatives there, or at least he's visited. He showed us slides of these huge structures called 'Rathas' that are like gigantic pagodas or chariots. Well, actually they are sort of like both."

Clara was getting tired. They'd been sorting through the attic for ages, and the dust was getting to her. "What are you talking about, Arundati? I think we've been cooped up too long. We're both getting batty."

"No, look, here are pictures, right in the travel pamphlet. These are exactly what I first learned about at St. John's. When Mr. Vargese showed us the slides of his trip there, I felt electrified. It was as though I'd been there in another lifetime."

"Here, give that to me for a minute." Clara took the booklet and started reading aloud. "Situated 60 kilometers south of Chennai, the monuments of Mahabalipuram, hewn out of rocks, attract thousands of connoisseurs of art from all over the world. Though ravaged by sea, wind and time, these sculptural treasures speak volumes about the magnificent heritage of ancient Dravidian art and temple architecture. Centuries later, they still bear silent testimony to the illustrious era. According to inscriptions, the marvelous monuments found here are the sculptural legacy left behind by Pallava king Mahendravarman I (580-630 AD), his son Narasimhavarman I (630-668 AD), and their descendants."

"Hey," Dottie interrupted, "hand over the booklet." She gently removed the tourist brochure from her friend's hand. Slowly and carefully, she turned through the worn pages. Clara had never seen Dottie so preoccupied. From time to time she pursed her lips and shook her head. She raised her eyebrows at some of the images.

"What is it? Why are you so interested in a piece of advertising? We have mountains of your aunt's stuff to still go through. Mountains!" Fingers splayed outward, palms up, she waved her hands to the boxes, chests and cabinets on either side of them. "Just look at all this!"

"I can't exactly explain it, but I feel like I've been to Mahabalipurim. Not in this lifetime, but in the past."

"You mean, as in reincarnation? I didn't know you believed in past lives."

Dottie sighed. "I'm not sure what I mean. After all, I might have been born Hindu, but I was never told anything about my origins. Are you saying that you have to be Hindu to believe in reincarnation?"

"I just meant that if you think your past is somehow connected to Mahabalipuram, going there might lead you to answers about your beginnings. I went to the Southwest to find out about my origins."

"You mean teaching at the Indian school? I thought that was a disaster. You said that the headmaster was murdered, you had to run from a hit man sent out by the bad boyfriend who was really a criminal. And you didn't find your mother?"

The two women looked at each other in silence. Clara's eyes filled with tears.

"You've summed it up pretty well. My year was a bust, when I learned that my birthmother had already died. I was too late. But on the other hand, I learned about myself, what I was made of, how I could hold together all my students while the school was sinking."

"Sinking? You mean metaphorically?"

"Yes, but now that I think about it, I was captain of a crew. My ninth graders and juniors; I had to keep them from being traumatized. We survived the school year in spite of what happened. Not just survived. The students grew from the tragedy. So did I."

"Hmmm. Whatever you say. I just know that I'm really happy that your ship came to shore in Santa Fe and that we became friends. If the school hadn't crashed I'd never have met you." Dottie looked around the attic room. "We need to concentrate on going through all this stuff. I told the estate lawyers we'd finish by Friday and it's already Thursday."

"Right. But before anything, I'm going to save this Mahabalipuram brochure for us. Who knows? We might find a way to actually travel there, and I can help you look for your birthparents. I've always wanted to go to India."

For the next hour, Clara and Dottie sorted through books, papers and memorabilia. It seemed that Aunt Miriam's attic was apparently a repository for decades of Dottie's adoptive progenitors. Some of the collection seemed worthy of a history library, other items were pitched after a brief exchange. The two adoptees worked steadily, speaking only when it was necessary to consult.

The name "Goldingham" appeared in many of the papers they came across, along with accounts of a tsunami that hit Chennai in the 1980s, uncovering remnants of an ancient city under the sea. As the afternoon turned into evening and light in

106

the attic room grew dim, they came across more papers, booklets and memorabilia about Mahabalipuram.

It was eight at night and they'd had no supper. Clara was the first to suggest that maybe they should call it quits for the day, "We can get an early start tomorrow and go through the remaining third of the collection," she told her friend.

"Yeah, I guess you're right, and I'm hungry and thirsty. But...why don't we tackle just one more box?" She shoved a beatenup shoebox to the area between them. "This is really heavy for papers. I think it's full of stones or pottery shards."

Clara cut through the yellowed packing tape that sealed both ends of the container. Small clouds of dust kicked up, and she carefully lifted off the lid.

"Voila," she announced. "These look like a bunch of gray stones. Please, can we go downstairs now? Aren't we done?"

"Wait, not so fast." Dottie picked up the fragments and laid them out on the wooden floor. "Look at these more closely. They're like body parts, stone body parts. Don't you think this used to be a statue?" One by one, she held up pieces of stone. "Oh, here's a head of Ganesh, the elephant god. Well, part of a head."

Clara shuffled through the broken bits of what they agreed was an ancient statue. "Voila! I found a hand, severed at the wrist. If this rubble was in fact a statue of the elephant god, what we have here is a hand of Ganesh. It's the most intact of the fragments. And now, I think it's officially ours.

"Wow. This goes along with the saga of a city under the sea, the story connected to Mahabalipuram. I once read that the Hindu gods were so jealous of the city's beauty that they sent a fierce storm to punish the people who built it, those who lived there. They placed it under a curse, and the next year a violent storm smashed everything to smithereens and wiped out everything and ended thousands of lives." Clara had obviously done her homework.

"OMG...I can't believe it. We may have struck gold." Dottie held up a sheaf of yellowed handwritten pages. "Here's a manuscript. It looks like someone started writing a novel. I know we can't take forever with this attic, but we've got to see what this is about."

"I agree," Clara said. "We need to check this out, at least the beginning. Let's take turns reading this aloud."

The two women sat side by side, the manuscript spread out on the attic floor before them. As Clara turned pages, a lone piece of paper fluttered out, raising motes of dust as it drifted. "Here's the novel I never finished writing. For my niece Arundati. May it help her unravel the tangled threads of her past. With more love than words can say, Aunt Miriam."

When they looked carefully through the papers they found articles about India, notes about Hindu gods and photos of Ganesh statues. A work apparently once in progress. There were plot notes and various chapter heading. The main plot thread seemed to be a scholar named Goldingham who salvaged a statue's hand washed up on the shores of the Bay of Bengal. He took the hand home to England and handed it down to his children. The hand brought ill luck to whomever received it, often death by drowning. Invariably the tragedy involved a wife or daughter. The only way the curse could be lifted, according to Aunt Miriam's plot notes, was for the stone hand to be returned to the Bay of Bengal.

"I'm impressed! What a great mystery this would have been," exclaimed Dottie. "This would have been a wonderful novel. It's no accident that these notes were waiting here for us to find them. This is a great discovery. If only Aunt Miriam were still alive, she might be able to explain the India themes running through this place. All this memorabilia stored in the attic. The whole Mahabalipuram thing, the broken statue of Ganesh, how it might have led to my adoption. But since Aunt Miriam, may she rest in peace, is gone, it's up to us to piece everything together."

"On a practical note," said Clara, "we need to eat something. I'm about to keel over. Let's just leave everything in place. We can tackle the attic again tomorrow."

"Great idea. Why don't we call for Chinese takeout? We'll be thinking more clearly after food and sleep."

# Chapter Twenty-one

Clara, much refreshed, awakened at dawn. Dottie was still sleeping soundly. Clara slipped into running clothes and slipped out of the bedroom they were sharing, pulling the covers up on her narrow twin bed and leaving her friend a note: "Out on a morning run (or maybe a walk). Back in less than an hour."

The chilly air made her face tingle. She took a moment to check out the surroundings. A mental snapshot, she reminded herself, was insurance against getting lost. Aunt Miriam's mansion was perched on a grassy hill and surrounded by gigantic oak and maple trees. Setting her stopwatch for 30 minutes, Clara bolted down the green slope toward a winding country road. Getting into the rhythm of running, she felt liberated. After the Jerome affair, the past she'd left behind in Santa Fe, and a cramped day in Aunt Miriam's attic, she needed to stretch her limbs. Her friend was probably even more exhausted than she was. Let Dottie sleep. She'd run half an hour out, half an hour back, and return to continue digging through the past.

At the bottom of the hill, she came to Conshohawkan State Road, where she turned right. At six a.m., there was no traffic, giving Clara extra mental space to think. She recalled beginning at the American Indian Academy, back when she'd hoped to find Greta Suina. She felt a pang of sadness that her search had led not to Greta but to news of her demise. Just as she might have been able to meet the woman who gave birth to her, death interfered. She was torn between sadness and anger. If only she could help Dottie find out about her birth family. Though she didn't know quite how, she sensed that Aunt Miriam's house might lead to a clue.

Steadily running, she stayed to the left side of the road. When she first started the sport five years ago, her friends–nearly all of whom were runners–warned her that one must always face oncoming traffic. It was a different life now, but running was the thread that connected her old self to the newer version. She'd failed to find family when she lived in Red Mesa, and now here she was trying to help Dottie search for her forebears. More and more, it seemed as though a trip to India would be in their future. The logistics escaped her, but the necessity seemed absolute.

As the sky turned from gray to a milky blue, Clara loped. She felt the energy of her strong legs and the head-clearing effect of moving through time and space. Running always gave her an opportunity to think things through. Today was no exception. How difficult would it be, traveling to the other side of the world? Where would the money come from? What about Dottie's academic work at St. John's College? Would India be overwhelming and confusing? Incredibly fascinating? Or maybe both?

According to her watch, she'd covered slightly more than a mile. While turning over the India question in her mind, Clara also noticed the surroundings. Maples and oaks lined the country road. She'd missed the russet, red, orange, and scarlet of an east coast Autumn, tree colors she hadn't seen since she was a teenager. Santa Fe, her adopted home town, had its own seasonal beauty, but this extravaganza surpassed even the golden aspen and cottonwoods of the Southwest.

When a loud clap of thunder broke her reverie, Clara realized her mistake. Why had she assumed that Pennsylvania's weather was stable? Apparently, it could be just as unpredictable as Santa Fe's. At home, she would never leave on a run without at least a hooded windbreaker. She'd have to cut her run short and get back to Dottie and the estate of Aunt Miriam as fast as possible. Maybe the coming storm would hold off. She'd been out only twenty minutes.

Despite her optimism, raindrops began splatting. She ran faster, suddenly noticing that the road forked after she'd turned around and changed directions. Strangely, she hadn't noticed anything but a straight road on her way out. This was going to be interesting. Just guessing, she veered to the right. After five minutes, she realized she'd chosen the wrong path. More clapping of thunder and a dangerous slipperiness to the oil-slicked road. Used to occasional mishaps of the road, Clara stayed calm. Business-like. Simply turn around and go back to the "Y," she told herself. Surely the left leg would take her back to the house. She imagined explaining to Dottie what happened, taking a hot shower and drinking tea to warm up. During her decade of running, she'd been caught in thunderstorms before. She'd always managed.

Her surroundings looked familiar, or so she hoped. Here she was at the "Y," where she had stayed to the left. Being careful to run on the most-gravelly part of the road shoulder, she managed to avoid slick asphalt. What had started out as a carefree morning jog had turned into a miserable slog. To her relief, at least the landmarks looked familiar. Here was the tan clapboard house with blue trim, there was the house all of gray stone.

The rain picked up, pouring in torrents, accompanied by an icy wind. As though running toward a finish line of a ten-kilometer race, Clara increased her speed. She felt as if her lungs might burst. Why on earth hadn't she taken a jacket when she'd slipped out of the house? At least she had her new running gloves. She slipped them from the waistband of her capris, wriggling her fingers to ward off numbness. In what seemed an eternity, Clara finally reached an intersection she remembered from earlier this morning. Just as she was about to sprint the last half mile home, her foot caught on a loose boulder and she fell sharply to the ground. Groaning in pain, she pulled herself up and dragged forward.

By now, the sky pelted icy sleet. If only she could find a shelter, she'd be able to rest enough to keep going. Despite the sharp pain in her left ankle, she barreled forward. As if in answer to her plight, here was a springhouse Dottie had mentioned. A two-story stone edifice from the 1900s, the spring house had been used to store produce. In the past, Dottie had explained, an actual spring ran through the ground floor. Now it was dry except for a trickle. Sinking to the muddy floor, Clara leaned, exhausted, against the stone wall. She moved her left ankle in a slow, painful circle. Not broken, but badly sprained. It would make it hard to crawl up and down the ladder to help Dottie with clearing out the attic.

The last thing she wanted is to be a burden to her friend. The tempest outside the spring house, from the sound of things, was beginning to let up. At least she could slip quietly into the house to let Dot sleep late. She felt for the housekey in her hidden pocket. Just inside the waistband of her shorts, it had seemed to be secure. Nothing there. Maybe she'd put it in one of her shoes. Removing them both, she checked carefully, even lifting out the orthotics she'd inserted for extra cushioning.

Nowhere. How could this be? She clearly remembered having the key at the start of her ill-fated run, but now it had vanished. Maybe it had slipped out when she stumbled into the springhouse. She looked at the ground, finding nothing. The key might have been covered up with the dirt she dislodged when she first arrived. While putting her shoes back on, she came across some rusty tools along one of the springhouse walls. She reached for a small, battered spade, and began to dig lightly through the dirt floor in front of the springhouse entrance.

The spade hit something hard. Something too big to be a key. She kept digging, soon discovering a metal box. Forgetting about the key, Clara pried the container out of its dirt grave, brushed it off and lifted the unlocked clasp. Inside, wrapped in yellowed tissue paper, was a small leather notebook. Inside were pencil drawings of the Taj Mahal, snake charmers, and statues of Indian deities. On the last page was a sketch of a statue's hand severed at the wrist. In neat print was a message: "The hand of Ganesh must be returned to Indian seas. Whoever makes the journey will be blessed with good fortune. Not returning the hand brings ill." Clara could hardly wait to show the notebook to Arundati. She felt that the notebook tied in with the attic's contents. All part of a shadowy past, a story whose full plot they might never untangle. One thing she felt sure about, however. Improbable though it seemed, they would someday be traveling to India.

When Clara reached Aunt Miriam's front door, she made one last attempt to locate her key. It had slipped from her waistband pocket to the lining of her running shorts. Ah, there it was. A satisfying click, and she was inside. She could hardly wait to share the notebook with Dottie.

## Chapter Twenty-two
## Santa Fe, New Mexico

As time passed, the two women drew closer. The bonds that had been started after what they called the "Aunt Miriam's attic experience" deepened. As adult adoptees, they shared many things that no one else seemed to understand. Clara felt robbed of a biological family tree. Dottie was bereft because of knowing nothing of her heritage.

During weekly sleepovers at Clara's, they discussed these problems late into many a night. Dottie felt mildly envious of Clara, she said. "At least you lived in New Mexico, the home territory of your late birthmother. You've seen petroglyphs, taught language arts at an Indian high school. You've been in the land itself. Your land."

"True enough. I am fortunate in that respect. But it amounted to nothing at the end. Greta died before I could find her. The curtain closed. The final act of my quest. Now I will never have a family tree. You know, one of those charts that shows who begat whom, so and so born to so and so. Different branches of aunts, uncles, cousins." Clara yawned deeply. "It's getting late. The guest bed is ready for you. Nothing about our conversation, but I'm feeling exhausted."

"Yes, I'm ready to turn in pretty soon," Dottie said. "Just one more thing. I'm not sure what would ever heal this hollow in my heart. I long to feel connected to something. I know it's far-fetched, but I feel that if I could go to India, to walk among the people, people who looked like me, it would make me incredibly happy. It's unlikely that I could ever manage to do that, but if it played out that I could, I would invite you to go with me. Aunt Miriam left me enough money to pay for both of us. You've got a good business head, and you could be in charge of finances. I feel like you're the sister I never had. But it's a ridiculous idea. We should call it a day."

"No," Clara said. "It's not ridiculous at all. But yes, we should call it a day."

# PART THREE


# JOURNEY TO INDIA

## Chapter Twenty-three
## New York City to New Delhi, India

Six months later found Clara and Dottie at JFK airport, sitting in excited anticipation. Clara had made inquiries and arranged the trip. Dottie, skeptical at first, finally saw the logic of going to India now rather than waiting. "After all," Clara had said. "You need to meet your biological mother while she's still on the planet. I'm ready to accompany you, and I'm a good traveler."

"If she's on the planet," Dottie gently suggested. "And it's a big if."

When Clara looked disappointed, Dottie added "Don't get me wrong. I am incredibly happy you're willing to go on this quest with me. If nothing else, we'll learn about the country of my ancestors." She hugged Clara, and it was settled.

They would fly from New York to Delhi, and then from Delhi to Chennai, Tamil Nadu. Early on in their planning, they decided that the brother of Dottie's close friend Sanjay, Narendra Patel, would meet them and act as their guide. Later, Sanjay said that Narenda couldn't be available but had found a professional guide for them, a Mr. Masterson. Clara wasn't sure whether Sanjay was an actual cousin of Dottie's or just a friend. Dottie, in referring to him, had called Sanjay both, interchangeably. If it didn't matter to Dottie, it made no difference to Clara. What they would do when they arrived was not mapped out. Their schedule was an open book.

They wanted to spend time at an *ashram*, then travel to Mahabalipurim and the famous Shore Temple. Maybe not in that order. They agreed that after talking with Narendra, a plan would emerge. The journal they'd discovered at Aunt Miriam's served as a kind of instruction manual. If the journal was right, the hand of Ganesh, now tucked away in Clara's cosmetics bag, came from a sunken lost metropolis. The city had been hidden by the Pacific Ocean for nearly three centuries. The journal stressed that the hand brought bad luck to decades of the Goldingham family. The bad luck was usually death by drowning. The theory was that when the hand was returned to the sea, the curse would be lifted. Why it had never been returned to the sea was a mystery.

"Nobody expected us to actually do this!" Dottie mused. She and Clara were waiting to board Air India. Their flight would leave in an hour.

"I don't think even we expected to actually do it," Clara said. "But once we got back to Santa Fe after settling your aunt's estate...well, everything just fell into place."

"I know," sighed Dottie, "I still can't believe she left me everything, way more than enough to finance our trip. And wasn't it nice of Sanjay to arrange for his brother Narendra's friend Lane Masterson to meet us?"

"Well, yes, I guess so. But we really don't know him and..." Clara trailed off. She couldn't present a solid argument against trusting this Lane Masterson, but she would have liked for their guide to have been Sanjay himself.

They'd urged him to come with them, but the trip was expensive, and besides, he had papers due at the college. "I've been goofing off," he said, and my academic future is hanging by a thread. You can believe I'd love to go with you. It's just not in the cards now."

There really was a chance the trip would help Dottie learn more about her roots. Clara had waited too late. Years of wondering and hoping had come to nothing. And now she was going to India with Arundati. Maybe that was what lit the fire. She might help her friend succeed where she'd failed.

Preparing for their epic journey had exhausted them both. They sat aboard Air India in business class, waiting for final boarding call and takeoff. In preparation for the fifteen-hour flight to Delhi, they tried to doze. Both of them were far too awake.

"Is this crazy or what?" Clara asked her friend. "You're going on this journey to find out about your roots. I'm going along because you're the best friend in the world and you invited me. And like I keep saying, since I failed in my mission, I'd love to help you find your original family. Ones roots are important. Just because those originals gave us up doesn't mean that they aren't our parents."

More passengers were trundling aboard, many wearing headphones around their necks. It was, after all, midnight, and maybe they expected to sleep. A *sari*-clad stewardess passed through the cabin passing out small pouches containing sleep masks, earplugs, minuscule tooth brushes and tubes of toothpaste, and even sleep booties to wear on the plane. Clara had just fallen asleep when Dottie's voice cut through her slumber....

"That's why the journal was in the springhouse," Dot was saying. "Aunt Miriam thought that since she couldn't travel to India to return the fragment, the next best thing was to put it in

116

near the stream that ran under the springhouse. I feel strongly that the hand was originally hidden in the spring and made its way to the attic.

"In 1900 there was an actual spring and the hand might have been under a great deal of water. With the passing decades, the spring dried up and the hand was covered by less and less soil. No one ever went into the springhouse. It was never used for anything, and my aunt was not able to get around toward the end of her life. She'd probably assumed that the curse had been lifted and the family would be free from future misfortunes. The chances of anyone ever unearthing that box were incredibly remote. You realize, this is all speculation. We can never really know what happened."

"And if I hadn't been caught in a storm and needing shelter," Clara said, "the journal could have remained there, undiscovered, for another thirty years. But something puzzles me...why was it kept in a box without the stone relic? Wouldn't it have been enough just to throw the hand into the stream and bring the journal inside the house?"

"You didn't know my Aunt Miriam. She put everything in containers, and I mean everything. Her theory was that things might or might not be important but if they were boxed, they wouldn't deteriorate and also that they'd be easier to find. Imagine if the hand hadn't been put with the journal and just thrown into the springhouse water. It would have made its way deeper into the stream bed and been lost forever. It's as though it was waiting for you to find it."

Dottie fell into a half sleep, occasionally answering Clara, but often remaining silent. Clara gave up on dozing. Instead, she started to watch "The Night of the Iguana" on the airplane's miniature screen. She found most contemporary films a waste of time and so she was delighted to find the Turner Classics channel in the film menu.

"Ha," laughed Clara. "And I did rescue that hand of Ganesh, you know. I put it in a small Tupperware container and packed it. If we go to Mahabalipuram, or I should say when, I will toss it into the ocean. The journal of Lord Goldingham said that the hand brought with it a curse. He wrote that the curse would be lifted only when the hand was thrown into the ocean closest to the shore temple at Mahabalipuram..."

"Yes," Dottie concurred, suddenly awake. "Where the waves dance to the symphony of stones. Maybe the curse being lifted will help me find out something, anything at all, about my birth family."

"We can only hope," Clara said. "I'll let you go back to sleep and I'll keep track of our flight's progress to the other side of the world." After Dottie nodded off, however, she closed her eyes and soon plunged into deep slumber.

The trip wore on and both women dozed. "I feel like the living dead," mumbled Clara. She and Dottie, between the two of them, had gotten perhaps an hour of sleep during the long journey from New Mexico to New Delhi. And it wasn't over yet. After a layover in Delhi, they would board an Air India flight to Chennai, where they were booked for a week. It would take them at least that long to plan exactly what they were going to do in the subcontinent.

A voice over the intercom, first in Hindi and then in English, reminded passengers to collect their belongings. "Maybe we can doze in-between flights," Dottie said unconvincingly. People around them were collecting hats, backpacks, books, briefcases and children. The two women joined the throng and stepped into the cavernous Indira Gandhi International Airport.

Clara was the self-appointed leader of their duo. She'd arranged the travel schedule and had a clear idea of where they needed to go and when. Dottie was good at following instructions and keeping them on track. As carefully as the trip had been planned, however, they weren't precisely committed to exactly what they would do once they were at Mahabalipuram. How would they go about looking for Arundati's family? Was it an impossible task, a chimera? Would they magically stumble upon clues?

A grueling but orderly hour going through Customs and rechecking their bags, voicing the thought on both their minds, Dottie said, "I'm excited about what we might find in the subcontinent. A quest! We don't know exactly what we're looking for and we have no idea what we'll find."

"In the meantime," Clara said, "we have to locate Terminal One. We could buy some snacks and magazines, maybe even nap."

"Good luck on that. I'm beyond feeling sleepy, but I could use food." Of the two of them, Dottie was more conscious of missing meals. For someone remarkably thin, her appetite was voracious. Clara envied her, as she had to run many miles a week to keep her weight down. No matter what she weighed, however, she considered herself stocky.

Overhead signs were in Hindi but also in English. "Good," Clara said. "We're headed in the right direction."

She removed a swath of papers from her backpack. "Let's see, it says here that we need to be at Gate 2 at eight p.m. and it's only five now. Let's go there and settle in. I need to walk after sitting for so many hours."

A half-mile later, they were in a newly remodeled terminal, complete with svelte waiting areas and beautifully patterned brown and gold carpeting. Every twenty feet there loomed an art installation set in the middle of a gigantic round platform. The floors of these circles were mirrored. A gigantic brass elephant mother appeared to be teaching her huge infant to walk. Those two figures were surrounded, on a low border wall, by smaller elephants processing around the circle.

"These are magnificent," exclaimed Dottie. "I can't wait to see the real beasts. I've always loved elephants!"

Clara had already walked toward the next circle. A mandala dominated its center, a mosaic of petals. The background was white and the petals were orange, green and yellow. "I love the use of color. I think it's preparing us for everything we'll be seeing when we visit villages. I read in a guidebook that housewives paint a new mandala outside their dwellings each day. It seems like Indians are born artists."

Now Dottie had gone ahead to the next display. "This one is like a giant coin on its side," she exclaimed. "Except it's got wavy spokes. Sort of mechanical looking. Wish I knew what it represents. There's a plaque, but unfortunately I can't read Hindi."

"If Sanjay was here, he could interpret everything. At first I was relieved that he couldn't come with us, but now I wish he had. It might make this whole expedition easier."

"What about Sanjay's guy, the man who'd supposed to be meeting us in Chennai?" asked Dottie. "Lane something? Sanjay said that even though he's from Amsterdam, he's lived in southern India for years and that he's worked as a tour guide. To quote, *I'd trust him with my life*. I don't think our friend would give us a bum steer. I mean, really..."

"Hmmm, I guess you're right. Or are we being naive to entrust ourselves with a total stranger? I just thought of his last name. It's 'Masterson.' Let's hope he's 'mastered' the art of getting around the subcontinent."

"Well, there will no doubt be all kinds of guides offering their services. It's not like we have a definite plan." Dottie stopped walking and stared at an enormous brass head of Buddha. "Oh my gosh, look at this next sculpture. I can hardly believe it. Should we get out our cameras and take a photo?"

Clara took her friend by the arm and guided her along. "No, absolutely not. First of all, I don't want to call attention to us. We're strangers in a strange land. Plus, we don't have forever. I'd rather just get to our waiting area. It's better to allow plenty of time." She tried to keep the irritation from her voice.

The crowd of people around them had suddenly grown dense. Women in brilliant *saris*, often with children in tow, men in *salwar kameezes*, men in business suits, women in Western dress. Walking swiftly, intent on destinations in the vast terminal. No one but Clara and Dottie paid attention to the airport artwork.

"I get the feeling we're the only ones seeing all this for the first time," Dottie said.

"No," Clara said firmly. " I imagine many of these Indian passengers might never have been to Delhi. Some of these them might not have traveled from this particular airport. Just think. We'll be seeing far more wondrous sights when we get to Tamil Nadu. I think we're close to our gate, but I'm not sure."

"Wait," exclaimed Dottie. "Look ahead. It's a yoga sculpture. Let's pause, just a moment. We gotta take it in."

"No. Stopping now could make us late."

"We can run the rest of the way, until we get to the right terminal."

When Clara saw the monumental sculpture up close, she relented. A scene in marble: spiraling upward and around were men and women in a variety of *asanas*. At the bottom, one of them was doing a downward facing dog. Others, at ascending levels, were in the cobra position, the plank, the tree *asana*.

"This is amazing," Clara exclaimed. "I learned all of these positions in a yoga class I took before moving to the southwest. I used to do them every day. Religiously." She looked at her watch. "When we get to Chennai, we'll be seeing the real thing. We might even spend time in an *ashram* if our guide can recommend a good one."

By now, they were jogging. Just when it looked as though they might be mistaken in their route, they spotted a sign announcing "Terminal One." Checking the departure listing, which was in both Hindi and English, they saw that their flight was leaving from "Gate C-3."

"Hooray," shouted Dottie. She sounded out of breath. Despite her high level of fitness, the last sprint had worn her out. The endless nature of this journey was wearing down both women.

As it turned out, they were none too early. Passengers were lining up to board, so they slipped into place at the queue's end, holding their boarding passes and checking their backpacks to make sure zippers were zipped and buckles buckled. The line wasn't moving fast. In fact, it wasn't moving at all.

"Oh great," grumbled Clara. "Now we can hurry up and wait. Just as soon as we board, I'm putting on my earplugs and closing my eyes. When the stewardess asks about meal choices, please tell her I don't want anything."

On board at last, the two women dozed until the plane descended to Chennai. The stewardess, a very dark Indian woman in a royal blue *sari*, awakened them.

"*Memsahibs*," she said, "You slept right through our meal, but now we are about to land, and you need to collect your belongings and prepare to deplane. Would you like a takeout box with some snacks?

"That's so kind of you," Clara said. "We have some granola bars. I think we'll be fine. Can you tell us what the local time is?"

"Yes, *Memsab*, it is twenty-one hundred hours. In other words, nine p.m."

Moving slowly with the throng of disembarking passengers, Clara and Dottie walked into the Chennai Airport. Minutes later, they were waiting at the luggage carousel looking for their bags.

"Hey," said Dottie, "there's a man over there with a sign reading 'Welcome, Clara and Arundati.' That has to be our guide. Lane Masterson. I hoped he'd be meeting us. I counted on it." She waved and smiled in the tall, blond man's direction.

"Oh, great," Clara said. "If you're sure this is what Sanjay set up, go over and talk to him. Meanwhile I'll stay here to grab our suitcases when they emerge."

Relieved that her friend had relaxed her usual skepticism, Dottie walked over to their welcome party of one. Clara retrieved first Dottie's maroon patterned bag, then her black one. They'd done minimalist packing, knowing they could buy clothes in India if necessary.

She wheeled both bags to Dottie, introduced herself to Lane, and was relieved to learn that he planned to escort them to the Chennai Palace Intercontinental. "This is such a relief, Mr. Masterson. Dottie didn't tell me we'd have a welcome party. Her friend Sanjay - well, he's my friend too - was going to come with us but at the last minute he couldn't. Guess he made up for it by arranging for you to ease our arrival."

The tall man smiled and shook hands first with Clara, then Dottie. "Please, call me Lane. Dottie told me in a phone call how carefully you planned getting here, but she said you don't have plans set in concrete. I'll help you get settled in your hotel, then I can meet you for breakfast tomorrow and offer some suggestions. India can be overwhelming for first-timers. She said she's hoping to find out something about her birth family."

"Yes, she's an adoptee, like me. I was too late. By the time I got a few clues about what I call my bio-mom, she'd already passed away. It's a long, convoluted story. We can tell you more tomorrow or..."

"Or not," Dottie interrupted. "Both our stories are convoluted, but we want to start from now. This is a search mission. I may not to be able to actually meet my relatives. I just want to find out more about the country that contains my heritage, my genes. I'm on my original parents' soil, the place from which they grew, from which I sprouted, to use a garden metaphor..." She trailed off, too tired to find the right words.

"You must be dead on your feet. That trip over from the U.S. is a beast. I'll drive you to your hotel and you can ring me up anytime tomorrow morning. For now, follow me." Lane had taken both their bags and was walking toward sliding glass doors.

"I'm so tired, I ache," said Dottie. "The sooner I can take a shower and collapse, the better." A long walk through corridors and across parking lots, and they arrived at Lane's large black SUV. He put their bags in the trunk and held the door for them as they wearily stumbled inside.

Lane Masterson, Clara decided, was too good to be true. In fact, she knew practically nothing about the man. When Dottie told her about Sanjay's friend and his offer to help them launch their exploration of southern India, she half-listened. Why hadn't she paid closer attention?

Well here they were, for better or for worse, entrusting themselves with Mr. Masterson. Dottie sat in the front seat of Lane's SUV, Clara in the back. Through the labyrinthian streets of Chennai they careened. Though it must have been midnight, tiny boutiques, no bigger than a closet, were brightly lit and ready for customers. They were open to the street. Some were mere stalls.

Here was a shop offering what looked like used car parts. Next to it, a place specializing in brilliant *saris* and shawls. The colors lit up the night: lime green, royal blue, red, yellow, lilac, sienna. Even at this hour, shoppers filled the streets.

"Wish it were daytime and we could stop to check out what's for sale," said Clara.

"It looks like everything's for sale," Dottie said from the front seat. "From what I've heard, there will be zillions of opportunities to buy. Sanjay said it right: India has become one gigantic market place."

Lane, who had been skillfully making his way through traffic, entered into the conversation. "Sanjay was right. There will be people selling you things from the minute you set foot outdoors. It's best not to purchase anything from street vendors. You'll be hounded from every direction. You two world travelers must be starving. I'll treat you to dinner at one of my favorite places in Chennai, then drive you to your hotel."

Clara wondered to herself, "Why is he doing this?" but said nothing to Dottie. They were both exhausted, for sleeping on the flight from New Mexico to New York to India had proved impossible. "Don't look a gift horse in the mouth," she admonished herself. Kindness existed, and people did kind things. Why shouldn't they be the recipients of the world's goodness?

Careening through the chaotic night traffic of Tamil Nadu's capital, Dottie and Clara peered through the windows of Lane's SUV. Meeting their eyes was a wild, teeming montage: pedestrians, animals, bikes and motorcycles, interwoven and kaleidoscopic.

"If you think this is heavy traffic," Lane told them, "you should see it in the daytime. Actually, you might want to take a day to sleep and adjust, or at least wait until afternoon before leaving your hotel. India takes time to wrap your mind around. I plan to take you to Kanchipuram tomorrow afternoon or the next day. The celebration of Lord Shiva is on Saturday, and that's a must."

123

"We have to get to Mahabalipuram," Dottie said. "Is that on our route? As we've been telling you, Lane, the reason we decided to make this trip is so Clara can help me sleuth about for information about my origins. Not sure what I'll be able to find, but it's about my family."

As though he hadn't heard her, Lane continued. "Kanchipuram is at the top of the list. It will open your eyes to the Hindu culture. Incredible temple architecture from Dravidian times, the legacy of Pallava kings. The five *rathas*, an entire history of the subcontinent written in stone. You know what Kanchipuram is called?"

"Well, fine," Dottie said, "but I really wanted to see Maha..."

"The city of 1,000 temples," Clara burst out. "Dottie, I know we'll get to Mahabalipuram soon...Mr Masterson lives in India, after all, and no doubt he has his reasons for taking us to the temple complex first."

"Please. Just call me Lane. Short for Tulane. My Mom wanted to go to Tulane, but she wasn't admitted. So my name was kind of a consolation for her. But - voila- we're here at last!" They'd left the brightly-lit main boulevards and were now in a dark, narrow street. "Don't be alarmed, ladies, this is my warehouse. I keep the car in a locked garage. We'll park, then walk to one of my favorite small restaurants."

# Chapter Twenty-four
# Chennai

Warehouse? Clara wanted to ask what that was about, but Lane and Dottie were already out of the car and waiting for her. She felt a vague unease, but said nothing. After all, Sanjay was Dottie's good friend or cousin or whatever it was. She trusted him and Clara trusted Dottie. Sanjay was the one who'd recommended Narendra, who'd recommended Lane Masterson. For better or worse, he was now their guide. They were two women alone in a foreign country. Lane Masterson was the only person they knew in this vast subcontinent. Maybe best not to start questioning.

"We're so grateful to you, Lane. I can't imagine being here without a guide, someone who knows the territory so to speak." Clara was appreciative, and her doubts might have arisen from extreme fatigue. The trip had been endless. She reminded herself that neither she nor Dottie had slept in two days.

"Yes," chimed Dottie. "Sanjay told us you came here ten years ago and fell in love with the culture and decided to stay. I can't imagine giving up everything and moving to another country."

They'd left the dark alley near Lane's "warehouse," and were now ascending stairs to an Americanized restaurant, Chennai Palace. Colorful signs in the stairwell advertised curries and chicken tandoori. "The finest Southern India cuisine!" "Tailored for the tourist but authentically Indian!" At last they were seated at a small table in the corner of a vast low-ceilinged room. As far as Clara could tell, there was only one other table of diners.

With an odd tone of melancholy, Lane said. "Well, looks as though we have the place almost to ourselves. It's after midnight, and most people who eat out in this part of town eat precisely at six, or eight at the latest." What he did not say is that "eating out" was mostly done by foreigners and not by the "regular" people of Tamil Nadu. Clara wondered why an empty restaurant would make him sad.

As they waited, Dottie talked with Lane about her birthparent quest. Clara observed the surroundings. Her usually quiet friend had suddenly become chatty. The walls of Chennai Palace were a satiny cream color decorated with handprinted flowers, birds and an occasional mandala. Recorded sitar music played softly. A fountain bubbled softly at one end of the dining

125

room. The host, a spindly man in a cream-colored *salwar kameez*, took their orders. "A large pot of *chai* to begin with," Lane said.

After their food arrived, conversation came to a standstill. They'd each ordered a dish to share and served themselves on individual plates: tandoori chicken, *alu gobi*, *saag paneer*, *chapatis*, mounds of fluffy basmati rice. By now, the restaurant was empty except for their table.

"You must try *kheer* for dessert," said Lane. "It's a delectable sort of rice pudding, flavored with saffron and cardamon. Even if you're stuffed, it tops off the meal. By the way, this dinner's on me as a welcome to India."

"I'm too full. More than too full," said Clara. "But I don't want to be the only nay-sayer."

"I'll have to stretch my capacity," said Dottie. "I'll throw caution to the winds and overindulge. So sure, let's have *kheer*."

Dessert was served. The best part of the meal, Clara thought to herself. She was winding down; she could barely keep awake. Lane was talking about the *Kumbha Mela* that would begin in a week. "You might want to seriously consider taking that in during your visit. It happens only every six or twelve years. A spiritual pilgrimage, a happening, The largest gathering of humanity on the planet."

Dottie came to the rescue. "Thanks so much for your suggestions, and I'm sure we'll want to seriously consider it. But right now we are more dead than alive. Please take us to our hotel." She got the reservation papers out of her backpack and showed them to Lane. "We'll be able to consider everything after a decent night's sleep."

"Or two," said Clara. "The way I feel right now, I could sleep for a week."

At last, aided by turbaned attendants, they checked into the Chennai Somerset Hotel. Though not opulent, Somerset boasted small touches of luxury. The squalor of the streets fell by the wayside as Dottie and Clara luxuriated, first Dottie and later Clara, in the sunken bathtub filled with hot water and suds from the in-house bubble bath. Everything was a creamy off white - the plush wall-to-wall carpeting, the heavy drapes, the satin bedspreads covering two queen-sized beds. A mirrored headboard made the spacious room look even bigger.

It was nearly two a.m. when they were propped up in their separate beds, trying to squeeze another few minutes out of the endless travel day. Clara started to write in her travel journal, but

126

her writing soon became illegible. Dottie was reading a guide to Tamil Nadu, but she nodded off before she could finish a page.

"You know, friend," Clara said. "We're done. I'm never too tired to write, but what I've put down so far is just scribbles. Everything's off till tomorrow. I hope we didn't tell Lane we'd pop right back and start our tour first thing in the morning."

Dottie yawned and put her brochures on the bedstand. "I'm so tired, I ache. Too bad if Lane has the impression we'll be ready to go in the morning, because I for one will not be. I could sleep forever." With that, she clicked off the reading light next to her bed, dropped her head on the pillow and fell asleep in less than five minutes.

"G'night," Clara sang out, even though her friend was gently snoring.

# Chapter Twenty-five

The phone's ring pierced through the hot Southern India noontime. Clara was the first to open her eyes. Dottie groaned and put a pillow over her head as her friend picked up the receiver.

"Well good morning, Ms. Jordan. Welcome to your first day in Tamil Nadu. This is your guide *Sahib* Masterson. You and Arundati have had at least 15 hours to sleep. Are you ready to rise and shine? The temples await us. The lavish festival honoring Lord Shiva will begin today at three. I can be by to pick you up in an hour...I promise, you'll be amazed."

Clara found Lane's fake Indian accent ridiculous. But she put on a pleasant voice. Speaking naturally, "Yes, good morning, Lane. Um, afternoon. Thanks again for taking care of us last night. An hour's too soon. I'm pretty sure we don't want to go anywhere till this afternoon."

"It will be afternoon in five minutes." Lane was annoyingly cheerful, but Clara reminded herself that he probably meant well. She ached from head to toe, and the last thing she felt like doing was sightseeing. Time for an attitude adjustment. India awaited.

"OK, Dot, swing into action."

Dottie roused herself and was soon ready to go with Clara to the Chennai Somerset Hotel's high-ceilinged breakfast room, fancifully called "Morning Glory." Like the floors in their room, Morning Glory's were polished marble, giving it a palatial aura. The breakfast itself seemed designed to what Americans would expect. Plentiful, perfectly edible, but nothing extraordinary.

They were ravenous after the twenty-hour trip of the last couple days, so they piled their trays high with scrambled eggs, bacon, fried potatoes, toast and croissants, bowls of oatmeal, and fruit.

"Sanjay warned us not to eat any uncooked fruit that couldn't be peeled," remembered Dottie. "And we can never, ever eat anything from the street vendors. No matter how tasty and delicious it looks or smells. I mean, I hate to sound like a nag, but if we're going to stay healthy on this trip, we have to stick to the rules."

Clara reached for a banana. She was still tired. Trying not to sound like a grouch, she said "Good grief. I wasn't born yesterday. You aren't the only one who's heard of Delhi Belly."

Lane appeared promptly at 1:30. "We'll take the bus to Kanchipuram," he announced. "You'll see why it's called The City of 1,000 Temples, and you'll experience the importance of the Indian god Shiva. There will be hundreds of Indians milling about. It's a real gathering place."

Along came a lumbering green city bus and Lane hurried them in. A mob had formed around them, including many children asking for "*baksheesh*." Women beggars held babies in arms. The latter group were the most tragic, thought Clara. The babies were skin and bones, and the mothers, with their sad, sunken eyes, looked exhausted. They pointed to their mouths, then patted their stomachs, indicating that they needed food.

"Pretty desperate, eh?" Lane commented. "No matter how long I live here, I never get used to the begging. It's pitiful. This is a country of extreme wealth and dire poverty. You just have to shut it out, and look for the beauty. But while we're rumbling along, let me tell you about Chennai and this part of ..."

"Let me guess," interrupted Dottie. "You're going to tell us that Chennai used to be called Madras and that it's the capital of Tamil Nadu. We did some research before our trip."

The bus swerved wildly to the left to avoid an elephant trudging along between the road and sidewalk. The traffic around them comprised a teeming mix of men, women, children, animals, bikes, rickshaws as well as cars, busses and trucks. "I get that you two studied up before coming here. But I bet you didn't know that Chennai is often called 'the Detroit of India'. It's home to a large part of the auto industry. I also bet you didn't know that it's a film production center. Like Hollywood, only here it's Bollywood."

"I guessed that," Clara said. "Our hotel is full of movie posters and images. Movies are kind of like a motif running through the whole place. I'll share a few tidbits I learned before we came here. Chennai is the fourth largest city in India. The British founded it in the 1600s."

"Well, go to the head of the class," exclaimed Lane. "It was established in 1639, to be exact. OK, enough of today's lesson. We get off in four or five stops and catch the state transport bus, Panjita Travel. Once aboard, it should take us an hour to travel to Kanchipuram."

A bespectacled elderly woman wearing a brilliant green *sari* had been silently sitting next to them, apparently listening to every word. She turned and addressed them with a small bow of her head, hands folded at her chin "*Namaskar*. Excuse me *Sahib*,

I live here and have many guests from America, and I must advise you to avoid Panjita Travel. My recent visitors, family members who've expatriated to California, were victims of Panjita. They were delayed time after time. People running the bus were rude and insulting. Because the bus kept breaking down, they spent hours at the roadside getting a tire fixed or the oil refilled or one of a million other things. No one maintains the Panjita coaches. They did arrive at Kanchi, but it was five hours late. Really, *Sahib*, it would behoove you to take Arjuna Overland instead. Panjita is guaranteed torture."

"Oh thanks," blurted Dottie. "You've saved us from so much time and inconvenience. I'm really glad we didn't have to learn the hard way."

Clara started to chime in, but before she could speak, Lane stood up and gestured for them to follow suit. "But here is our stop. We will take your advice into consideration, *Memsab*. *Dhanyavad*." He pushed Clara and Dottie ahead toward the steps to disembark.

"You've been warned," murmured the green-clad lady.

Once out on the teeming sidewalk, Clara and Dottie turned to Lane and persuaded him to heed the unsolicited advice. He was clearly not happy about it, but he admitted that he had not traveled with Panjita for several years. "Actually, it wasn't so good. It was not first class, it was not second class. It had no class. Obviously, it has gone downhill even from then. I guess we'll track down this Arjuna Overland Company and try to book travel to Kanchi."

That was more easily accomplished than any of them might have guessed, and after a quick lunch of *chai*, rice and *dhal*, they were on an Arjuna coach rumbling toward the city of 1,000 temples.

"Before you launch into a travelogue," Clara said. "What does *Dhanyavad* mean?"

"I believe it's *thank you* in Hindi," said Dottie. "I learned that from Sanjay."

The Indian countryside, flat and green, stretched out on every side, teeming with people working the rice fields. The roadside was the scene of much activity as well: bicycles, rickshaws, donkey-drawn carts, an occasional elephant. Clara gazed out at the kaleidoscope of activity until sleep overtook her. It had been an exhausting four days. Just getting here.

The next thing she knew, Dottie was gently shaking her shoulder. "Wake up, friend. The city of 1,000 temples awaits us."

Lane, who was sitting in the seat ahead of them, turned around. "OK, ladies, make sure you have your backpacks, cameras, water bottles, whatever you brought on. Put everything possible inside your packs. Thieves are on the lookout for tourists, and I'm afraid we don't exactly blend in."

Following his own advice, Lane picked up a package wrapped in brown paper and tied with string and shoved it into his canvas pack. It was half the size of a shoebox, Clara observed. She wanted to ask what the box contained, but it was none of her business. Something about it, so unlike the usual travel paraphernalia, seemed odd. Clara hadn't seen the package earlier. It was as though he'd picked it up somewhere along the way. Really, it was Lane's concern, but still...

Clara, Dottie and Lane stepped out of the bus at the entrance to the vast temple complex and were assailed by dozens of vendors. "*Pashminas* of finest cashmere, no better prices anywhere. Two for ten dollars!" "Inlaid boxes, the perfect souvenir, made by top Tamil Nadu artists!" "Mobiles, postcards, *salwar kameezes*!" The three travelers could barely move through Indians hawking their wares.

"Dottie," yelled Lane. "Do not look at anything. Don't talk to any of these pests. If they think they've got a customer, we'll never get rid of them. No eye contact. Come on, let's go." He had already paid admittance through a travel agent on the bus, so they plowed through the entrance into a vast open plaza. Temples and monuments, as far as the eye could see.

"Here we are!" Lane exclaimed.

"Kanchipuram looks like the India of my dreams." Clara sighed and looked around with wondering eyes. "Murals, carvings, stone sculptures, throngs of people and a million other sights —everywhere. I can hardly take it all in."

Dottie was gazing upward. She pointed across the esplanade. "What's that tall, skinny pole? Looks like some kind of needle, maybe a tower? It's being held up by tiny elephants. I could stand here all day and study the base."

"You're on the right track," Lane said. "The name escapes me, but the pillar is symbolically connecting heaven and earth. The connection features large in Hindu mythology."

"Look over there!" Clara waved her hand to the left. "A whole flock of Indian women in gorgeous red and gold saris. It looks like a field trip for ladies."

"You might say it is a sort of field trip. Those are probably teachers out from school to visit holy places. This is *Margazhi*, one of the most important—no, the most important — festival in Chennai."

"What's it about?" asked Clara. "The only festivals I've heard about are *Divali* and the massive *Kumbha Melas*."

"The best way to describe it might be the largest music festival in the world. It features over 3,000 music performances. It's also a kind of celebration of the season. Mid-December through mid-January, best time of year in Chennai. Top-notch musicians from all over the subcontinent vie for performance spaces. Really competitive."

Lane was just warming up to his topic, and it became clear that he wanted them to immerse themselves. He began to elaborate on a nearby restaurant where one could "enjoy the *ragas* while devouring *dosas* and *vadas*."

Dottie interrupted. "Very interesting, but in addition to sightseeing, we are here on a private mission. I need to search for information and people who can lead me to someone I'm related to. We've been talking with you about my birthparent search. Were you hearing us?"

Her friend chimed in. "Don't get us wrong. Of course, we want to learn about the culture of this wonderful country. On the other hand, we don't want to get sidetracked."

"The problem is," Dottie explained, "We know in a general sense what our mission is, but we're a bit clueless as to how to go about it. We're looking for inspiration."

"Maybe for an epiphany," Clara said.

An eerie sound cut through the hot, overcast afternoon. A bare-chested young man wearing a white sarong and beads around his neck was blowing into a conch shell. The sound that emerged was long and deep. He faced four directions, sending a clarion call toward each.

The crowd stopped milling and stood in rapt attention. "It's a summons to pay respect to Lord Shiva," Lane whispered. Standing on a raised stage, the first of two dancers began to perform. A musician, sitting cross-legged at the corner of the stage, played a sitar and sang.

The lead dancer moved slowly, with outstretched arms and a solemn expression. Gradually, she became animated. Lithe and graceful, she waved her way through an intricate pattern of gestures. She danced with her bare feet, her arms and hands, and her eyes. The pace of her movements accelerated and grew wildly exuberant. After a long series of steps, she returned to a statue-like mode, retreating to give the stage to an older, more sturdily built dancer. The second dance was slower and more lilting than the first.

Transfixed, Clara whispered to Lane, "Are those what are called *guptas*, those hands doing all kinds of movements?"

"Yes, and they're really important, part of the devotional homage being paid to Lord Shiva."

The music, drums and stringed instruments providing the background for a high-pitched, slightly nasal singing. "I have no idea what they're expressing," Clara confided, "but for some reason I find the melodies irresistible."

"Mesmerizing, magical, miraculous," agreed Dottie.

Suddenly the music and dancing came to a halt. The conch blower once again sounded a summons. A ten-foot tall cart, pushed by three small men, rolled across the brick palisade toward two stages. Inside was a bronze-faced statue wearing a towering black and gold crown. Down the front, from neck to foot, the statue wore a slender gown emblazoned with gold medallions. "An interpretation of Lord Shiva," Lane told the women. "We need to stay right here. Then, when the crowd begins to form a queue, we can be blessed by a holy man. That is, unless you don't want to."

"We do want to." Clara and Dottie both replied.

"We need all the help we can get," Dottie reaffirmed.

They were the only white people in a sea of Indians, but no one seemed to take much notice of them. The worshippers' expressions were solemn, joyous and every emotion in between. All were paying close attention. Men, women and children formed a line before a small man perched in front of the Shiva image. One by one, he dabbed their foreheads with a white substance that looked like ash.

"I can't believe this is happening," Clara said as her turn approached. "I feel like I should make a wish."

Lane, standing right behind her, whispered "Do. A blessing from Lord Shiva is powerful. It is about hopes and dreams. Concentrate on what your heart most desires."

"But it's just this little guy in a white diaper," Clara said.

Lane laughed. "It's a *dhoti*, not a diaper. That's Shiva's anointed, his administrator, his anointed Holy Man. The blessing comes through him."

Within the next five minutes, Lane, Clara and Dottie were all wearing white *tikka* marks on their foreheads. All afternoon, Clara had been depressed. The search for Dottie's ancestry seemed like mission impossible. She'd bungled Mission Greta, and this madcap trip to India might be a fiasco. But after receiving the *tikka*, Clara felt oddly refreshed and energized.

With Shiva's blessing, her outlook changed. True, it would be difficult to find answers, but she and Dottie were a strong pair. They would do whatever it took. As the threesome walked through dozens of temples and carvings, she allowed herself to feel mildly hopeful. She looked up at the towers of a blue, pink and tan building. The top tiers, Lane said, were a medley of scenes from Hindu mythology. Like the world around them, the painted scenes were teeming. Except in this case, the beings—celestial, animal, and human—were stone.

"While we're still living and breathing," she confided to Dottie, "we'll get to the heart of things. If we can't find anyone to interpret, we may have to invent an 'origins story' for you."

"I'm not sure I like that idea at all," Dottie said. "I think the truth is out there waiting to be discovered. Not invented. Discovered."

As he led them toward the inner temples of Kanchipuram, they followed closely behind Lane. More than once, he reminded them, "Stick right behind me. The crowd around us is only going to grow denser."

He continued, "You'll be happy to know that we're headed to Mahabalipuram now. Isn't that where Dottie thinks her family might be located?"

# Chapter Twenty-six

"Just a wild hunch," Clara told him. Bracing herself against the mass of humanity on every side, she turned to Dottie and whispered, "How could we ever explain your dream and the statue hand of Ganesh?" Dottie shrugged.

Lane turned around, looking displeased. "Please stick with me. We can't afford to get separated, and this crowd makes it necessary to concentrate. I have to find the right bus to take us to the Shore Temple."

After speaking with several different pedestrians, Lane shouted, "Here! The bus. The red bus... Hurry, run, we can't miss it." Clara and Dottie hustled, and the three of them squeezed in just before the doors clanked shut. Some young Indians in western jeans and t-shirts, college students thought Clara to herself, got up and indicated for them to take their seats. Clara and Dottie took advantage of the offer. Lane declined.

"Nice people," he said to no one in particular. "The civility of most Indians never ceases to amaze me." Twenty minutes later, they were still barreling through traffic. Clara noted, not for the first time, that Lane was still carrying the package wrapped in brown paper and bound with string.

Clara wondered what that was about. She felt a growing resentment toward Lane. Finally, she blurted, "We don't seem to be going anywhere near a body of water. I thought the shore temple was on the Bay of Bengal. It looks like we're going inland."

"Speaking of water," Dottie said, "I'm feeling really dehydrated. Is this bus ride ever going to end? And where?"

Lane's florid complexion turned even rosier. "My apologies, ladies. I remembered that I had to deliver something to an herb expert in a place called Cardomon Inn, and it needed to get there before five. I didn't want to just leave you to find your own way to the Shore Temple, and it was too complicated to explain. No worries, my dears. If we run out of time today, I'll be your guide first thing tomorrow. Sorry if you feel like you're being dragged along, but we had too late a start. Get up now, the next stop is ours."

What choice did they have? Though she tried to silence her doubts, Clara was beginning to feel uneasy about this Lane person. Why had they entrusted themselves to him? Once they were back at the hotel, she and Dot would have to hold a business meeting. Maybe they'd be better off on their own. There seemed to be any number of freelance guides available. They advertised in the hotel lobby and, it seemed, on every street corner.

Lane escorted them off the bus and into the jumbled sidewalk crowd. "Just follow me. This won't take long." What "this" referred to was a mystery. They arrived at an area of greenery with a shaded path leading into a sort of mini-jungle. The air was filled with the perfume of spices and herbs. They walked down an embankment of red clay, past plants with labels in English: "cinnamon," "tumeric," "ginger" and dozens more.

"Ladies, I owe you an explanation for my schlepping this package. I have a few American clients who've asked me to be their buyer for spices," Lane said. "Some of them have given me samples of what they think they want. That's what's in the box."

The proprietor, a bear of a man wearing an orange shirt, greeted them and took the package from Lane. "*Namaskar*," he said with a slight bow, palms held together in front of his heart.

"*Namaskar*," chorused Clara and Dottie, both offering their version of *Namaste*. Apparently, this was going to take awhile. "Forget about the Shore Temple for today," Clara whispered to Dottie.

Out of nowhere appeared a stunning young woman wearing a white *sari* trimmed in gold. "And here is my granddaughter Dina," said the proprietor. She would be happy to give you a tour of our spice shop. We can offer you many free samples."

"No, but thank you," said Clara. "We have to get back to our hotel in Chennai, as we're both suffering from jet lag."

"Jet what?" The proprietor looked puzzled.

"She means that we are tired," said Dottie. "Exhausted. And, I have to ask you, may I use your toilet? I've been drinking too much water."

"Yes, Dina will take you. It is Indian style, very simple. A hole in the ground. Meanwhile, *Sahib* Lane, may I show you the newest plants I am growing?"

"That's fine," said Dottie. "We're used to Indian style. What I mean is, at home, we go camping a lot and we rough it."

"Just go. Follow Dina," Clara interrupted. "I'll stay here with your backpack." She found herself next to a little shelf covered with papers and the box that Lane had been carrying. Making sure that Lane and the herb shop proprietor were not nearby, she quietly opened the box to inspect its contents. An order for herbs sounded fishy. Sure enough, underneath a few sprigs of leaves, there was a stack of four by six color photographs. Intricate chokers and necklaces, small statues, letter openers, the objects appeared to be ivory.

The two men, conversing in Hindi, were walking toward her. She quickly closed the box and pretended to be fumbling with Dottie's backpack. "I can't believe my friend is so careless. She leaves all the pouches of her pack unzipped. Anyone could reach in and steal anything."

"Ah yes, *Memsab*," said the proprietor. "This is a country, alas, of many good people but also of many pickpockets. One must always be on guard. Busy hands are everywhere. Necessary to be always careful."

Clara thought wryly of how not careful Lane had been to leave his box unsealed and right next to her. She hoped he didn't suspect that she was beginning to doubt him. Not just his flimsy explanation of the package, but everything so far. After all, he was not getting them to the Shore Temple, which is the only place they'd asked for specifically. Maybe she and Dot should just go on their own? Make excuses tomorrow or just leave without telling Lane?

Meanwhile, Dottie, escorted by Dina, had joined them. Clara could hardly wait to talk to her in private. She no longer trusted Lane, but on the other hand, they might need him at some point. It wouldn't do to let him know that they doubted him. Being on their own might be worse.

After a seemingly endless journey, off and on various busses and lots of walking in between stops, they were back at the Chennai Palace Hotel. It was amazing how their hotel had come to seem like home.

"Thank you so much, Lane, for a fascinating first day exploring India." Feeling like a hypocrite, Clara shook Lane's hand. "Tomorrow, we are just going to rest up. We have your number and we'll call you if we need to. I think we'll use the hotel concierge. We might want to do some shopping and if you're like every man at home, that's a cruel and unusual punishment."

Lane grimaced. "You misjudge me. I don't mind shopping at all. In fact, I know the best places and I can keep you from paying too much. Really, the tourist here is an easy target."

"Lane, you're so kind," Dottie said. "But we are big girls now. We learned to barter in Santa Fe, where we're from. We've had loads of practice bargaining with Native Americans for pottery and turquoise jewelry. We 'll be fine. Thank you so much for all you've done for us."

Together, the two women gently ushered Lane out the Chennai Palace Hotel entrance into the teeming crowds. Not only the sidewalk but the road beyond was in a state of mild chaos. "It's as though everyone in the outside world is on the way to a big event," said Dottie.

"And I'm glad we're not invited. I've got a great idea. Let's order dinner brought to our room, a real Indian feast. Tomorrow we will go to Mahabalipuram. On our own. Here's the restaurant, and it seems to be open. Let's place an order for an hour from now."

They ended up choosing mung bean curry and rice, *paddu*, *laddus*, and Indian beer. By the time their food arrived, both had showered and were in slippers and robes. "A pajama party for two," Dottie said, as she sipped pale ale and delved into their take-out dinner. "Who ever thought that a lentil and rice puff would be so yummy? I don't know about you, but I was starving."

"Mmmm, wait till you try this curry," Clara said. "It is better than anything I've had in Indian restaurants at home. By the way, there's something so weird that happened today, and I almost forgot to tell you about it. Remember when you had to go to the restroom while we were at the herb shop?"

Dottie reached for the *laddus*, round sweets filled with nuts and raisins. "Try one of these delights. Heavenly." She chewed, swallowed, and finally replied, "You mean the hole-in-the-ground restroom? Yeah, that was quite the experience. You weren't the one to endure that dismal bathroom, but you looked so happy when I rejoined you. What happened?"

Clara drank deeply from her bottle of Indian ale. "I think Lane isn't quite honest. He may be a tour guide, but he's also may be dealing in ivory jewelry. You know. Ivory. Elephant tusks. Illegal dealings?"

"Good God," Dottie groaned. "Not again. First you had horrible Henry in your life, the pottery smuggler. And now another kind of confiscator? What makes you think Lane's doing that? He's not a poacher, is he?"

"Well, maybe not directly, but making anything from elephant tusks is illegal, and Lane might be into selling illegal stuff. The so-called herb order was just a front. While you were at the hole-in-the-ground, I peeked into the box he was carrying around. It was mainly full of photos of ivory artifacts. Either he was giving them to the herb guy to place orders or else he had the originals and wanted the herb man to make an offer. I wish we could have heard what those two were saying."

"Or understood it, you mean," Dottie corrected. They'd tried to learn a bit of Hindi on their own before coming on this trip. St. John's, her college, did offer Hindi lessons as part of the Graduate Institute, but from what she gathered, the process of learning was painstakingly slow. They would have needed to start at least a year before their trip.

"Well, at least we don't have to be with Lane tomorrow," Clara said. "Maybe he is doing something illegal. Just so he doesn't get us involved, or put us at risk. Surely he won't endanger us."

"I hope you're right," Dottie said. "He's probably just a minor crook, maybe not a totally bad person. I think it's important for us not to let him suspect that we're on to him. In other words, the more that we can do on our own, the better."

"Let's drink to that," Clara agreed. The two friends clanked bottles together and shortly after that went to bed. Their sleep was long, deep, and dreamless. In the Hindu culture, it would have been called a little death.

# Chapter Twenty-seven

"How can I help you, *Memsab*?"

The young concierge at Chennai Palace's front desk, stood attentively on the other side of the counter. To Clara, he seemed as gracious and charming as Lane was abrupt and remote. Dark eyes and chiseled features, slender and wearing a crisp white dress shirt and navy suit, he looked to be about the same age as the American Indian Academy students she'd taught last year. Ninth graders. However, he was probably in his twenties.

"Yes, Mr..." She looked at his name tag: Balram Iyer. "My friend Arundati and I are guests fairly newly arrived in your city, and we need a tour that will take us to the Shore Temple at Mahabalipuram. Our regular guide had to take today off." This of course, was not true at all. They'd had to convince Lane to leave them to their own devices today, and it hadn't been easy.

"Ah yes, *Memsab*. That can be most easily arranged. There is a bus that will be leaving at ten a.m. precisely. Your fellow passengers will be mostly British, along with some Japanese. That will be for two, right?"

"Yes, and I have *rupees*."

"Ah, very good, as your cost is less if you pay in Indian currency. Or if you like, I can simply add it to your hotel bill. For two, it comes to 2,500 *rupees*. More or less seventeen dollars each."

"Fine. Just add it to our tab, Mr. Iyer. Any suggestions for what to take?"

"Yes *Memsab*. Be sure to have an umbrella, as it can rain at any time and, if it does not rain, you can use the umbrellas for protection from our blazing hot Indian sun. Bottled water, sunglasses, sunscreen, comfortable shoes, camera, a sweater. You appear to be a seasoned traveler. No doubt you are accustomed to being prepared."

Clara never ceased to be amazed by how reasonable prices were in India. Back in the room, she told Dottie about the bargain rate for going to Mahabalipuram. "I kind of wish we didn't have to deal with Lane at all. We might need him at some point. For the nth time, let's think about breaking out on our own."

"Um, maybe it would be for the best. I can't decide," Dottie mumbled vaguely.

By 11:30, they were on their way to Mahabalipuram, seated in a large tour bus along with other tourists. Their driver, a young Australian woman wearing capris and an enormous sun hat, began a nonstop travelogue. "Where the wind meets the waves, this is my favorite site in Tamil Nadu...when we arrive, you'll see why this locale has been proclaimed a world heritage site. It dates back to the Pallava dynasty, 800 years B.C. Unimaginably ancient! Just wait until you see the temple itself, a tower to antiquity..."

They came to a bridge, at which point the bus practically stopped. A line of vehicles ahead of them was barely moving. "Nothing serious, folks," announced their cheery driver. "People are just stopped to witness the mid-river breakdown." Outside and below them, an ox cart was mired in the muddy water. Apparently, the back wheel had fallen off and the cart was partially submerged. The cargo, which appeared to be a wagon full of sand, remained intact. The driver climbed off his perch and walked into waist-deep water to inspect. He was soon circled by curious villagers. Men. All of them wearing tee shirts and turbans, along with jeans. Vainly they were trying to lift up the back of the wagon.

"In America," Clara announced, "we call these events looky loos. If anything happens on the side of the road, people have to slow down and gawk. "

"Yes," Dottie added. "It must be a universal trait. Oh , here come more helpers. They're pushing the cart to a more shallow part of the river. And here comes someone with a new wheel. A traveling mechanic."

"How can it be a mechanic?" Clara asked. "This is pre-mechanization. Like something from the Middle Ages. Or even the Dark Ages. Wow! They've actually lifted the rear part of the cart up. I think they're changing out the wheel." A cheer arose from the bus's passengers and slowly the gridlock lessened. Once again, they rumbled along the two-lane road.

Still no sign of a shore temple. Instead, the bus came to a halt. "OK," yelled the driver. "Everybody out. We're almost there, but your visit to this part of India would not be complete without visiting a traditional fishing village. It's how people along this section of the Bay of Bengal make their living."

Clara started to protest. Dottie, sensing her friend's impatience, whispered "Let's just go with the flow. When will we ever have a chance to see something like this again? I'm sure we'll eventually get there."

"Yes, you're absolutely right. I'm still living the hectic pace of home. Driven and trying to pack everything in. India manages to be both bustling and laid back. A fascinating combination. Let's go see what life is like in a southern Indian fishing village."

Everyone piled out of the bus and waited for instructions. "We'll spend twenty minutes here," announced their driver. "If you need the restroom, you can use one at the general store but you must first buy something." She waved her hand toward a shack of weathered gray wood. A Coca-Cola logo adorned the screen door.

First Clara, then Dottie used the facilities. Then, on to the village. Along with the other bus passengers, they walked toward a wide beach of golden sand. Unlike the muddy river water, the water before them was a dazzling blue. White breakers pounded the shore. Men and women were sitting by long canoe-like boats. Many were scowling.

"No catch today," complained a gray-haired man. "We are hoping our luck will change." It never ceased to surprise Clara when the Indians spoke English.

"*Enshallah*," said the friend next to him.

"*Enshallah*," Dottie told him. She turned to Clara. "That's kind of a universal term that means 'God willing."

"Well, actually, I knew that. Hey, let's check out the walking path. It looks a lot more pleasant than standing here with this dispirited crew."

The two women strolled around a neighborhood of stucco dwellings. A tidy path connected the well-tended homes. In front of each small house, at the front door, was a design in brilliant pastels, each one unique. Some were being created as they walked by, all of them painted by village women.

"You speak English?" Clara asked one of the folk artists.

"A little," replied a woman looking up from her work.

"Do you make a new drawing every day?" Clara asked.

"And do you use a pattern or just make designs up as you go along?" Dottie wanted to know.

"Ah, yes," the woman said. "I understand. You wonder do we make new designs each day. Also where we find designs."

Clara and Dottie nodded.

142

"Some of us in our village do a new drawing every day, some of us once a week. I like to do one every two days. All different, no drawing like the one before. No pattern. They come from inside us." She tapped her right temple and smiled.

"They're beautiful. Wish we could have something like this at home." Clara got her camera out. "Do you mind if I take a few photos?"

"No *Memsab*. It is very fine. Should I stand by my door?" Clara moved back to capture the woman's lavender, blue, and white *sari* as well as the brilliant bird drawings at her feet. She took some close-ups of the doorstep artwork. The birds, one each in fuchsia, turquoise, navy blue, and yellow radiated out in a wheel pattern.

Two curious neighbors looked on. Both were smiling. They wanted their photos taken as well. Clara asked their permission, having no idea if they understood. The English-speaking woman said something to them in Hindi, then turned to Clara. "They said yes. They would like it very much."

"If only we had Polaroid cameras."

"Here's something almost as good." Clara, with a few clicks, got to the screen with the Indian women smiling at their doors. She beckoned them to come look as she held her camera and pointed to the display screen.

# Chapter Twenty-eight

Their day in the village ended without a visit to the shore temple. "We simply ran out of time," the guide explained. "I can schedule another visit in one week from now, when there will be dances and another ceremony. I can sign you up now." Clara and Dottie opted instead of signing up to revise their decision to ditch Lane. After all, they did want to see as much of the subcontinent as possible and Lane knew the territory.

"Maybe an attitude adjustment is in order," Clara announced to no one in particular.

Back at Chennai Palace, they met Lane for dinner. Chicken tandoori was featured and all three found it delicious.

"We've gotten a little off track," Lane said at the end of their day in the village. "I'll book us in a place called Cardomon Inn. Don't worry about the expense: I know the owners. It's on me."

After dinner, Lane said he had to meet a local business man. "Some tourists from Holland, clients of the business man, will be needing a guide in a few months. You may need to be on your own for a bit but I'll always be here for you."

Clara felt relieved to have time alone with Dottie. An idea was forming, and she needed to run it by her friend. The two went to their room and collapsed into armchairs next to a round coffee table. Both of them sensed the trip was not going well.

Silence reigned for a few minutes. Finally, Clara spoke. "With Lane Masterson, we don't seem to be getting any closer to finding your original family."

Dottie took a large sip from her water bottle. "I'm really glad you mentioned that. I've been wondering about the same thing. Somehow, I don't have the feeling that with mysterious Masterson at the helm it will ever happen. What if we just went off on our own, maybe spent time in a quiet place of devotion and learning, maybe an *ashram*?"

Clara brightened at the suggestion. "With the money he requires, we could instead pay local guides who could possibly help more with finding your original family. I've paid for his so-called services until the end of this month. Knowing him, he would be just as happy to not have us on his hands. We don't have a written contract for any particular amount of time."

"Right. It might be a win-win. He could go off with those new tourists he was going to meet and we'd have our freedom."

144

Clara sighed heavily and sank deeper into the armchair. "We'd also have the responsibility. We don't know what we're doing here. It's alien. Beautiful but bizarre. On the other hand, we really don't know this Masterson character. I feel like I've let you down. It's your inheritance we're spending and, so far, we're not getting any closer to finding out about your origins. You could have hired a detective. It might have been cheaper, and it might have resulted in something." She began to cry, softly at first, and then all out. "What have I gotten us into?" She transferred a pillow from behind her back, put it on her lap, and buried her face.

Dottie reached across and patted her friend's back gently. "Quit blaming yourself, friend. This quest was the idea of us both."

Clara lifted her head from the pillow. "I was the stronger advocate. Because I failed to finding my original mom, I tried to make up for it by helping you. Okay then. We are far from giving up. More and more, I agree that we need to make a break from the mysterious Masterson. He has too many hidden agendas." Clara sniffled and blew her nose.

Dottie agreed. "And helping us isn't one of them."

"Exactly. I'll make us some tea and then we can go to bed early. We won't have to see Masterson until tomorrow morning and by then one of us might come up with an actual escape plan. We'll sleep on it."

The next day, Clara and Dottie slipped into the Cardomon's buffet breakfast at opening time, 6:30 a.m. They hoped to talk privately before seeing Lane, but they were too late.

"Good morning, *Memsabs*," Lane chirped from across the room. "I guess we're the early birds today. I trust you slept soundly. Wait until you hear my plan for today. I think you'll like it."

"Well maybe," said Clara, "but it seems like we've lost sight of our reason for taking this trip in the first place."

Dottie chimed in. "Of course, we want to see the real India, but we want to do things that have the most possibility of my meeting someone who looks like me, who might be related. You see, we have this artifact, a hand of Ganesh. I mean a fragment of a statue of Ganesh, and it belonged to my family."

Clara glared at her friend for telling Lane so much. She sent a silent message to Dottie: Just keep quiet. She looked directly at Lane. "Let me do the explaining. What she's trying to say is that we have good reason to suspect that Dottie, whose

145

actual name, as you know, is 'Arundati, might be from a family in southern India. We thought if we met people in Chennai, the town near where the artifact actually came from, we could maybe come across Dot's relatives."

"No matter how distant the relatives," Dottie said, "they might remember when a small girl disappeared from their village and who the girl's parents were. Even if the parents were dead, people could lead us to the next of kin. I'd ask about my original mama and papa. You can't imagine how greatly that would help me."

Lane hardly seemed to listen. He was shuffling through receipts, papers that looked like bills of sale. "Well yes," he said. "You just need me to be an interpreter in this wild goose chase of yours. I can do that, but first I must get something important to Jaipur, to the Chand Baori Stepwell."

"The what," both women asked at once. "What is a stepwell?"

"An ancient subterranean edifice," said Lane. "You will not have really seen India unless you've seen one. I realize, however, that you're obsessed with this Mahabalipuram idea. I have to meet a business partner in Jaipur and since you're not interested in the Chand Baori, I can book you with one of my friends, an accomplished guide with very good English. He can take you to the Shore Temple. I'll cover the cost. My friend owes me a favor. Just let me know and I'll make the arrangements."

Clara could barely hide her astonishment. This was a new Lane, one who seemed to be almost relieved to be free of them for a day. She thought back to the mysterious box at the spice garden near Cardomon Inn. Could it be that his real business was not tour guiding at all? Maybe that was a front?

Clara tried to put her thoughts to rest as they went through the sumptuous buffet line. There were vegetable dishes, rice pilafs, salads and puddings. Western style breakfast offerings adjoined the Indian cuisine: eggs scrambled, eggs benedict, pancakes, bacon and sausage, oatmeal, granola, dry cereals, breads and rolls.

"This should hold us all day," Dottie commented. "I didn't realize how hungry I was."

Clara agreed. A great idea to leave well-fortified for their day's adventure. She noted to herself that a new harmony reigned between Lane and his two clients. Something had shifted, and she wasn't sure why — but she was grateful. An invisible release. He

146

no longer seemed to be micromanaging them, but instead made arrangements for them to branch out on their own.

Breakfast finished, the two women climbed into a tour bus that would take them the 60 kilometers to the Mahabalipuram shore temple. Other passengers seemed to be from all over. No Indians, but dozens of Japanese and what appeared to be Europeans. Most were married couples. Clara and Dottie appeared to be the only women traveling alone. Like the other tourists, they were outfitted in slacks and wearing sun hats. Cameras and backpacks were the universal accessories. The two women relaxed into their seats.

"As much as I enjoy the kaleidoscope going on outside," said Clara, "being in the bus feels relaxing."

"Yes," Dottie replied with a deep yawn. "I'm closing my eyes for a bit. But don't worry, I'm still listening to you."

Clara, though she suspected that she was losing her audience, continued. "India assaults the senses. Not that it's bad, it's just relentless. So many colors, smells, vehicles, animals...the beautiful and the trashy, all jumbled together."

"An overabundance," murmured Dottie. She yawned again as she leaned her head against Clara's shoulder.

"Exactly," said Clara. Being careful not to move quickly and awaken the now-sleeping Dottie, she slipped her travel guide from a backpack at her feet. "Maybe you're only half-sleeping, friend. Not sure you'll hear this, but I'll read aloud anyway. You can listen in your sleep. It says here that Mahabalipuram is a World Heritage Site, one of 16 in the entire world. And listen to this: The visitor to this sought-after tourist destination never fails to experience the rare symphony on the rocks created by the Pallavas. You know, the line of leaders who ruled India for centuries."

At the mention of the Pallavas, Dottie woke up. "Yes, I remember a lecture back at St. John's College when I took a seminar. They ruled between the 3rd and 8th centuries. The stone artwork we'll be seeing is Dravidian."

Now Clara was yawning. "I could read on but I think instead I'll wait till we see everything with our own eyes. And speaking of eyes, now I need to close mine. You're got the right idea. Time for a power nap."

Twenty minutes of rumbling through traffic-clogged streets filled with motorcycles, busses, cars, pedestrians, bicyclists. All of which Dottie and Clara, in their slumber, missed seeing. The extra vigilance that India seemed to require had drained their energy. All too soon, the bus driver's announcement broke through their respite.

"Dear ladies and gentlemen, we have now arrived at our destination, the magnificent Mahabalipurim, gem of Southern India. Included within your bus fare, you will have the service of guides along the way as you explore this vast complex. Dear ladies and gentlemen, it is a repository of history and art, far too vast to be absorbed in the mere four hours of our stay. It would take four days to even begin to appreciate its wonders."

The passengers were growing restless. Some of them started putting on hats and backpacks and standing up in their seats. Clara spoke for all them, gently interrupting. "Dear *Sahib*, please excuse me for interrupting, but could you tell us exactly when we should meet back at our bus and if we will have a guide as we stroll through the grounds?"

"Ah yes, dear travelers, you must make sure your time devices all say 1 p.m. You must be back in the bus by 3:30 p.m. It is most important to be on time. I will release you to explore the wonders, but first I will introduce James, your local guide for the Shore Temple and surroundings. He is a lifelong student of the art and culture of Southern India. He is kind and helpful and infinitely knowledgeable." A short, very dark man in western clothing, slacks and a sports shirt, a small microphone hanging from his neck, stepped into the front of the bus next to the tour guide.

"*Namaste*, dear visitors. I will stand outside the bus and give a brief overview of all that we'll be walking through. You must stay with the group and be within listening distance of my voice. Please step out and gather by me at the first of the *Rathas*, those stone shrines to the right. He pointed to a group of massive stone chariots. I'll hold up this flag." Demonstrating, he waved a pole festooned with a red pennant. "You will always know where I am by the flag and I beseech you to keep it in sight."

At last, the exodus began. Even though the bus driver said it was safe to leave things on the bus. "It will be locked and I will be inside it the entire time." Clara and Dottie scooped everything into their large backpacks, to take with them. James stood next to a pagoda made of stone. The other passengers were peppering him with questions.

The seated crowd had become a standing one. "Dear esteemed visitors, instead of answering your individual queries,

148

please give me a few minutes to address everyone. I request most humbly your attention. We will stay at these *Rathas* — a term that basically means 'Chariots' — for half an hour, and then we'll move on. Feel free to climb and walk on them, but be safe and careful. Oh yes, at the end of the five *Rathas*, you will find public toilets, Indian style, should you need to answer nature's call.

"Having said that, I will now introduce you to the Dharmaraja *Ratha*, the tallest of the five. Please observe the exquisite carving of the pavilions and row or Chaitya windows that adorn this gallery of art..."

Some of the bus passengers were beginning to wander off on their own, and the tour guide, taking that as a cue, announced that they could simply ask questions of him rather than being lectured to. "Feel free to wander among the *rathas*. I see that some of you are taking photographs of the family of tiny owls that are nesting in the arches and eaves. They are here every season, they or their progeny. Please be mindful of the time, do not wander very far from the group. I will be standing here with my flag plainly visible."

Clara and Dottie wandered to the end of the rectangular *Ratha* area, glad to have some time away from the droning guide. "So these ancient sculptures are like pagodas," said Dottie. "I read in our guidebook that they are shrines, some of them are dedicated to heroes of the Mahabarata."

"The maha...what?" Clara asked.

"We studied it at St. John's. It's a famous Sanskrit epic, sort of like the Bible in importance. We read it in an English translation but we also had to study enough Sanskrit to read parts in the original. It's all about warring cousins, full of battles and Hindu dieties. We barely scratched the surface, but..."

"It sounds fascinating but pithy," interrupted Clara. "Like something that would take a lifetime to study."

"Maybe several lifetimes. If I'm reborn, I'd like to be a Hindu scholar and devote my life to study. I've read part of the Mahabarata. I plan to read the other famous Indian epic, the Ramayana. I'd love to become an authority."

"Meanwhile," Clara said, "I think I'll take a stone cow ride." She handed her camera to Dottie. "Take a photo after I'm a little further up this behemoth of a cow."

Dottie laughed. "That's not just any cow. I think it's Nandi, the vehicle for Shiva." Clara climbed wide steps and hoisted herself up to sit on the wide stone back. "Hey, that looks

149

great. Just slide up a little more and maybe take off your hat and wave it in the air with one hand. Sort of like a rodeo cowgirl."

"I can't get up any further." Clara was overcome with a fit of laughter. "You try it, Miss Hindu religion expert. See if Nandi likes you any better. The back of this beast is slippery...and I'm slowly but surely going to land on my rear." Dottie snapped more photos as Clara begged her to stop.

Finally, she slid all the way down and was sitting on the stone step. "Well this is better than the last time I fell off a four-legged beast. Did I tell you what happened with Jerome?"

Dottie held out her hand and helped Clara to her feet. They walked on to the second of the five *Rathas*.

"You mean that sometime boyfriend?" asked Dottie. "I thought you were finished with him."

"Jerome was great until we went on a horse ride. After that, our relationship went downhill. It plummeted. But here we are at another one of these statues. Are you sure you want to hear about this?"

"Yeah, I do. Unless it's too painful to talk about."

"I don't want us to miss seeing everything. But we can continue wandering through the sculptures and talk at the same time. It really helps me get over it. The breakup, I mean."

Clara continued. "I should have known Jerome was obsessed with horses when we went to a display of Native American and Spanish bridles at the Wheelwright Museum. When he suggested a horse ride, I told him I wasn't an equestrian, that I'd only been on a horse a few times in my life. Finally, I agreed to go with him one Sunday afternoon, someplace flat and not challenging. I insisted on a gentle steed, maybe an old nag.

"We went to this place called Bishop's Lodge and were matched up with horses. The horse manager gave me some pointers, and Jerome had to chime in. My horse was a chestnut mare with white markings on her face. They told me her name was Harriet and that she had a reputation for being gentle and patient.

"Well, maybe she was. But Jerome wasn't. We trotted along for maybe half a mile — a reasonable enough pace — but then his horse started going faster. Egged on by him, I'm sure. I yelled out to please slow down. Harriet was right behind Jerome and his black horse. I never did catch his horse's name. He yelled back at me, 'Hey, you're doing great. Just enjoy it. This is the only way you'll know what it really is to enjoy riding.' He shouted that, and...and then he was off."

Dottie interrupted. "Let me guess. You fell off Harriet and nearly got trampled."

"No, I stayed on, but I did the exactly wrong thing. I pulled on the reins, which made Harriet think I wanted her to gallop faster. I was sending the opposite message of what I meant. By now, I was terrified. I was crying and screaming for Jerome to stop. He didn't hear me, or he just ignored me. I was nearly beheaded by a low branch. My heart was pounding. The more I wanted Harriet to slow down, the faster she went. Finally, my screams got through to that idiot Jerome and we slowed, then stopped."

Clara started to tell Dottie about some disastrous hikes with Jerome, but then stopped herself. "We're here though. Enough of hashing over the painful past." She jogged toward the next *Ratha*. Dottie trailed after her.

"That's terrible. I had a boyfriend like that once. He was always dragging me along to things I wasn't interested in. The worst was running. He was fanatical, and we'd have to do at least three miles every morning. I would have enjoyed it, but he kept introducing speed work, as though I wanted to keep bettering my time and compete in races."

"Just like Jerome," Clara said. "Did you tell him no, that you were happy just to go jogging, to enjoy the scenery and fresh air, to be able to carry on a conversation?"

"Oh, here we are at another one of those *Rathas*. I'm going to climb on the Nandi and you can take my picture." Dottie handed her camera to Clara. "I just remembered his name, Billy Wells. He finally got me to run a 5-kilometer race with him, and I thought I'd die. Actually, I did pretty well, third in my age group 25-30."

Clara snapped a few photos of her friend and handed the camera back. "What's wrong with these men who insist that you just love what they want to do? Did that experience turn you off from running?"

"No, but it definitely turned me off from Billy. He pretended to be nice but he was really a total jerk. We never could have a serious conversation about what really mattered. Every time I tried to explain to him what it was like to be adopted, he tuned out. He had no sympathy for any of my concerns, and yet he yammered on endlessly about what a tyrant his father was, how

151

awful that his father preferred his older brother, and how it ruined his childhood...on and on. He would say dumb stuff like 'I wish I were adopted. I don't fit in with my family at all.' It made me mad. At least he had a family that he was actually related to. Blood relatives."

# Chapter Twenty-nine

They walked on to the end of the *Rathas* and turned back to meet up with the tour guide. "We can continue this conversation later," Clara said. "I've never found anyone who understands what it's like to have been adopted. I mean, it's an important part of who I am."

"Of who we are," said Dottie. "I'm beginning to like the idea of reincarnation. Even if I never find anyone I can be sure is related to me, maybe there will be someone who looks similar. Does that sound crazy?"

"No crazier than my traveling to New Mexico in search of roots. I've told you how disappointed I was about being too late. When I thought at last we could have a reunion, the person I thought was my original mother was already gone. The next best thing was to meet Native Americans who knew her."

Joining the other bus passengers and following the tour guide, Clara and Dottie admired wall after wall of stone carvings. "Here," the guide announced, "witness the beautiful open air reliefs featuring thousands of glorifications of Shiva. And here's one called 'The Descent of the Ganges.' Look into the overhead niches, you'll see the tiny owls that seem to love making homes here. Real owls, not sculptures."

Cameras clicked away but instead of photographing, Clara and Dottie opted to get a head start to find good seats. Dottie was disappointed. "I thought we'd get to walk around on the beach surrounding the Shore Temple. It's not enough to just see it from a distance."

"We'll come back on our own," Clara told her friend. "You're right I thought this tour would be more in depth about Mahabalipuram. But we might as well learn about other parts of India."

"Yep," Dottie sighed. "I guess our new motto will be to go with the flow. I'm not sure how I expected to find out anything about my ancestry by just being here. Weren't we going to return the hand of Ganesh to the ocean, hoping that the Deity would somehow help us remove obstacles? Do you still have it in your backpack?" Clara nodded yes.

By now, the two women had front-row seats on the tour bus. It took fifteen minutes for the returning passengers to re-board. A few were overweight and moving slowly. Vendors had surrounded the bus and were hawking their wares. "Glad we got in the bus before being mobbed," Clara said. "And I assure you, I do have the hand." She rummaged through her backpack and pulled out a ziplock bag. "See, here it is, this ancient artifact. I need to put it back right away, as it's too precious to lose. We don't know when we'll need it, but right now it seems to be like a talisman."

"By the way," Dottie said, "this is apropos of nothing, but I learned that our guide's name is Darsaka. I have a *rupee* to tip him at the end. He announced that he'll give a lecture while we're on the road to Pondicherry."

The last of the passengers made their way to empty seats. Many were carrying postcards, *pashmina* shawls, mirrored flags, and *salwar kamizees* in plastic bags.

Darsaka held up a small microphone. "OK, ladies and gentlemen, we are all here now, and I apologize for the aggressive hawkers. I'm sure you've noticed the effect of our dense population. You're never alone in India. Wherever you look, at any time of day or night, you always see people. Visitors are a natural target for vendors, who are often feeding large families."

The bus driver shifted into gear and they lurched away from the temple complex. "We will now travel south to Pondicherry," said Darsaka. "India is the seventh largest country in the world, 1,900 miles from north to south and 1,839 miles from east to west. There are 5,000 miles of coastline. The seas around the Subcontinent are the Arabian, the Indian Ocean, and the Bay of Bengal. We are a young country, with 56 percent of inhabitants below age 25. India has 863 political parties..."

During the lecture, Clara dozed off. When she awakened, Darsaka was still talking and Dottie was not in the seat next to her. She stood up and scanned the seats behind. There was her friend, in conversation with a young man at the very back of the bus. Oh well, she probably needed a break from their constant togetherness. Besides, he looked like a nice young man. Dark eyes and hair, olive skin. Obviously Pakistani or East Indian.

The countryside was less crowded with people and more with vehicles. For half a mile, there were trucks lined up along the grassy roadside. "They are delivering rice to the villages," explained Darsaka. "The drivers are on strike for better wages. They are waiting until their demands are met while in the meantime, the villages who are waiting for rice are growing angry. It is a big mess. But now I will introduce to you my friend

James, who will be taking us around the Bridhadisvara Temple, a 13th century complex dedicated to Lord Shiva."

James, a very westernized-looking Indian, took the microphone from Darsaka. "Ladies and Gentlemen, welcome to this fascinating part of the great country of India. I will read you a quote 'India, land of dreams and romance, palaces, famine and pestilence, tigers, elephants, the cobra, the jungle, 100 castes, creeds, and colors. Three hundred and sixty million gods...'"

The bus lurched to a stop and suddenly it was time to tour another wonder. Passengers were putting on backpacks and preparing to disembark. Dottie squeezed through the center aisle before most people had stepped into it. She raced up to Clara and sat down beside her. "Sorry I disappeared, but I was in the back with a super nice Indian American man who told me about this amazing event and we've got to go!"

"Let's just get off the bus and you can tell me more."

They stepped out onto a dirt plaza surrounded with stone friezes and miniature temples. A group of women in brilliant red and gold *saris* drifted by. "Those are school teachers on holiday," remarked James, who now seemed to be sharing guide duties with Darsaka.

"Here we are, ladies and gentlemen." While James talked about the Chola Empire and the stories carved in stone, Dottie told Clara that they had to go to the *Kumbha Mela* that was beginning in a few days. "We can go with Shubi, the guy I was talking with in the back of the bus. While you were taking a nap, we struck up a friendship, and he told me all about it."

"Are you crazy?" Clara took her friend gently by the shoulders and looked into her eyes. "Those are pilgrimages for Hindus. Millions of Indians in a frenzy of religious fervor. We'd be swallowed up and never seen again. What makes Shubi think it would be safe for two American women?"

"I think you have a completely wrong impression, Clara. Shubi told me that it's helped him with his worst problems, that it's given him a moral compass, that it's all about truth-seeking. There are *sadhus*, *gurus*, wise men and scholars, ascetics, sages there to help people just like us. To help them learn who they really are. After hearing about it, I really feel it's what India is all about."

Clara was irritated. She didn't want to miss out on hearing details of the Bridhadisvara temple. "Who is this Shubi character and why should we listen to him? Can't we talk about this when we get back to the hotel? In the meantime, let's just be here now. When will we ever come this way again?"

"I invited Shubi to join us for dinner when the bus takes us back to Chennai. I think when you learn more, you'll see things my way."

Clara didn't reply. Instead she let out a deep sigh and whispered to herself. "What the hell," a comment Dottie pretended not to hear.

After 30 minutes of touring about the temple grounds, Clara and Dottie, along with everyone else, got on the bus. Dottie sat next to the window, staring out moodily as the Indian landscape rolled by. Clara said, "OK, I'd like to hear why you think this *Kumbha Mela* is such a must. Let's keep Shuti out of this. We don't know him and how do we know he has good advice?"

"It's Shubi...Shubi, with a 'b' and I'll just uninvite him. I'll tell him my travel companion made other plans. I'll try to remember everything he said. Really, though, why are you so suspicious? What's in it for him if we go or don't go?"

"That's what worries me. This Shubi must be promoting his own agenda. It's bad enough that we have Lane as our so-called guide. The last thing in the world I want is someone else interfering with our India experience."

Several hours later found Dottie and Clara back at the Cardomon Inn. They were happy to learn from the desk clerk that Lane had, according to the desk clerk, been "called away on business." No interference or unsolicited advice from Lane. They treated themselves to the hotel's Aryuvedic Massage salon, ordered room service for dinner, and obtained some free maps from the Cardomon Inn's front desk.

The night was young and even though they were of opposite opinions about going to the *Kumbha Mela*, they would have time to debate the pros and cons. Clara continued to resist, but she listened to Dottie make her case. "First of all," she began, "the *Kumbha Mela* is maybe the biggest celebration in the world, but it's also a pilgrimage and a quest for spiritual growth. It attracts pilgrims from everywhere on Earth. Nearly everyone is Indian, but after all...I'm part Indian."

"Do you even know where this massive event is held? We'd have to store most of our belongings and take a plane. I refuse to travel hours and hours by bus."

Dottie pulled out a map of India and spread it out on their spacious coffee table. "Here we are in southern India. She pointed to Periyar and then traced her index finger upward to Uttar Pradesh and Allahabad. This is the center of the event; it's where the Yumana and Ganga rivers converge. A vast temporary city springs up and lasts a month. There are feeding tents everywhere. *Gurus*, both men and women, lecture, addressing life's most perplexing questions. They hold forth 24/7 for people seeking answers."

They had finished the *roti*, curry, and vegetarian dishes and were now enjoying *chai*. Clara took the tray, now stacked with empty dishes, and put it outside their door. "OK," she said. "This all sounds very lofty, but how exactly will it lead you to find your birth family? Or anyone related to you? I admire you for wanting to go to this *Kumbha Mela*, but I don't see how it's going to get you any closer to your goal. I want to help you, but I also feel it's my job to keep us safe. This seems a risky business."

Dottie took a long drink of *chai* before answering. "I have a confession to make. Even before inheriting from Aunt Miriam and our planning of this trip, I was intrigued by the *Kumbha Mela*. When I was at St. John's College, I studied it and talked to some Indian students who knew a lot about it. My quest for roots has gone from finding one particular person to a more general quest. Who am I? Why am I here? What am I going to do with my life? Even though I am not a direct citizen of India, I feel that it's shaped me. It's the country of my original mother. I have a longing to know my own land. Mine, even though I didn't grow up in it."

Clara was softening. "I know that's how I felt when I arrived at last in the Southwest, in New Mexico. True, I was too late to connect with Greta but..."

Dottie interrupted. "I'm almost reaching a willingness to not know thoroughly who I am and exactly where I originated. It's giving me a sense of possibility..."

"I'm not sure what you mean," Clara broke in. "How can wandering around with millions of pilgrims lead you to anything but more frustration? Have you decided to find Mother India instead? This seems like a colossal effort for nothing. I think you need to sleep on this. I'm not on board with it."

Dottie glared at her friend. "Whatever. You don't need to sound so angry...Look, if you can't see things my way, you can just play tourist while I do it on my own."

"Now you've really gone around the bend." Clara left their room, picking up the room key and slamming the door behind her. She walked the lush grounds surrounding The Cardamon Inn. Peering into the twilight, unable to detect beyond the wrought iron fence, she suddenly felt hopeless and alone. Why had she considered this trip such a good idea? Maybe she would let Dottie go on her own, but on the other hand, if anything happened to her, Clara would feel responsible.

"*Memsab*?" said a soft Indian voice from the deepening penumbra. "You must not be out here. We are having a mosquito invasion and it is recommended to stay indoors at night. Is everything satisfactory? I am the hotel's security guard. May I help you?"

Clara was caught off guard, but she didn't want to be like some of the clueless, bumbling tourists she'd observed on the day's bus ride. On the other hand, she was feeling desperate and she did need someone to talk with. "Um, my travel companion wants to join a *Kumbha Mela*, and I don't. Can you suggest something near here that would be good to see. I'm hoping to suggest an alternative."

"Ah yes, *Memsab*, you are near one of India's finest natural treasures: Periyar Wildlife Preserve. If you like, I will book a tour tomorrow for you and your friend. I can speak to the concierge. There is much to love in the park. It is a sanctuary for tigers. In order to view those creatures, one rides about with a naturalist in a covered jeep. Also, the park is home to elephants, rare lion-tailed macaques, sambar deer, leopards, Indian bison. When in this part of India, it is what you call a must."

"Amazing. I would love to explore Periyar, but let me talk to my friend first. Maybe I can persuade her to give up on the *Kumbha Mela* idea."

"Forgive me, *Memsab*, for saying this, but I think it is a very bad idea for two young American women to enter into the processions. It is for the most part safe and peaceful, but you would — if you'll excuse me — stand out like a sore toe."

"You mean like a sore thumb," Clara said.

"Yes, yes, a sore thumb. It is hot and dusty and uncomfortable. Do you want to dip in the Ganga River? That is for Hindus. But, we do have occasional Europeans and people from all over the world who want to do it."

Clara felt exhausted and slightly angry. The conversation was leading nowhere. She would try to convince Dottie to tour the park and put off deciding about the pilgrimage. If that didn't work, she might just book a tour of the wildlife refuge for herself. She seriously doubted if Dottie would be foolish enough to tackle the pilgrimage solo. In fact, she was almost certain. She said good night to the security guard and walked back to her room.

She'd prepared exactly what she'd say to Dottie, but it would have to wait until morning. All the lights except the small lamp on her nightstand had been turned off. Her roommate was tucked under a sheet and sound asleep. Very quietly she donned pajamas, brushed her teeth and slipped into the single bed across from the now gently-snoring Dottie. It took a long time to fall asleep. She dreamed of being alone in a crowd and not knowing where to go or what to do.

When she awakened, long after her usual seven a.m., Dottie had already left the room. This was worse than the nightmare. To be in India with an impossible travel buddy was unthinkably bad. Horrific, in fact. Clara closed her eyes, pulled up the bedding and tried in vain to go back to sleep. She would have to call on inner strength to figure this one out. Maybe she could somehow keep the situation from spinning more out of control.

She took a shower, something that always made her feel better. Hoping that Dottie would be in the hotel dining room, she ambled through a vine-covered arbor leading to the breakfast buffet. No sign of her friend. She felt oddly betrayed, but decided it was better to play detective on a full stomach. Strictly American style this morning: coffee and a generous bowl of yogurt with sliced strawberries and a heap of granola.

# Chapter Thirty

In a mild state of panic, Clara went to the front desk. Hotel guests had been advised to leave room keys with the clerk on duty if they left the premises. "Did Arundati Smith check out for the day?"

"No, *Memsab*. Miss Smith has not been by this morning. Was she not in your room?"

"Well, no. And she seems to have vanished. I'm getting a little worried."

"Ah yes, I understand. Did you check the nature trail out behind the inn? It is an outdoor museum of plants and herbs native to India, a self-guided adventure. Many of our guests like to take advantage of it. Your friend might be educating herself on our local foliage."

When Clara didn't respond, the clerk, his brow furrowed, said "Let me know how I can help."

"Um yes. Thank you. I will try the nature trail."

"Please let us know if we need to send out a search party. Or even if we need to call the local police. To get to the trail, take this exit to my right." He waved his hand to a double glass door that led to more of the Cardomon Inn's lush gardens. Enchanting vine covered gazebos, a trickling stream running alongside the path, flowering shrubs, towering sal trees, birdcalls...Clara felt she'd stepped into another universe. If she hadn't been so worried about her friend, she would have enjoyed this walk into tamed wilderness. Every time she thought of Dottie, however, her good humor vanished. She vacillated between fear and anger, with a dash of indecision. Maybe she was wrong about the *Kumbha Mela*. Maybe she needed the ego-dissolving that surely would result from such a massive event. Still, she thought of their vulnerability, their relative lack of experience.

"Dottie!" she yelled into the void. "Dot. I'm sorry I nixed your idea. If you're set on the *Kumbha Mela*, I can reconsider. Just don't disappear on me." No answer. She called out again. "Hey Arundati.. Dot! Your roommate is looking for you."

She started to walk faster. A marker indicated that she'd covered one mile. No sign of Dottie, no sign of anybody. The path was undulating, a little bit downhill, a little bit up. Thick foliage overhead created an eerie dimness. Clara called into the void even as she quickened her pace. By now she was practically running.

A sign announced the two-mile mark. Her mind raced wildly over the possibilities. Maybe that demented Dottie had set off on her own with the crazy *Kumbha Mela* plan. But no, that couldn't be. She remembered seeing her nightgown on the rumpled empty bed next to her and Dot's backpack hanging on a hook. If Dottie wanted to pay her back for resisting the *Kumbha Mela* idea, she was succeeding.

She raced along the path, which was now circling back to the inn. Passing the three-mile marker, Clara thought back to all the 5-kilometer runs she'd done in New Mexico. Then, all that was at stake was bettering her personal best times. Now, the stakes were higher. Either she would find her travel companion or everything they'd hoped to accomplish in India would come to a screeching halt. "Everything" was undefined. Maybe it could best be described as coming to terms, accepting the vagueness. Maybe they would not ever know thoroughly who they were and where they came from. Maybe it wasn't essential. They could be heartbroken forever or they could make the best of it and get on with life...

By now Clara was back at the Cardamon. She picked up her key from the desk clerk and walked across a wooden deck to the room. To her astonishment, Dottie was there, sitting at the round hotel table writing in a small spiral notebook. She looked up sheepishly at her friend. "I know I've been a jerk, and I apologize. I don't want to ruin our trip. I am going on the *Kumbha Mela* even if I have to go on my own. On the other hand, I don't want you to hate me forever. Shubi, who I feel is as trustworthy as Lane is slippery, is helping me make arrangements. You are most invited. I want to share this with you. In fact, I was going to write you a note saying just that."

Clara took a few minutes to respond. "First of all, where were you? Also, I've been out on the trail and I decided against my better judgement that I'll go with you. It's insane and risky at best. But who knows, we're already in no man's land. Might as well throw ourselves into the melee."

"I was on the trail myself. I woke up before dawn and slipped out quietly. We must have just missed one another. I've been making a list of all I have to do — now it would be all we have to do — before leaving for Allahabad."

"I've got a million questions, but you've probably got answers. And I want to hear them. I guess Lane's still away on business. I'm actually kind of glad. We've paid him for everything to date, so who cares? One thing that comes to mind is that we can't take everything with us. I'm pretty sure we have to downsize to one backpack each." Clara wasn't sure why, but she was warming up to this idea of Dottie's. It was the greatest spiritual gathering on the planet, something they'd never have another opportunity to join.

"You're absolutely right about that. But guess what, I've done some research. There are special tourist camps at the event. There are tents, so-called 'luxury tents,' with bathrooms attached. Guides and assistants can be hired. Supposedly, there is tight security at these tourist camps."

"And all our stuff," Clara wondered. "What do we do with it while we're at this *Kumbha Mela*?"

"You'll be glad to know that I have a plan, one that I ran by Shubi. We can fly on Air India to Chennai and pay the hotel to store our regular clothes. We'll have to buy traditional Indian garments to wear on the pilgrimage. Not *saris* but *salwar kameezes*."

"You mean we can't just wear jeans? After all, we'd be going as tourists."

Dottie sighed. "You don't quite get it, Clara. This is a religious festival for these millions of Hindus. Their hope to be forgiven of all sins comes with bathing in the rivers. The Ganga, the Yumana. Their hopes of being reborn into better lives. It's a weird combination of celebrating and enacting the most sacred rite, the bathing."

"Hmmm." Clara didn't sound convinced. Instead, she sounded a little annoyed that her friend knew so much about the big event and she knew so little. "I know what a *salwar kameez* is, so you don't have to explain that to me. But do we have to dip into filthy rivers? I mean, if one is Hindu, they're probably not so bad. But if you're Western or European, you can probably pick up some pretty nasty bacteria."

"Calm down, friend. You don't have to do anything like that. We might not even be allowed to. The main thing is to just go, be respectful, listen to the *sadhus* and *gurus*. Shubi told me that many of them are lecturing in special tents, and in English. We can go from *guru* to *guru*, like an open-air university in eastern air spirituality. It will be daunting but magical."

Clara swallowed her doubts, at least temporarily. She was relieved to be back on even ground with her traveling companion. The emotional atmosphere improved even more when Dottie

162

agreed to go with Clara to Periyar Wildlife Sanctuary. "But don't forget that we'll need to spend several days buying the proper clothing and other supplies before flying to Allahabad for the *Mela*. It starts January 15. Shubi will meet us at the airport and help us connect with an assistant who will book us with the tourist camps. Can you be in charge of the airline reservations to Chennai and then Allahlabad?"

"Sure," Clara agreed. "You know how good I am dealing with airlines." She didn't add that she'd done all the arranging for their flight to India, so much that it became a bit burdensome. "So, let's hire a taxi to the wildlife refuge. While you've been plotting and scheming to get us to the mad celebration of pilgrims and ascetics, I've been reading about Periyar."

# Chapter Thirty-one
## Periyar Park

An hour later found the two women at the entrance to a shade filled jungle with wide asphalt walking paths. An unusually tall Indian in an olive green uniform greeted them. "Hello *Memsabs. Namaste.*" He placed his hands together over his heart and bowed his head. "My name is Pratik and I am in a training program to be a naturalist guide. What I think you Americans call an 'intern.' Do you mind if I stroll along with you in Periyar? I know a lot and can help your enjoyment."

Surprised, Clara and Dottie chorused "Yes, we'd love it." and "Sure, and we don't even mind that you knew we were Americans. It's our first time to your country and we'd love to learn about nature as well as culture."

Clara was delighted. Now she wouldn't have to listen to Dottie's doubts about spending the time in Periyar. Dottie wouldn't have to listen to her reflections on why going to the *Kumbha Mela* was a bad idea. This was actually perfect.

"These trees towering over us are called *sal*. They are native but more prevalent in northern rather than southern India. These are transplants. We want to give our visitors an overview of all of India, not just the southern part of our vast subcontinent. India has fourteen different kinds of forests. The plants along this section of the preserve have signs translated into English, so I recommend reading them to get an overview."

Though the plants were interesting, Clara preferred looking at people out on a midday stroll. There were a few dressed in jeans and t-shirts, but most of the women wore *saris*. Children in strollers. That fit her preconceptions about the Indians' love of children and desire for progeny. *Stop*, she told herself, *quit buying into your own stereotypes.*

Time to tune back into the walk through the park. Dottie and Pratik were chatting about a giant spiderweb spanning the space between large ferny plants. She saw that the web was occupied by a black spider that reminded her of the black widows at home. She tried unsuccessfully to suppress a grimace.

Pratik noticed right away. "No worries, *Memsab*. That fellow is not poisonous. He is just trying to catch flies and bugs to stay alive."

"Or she," Clara couldn't resist adding.

"Ah yes, *Memsab*. Or she. But you know, really most of our spiders will not be harmful. The worst one is the wind scorpion, also known as a sun spider. In all my years of walking in the woods and jungles of Tamil Nadu, I have never seen one. They do not like people and keep — how do you say — a low profile."

"What about animals?" asked Dottie. Clara was glad to observe that her friend was thoroughly enjoying the park. "The only species we've seen so far are elephants and monkeys. They're roaming around the streets, sort of mixed in with the traffic."

"Yes, but in the jungle we have six different kind of monkeys, wild boars, and panthers to name but a few. And of course, deer. There are swamp deer and sambar. Their ears are funnel shaped to catch the more muffled sounds in dense jungle. And we have many, many kinds of birds. For example, the Malabar Grey Hornbill, the White-cheeked Barbet, the Nilgiri Wood Pigeon. I'm trying to learn to recognize their calls. Oh, here we are at the river dock. Would you like to cross and go into deeper jungle? I will rent *gaiters* for us and you can reimburse me later."

Clara and Dottie looked at each other.

"Why not?" asked Dottie

"How much?" was Clara's question.

"I can get a special price," said Pratik. "For you it will be just one *rupee* for both. I guarantee you will find it fascinating, a once-in-a-lifetime opportunity. The next raft leaves in 15 minutes."

"We're this far in," said Clara. "Might as well..." She and Dottie sat on the wooden benches outside the launching shack and laced up the tan khaki *gaiters*, protection from leeches. Guided by a ranger dressed in camouflage, a raft drifted to shore and the small awaiting group stepped aboard. The raft was small and they had to stand.

In addition to Clara, Dottie and Pratik, there were a husband and wife and a tall blond young man. Instead of crossing the river directly, they floated downstream for a short time. The raft seemed flimsy and unsafe. To allay her nervousness, Clara started a chat. Dottie joined in.

"We're from New Mexico," Clara volunteered. "Where are you folks from?"

"Texas," said the husband.

165

"I'm from the Netherlands, and I'm here on a break from college," said the young man. "Has anyone been to this part of India before?" No one had. The raft was now rocking, and the more crazily it moved, the more the conversation increased.

After what seemed an eternity, they pulled into the other side of the river, stepped out onto a dock, and began their walk through the deep jungle. The green leafiness added to a sense of mystery. Pratik advised them to keep silent or, if they had questions, to whisper. "We will increase our chances of seeing wildlife if we make no noise."

Dense trees and dusky shadows. Dark, cool, inscrutable. The jungle was all of these. They followed along on a path, the earth and moist under their feet. "Elephant tracks," said Pratik, pointing to large rounded pockets in the mud adjoining the path.

They walked on, inspired to remain silent. Abruptly, Pratik stopped and pointed to a large bush a few feet to the right. A gray hunk that looked like the carcass of some kind of beast. "A sambar," he said. "A fresh kill, probably by one of the park's resident tigers. The big cat will come back and eat for several days."

"Yikes," exclaimed the wife. "Are we in danger of its coming back to snack on us? Are we safe out here?"

"Oh yes," said Pratik. "We are extremely safe. I have a laser that can ward off just about anything. These jungle animals do not like humans. They have plenty to eat and so they are not after us. Besides, it may have been a wild boar that got the sambar. Let's be very quiet. Maybe we'll get to see a boar."

Dottie and Clara spoke to each other in whispers. The married couple and Dutch college student shushed them. The silence deepened and the sun slipped behind clouds. Pratik stopped abruptly and turned around to face them. He pointed toward the left. "Look, there it is, up ahead. It's a patch of gray. Not moving but if you study the left of that ridge, you'll spot the boar."

They stood for what seemed a very long time. Clara saw a slight rustle in the tall grasses. Whether it was the boar or not, she wasn't sure. Dottie admitted to Clara that she saw nothing but the forest. The others didn't comment. They walked on in silence, hushed by the expectation of wildlife. Birdcalls overhead, occasional rustles in tall grasses, but no more sightings. From time to time, Pratik would comment on particular leaves used to make dyes or grasses used in basketry. After twenty minutes, they turned around and circled back to the river.

"Well, not very eventful, folks," Pratik commented. But that's how it is with jungle walking. Sometimes all you hear is the silence and all you see is a rustle in the high grasses. Other times, a distant roar or laugh of a hyena."

"I enjoyed the bird calls," said Dottie. "There were so many different kinds. It was like being in an exotic aviary."

"And it was fun spotting a boar, even though it was far away," said Clara.

The couple and the blond young man said nothing. A sense of gloom settled over the small group. Disappointment that the wildlife they'd hoped to witness was so elusive, mere glimpses. Clara, ever the cheerleader, tried to lift the mood. "The jungle felt mysterious to me, filled with a sense of boding and watchfulness."

"Ah yes, *Memsab*. That is an excellent way to describe it. I myself find it brings a kind of peacefulness. But, dear visitors, here we are back at the raft for our journey upstream to the start of our walk. Stay lined up here at the bank. I will pull the raft up and help each of you on. Do go to the center and once we're afloat, make no sudden movements."

The upstream paddle seemed much shorter than their trip to the jungle side. By now, late afternoon sun broke through the clouds, and the muddy water reflected its golden light. As they neared the boat shack, Clara got a *rupee* out of her money belt to pay Pratik and realized that she knew what they had to do next.

As if reading her friend's mind, Dottie said, "And since there's still daylight left, we need to go into the shopping area to buy a few things for the *Kumbha Mela*. Pratik, could you direct us?"

They stepped from the raft to shore and removed their *gaiters*. Clara paid Pratik, adding a few coins as a tip. She dreaded taking actual steps toward what she now thought of as Dottie's mad adventure, but part of her was looking forward to it.

"Please wait while I settle up with your raft mates and I will direct you to the best shops. In fact, I will be happy to take you to Kumily, which is the nearest place with stores. You mentioned that you're planning to go to the *Kumbha Mela*, and my friend Kala Devli just opened up a boutique that sells *salwar kameezes* that would be perfect for the heat and dust of the pilgrimage."

While Pratik, their "new best friend" — as Clara would say later — took payments from the college student and the couple, the two women waited in plastic lawn chairs next to the boat shack. This was clearly not a luxury operation. A young boy, apparently the son of the raft operation owner, brought them some Coca-Colas in bottles.

"This hits the spot," Clara said. "I never drink cokes but every now and then. they're just the thing." When Clara was rummaging in her fanny pack for a few coins for the boy, Pratik interrupted with assurance that he would take care of it.

"I am a package deal, you will find, and cokes are included. For some reason your fellow passengers refused them. They seem to be super afraid of germs. Actually, I don't think they are well-suited to visit Mother India. You two, on the other hand, seem open to new experiences. Having said that, here is our jeep for the shopping trip."

It was all happening very fast, Clara thought, this *Kumbha Mela* plan. Yes, they were going through with Dottie's crazy idea. No backing down now. Shopping was something they both loved to do, and it would take her mind off the upcoming event, which she still could not quite believe.

She and Dottie climbed in the back of Pratik's jeep. "Welcome to my jalopy," he joked. "It will be a bumpy ride, but I guarantee you will love the clothing that my friend Kala Devli and her ladies create. They are sturdy cotton, organic cloth, and will be perfect for your adventure. She is very good, so I've heard, at finding clothes that flatter her customers."

They rumbled alongside the path into Periyar, going the opposite direction of late-afternoon visitors. The sun nearly down, the trees were dark and shadowy, almost a ghostly presence. Clara wondered to herself how cotton material could be anything but organic. Instead of asking about that, she said, "We certainly want clothes that flatter us."

"Right," chimed in Dottie. "And if they're cotton they'll be sturdy and good in the heat." To Clara, she whispered, "This is going to be fun. With all the strangeness of India, shopping is something familiar."

"Yeah, shopping. It kind of crosses international boundaries," Clara said. "We probably need two outfits each. Didn't you say the *Kumbha Mela* is for a month?"

"We don't have to do an entire month," Dottie said. "We could go for a couple weeks and see how we do. I mean see how we like it."

The jeep came to a screeching halt. "Here we are *Memsahibs*," said Pratik. They found themselves at a row of storefronts. Instead of a building, these small shops comprised a wooden platform with a tent for a roof, the inventory neatly arranged in shelves and cabinets. The interiors were surprisingly deep, the fronts open to the night air. Clara and Dottie stepped up from the dirt road into Kala Devli's shop. "The Market," a sign announced, "A women's cooperative, Since 1978."

"*Namaste*. Good evening. How may I help you?" The speaker was a tallwoman wearing a pink embroidered tunic top and black jeans. She was the only person in the shop, so they assumed that she was *Memsab* Devli, the owner of the women's cooperative.

"Welcome to the Women's Market," she said with a broad smile. She had perfect teeth and her dark brown hair fell to her shoulders. "All of our clothes are made by women artisans."

Pratik excused himself to go visit with an adjacent shop owner. "My sister's husband," he explained. "I can be back whenever you say. Would twenty minutes be enough time? Or should I say an hour?"

"Knowing us, closer to an hour." Dottie was already rifling through a stack of *pashminas*. "*Memsab* Devli, we two American women are going as tourists to this year's *Kumbha Mela*. We need to be wearing appropriate clothing. My friend doesn't really want to go, but I talked her into it."

"Hmmm," Clara said to herself. "Sort of."

"Ah, you are very wise to go. It will give you a sense of the real India, you'll experience the spirit of this country. These events are life-changing. And I have just the right kind of garments. Not too fancy, very suitable, and also nice-looking. Leave it to *Memsab* Devli. I will outfit you. Which of you would like to go first?"

"You begin," Clara said. "Meanwhile, I will be looking at the different kinds of drawstring pants. There are many racks to go through."

"Sizes," said *Memsab* Devli, "are very general. Small, medium and large. Looking at you two, I would say you'd wear small. In some styles, however, you'd be medium. They vary, so the best thing is to try them on. Our fitting rooms in the back."

While she was talking, an Indian teenager emerged from the inner depths of the shop. Slender and graceful, she had the same perfect teeth, dazzling smile and long dark hair as *Memsab* Devli. "*Namaste,*" offered the girl, placing her fingertips together, touching them to her forehead, and slightly bowing.

"My niece Rita will help you with the fitting. Like her auntie, she is an expert at finding what flatters. Her sense of color and line is extraordinary."

170

Dottie was the first to start trying on outfits, some selected by her, others by Rita. She came out of the dressing room several times, the last in white pants and a jade jacket over an azure camisole. "I love this," she told Clara, "but it doesn't seem quite right. It's more like something I'd wear to a party than on a spiritual pilgrimage."

"Try what I found for you. I think this might be perfect." Clara handed Dottie a chambray blue tunic. "This is called a *kurta*. It will be perfect with the white pants of your last outfit. Or maybe black will be more practical. White will show dirt."

Dottie emerged from the dressing stall smiling broadly. The *kurta* suited her beautifully. "I love the side slits and the three-quarter sleeves," she said, twirling around for Clara, Rita and Devli. "It's so comfy. If you have the pants in black, I'll take one in white and another in black."

Meanwhile, Clara had fallen in love with a garment called "*Dhulla* Pant," with a drawstring waist and bell-shaped leg. Rita picked out a sleeveless notch-neck jersey top with contrasting yoke. Cloud blue, it had cap sleeves. "It's light and airy, I could walk for miles in this," Clara exclaimed. "I'll also take the white V-neck top with cap sleeves." She pointed to the wall-length rack of tops with her favorite displayed on an out-facing hook.

"Whew, we did that just in time. Here is Pratik." Clara counted out *rupees* and went to talk with their guide. Dottie, next in line, asked *Memsab* Devli if she could take dollars rather than *rupees*. Or possibly she could pay with a credit card?"

"Yes, although you will pay slightly more." We have to pay a fee at the bank to have dollars converted. "But yes, you may pay either way. *Rupees* or dollars. Unfortunately. we are not set up to take credit cards."

"Time flies when ladies are shopping," Clara said to Pratik as Dottie finally completed her transaction with *Memsab*. Purchases were wrapped and carefully packed in drawstring shopping bags. After farewells, the two women and Pratik were finally on their way back to the Cardomon Inn. The jeep rumbled quickly along. A full moon shone brightly, nightbirds sang and monkeys screeched.

"This," Clara said, "is heavenly. I feel like we've finally arrived."

"The India of my dreams," agreed Dottie.

171

The shopping trip with Pratik was only the beginning. After a good night's sleep, Clara and Dottie dedicated themselves to preparing for the *Kumbha Mela*. They needed not the just the right garments to wear but supplies. Clara made up a list, including sunscreen, jerky, hand sanitizer, small packs of tissue, and more. The distances from the Cardomon Inn to Kottayam or Thekkady were long.

"I've got a great idea," Clara said. Now that she'd resigned herself to the *Kumbha Mela* plan, she was taking a lead in their planning. "Let's fly back to Chennai, maybe store our stuff with the same hotel we stayed at when we first arrived, shop for those necessary items we listed and then fly from there to Allahabad. We can say goodbye to Lane in the morning and thank him for his help."

"Help shmelp, he hasn't been the greatest. I think Shubi will be better. I spoke with him by phone and he said he'd make a reservation for us at a tourist camp. He's Indian, and he's gone to *Kumbha Melas* before. He knows the territory."

Clara told herself not to make a disparaging remark about Shubi. She would try to be of one mind with Dottie. She quieted her doubts and mentally rolled up her sleeves. Together, they could do this. They bid Lane a hasty farewell the next morning at breakfast, packed their bags - including the new outfits to wear during the *Kumbha Mela*, checked out of the Cardomon. It was sixty miles to the Madurai Airport. Shubi had hired a driver for them and, thankfully, told them how much to pay.

The short air flight to Chennai, checking back into their hotel and making storage arrangements went smoothly. "We're getting to be seasoned travelers," quipped Dottie. "I told Shubi we could be ready in a week to leave for the *Mela*. We need to have everything in our backpacks for the January 4th pickup. That'll give us enough time to shop for whatever we'll need and also to rest up."

"*Namaste, Memsabs,*" said the desk clerk at Chennai Palace. It was not the man from before but a young woman in a red silk *sari*. Her name tag read "Ondra." She opened the guest registry. "I see you've stayed with us before. Are you leaving India so soon?"

"No," volunteered Clara. "We like it so much, we're staying longer."

"In fact," added Dottie, "We've decided to go to the *Kumbha Mela*. We'd like to rent storage space from you for one, maybe two weeks, as we'll take very little with us."

Ondra looked surprised, then pleased. "You are very adventurous, *Memsabs*. But you are not the only ones. We have another guest who will be going to the *Mela*. Perhaps you'd like me to put you in touch with her?"

"Yes, that would be perfect," Clara said. "The more we can learn ahead of time, the better."

"Very well, I will send a message to her, a Ms. Samantha Owens. If it's OK, in one hour, I'll give her your room number and tell her that she can look you up."

"Sounds like a plan." Clara signed the registry and they made their way to Room 322. The Chennai Palace seemed like a relic from another era. A creaky elevator took them to the third floor. Exhausted, they stretched out on the twin beds even before packing. In no time, they were both asleep.

Clara heard it first: a gentle tapping at the door. "Who's there?" Dottie bolted up and stood next to her friend.

"It's Samantha Owens. You can call me Sammy. I've adopted India as my spiritual home. The desk clerk told me about you two. Seems like we're all planning on the *Kumbha Mela*. I tried to phone you but couldn't get the phone to work."

It seemed rude to be talking through the door, so Clara opened it. Samantha was a tall blonde with piercing blue eyes and a pixie haircut that made her look about twelve. She apologized for "just barging in," but both Clara and Dottie swept her qualms away. They were happy to find a kindred spirit, someone who did not consider going to the *Mela* an ill-advised, risky venture but rather the key to grasping the real India.

The three of them adjourned to the hotel bar, settled into the cushioned wicker chairs, ordered sodas and talked about why they were going to the pilgrimage. Clara went first, relating the story of hoping to learn about her origins in New Mexico. "It was a failed mission. I discovered, sadly, that I was too late. My mother had passed away. I was devastated that I never got to have a reunion with her. I was five when I was adopted so I had just distant childhood memories."

Samantha had also lost someone, it turned out. She crossed her sandaled ankles, took a large drink of ginger ale and

173

began. "I am an India-phile and have been for a long time. My love of the country began years ago when my Grandfather told stories of serving in the China-Burma-India theater of World War II. He was a clinical psychologist in charge of a neuropsychiatric ward and part of his job was taking shell-shocked soldiers on walks around Calcutta.

"I thought you said he was in the war," Dottie said.

"He was, but India was a staging area for planes flying the Hump — that's the Himalayas — over Burma to China. The Allies had to keep Chiang Kai Shek in the war fighting the Japanese. Anyway, Grampa was in the Army Airforce for almost two years. About the same time I became so interested in India, my younger brother died in a car crash. I blamed myself, and I never got over it."

"How on earth could that have been your fault?" Clara wanted to know.

"It sounds odd, but it's because I wanted strawberry ice cream at my thirteenth birthday party. I threw a fit, and Craig couldn't stand it. There was a big family blow-up and he stormed out of the house to buy some. A drunk driver smashed into him going the wrong way on a two-lane road. I've never been able to forgive myself. In a way, I'm doing the *Kumbha Mela* pilgrimage as a path to peace. A spiritual making-right."

No one said anything. What could they say? A waiter appeared and announced that the restaurant was closing in fifteen minutes and would they like to order from the bar menu.

"That's a great idea," Dottie said. "Do you two agree?"

"Why not?" Samantha asked. "Their *samosas* are wonderful. With a couple plates of those, we'll have a dinner." She picked up the bar menu and passed it over to the other two. "I've had their Best Indian Punjabi *Samosas*. Stuffed with mangos, potatoes, and curry leaves. Completely delectable."

Clara chimed in "They sound great. I'm suddenly very hungry."

"Yes," Dottie said. "We could also order the Baked *Samosas*, with curry powder, potatoes and tomatoes. I'd like to buy us a bottle of white wine to share. To celebrate our friendship."

"And to drink a toast to the *Kumbha Mela*" added Clara. "I guess it's Dottie's turn to share. And next we have the charming Ms. Arundati Smith..." She handed over an imaginary microphone.

Before Dottie could tell her story, the waiter appeared to take their order.

Samantha pointed to the Punjabi and the Baked *Samosas* on the menu and asked about a good white wine.

"I assume we all want white?" The other two nodded yes.

"This is my treat," Dottie said, "but we can all make the selection."

"We have both very expensive and more reasonable Chardonnay and Sauvignon Blanc," said their chubby turbaned waiter. "India is becoming known for its wines and outstanding vineyards. On the pricey side, we have a superb Fratelli Vitae Chardonnay. It's from Karnataka, our best vineyard here in the south. But for something still quite good but much less costly, I recommend the Sula Vineyards Sauvignon Blanc. It is a favorite with many of our guests."

They decided on the Sauvignon Blanc, and Clara once again handed Dottie the imaginary microphone. "I'm like you two in a way. I came to India in search of a person. I wanted to know about my birthmother. Maybe it was naive to think I could find her, but I thought by being in her native land, being in India, I could get closer to knowing her. I know it sounds sort of vague. It's your turn, Clara. Tell Sammy about your longing for roots."

"Yes. In fact, I moved to the Southwest hoping to track down my origins. Unlike Dottie, I managed to find a name - Greta Suina. I taught at a Native American school and lived through the murder of its headmaster - but I never found Greta. She had already died. I met her people, at least that."

Samantha took Clara's hand in hers. "How sad for you, after changing your life for this quest. You must have been heartbroken to learn that you were too late."

"It was incredibly disappointing. Even though it wasn't my fault, I took it as a colossal failure. That's one reason that I wanted to help Dottie with her quest. I don't want to bomb a second time."

The wine arrived, along with steaming platters of *Samosas*. The waiter poured out three glasses of Sauvignon Blanc, and the women held their glasses for a toast.

"To a safe and enlightening *Kumbha Mela* experience," offered Clara.

"To our friendship, and to the lost daughters, adoptees of the world. To women and men who are searching for birthparents. We may never find the mothers who brought us into the world, but may we find inner peace and forgiveness. These losses are not our fault. May we replace guilt with love."

"To us, and our journey," offered Dottie. "Even if I never find anything about my original family specifically, may I find answers. I had this belief that when I came here I would see people who looked like me and that miraculously, I'd encounter someone actually related. I'm realizing now how impossible that might be."

"What about your adoptive parents?" Samantha asked. "Couldn't they give you any clues? I mean, they got you from somewhere. Did they tell you anything at all that might be helpful?"

Dottie took a deep sip of wine. "Right. I didn't fall out of the sky and just land on their doorstep. I was an infant and my parents got me from a Catholic home for unwed mothers. My adoptive mom and dad were great, but they believed that the secrets of my Indian origins were best kept concealed."

"Like my parents," Clara said, "they felt that nurture was more important than nature. Isn't that right, Dot?"

"Completely right. But in retrospect, they did their best. They exposed me to all things Indian. Music, food, art, culture. It was like they appreciated where I was from, or at least where my birthmother was from. But they couldn't actually imagine going to the home for unwed mothers to track down records of my birthmother so I could meet her. They couldn't talk about it and whenever I broached the topic, my mom would get tears in her eyes. I felt guilty for wondering.

"Years went on and my questions went unanswered. When Mom and Dad died, I finally decided that I would someday, somehow travel to India. I would learn what I could about my mother's country of origin. I was sixteen when I lost my adoptive parents. It was the end of the world.

"It was after my Aunt let it slip that I found out. I had darker skin, but they explained it by lying about a relative on my Dad's side who was Egyptian. I never really questioned that, but I did wonder. Finally, they had to tell me they had no idea who my father was, and it was a shock. It was after that when they started with the cultural touches - this from India, that from India. But just as I was absorbing the news that I was adopted came a bigger shock. I mean, it was not right away, but..." Dottie's voice grew hoarse and she stopped talking. She couldn't say more.

The really sad part of Dottie's story, Clara thought to herself, was that her parents didn't tell her she was adopted until she was eight. She jumped into the conversation. "She lost both her adoptive parents in a sailing accident. They died before Dottie could find out much at all. That's one thing that drew us together. We both felt that we'd become orphans for a second time. Part of our motivation in coming to India was to lose ourselves. Maybe even to reinvent ourselves. I know that may sound weird."

"Not at all," Samantha said. "You know, I've been wandering around this country for a year now. In a way, I think I'm finding myself by losing myself. Nothing at home was keeping me there. I haven't lost my parents, but we don't get along. They do put money in my bank account every month, so I guess that shows that they love me. They always cared more about my brother. My escape to India drove us even further apart."

By now they'd eaten the *samosas* and drunk the last drop of wine. After another hour of comparing stories, they retired for a long night's sleep. During the next couple days, Samantha, the seasoned India traveler, took them to shops. They bought shawls, snacks, extra sunglasses, hats to ward off the sun. On the fifth day, they boarded a plane and flew to Allahabad, where they were met by Amitav, Samantha's pal, and Dottie's friend from the bus, Shubi.

Amitav was the only one of them who'd been to the *Kumbha Mela* before. Shubi, it turned out, had been planning to do the pilgrimage twelve years ago but had to stay home and tend his ill mother. She was gone now, and he would walk this in her honor. "My mother was the most wonderful woman," he said. "She was my spiritual inspiration and what kept us together as a family, me and my five brothers and sisters. She always wanted to do one of these pilgrimages but never did. So, I'm walking it for her."

They comprised a small group of tourist pilgrims that over the next weeks would become a close-knit family. Amitav was tall and lean. Dressed in a short sleeved white shirt and cotton *dhoti*, he fit in with dozens of Indian men similarly attired. "We will walk about a mile until the eastern gathering point. Then we'll be meeting with another large group of people coming from the north. It starts slowly but will soon become a moving mass of humanity. You will see."

Shubi, much shorter than Amitav and a bit stout, was dressed in jeans and a red t-shirt. He had a cotton shawl wrapped

177

around his head and shoulders. Dottie, Clara, and Samantha wore *salwar kameezes* and sun hats. They were a handsome group, and clearly enthusiastic about doing the pilgrimage. In days to come, as they melded more and more into the mass, their enthusiasm would grow.

The airport marked the beginning of what would be a walk of many miles. "Are we at the starting point?" asked Clara. "I'm used to walks and footraces where there's a beginning, middle and end."

Amitav laughed. "You are at the beginning. The whole *Kumbha Mela* is the middle. And the end is whenever we want to stop walking. I assure you, we will not want to walk the whole month. Maybe a week, two at most. But in answer to your question, we have about a mile before we meet the pilgrims coming from the north. In the meantime, let me fill you in about this massive event. There is nothing else like it in the world."

"Yes," Clara said. "We've done some reading, but it's a lot to wrap one's mind around. I'm all for getting more background." The others agreed, and as they walked in a loosely gathered moving crowd, all chattering away in what Clara assumed was Hindi or Urdu, Amitav expounded.

"As you know from your reading, this event started several hundred years B.C. It's the longest running religious festival and the biggest gathering of people in the world."

"Wow," exclaimed Dottie. "I knew it went way back. Ummm, Mark Twain went to one in the nineteenth century, sometime in the 1890s. He could hardly believe the people who, as he put it, 'plodded on for months to get here, worn, poor and hungry'."

Amitav continued, "The *Kumbha Mela* goes back to 500 B.C. The story on which it's based is pretty simple. The gods were carrying a pot that contained the secret of immortality. For twelve days, they were pursued by demons and four drops fell to earth from the pot. The locations of the drops are where the festivals are held."

"And Allahabad, which used to be Prayag, is one of them," Samantha added.

"The reason the *Kumbha* is held every twelve years," said Dottie, "is because the chase lasted twelve days and every day is a year in the gods' time. At least that's what I've read."

"You are absolutely right," Amitav said. More and more people were congregating, walking purposefully. On either side

178

of the dusty road were shops and boutiques, one after another, full of scarves, sunglasses, postcards, and cellophane packages of nuts and snacks. A scrawny turbaned man with necklaces draped over his elbow shuffled in front of Dottie. He held one of his necklaces in her face. "You buy? You buy? Only one *rupee*."

A woman in a lime green *sari* stationed herself in front of Clara. She was selling embroidered purses and waved one of them in front of the entire group. "You buy? Handmade. Fine quality. Good price."

"Don't stop. Just keep walking," Shubi advised. "These peddlers will drive you crazy. This is supposed to be a religious pilgrimage, but whenever there's an opportunity for commerce, the buying and selling are bound to be there."

Clara pushed forward. Surrounded by the others, they formed a tight cluster. The crowd grew ever denser. They moved en masse to either side of the wide dirt road. Clara's group were swept along. They held hands, so as not to get separated. In the distance sounded a faint chant, *Har har Mahadev*, repeated over and over. As that grew louder, another chant blended in: *Har har Ganga*.

"You won't believe this," said Samantha. "It's the approach of the Nagas. They're naked ascetics, some of the holiest of the *sadhus*. There are hordes of them, on their way to take a dip into the Ganges. This is only the beginning. We will see processions all day long. Every religious sect will be parading by the public. They range from naked to vested in ornate robes. But I'll quit talking. Just feast your eyes."

A kaleidoscope of *sadhus* and other holy men paraded by. Many of the *sadhus* were carried atop pagodas and platforms. A few women ascetics - *sadhavis* - were pointed out by Samantha. All wore brilliant saffron *saris*.

"I can hardly believe what I'm seeing," Clara said. "I love the splendid robes, the gold chariots, the umbrellas."

" ...and the camels and elephants." continued Dottie.

The din of so many pilgrims made it nearly impossible to be heard. Bells pealed, chants resonated, mantras rumbled. Shubi shouted, "If you could understand Sanskrit, you would hear the *Vedas*."

Dottie shouted, "Aren't they some of the most sacred and ancient hymns in India? I studied them a bit at my college." A huge gong resonated, followed by ever more energetic chanting. "St. John's," she added, before giving in to the outside din.

179

All the time they'd been talking, Dottie, Clara, Samantha, and Shubi were getting closer to the Ganges River. Amitav had vanished. From a vantage point fifty people deep, they witnessed the *sadhus* plunging into the brown water. Gongs, chanting and jubilant chants arose from the crowd.

"So are we next in line?" asked Dottie.

"Don't go near that water," Samantha exclaimed. "Indians have an immunity. For westerners, it would be a death sentence to take a dip in the Ganges. Or at least a recipe for illness. I used to be a nurse practitioner, think I told you that, and I've managed to survive here in the subcontinent because I'm really careful. You can witness the pilgrims, but just witness."

"Dottie, I can't believe you'd even think of it. We have been living in a western sanitized world. These germs aren't the ones our bodies are used to. We can just watch from afar. Maybe get 'secondhand enlightenment'."

"We're just about a mile from the tents where different *gurus* will be holding forth," Shubi said. "Every one of them will be delivering a spiritual message. It will be a million times better for you than plunging into Mother Ganges."

"But aren't you going to do a ritual bath?" asked Dottie.

"Yes, but it's different for me."

"Because you're Hindu, right?" Clara was eager to disabuse her friend of the notion that she should plunge into the brown waters. They'd talked about Dottie's Indian heritage and how certain cultural traits might be part of her DNA. Surely her friend didn't think that DNA could protect her from catching a disease? Or did she? It was more than a little bit worrisome.

After an exhilarating day of walking alongside the cavalcade of *sadhus* and their followers, Dottie, Clara and Sammy were glad to see the tourist camp. They'd sat with Indians and eaten the free vegetarian food served on large green leaves and, as the sun was going down, the thought of sleeping on mats in the tourist tents was heavenly. Amitav had reappeared but would be leaving them tomorrow. He and Shubi had retreated to the men's tents.

The three women walked to their designated tent. After and a visit to a rustic but clean washroom, sat side by side on their mats. At least for now, they would sleep in their clothes.

"I can hardly believe this day," Clara said, "as they finished the last of their rice and vegetables. "How can they feed us all?"

180

"And how many Hindu sects are there? Was there a *sadhu* representing every one?" Dottie asked.

"I've never been able to find out how many branches there are of Hinduism," mused Samantha, "but there aren't just Hindus in the *Kumbha Mela*, there are also Sikhs and who knows what else. As you witnessed, it is free-flowing and I believe it's amazingly inclusive. Did you find anyone looking at us skeptically because we're westerners? No! And the meals are prepared by volunteers. They're much safer than street food. The servers of free food are creating good karma for themselves. I've heard they do it out of love."

Other women in the large dormitory tent were sitting cross-legged and chatting. Clara asked a question she'd been wanted to pose ever since they met Samantha at their hotel. "How did you get interested in India in the first place? What was the main thing that called you here?"

In the distance, there was faint chanting and an occasional gong. Didn't these pilgrims ever sleep?

"I thought I'd told you. There was the early curiosity. Then, later, when I was a practicing Sikh, I first came to India to study yoga. I've been coming back for ten years and now, I guess you could say I've expatriated. With all its problems and vastness, I find it a far more reasonable place than America. You might say I've fallen in love with India. I became part of the Sikh community in northern New Mexico after I graduated from the University of New Mexico."

# Chapter Thirty-four
## Kumbha Mela

After a restorative night of sleep and a communal breakfast, Clara, Dottie and Samantha joined Shubi for a long day of walking. Shubi sounded like he'd been up for hours. He looked well rested and wore a smile, along with a fresh *kurta*.

"Hey, ladies, forget about the Ganges for now. In a short time, we'll reach the tent of Pilot Baba. He's surrounded by followers but I see some room at the far right. Let me remind you that one never enters a holy place wearing shoes. Leave them outside and let's slip in before Pilot Baba begins."

"What? How do we know we'll be able to find them when we get out?"

"Believe it or not, it's perfectly safe." Shubi untied his Nikes and placed them next to a large pair of leather sandals. I will be responsible for finding them when we leave the discourse. I read the sign, and this will indeed be Pilot Baba."

The three women and Shubi, now barefooted, sat next to what appeared to be a very large family. A mama, papa and children who ranged from nine or ten to teenagers. Or so it appeared to Clara, who was taking careful mental notes for later journaling. She'd bought a blank book in Chennai but had yet to make her first entry. Today would be the first to be documented.

Pilot Baba, wearing a red beret and khaki shirt and pants, sat cross-legged on a raised platform. He had a salt and pepper beard and sunken dark brown eyes. The pilot attire contrasted sharply with the marigolds stranded around his neck. The followers were viewing him with reverence and chanting softly. *Samadhi...samadhi...samadhi.*

"What is the hat about?" whispered Clara to Shubi.

"He actually was a pilot in one of the Indian forces, a fairly high-ranking officer. Then he realized his calling and decided to devote his life to seeking *Samadhi*. That means enlightenment. But I'll tell you more about it after the discourse."

The gong sounded and Pilot Baba began. "World Peace. It is our mission, and it comes through inner peace. Our individual inner journey. Western society does not have time for this journey, but it can be attained. We must take time. We achieve this through practicing yoga and meditation."

Pilot Baba closed his eyes and took slow, deep breaths... for several minutes. The followers closest to him did the same.

Some of the women bowed their heads and whispered what sounded like prayers.

Pilot Baba opened his eyes and began. "I wish the union of many spiritual worlds. How can this happen? Supreme inner peace. That is the answer. Supreme inner peace can be attained by every person. It is necessary to face and overcome obstacles. The one who seeks spiritual growth walks with or without food, with or without sleep because he knows that on the spiritual path difficulties are there. On the spiritual path there are hardships. On the spiritual path to God there are hardships but after that there is only contentment and joy."

A follower raised his hand. "How difficult is it for me to experience this. It sounds impossible."

"It is not difficult, but you must meditate. You must do yoga. You must sit each day for three hours in silent meditation. If you practice this daily, you will see the benefits. Practice breathing. It will not happen in a day or two. It will not happen in a week or two."

As the discourse wound down, the mood changed. From the side of the tent, a man brought in a rectangular box and handed it to Pilot Baba. The sound of cymbals came from within the crowd and several women in white *saris* got up to dance. Clara started getting up to join the dancers, but Samantha gently tugged on her long blouse and whispered, "Sit down. This is a sacred event, and we don't want to make ourselves conspicuous."

Dottie whispered, "I think we're already conspicuous, just by being here. Maybe we need to just be flies on the wall. Think of it as auditing. We're not Indians. Well maybe I'm half Indian, but you know what I mean."

The dancing stopped and the music died down. "Very well, ladies, let's get out quickly and reclaim our shoes. We'll want to hear Purna Praghnamataji. She has an even bigger following than Pilot Baba. Her discourse will focus on *dharma* and *satsang*. We have to walk about half a mile, I think, through a market area. We need to move fast to find seating. Of all the *babas* and *babarinas*, Purna us the most revered. We'll be very lucky to be in her presence. Just being there will be a blessing."

Samantha led the foursome outside the tent. "You've got to be kidding, Shubi. There's no such word as babarinas."

"Yeah, you're right. Just thought I'd make a joke. Remember, I'm a native Indian but I grew up in America. It's the kind of joke an American would think was funny."

Clara, Dottie, Samantha and Shubi all reunited with their footwear and moved in a tight line through masses of people. Dottie strayed off to one of the vendors and nearly got separated from the other three.

"I really need one of these *pashminas*," she said. "I got chilly last night in the camp and I didn't want to wear my coat. Really, it won't take but a minute for me to buy a couple."

"No, absolutely not," Shubi said. "First of all, you'll pay twice as much here unless you bargain. We don't have time for that. Also, there are millions of *pashminas* sold all over India by millions of vendors. Now isn't the time. Really."

"Yes, friend, let's go on to the next discourse. I'll give you one of my *pashminas* tonight. I brought a couple. Now's a time we really need to stick together. Once you get separated in this mob, good luck on ever getting reconnected."

Before Dottie could answer, Samantha was herding them toward the tent of Purna Praghnamataji. They couldn't find a place at the back of the tent, so had to crowd into an opening toward the middle. Purna's followers made room for them, often with a greeting of *Namaste* or welcoming smiles.

"Wow," exclaimed Clara. "I can't believe these people, they're so friendly and forgiving. If this were America and you tried to crowd into an audience, you'd get ugly glares and rudeness."

"Yes," Shubi agreed. "We Indians are often very gracious. But let's repay the kindness by keeping still and listening. It is a rare privilege to hear Purna Praghnamataji expound on *Dharma* and *Satsang*."

Seated on a platform, cross-legged and straight-backed was a small woman. She was shrouded in a tan *sari* edged in gold. Her black hair was parted in the middle, pulled back in a bun. Round, gold-rimmed spectacles lent a scholarly air. She looked to be in her late 50s.

"*Dharma*," she began. "What is the meaning? It means behaviors that align with a child of light. *Dharma* makes life and the universe possible. *Dharma* means virtue and a right way of living. *Dharma* is pure knowledge, pure bliss. It will always give you light. It leads to the knowledge that we are all one. There is only one soul."

A follower next to Samantha raised his hand. He was a very dark-skinned Indian teenage boy. Purna looked at him and nodded an acknowledgement, and he spoke up. "Do you find this knowledge by meditation and prayer?"

"Not only that," said Purna, "but by *Satsang*. That means being in the company of those people who are spiritually awakened, who are spiritually divine. So, the truth will come to you. Don't be with worldly people. Your intellect will become awakened."

A middle-aged woman in a blue and gold *sari* raised her hand. Purna noticed and nodded her head toward the questioner. Outside light was growing dim and sometime during the discourse, white lights all around the top of the meeting tent had been turned on. Their reflections twinkled on Purna's spectacles.

The blue-*sari* woman asked, "How will I find a teacher? Will everybody find their own *guru*?"

"The answer is yes. If you have a real desire, you will find your *guru*. But, it is not good to go and find a *guru*. First you must have the desire for supreme consciousness. It is necessary that you evolve. If the qualities of supreme consciousness come in front of you, the *guru* will be there. You should say to yourself, 'Clarity, that is my goal.' Practice *satsang*. Listen and do not be in a hurry to find a *guru*. If you hurry, you may find yourself changing *gurus* and that is not good. Use an intellectual process, a rational approach."

Clara whispered to Dottie, "I think that's like the saying 'When the student is ready, the teacher will appear'."

"Shhhhhsh," Samantha hissed. "We can discuss this afterwards."

"What is required?" Purna raised her voice ever so slightly. "Mental hangups remain with you for a long time. You have to give them up. Singleness of purpose and purity of heart are required. If you are not ready to renounce anything, you will not achieve supreme consciousness."

The meeting dispersed and the four friends rejoined the moving cavalcade of pilgrims. The smell of incense and sweat filled the air. Small bonfires, beggars crouched next to them, lined the dirt road. A float topped by a large Nandi, a white seated bull, lumbered through the crowd. "Ah," exclaimed Shubi. "That is the vehicle for Lord Shiva. Nandi is the bearer of truth and righteousness. It looks like solid brass, but it is hollow inside." A diminutive wizened man, most likely a *sadhu*, sat precariously atop a stool placed directly in front of the *nandi*.

Although it seemed impossible, the crowds were even denser than before. More than once, they lost track of one another. The human river proceeded at a lumbering pace. Clara shouted to be heard, "One thing this is bringing home to me. You're never alone in India. It wasn't quite this dense, but the streets of Chennai were just as packed with people."

"Right," Samantha shouted back. "That's the subcontinent for you, wherever you look, no matter the time of day, you always see people. Speaking of people, I don't see our other half. Where are Dottie and Shubi?"

Clara looked frantically to her immediate right. "They were just here. Dottie asked Shubi to go with her to bargain with a street vendor. Still the *pashmina* obsession. "Just one minute,"Shubi said. "I used to help my sisters find *pashminas* and we can shop fast. Just move slowly and we'll be back with you. Let's backtrack a bit. Stick together and look in every direction. Call out both her names, Arundati and Dottie. Let's stand in this spot for awhile. I was always taught when you're lost to stay in place."

"Dottie, Arundati, Shubi. We're here. Come back, we're here!" Their shouts fell on deaf ears except for one Indian woman clad in a pink *sari*, who came up to Clara and said, "I am Arundati."

"Thank you, but we're looking for an American Arundati. She was just here and now she's gone."

# Chapter Thirty-five

Dottie found herself alone. If you could call being in a crowd of millions alone. How it happened, she wasn't sure. She checked her shopping bag of *pashminas*, one for each of them, and the next thing she knew, Shubi was not next to her. He had been swallowed up by the relentless stream of Indians surging toward the Ganges River. She called her friends one by one: "Clara, Samantha, Shubi... It's Arundati, Dottie. I'm looking for you. Here, by the *pashmina* vendors." Over and over, she shouted her plea. The pilgrims plodded on, some looking at her with pity, others with mild amusement.

She was about to break down in tears when, finally, an English-speaking Indian woman came up to her. "*Memsab*, you are not well. Is there anything I can do to help?"

"I've lost my people. We were all together and now I can't find anyone." Dottie choked back a sob. "I've called and called. They may think I'm ahead. We got separated, but they knew I went over to the vendors. But...but..." She stopped, unable to say anything that would make sense.

"Yes, *Memsab*. You are American and staying at one of the tourist camps, right? It is hard for outsiders, and yet they keep coming to these festivals. I have helped lost Americans before. I will try to help you."

Dottie could hardly believe her ears. How could this complete stranger possibly help her? Could she trust her? And yet, what choice did she have? An onlooker in white garments, a *salwar kameez* and baggy pants had joined them. Alarm bells went off, but the American woman told herself to ignore them. "Your only chance. Your only chance," she repeated silently to herself.

"My name is Dina, and I have American friends." The man, also wearing white, drew nearer. "And this is my brother Javeen. We were teenagers when we last went to *Kumbha Mela*, and we want to bathe in the holy water of the Ganges a second time. We can help you locate your tourist camp, but first we must bathe. I advise you to join in, as it will wash away the troubles of your past. You will emerge a new person."

Javeen looked at his sister and nodded his head. His eyes were jet black, Dottie noticed, and his teeth very white. Standing side by side, he and Dina looked like fraternal twins. Her head ached. Fear, exhaustion, anticipation.

"Yes," Dina said, "this is the chance of a lifetime. You may never have this opportunity again. People in India spend their whole lives anticipating such an opportunity."

"But...," Dottie began. "How will I ever find my friends? I believe it would be wonderful to bathe in the sacred waters, but they will be worried about me." She wondered if she was losing it. Ending up here, alone, with total strangers? Yes, strangers - even though she felt she'd known them for much longer. Maybe in another lifetime? Dottie took a deep drink from her water bottle, realizing that it was almost empty, and decided to go along with the brother/sister combination. She knew that she shouldn't take a plunge into the murky water. She would wait for them and then rejoin Clara and the others. Dina and Javeen assured her that after bathing in the sacred Ganges, they would escort her to the tourist camp. It was settled.

Slow-moving but relentless, the push toward water was itself a rushing human river. Dottie did not resist when Dina and Javeen, on either side of her, held her hands. Indians next to them, ahead, behind — all with a single intent. A jubilant din filled the air. Loud chanting began. "*Sat Chit Ananda...Sat Chit Ananda...Sat Chit Ananda.*"

Dina spoke loudly into Dottie's ear: "The mantra they're repeating translates as 'Life is absolute bliss consciousness.' It's affirming the self, realizing the self, removing the metaphorical dust from the mirror. It is basic to our philosophy. You can join in. Everyone, Hindu or not, is invited."

They were getting closer to the water. Dottie imagined that she could hear splashing. It was impossible to see through the dense wall of bodies. At first, she'd felt silly holding the hands of Dina and Javeen, but as the crowd became more frenzied, she was grateful for the connection. To her surprise, she joined into the chant: *Sat Chit Ananada...Sat Chit Ananda...Sat Chit Ananda.*

Suddenly her feet were in water. It was time to let her friends plunge into the river as she stepped aside. But there was nowhere to step. She let go of the brother and sister hands and tried to back off. First Dina, then Javeen plunged into the Ganges. Total immersion. They disappeared into the water, then reappeared, each time lifting their faces to the sun and shaking their heads. Their eyes were closed and they wore expressions of bliss.

Dottie stood, fascinated, until, abruptly, she found herself in the very water she'd vowed to avoid. When a large man rushed

188

beside her and dove forward, she lost her balance. The water was freezing cold and after taking a deep breath, her first thought was to locate Dina and Javeen. Her second thought was making sure her backpack was still there. "I can't believe it. I didn't mean to, to...."

"It's OK. We're here." Javeen put a blanket around Dottie's shoulders. He and Dina were by her side. Where Javeen's blanket was from, she had no idea. To her relief, her backpack, a bit soggy but intact, was still attached to her shivering body.

"I can't believe I took the plunge. Well, compared to your bathing, it wasn't much. I'm not sure it even counts. Somehow I've got to find Clara." She was shaking badly and her head was pounding. This was like a bad dream, but she couldn't wake up. Dottie tried to hide her growing fear from Dina and Javeen. "Can you help?"

"Not to worry, dear *Memsab*. We will get you to the tourist camp, but it will take a little walking from here. You look very tired. Shall we stop for a short time at the *araam ke lie padaav*?" Javeen cast a worried look at Dottie.

"He means, how do you say it in English, a rest stop," said Dina. "We will get you some hot tea and then we'll take you to find your friends. Please do not worry. Everything will be OK."

There was nothing to do but trust that it would be. Dottie announced that she wanted to use her full name from now on. "I am Arundati. My childhood name no longer suits me." She was comforted by sitting on folded blankets in the *"araam"* or whatever it was called. The tea restored her spirits and for awhile she felt that everything would be fine. But after the sun went down, her fear returned. Would she ever be reunited with Clara and Samantha? She was so far from finding answers to anything. Instead, cold and miserable, she was thousands of miles away from her New Mexico home and her best friend Clara. She might as well be on a different planet, another universe, a different galaxy.

Dina recognized her exhaustion and spoke to her in soothing tones. "My dear Arundati, you must rest a bit. We will take you to find your friends after you have taken a nap. Javeen is a friend of the police who work at night guarding the security of the pilgrims. If necessary, we will solicit their help. You are still damp from being in the Ganges, and I wish I had some dry clothes for you. But here, I have borrowed a quilt and I will cover you well."

In the past, Arundati - as she now thought of herself - would have protested lying under a strange less than clean comforter. But what mattered in the past no longer seemed important. The American woman clutched her backpack, pulled the quilt up to her chin, curled into a fetal position and was asleep in less than five minutes. She dreamed of lying on a warm beach with waves lapping gently around her. Their touch was gentle, soft, comforting. In her dream, strong arms picked her up and carried her inside a house. She felt safe, cared for. She wanted to know who her rescuer was but instead, she awakened with a start. Instead of strong arms carrying her, Dina's gentle hand was shaking her shoulder.

"Arundati, wake up, wake up. We will find your friends. Please trust us. We can help you." Javeen left Dottie with his sister and went in search of a policeman. Arundati drifted in and out of consciousness. Had she really bathed in Mother Ganges? Well, maybe it was an accidental bathing...maybe just a dip. After all, she didn't intentionally go into the river...Or did she?

"Javeen has located a police lady, Yogita, who knows where all the tourist camps are. She will take us to one, then to another, until we locate the correct one. We will go with you and not leave until we see that you are once again with your friends."

The hours following, when Arundhati tried later to recall them, were a blur. Held up by Dina and Javeen, she trudged on through a scorching hot afternoon. She felt dizzy and feverish. She would remember another person, a lady gendarme named something like Yogita, directing them. The walk was long and torturous, but just as nightfall began, they reached a tourist tent camp.

Many exchanges in Hindi and wandering about to groups of people brought them at last to Clara and Samantha. They were camped in the women's section under a giant canvas pavilion. They were sitting on a straw mat, clothes wrinkled, hair awry, with their heads bowed. Samantha was chanting and Clara sobbing very softly.

Dina interrupted, "I have your lost girl. It wasn't easy, but we've found you at last."

Clara, her face wet with tears, sprang to her feet and gently hugged her best friend. "Dottie, my God, we searched for you all afternoon. We were worried sick. What happened?"

"I'm Arundati from now on," the exhausted woman said, right before she collapsed. Clearly, now was not the time for an

190

interrogation. Instead, Clara put a makeshift pillow under her head and covered her with a light blanket.

"I can't believe you found her...and then found me," Clara said. "I thought I'd never see Dottie...I mean Arundati.... Did she really bathe in the Ganges? She promised me she wouldn't."

Dina smiled tiredly. "Your friend was with me and my brother after she got separated from you. She was wandering through the crowds and calling your name. It was not safe for her. Even though the *Kumbha Mela* is a religious event, there are *goondas,* bad guys, everywhere. What do you call them...bad actors? And so, Javeen, that's my brother who is doing the pilgrimage with me, we adopted her. We promised we'd go with her as she searched. But we had to bathe in the sacred waters first. Mother Ganges. We'd been planning for this moment our entire lives."

"And it was then that Dottie, I mean Arundati, fell into the water?" Clara was increasingly worried about her travel companion, who remained dead to the world. Arundati was asleep on her side. Clara gently massaged her slender blanketed back.

"Did she intentionally take the plunge?" asked Samantha. "Are you sure it was an accident? Maybe she felt it was important and therefore allowed herself. She might have been inspired to 'seize the moment,' as the saying goes?"

"I think it was predestined," Dina said. "Your friend knew she was searching for her mama, she told us. Maybe all along, her mother was the Ganges. Many of us feel that connection. That's why the *Kumbha Mela* draws us, that's why the water is so important."

Clara wanted Dina to go away, but she didn't want to hurt her feelings. This entire day had been a disaster, and she was at the end of her patience. "Dina, we need to sleep now. I cannot thank you enough for coming to the rescue. Without your help, I might have lost my dearest friend forever. May I pay you back somehow?" She reached into her backpack and pulled out a wallet.

"Oh no, no, no. It was my good fortune to be in the right place at the right time. I am glad to have come to the rescue. It is very good karma for me and my brother Javeen. I ask you, however, to consider the possibility that Arundati deliberately bathed in the sacred waters. She told us she was searching, and there is great power in Mother Ganges. It is said that after bathing, people are not the same. It brings about transformation."

"Speaking of transformations," Clara said. "I am about to turn from awake to asleep. Again, my deepest gratitude to you, Dina, and to your brother." She bowed her head and held her hands together in a gesture of *namaste*.

Dina stood up to go. "You know what we say in India about sleep? That going to sleep at night is a little death. Goodbye, Clara, Samantha, and sleeping Arundati. Please tell her in the morning how much I enjoyed being with her. Good luck to you all." Dina backed gracefully out of the tent and disappeared into the night.

# Chapter Thirty-six
## The Ganges River

Clara awakened before the others. She dug a mini-flashlight out of her pack and read her watch. Four-thirty a.m. She stood up and looked across the Ganges River. The sights and sounds were mesmerizing. Bells, strings of white lights, flaming torches, and chanting. An extravaganza. Early risers were already bathing in the sacred waters.

She stood outside the tourist tent for what seemed like hours. Clara had been dreaming of being back in New Mexico, teaching at the American Indian Academy. But that was long ago and far away. Here they were, on the other side of the world, she and Dottie. No, make that Arundati, along with their new best friend Samantha. Those two were still dead to the world. She smiled to herself, crept onto the sleeping mat and pulled up the soft blanket that covered all three of them.

Tired as she was, sleep would not return. There was too little time left before dawn, and she could still hear the river ceremonies. Maybe letting her mind wander would court sleep. Productive musing. She created a mental travelogue, details that she'd might use in a future memoir. A review of all they'd done since traveling to India. Before leaving America, the *Kumbha Mela* had not entered into plans at all, but now that they were here, it might turn out to be their most meaningful experience. Certainly, it was not what most tourists would choose to do.

Samantha looked healthy, her blond pixie cut fresh and lively, just like the woman herself. Arundati, on the other hand, did not look well. Her face seemed drawn and gray, and she was sweating. Bathing, or accidentally submerging, whatever it was, in the Ganges, might have been a terrible mistake. When Arundati awakened, she would try not to raise fears, but she would observe her closely. Also, she vowed to let Arundati tell her whether or not the plunge was intentional. It might have been a bit of both. Her friend was more impressed with the *baba's* discourses than she was and was dealing with the ever-diminishing hope that she'd learn about her origins. How well Clara knew about that hope.

Both Samantha and Arundati began to stir. Clara wanted to let them awaken in private. Soon enough, they'd be back in the human river of people. She took a brief stroll around the periphery of their tent. Inside, Samantha and Arundati stretched and got back into daytime garb.

"It is amazing," Samantha yawned, "how *salwar kameezes* go so easily from being night to daywear. That's one of the many reasons I love India."

"I think I'll want to wear Indian clothes even when I'm back home," Arundati said. She pulled a light blue tunic over black drawstring pants, then drew her shoulder-length black hair back into a pony tail.

Clara stepped back into the tent. "Here, let me turn that pony tail into a braid. Then people will think you are from here. Doesn't she look more like the native people every day?" she asked Samantha.

"Absolutely. Of the three of us, she's the one who blends into the crowd. All she needs is a *tikka* mark on her forehead. Even with the proper forehead marking, obviously, I wouldn't convince anyone. Clara, with your beautiful black locks and olive skin, you could be one of the northern Indians."

It was going to be the hottest day yet. At seven a.m. the sun was already intense. Dawn brought an end to bells and chanting coming from Mother Ganges, but now the human voices came from various tents of the *babas*. Just as they had every day of the *Kumbha Mela*, they continued the discourses that had lured Arundati. While she was pacing around the tent, Clara realized that she didn't want to continue the *Kumbha Mela*. The heat and dust were intense, the crowds relentless. What at first seemed fascinating was now exhausting. She'd had enough.

When Clara came in from her walk, both Arundati and Samantha had returned from the camp's restroom facilities. Backpacks in place, they looked ready to carry on. Clara dreaded telling them about her decision.

"You two look so much better than I feel," she began. That wasn't exactly true, as Dottie-Arundati didn't look at all well. No need to point that out. "I don't know how to say this, but I can't continue with this *Kumbha Mela* adventure. After yesterday, I wanted to quit, especially since we got separated, but I couldn't find a way to tell you. I mean, we were so incredibly glad to have Dottie, I mean Arundati, back with us."

To her relief, Samantha and Arundati didn't look disappointed. In fact, they both smiled. Samantha rolled her eyes and laughed. "You won't believe this. We had just been talking about 'a little *Kumbha Mela* goes a long way.' We've had enough

194

as well. I have the perfect suggestion. After the madness of all these pilgrims, we could go to an *ashram* I know about. It will be restorative and calm. Also, we'll practice yoga and meditation every day. I've spent time in *ashrams* before, and I've come out feeling like new. What do you think?"

"Wow," Clara said. "I think we should have done that instead of all this wandering around. But Arundati, you're the one who had a specific goal, finding your birthmother. Nothing we've done so far has led us anywhere in that quest. Would this seem like giving up to you?" Dottie shrugged her shoulders.

By now, the three women had rejoined the milling stream of pilgrims. Samantha assured them that she knew of an *ashram* they could enter without a previous reservation. "I spent the better part of a year there when I first came to India. I know they'll remember me, as I started out as the worst yoga student. Also, I complained about having to scrub floors and peel vegetables. As I stayed on, all that changed. I ended up being an assistant yoga instructor."

The plan was to spend one more day on foot, maybe going to hear some discourses along the way. They would go to the *Mela* Grounds, a vast tented area with information and guides. From there, they would decide exactly what to do next.

"I might be leaving you," Samantha admitted. "Sorry I didn't tell you this till now, but I'm engaged to be married, and I told Rajeev - he's my fiancé - that I'd be with him before December. I've kept it a secret, as I wasn't sure. But last night I realized that this is my future, my life. There's nothing back in the states for me. I have no family ties, no property. India is now my home."

"Congratulations, Samantha." Clara gave her a gentle hug, pretending to be far more cheerful than she felt. It was no surprise that Samantha would choose romance over wandering around India with two lost souls, adopted souls at that.

"Hooray for romance," Arundati said. "I'm happy for you. We would love it if you could be our sister traveler forever, but nothing lasts forever. If you could just help us get to the *ashram*, that would be fantastic."

"We'll be at the *Mela* Grounds by five," Samantha assured them. "You may wish to go to another *ashram* than the one I first mentioned. There will be options there and busses to take you. Believe me, from years of doing this, I know it's not so hard to get around India as you might think."

"But you speak some of the language," Clara said. "We just know English. Also, what's the name of the *ashram* you stayed at? You never told us."

They were walking swiftly now, as though racing against the blazing sun. All three women carried water slings over their shoulders. Whenever they ran low, they stopped and bought fresh bottles. They were getting down to the last of their trail mix, jerky, and protein bars. When Arundati suggested buying some Indian snacks from street kiosks, however, Samantha quickly discouraged her.

"Just because it's in a cellophane bag doesn't mean it's OK to eat. One reason I've stayed healthy is that I never, no matter how hungry I am, eat or drink anything from a street vendor. You look worried. Is it just because you're tired and hungry?"

"I am worried," Dottie admitted. "Yesterday, when I was with Dina and Javeen, I did eat from a street vendor. I thought because it was food they said was fine that it would be okay. I mean, it was cooked. Just a little baked pastry filled with potatoes and lentils."

"Oh, you mean *samosas*? They're the most popular street food in India. If they were just fried and still hot, they were probably okay, But as a rule, never eat from the street. I'll repeat myself. I've lived and travelled in India for quite awhile, and I still don't do it."

"Why do you think we wouldn't like the place you stayed at?" Clara asked. "We should have researched the possibilities before leaving home, but we never seriously talked about doing that as an option."

"Actually, it would probably be fine. I went as a yoga teacher, and focused more on the research division. There was a section devoted to those who just wanted to go as a retreat. The place I'm thinking of is accessible from Allahabad. There are some wonderful *ashrams* in the southern part of India, particularly Kerala, but it would take way too long and be a little complicated to get there. You two need to seek refuge sooner rather than later."

Arundati stumbled, falling against Clara. "Just a bit of gravel in my shoe," she muttered. "Or maybe my shoe's falling apart. Let's go over to the edge of the crowd so I can see what's wrong."

Holding hands to avoid being separated by the ever-moving press of pilgrims, Clara, Arundati and Samantha moved

196

to the side of the wide dirt road. They sat on the ground, on a scruffy patch of grass, while Arundati took off her worn out Nikes. She emptied them out, shaking a few sharp rocks to the ground. "Sorry for the smelliness," she said. "I need new shoes." She held up the running shoes. "These things have had it."

"I could use new feet!" Clara exclaimed. "The sooner we can get to a place of retreat, the better." She secretly worried that it was more than Arundati's shoes that were the problem. Her friend was getting slower at walking, and she looked frazzled. They were all worn down by the relentless heat and dust.

"Let's buy some more water before we forge ahead," Samantha urged. "One thing we have to avoid is getting dehydrated. That and not eating enough." She pulled out a package of beef jerky and offered it to the others.

"Up ahead, look up ahead!" Clara thought she spotted a divergence of the crowd. "Is that the Old Naini Bridge?" she asked. "Isn't that where we veer over to Allahabad?"

"No, there's another crossing of the Ganges that will get us closer," Samantha said. "I promise. We can go to the Yogoda Satsanga Ashram and get you established. Then, dearest friends, I must leave you to go meet Rajeev. He is introducing me to his family in one week and I will have to prepare. As you may know, traditional families usually pick out their sons and daughters' partners. So, we are bucking the trend."

"Does that make you nervous?" asked Arundati.

"No, it just makes me more determined to make a good impression. I have to pass the 'future daughter-in-law' inspection. Rajeev's parents, even though they're traditional, have a younger son who's in the states getting a double degree in computer technology and pre-med. Rajeev has enlightened them a bit. But...an American bride. That's a big leap. Okay, gang, we need to veer left. The new bridge is just about a quarter mile from here."

Arundati, who'd been walking very slowly, stumbled and fell against Samantha. "Sorry, I'm feeling a little bit weak. My stomach hurts. My head aches. I'm basically a wreck." She laughed weakly. "It may have been something I ate or drank. After my immersion in the river."

Clara rushed over to Arundati's side. Samantha held her on the right, Clara on the left. All the while, they moved steadily toward the massive bridge that would take them to Allahabad. Hundreds of pilgrims surrounded them. Women in flowing

197

*saris*—red, purple, blue and a myriad of other brilliant colors. Men in *salwar kameezes*, simple drawstring pants and shirts which had once been white but were now a dusty tan. An occasional adolescent boy or girl in conservative western jeans and tee shirts or tunic tops.

With Arundati fading fast, they resisted the lure of more *gurus* giving discourses. They passed signs luring the faithful: "Meditation is a superb spiritual immersion - A cleansing and rejuvenation of body, mind and soul." Shortly after crossing a massive bridge whose name Samantha didn't know, they came to a surprisingly peaceful residential section of what must have been Allahabad.

"We're nearly there," Samantha told them. "The Vrindavan Satsanga Ashram and Research Center. It's where my dear friend Vivian went to perfect her meditation practice. She literally 'found' herself there. It was a complete transformation. She was wasting her life and talents before the *ashram*. I remember her saying that she wanted this to be a spiritual journey that said yes to everything."

# Chapter Thirty-seven

Clara and Arundati were both amazed at Samantha's ability to navigate the intricate streets of the city. She could actually read the street signs enough to ask directions of the Indians around them. By now, they had escaped the *Kumbha Mela* crowd. The streets were dense with pedestrians, cattle and an occasional elephant, but this was the bustle of everyday life. The incense, bells, and chanting were replaced with the honking, roars and jingle of cars, carts, cyclists, and motorcycles.

Clara shared the last of her beef jerky with Arundati. "You're going to make it, friend. We'll be like Samantha's friend Vivian. Saying yes to everything. By the way, what happened to her, Vivian, that is?"

"Well, the last I heard, she was teaching meditation classes in San Diego. She was hugely successful. Always had a waiting list to get into her workshops and retreats. I was hoping she'd come back to the subcontinent to travel and explore with me. We were like sisters. Sadly, we've been out of touch for a couple years."

After turning right off Yogita Lane, the English word a nod to Western culture, they were at a tall wrought iron gate. Beyond the gate, tall shrubs, towering palm trees, and lush greenery blocked a view of whatever was beyond. with a brass sign at the top that read "SIVANANDA VRINDAVAN HEALING ASHRAM."

Samantha pushed a buzzer attached to an intercom box. "*Namaskar.* My name is Samantha Owens and I have two pilgrims with me who would like to inquire about staying at your *ashram.*"

"Yes, welcome Miss Samantha. Do you have a reservation? Also, may I have the names of your friends?"

"No, we just came from the *Mela.* My friends are Clara Jordan and Arundati Benet. They are the ones who would like to stay. I am their escort."

A buzz sounded and the gate opened. A turbaned man who apparently worked for the *ashram,* greeted them with a 'Namaste' and put their backpacks in a cart. "Welcome, *Memsahibs.* I will take you to reception."

"I can't believe it!" Clara exclaimed. "I've always imagined that I'd someday go to an *ashram,* and now it's actually happening."

In her excitement, Clara failed to notice that Arundati was looking pale and depleted. Samantha, who did notice, was alarmed at Arundati's rapidly deteriorating condition but deliberately said nothing about it. She didn't want them to be turned away. They greeted the young man at the reception desk. His name tag identified him as "Ravi." Samantha, by silent assent, was the designated spokeswoman. "My friends would like a residency for probably just a month, maybe longer. I will be staying just three days, to get Ms. Jordan and Ms. Smith settled, and then I have to prepare for a wedding."

"Ah yes," said Ravi. "And is this someone in your family, this wedding? Forgive me for prying, but we Indians are very fond of wedding celebrations."

"Actually, it's my wedding. I'm a transplant to India, as you have probably suspected. I am meeting my fiancé's family and we'll be setting a date. He is from Kerala."

"Congratulations, *Memsab*. What a lucky man your fiancé is, and his family I think will be happy that he is following his heart. We modern Indians honor very much the traditions of our families, but we also realize that times must change. Here is the guest registry for you to fill out. When that's done, I will show you to our residential section. You will each have your own separate room, unless you wish otherwise."

Samantha interrupted Ravi's marching orders. "I've been wanting to invite you, Clara and Arundati, to my wedding. It's in Tamil Nadu, Chennai. If it's before you fly back to the states, you'll be my honored guests. It's going to be an awesome event."

"We'd love to, but we're not sure exactly when we'll be in Chennai. Our luggage is being stored in a hotel there and that's where we catch an outgoing flight." It was obvious that Arundati was intrigued by the idea of an Indian wedding. But that was in the future. The Sivananda Vrindavan Healing *Ashram* was here and now.

Samantha's invitation was left hanging in the air. As the paperwork finished, the three women followed Ravi upstairs and down a long corridor to the end of a hall. A *wallah* followed with their backpacks. Ravi filled them in on the schedule. It was the same for all guests, newly arrived or long-term residents. "We are very disciplined here at Sivanandra Vrindavan and the schedule, which is posted inside every door, seldom deviates. It is a routine that allows for spiritual growth and healing. Usually, after a week of getting used to our routine, guests are encouraged to move into our single-sex dormitories. The shared living space is part of the experience. You will see. Please come to the office if there is anything you need or if you have questions. You are most welcome, and now I advise you to rest. Our communal dinner is at 6 p.m. and wakeup call in the morning is 5:30 a.m. Dear *Memsabs*, you are most welcome, and now I advise you to rest."

And rest they did, each in her rooms, each lost in private musings. Samantha dwelled on her upcoming meeting with her fiancé's people, the traditional Hindu wedding, which would be the extravaganza of a lifetime. Clara and Arundati, in their separate reflections, both realized that after the retreat, it might be time to go back home and pick up their lives where they'd left off. Or, to invent new lives. Arundati's dream, had not been realized, and probably it never would be. On the other hand, she had absorbed the sights and sounds of India. She had seen any number of Indian women who might be distantly related to her. She had reached the point of feeling that it might be enough.

Maybe "Mother India" is the only parent I need, Arundati told herself. Somewhere she'd read that to be fully alive, fully human and completely awake was to be continually thrown out of the nest. To be always in no woman's land. In the next room, Clara was recording her thoughts in a journal. "Who am I?" she wrote. "Why am I here?" "How shall I live?"

# Chapter Thirty-eight

The gong reverberated through high-ceilinged corridors and a vast reception hall. A deep sonorous voice was reciting a morning prayer. Or was it a *mantra*? Maybe a little of both. The fragrance of incense wafted into the sleeping quarters, surrounding the great hall. Arundati, Clara, and Samantha, in their separate rooms, awakened with the realization that they had just minutes before it would be time to join the group meditation. *Chai* and a vegetarian buffet would be available at ten a.m.

Ravi was outside their doors as, one by one, the women emerged from their rooms. "You are the newest guests, so I wanted to make sure you're doing well. After the meditation, you are free to walk the grounds and familiarize yourself with everything. Then, before morning *Satsang*, you are encouraged to meet by the tea tree—he gestured toward a garden outside the central courtyard—for assignment of your tasks. You notice that we do not have staff here at Vrindavan Ashram. We are the staff. Part of our discipline is performing the most mundane chores with reverence."

Ushered into a great hall, the women took their seats on yoga mats near the front. Samantha managed a full lotus position, Clara sat cross-legged, Dottie stretched her legs out in front and crossed her ankles. Incense, a piney fragrance edged with cinnamon and other spices, sent an aroma through the cool morning air. A gentle, pulsating drumming and an occasional gong came from hidden speakers.

Ahead of them, on a small platform sat a woman dressed in orange and marigold. After a final gong, she began. "*Namaste*, my friends. Today is a brand-new beginning and a chance to count our blessings, to breathe deeply and feel the life-giving *prana* of the universe. Make yourselves comfortable. Sit tall and give your diaphragm room to inhale and exhale slowly and deeply. Close your eyes. We will repeat *Om* three times, then I will ring a soft bell. When our time is up, some twenty minutes from now, you will hear the soft bell again and it will be time to open your eyes."

As one, led by the lady in orange, the group softly intoned...

"Ommm...ommmm....oooommmm."

After the bell sounded, there was only the sound of breathing. Time stood still as each student sank into contemplation. The outside world seemed far away, the past a distant memory, the future irrelevant. There was only now... After what seemed like far more than twenty minutes, the bell sounded once again.

For the new guests at the *ashram*, there would be free time before the meal at ten. After the first week, which was considered orientation, they would be practicing daily yoga for nearly two hours. Clara and Arundati decided to spend the time between meditation and the morning meal with Samantha, as she would be leaving the next day. They went to her room for what might be their last chance to visit.

"I can't believe that we're actually here, in an *ashram*," Clara said. "It's hard to say why, but I feel like this is where we should have been all along. The time we spent with Lane Masterson, that fake guide in Chennai, was something of a waste. I'm not even sure he was really a guide. He just took our money and carried on with his illegal business using us as a front."

"Yeah, really," chimed in Arundati. "Remember what he was carrying around in a box he tried to keep hidden from us? It looked like ivory carvings and jewelry. Illegal. I think ivory was his real business." She paused, sighed, closed her eyes. "You know, guys, I really don't feel too well. I think I'll have to take today off and just sleep. Can you tell Ravi I'm under the weather? I hate to be a wimp, but I have to lie down..." With that, she collapsed on the bed. She shivered and started to cough. "You two make my apologies. I'm sorry to be such a wimp. Can you find some extra blankets. Not sure how I can be having chills when it must be 100 degrees out..." Her voice grew weaker and then stopped. She was asleep.

Samantha found some extra blankets, soft woolen throws, and put them over Arundati. Clara held the back of her hand against her best friend's forehead. "She feels feverish. I think I'd better stay with her. You can go to the meal and maybe bring me something back." Her eyes glistened with unshed tears. "This is all my fault. I'm the one who thought it would be such a great idea coming to India."

"Please. It is not your fault. You and Dottie, I mean Arundati, decided this together. You told me enough about how this trip was launched. You're both responsible for being here, and I'm sure there's a doctor somewhere in this *ashram*. At the others I've stayed with, there was always an *Aruvedic* practitioner and also there were doctors of western medicine staying there.

You'd be surprised how many of them like to practice both western and eastern medicine."

"I don't need a doctor," murmured Arundati. "Please don't let me ruin your first day here. I just need to go back to sleep. I'm feeling nauseous. I don't think I can keep anything down." She groaned and pulled the blankets over her head.

Reluctantly, Clara and Samantha went without their friend to a vegetarian buffet in the main hall. There they talked with other guests and filled their plates with rice, curries, pilafs and *samosas*. To drink, the choices were *chai* or water; they both chose the former, then sat at a long white table on folding chairs.

"Mind if I join you," asked a young woman who introduced herself as Penelope. "Just call me Penny. I'm from London, where I am enrolling in a music program next semester. This is what I think you'd call my gap year."

Clara held out her hand and shook Penny's extended hand. "Clara Jordan here and my friend Samantha Owens. We just arrived, and are taking today to get oriented. Have you been here very long?"

"A week's all, but it feels much longer." She noted Clara's raised eyebrows and hastily added, "I mean that in a good way, There's such a predictable routine here. Early rising, meditation led by Swami Ji, his wife, or one of the advanced *Yogis* who lives here year-round. Then *Asana* - that's yoga - twice a day, at 8 a.m. and 3:30 p.m. I'm glad this is Friday, because every other day we eat our meals in silence. I wouldn't have wanted to miss the chance to talk with you."

"I don't feel OK leaving Arundati, alone while we just go about our business," Clara said, even as she prepared to do just that. "During the day, with Penny helping us, maybe we can make contact with a doctor. Arundati's quite a strong girl. She's stubborn as an ox. If she doesn't want us to bring a doctor to her, she means it."

"I don't care if she's an ox," Samantha said. "there are illnesses in this country that have humbled the best of us. I should know; I've felt at death's door. You live here long enough, you either build up immunities or you give up and go home."

"Wait." Clara tiptoed over to now-sleeping Arundati. She pulled a blanket up around her friend's shoulders, kissed her softly on the cheek, felt her forehead with her palm. "A little warm, but I don't think she has a fever." She went to the washbasin, poured a glass of water and put it on the nightstand. "We'll be back soon to check on you."

Quietly, Samantha and Clara exited and then made their way to the great hall. A couple dozen others were already on their yoga mats, sitting meditatively or lying prostrate in *savasana*, the corpse pose. The instructor, a willowy young man with blond hair pulled into a topknot was seated in the lotus position at the end of the hall. He appeared to be deep in meditation.

Silence reigned. Late comers entered on silent feet and spread their mats at the back and edges of the hall. The instructor, after a few minutes of stragglers, rang a soft bell. He folded his palms, fingertips to his chin. "*Namaste*, and welcome. My name is Alex, but my Indian name is Sundeep. Swami Gi asked me to take his class this morning, as I need to lead five classes for my final certification. I have been a student of yoga for twenty years and have been at the *ashram* for the past twelve months. If you're new, please be aware that yoga is not a contest. The *asanas* do not need to be done perfectly. We all do the best we can. Thank you all for being here.

"We will begin silent meditation. I'll ring a soft bell at the beginning and the end. If you can achieve the lotus position, fine. If not, you can sit cross-legged or with your legs out in front of you. Aim to keep your core erect and your back straight. Aim for a personal best. Keep your eyes closed or downcast. We will begin with repeating '*Om*' three times."

"Ommmm...

"Ommm...

"Ommm..."

After a soft bell sounded, the room fell into deep silence. Clara, after first worrying about Arundati, then sank and into thoughts about her own life. Possibly their trip to India hadn't provided answers. Certainly not for her friend, but also not for herself. And yet maybe they were coming to a certain kind of acceptance about their rootless state. The old question of nurture versus nature. The parents who raised them: weren't they even more important than those original parents, the feckless couples who'd brought them into the world and then passed them on to someone else...

Did it really matter that they had unanswered questions about their origins? Would knowing change anything? And what if Arundati, by some miracle, found her mom and was disappointed? She would never forget her despair at learning that her own birthmother had passed away. After finally tracing her, she was too late. But what if she'd been disappointed, what if Greta Suina hadn't been happy to see her? What if she'd been rejected all over again?

In her mind, Clara traveled back to New Mexico. She relived her entire school year at the American Indian Academy, the death of headmaster Joseph Speckled Rock, her disastrous affair with Henry DiMarco. She'd been so glad to move to Santa Fe, and even happier to meet Arundati Smith — Dottie, who was the sister she never had. And, finally, she was surprised to admit to herself, she was glad to be here at this restful place.

The ringing of a soft bell brought her back to the present and along with Samantha and the couple dozen other yoga students, she stood for a slow salutation to the sun. Stretching to the high, vaulted ceiling of the great hall, Clara realized that despite her happiness in this moment, she had a serious obligation. Arundati, despite her protests, needed help. Somehow, unless her condition improved, they must find a doctor. In fact, maybe she shouldn't even be here, calmly doing yoga.

But she silenced that nagging voice and continued the morning *Asana*. Stretching, bending, reaching: it felt wonderful. "Free time, ladies and gentlemen until this afternoon at three p.m.," announced Alex/Sundeep. "If you are new to the *ashram*, continue your self-orientation. We all share the workload here. Find out from the front desk what tasks are not already claimed, and volunteer for whatever you feel best suited for..."

"Can you sign me up for whatever you decide to do?" Clara asked Samantha. "I have to go check on Arundati. I just don't feel right about letting her tough it out. She really did not look good at all."

The two women stood outside the great hall, other yoga students milling around them, and finally decided that Samantha would try to sign them both up for kitchen duty. If that wasn't possible, Clara said she wasn't averse to scrubbing the bathrooms. Not that it was her top choice, but she could imagine that there would be plenty of vacancies for that duty.

"What about gardening? They grow all their own vegetables here, and I love working in the earth. I've had lots of experience, and I'm strong."

"Dear, I don't think the point is whether or not you've had experience. We are talking about pretty basic labor. I'll see what I can do for you. In the meantime, go rescue our friend..."

While Samantha went to a meeting in the outdoor courtyard, Clara rushed down the corridor outside the cavernous yoga room. For a moment, she felt disoriented. It was the first time in days that she was without friends at her side. Was it correct to turn right for the stairwell to their rooms? Or was it left? She tried to backtrack in her mind and to recreate how they'd gotten to yoga. Instead, she kept thinking of the sign posted outside the yoga room: Meet at the Tea Tree at noon for assignments: Mundane tasks done with Reverence.

Wasn't she on a task? It wasn't mundane, maybe it was even a matter of life and death. Despite the relaxing two hours of yoga, she felt her heart beating faster. Why hadn't she insisted on staying with Arundati? Here she was at the end of the hall, but there was no stairwell. She must have turned the wrong direction. Nearly running, she backtracked and went to the other end of the corridor. Yes! Here was a stairwell. She raced up, two steps at a time. The doors all looked the same and the numbers — theirs was 300 — were all in Hindi, or maybe it was Urdu. As usual, there was no one around to ask. Everyone was getting their mundane task assignment.

She walked quickly up and down the hall hoping in vain for a detail that would jog her memory. To no avail. Everything looked the same. Desperate, she decided to call out. "Arundati! Dottie! It's Clara. I'm coming to see how you are, but I can't find our room..."

No answer. She tried again, walking up and down, calling at every door. Finally, from the third room from the end came a low groan. Of course, Clara reminded herself, they'd left Arundati in Samantha's room. She rapped softly and called "Dottie, it's me, Clara. Sorry I left you alone..." She opened the door, but Dottie wasn't in the bed.

"I got up to use the restroom and tripped. I tried to get up but just couldn't. I need water...'

Clara helped her friend get up off the floor, took her to the bathroom, sectioned off in one corner of the room, opened a bottle of water and had her drink the entire contents. "Let's move you next door to your own room. I told Samantha to fill in for me this afternoon. You need to get comfortable and rest up." She placed a palm on Arundati's forehead. "You're really feverish. Once we get you settled, I'll go to the reception area and see if they have a medic who can advise us." She gave her friend a gentle hug, rubbed her back, and led her next door to her assigned room.

Arundati collapsed on the single bed. "I need to take a shower but can't do another thing right now." Suddenly she sat up. "Please don't tell the desk people how bad I am. If they think I'm contagious, we might all have to leave. I'd hate to ruin this for all of us." She sighed deeply and fell back in a prostrate position. "I'll be fine...really," and then she was asleep.

Clara had handled emergencies before. She remembered her year of teaching at the American Indian Academy, the year that began with a dead body on her classroom floor. She was smart, she reminded herself. She was resourceful. As she went downstairs and made her way to the reception desk, she prepared what she'd say. Not too much, but enough to muster up a medical person.

The slender young woman's name tag read "Meera" and she stood regally at the desk talking on the phone and taking notes. When she saw Clara and read the alarm on her face, she quickly ended the conversation. "Yes, madam, is something wrong? Did you get your cleaning or cooking assignment this afternoon? How can we help you?"

"*Namaskar*, Meera. I'm Clara Jordan and..."

"Yes, we know who you are," interrupted Meera. "Why don't you come around to this side of the counter and I'll bring you a cup of *chai*?"

"That's so kind. I gladly accept." She walked around the counter and sat in a rickety metal folding chair across from the elegant Meera. "I'm sure Arundati will be fine, but right now she is a bit ill. I think it's just fatigue, but is there a doctor here at the *ashram*? Someone who could examine her? Maybe prescribe a homeopathic or herbal remedy?" Worried about not taking a chore assignment, she added "Samantha said she would sign me up for a work detail. We don't want to disrupt the orderly routine."

"Please do not worry about that. Your friend is not the first resident to become ill here. She won't be the last." Meera's smile was dazzling, Clara noticed. Something about that smile reminded her of Arundati when she was feeling better, not the ill, diminished version.

As Clara nervously sipped a cup of hot *chai*, Meera explained that there was no doctor currently in residence at the ashram. "We had Dr. Patel for nine months, but his mother was ill and he had to go to his hometown in Kerala to help the family. How would you feel about a medical student? Ashok Gatwande is a medical student, or maybe he's an intern. He is going to school but now on break and staying here for a couple months. He's a brilliant guy, and I'm sure he can give you an expert assessment and advise you on what to do." She paused. "If it is something contagious, we must have her leave and go to hospital or clinic."

Trying not to focus on Meera's last words, Clara finished her drink and hurried back to Arundati's room to await the visit from Mr. Gatwande. Ashok. Her friend was immobile, asleep on her side in the narrow bed. The room was hot and stuffy, so Clara opened the window. She felt Arundati's forehead. Not as hot as before, but still warm. Of course, it could be the rising external temperature.

A gentle knock announced the arrival of Ashok Gatwande. Clara cautiously opened the door. "*Namaste*," said the sturdily built young man before her. "I am taking a break from my third year of medical school, an *ashram* break. I am here to help."

"*Namaste*," replied Clara. "Our patient is sleeping, but I can tell you what has happened. Thank you so much for coming."

"No," called out Arundati from her sickbed. "I'm not asleep anymore. I can tell you what happened, Mr. Gatwanda."

"It's Gatwande. Call me Ashok. I'm sorry you are sick. Your friend said that you had bathed in the Ganges River while you were walking in the *Kumbha Mela*. She thought maybe you'd accidentally swallowed water then."

"Well, I didn't exactly take a dip in the river on purpose. Partly I wanted to, as I was curious, but actually I was jostled by the crowd and fell in by accident. I'd gotten separated from my friends and was trying to find them. They were also trying to find me. Obviously, we reconnected."

"Yes. You were very adventurous to join in. It is very rare for westerners to do that. But what I really need to know is about your symptoms. Diarrhea? Nausea? Vomiting? Chills?"

"Yes, I have diarrhea, no vomiting. I have pain in my abdomen. All morning I had terrible chills. Mainly I'm tuckered out. Weak. I feel terrible that I can't do any of the activities, and I'm a burden to Clara and Samantha." She was about to cry but pressed her lips together and closed her eyes.

"Please try not to be stressed. I know how hard that is, but trust me, everything will be fine. It sounds like you might have contracted amoebic dysentery. I'll ask you some questions that can eliminate cholera, malaria, schistosomiasis and some other diseases." After a question and answer session, Ashok checked Arundati's pulse and took her temperature.

"Have you been eating? Drinking lots of water?"

"Neither," Clara answered for her. "We haven't been able to get anything down her. And...I hope you don't find this offensive...we haven't been able to get bottled water for her. I know the Sivananda Vrindavan probably has pure water, but maybe it's not so good for our sensitive western stomachs."

"The water situation can be solved. I'll ask one of the couriers to bring you a case of water. It is very cheap from the market, but please remember when you pay him, also to tip. As far as eating, Miss Arundati, here is what you need to eat: bananas, rice, applesauce, and toast. It's easy to remember: BRAT. A tried and tested regimen that will help you keep up your strength and settle your gastrointestinal system."

Clara volunteered to go downstairs and make a request to the kitchen as Ashok continued, by discussing with Arundati where she'd been and what she'd consumed, to eliminate possible diseases. By the time Clara returned, bearing a bunch of bananas, he had eliminated the possibility of schistosomiasis, typhoid, cholera, and malaria. "This dysentery may resolve on its own, without treatment beyond the BRAT diet and rest. Lots of rest. Also, make sure our patient is staying really well hydrated."

As if on cue, a knock at the door signaled a *wallah* bearing a case of bottled water. Clara paid the man and brought over an opened bottle. "Here," she said to Arundati, "drink this. All of it, if you can."

"That's exactly what she needs to do," Ashok told them. He looked at Clara. with a pained expression, his brow furrowed. "Here's an idea. You go on to the afternoon *Asana*. I'll check with the reception staff and explain to them that Arundati needs time to recover from food poisoning. That's better than announcing that she has dysentery. It can be contagious, and since there's a danger of it spreading, you might have to leave."

"But if it is contagious," Clara said, "how do Samantha and I keep from contracting it? We don't want to leave, but we don't want everyone to get sick."

"I'm here, and I should have something to say about the situation." Arundati had shifted in bed to a sitting position. "I haven't died yet, and I already feel better. You can more or less isolate me. Just make sure to bring the rice and whatever and keep me supplied with water. Clara can follow the routine and cover for me if the desk people grow suspicious."

"What about your other friend, Stephanie, Simone...whatever her name is? Isn't she in on everything? Weren't you traveling together? You'll have to let her in on what's happening."

"You didn't know? She is just with us another day or so. She's going to meet her future in-laws."

Ashok looked puzzled. "In-laws?"

"That's the mother and father of her future husband. In America, we call it 'extended family.' Samantha's been wonderful. We'll miss her." She looked over at Arundati, who was now sleeping. "I guess it's OK with the *ashram* if I participate and my friend here just recuperates."

"They're very kind and forgiving. I will tell Meera—she's the one in charge of the reception desk—that I'll be monitoring Arundati. Then, when she's better, she can join in. This is a wonderful place, a place for healing and inspiration. You'll see."

Feeling slightly guilty, Clara left Arundati in the care of Ashok. She went to the main hall in search of Samantha. It had been cleaned, yoga mats placed in rows for the afternoon's session. For the first time, she began to notice the beauty of the *ashram*. Hadn't she heard that it used to be the home of royalty, a building repurposed? Tall pillars on either side of the cavernous room, ornate carvings at the top of each. What were they called? The capitals? The arches on either side were elegant and graceful. Everything was painted a creamy pink.

# Chapter Thirty-nine

Leaving the yoga room, Clara wandered outside, in search of the so-called "tea tree". Wasn't that where the jobs were supposed to be assigned? Somehow, she must have taken a wrong turn. Here she was in an entirely different wing of the complex. The walls around her were lined with books. A file cabinet and a wooden table and chair occupied one corner. Nothing high-tech about this place. Clara picked a book from the shelf, a hefty tome with a royal blue cover. Although she recognized letters in Hindi, she could not make out a single word. She paged through and studied several drawings, illustrations featuring human faces. The first drawing featured a thumb over the right nostril, the second with an index finger over left nostril. Yes! It was a demonstration of yogic breathing. In on one side, out on the other. Samantha had mentioned them that some of India's *ashrams* included research centers. This must be the case with Sivanandra Vrindavan Ashram.

Time was slipping away and she still hadn't found the tea tree. Much to her relief, Samantha found her. "Oh, here you are," she exclaimed. "I've been searching all over. I signed you up for scrubbing the dining area floor, every day after the evening meal. I hope that's OK, I mean every other job was even worse. I'll be scrubbing with you in the few days I have left." She took Clara's elbow and ushered her back into the main building. En route, they passed through an open courtyard. Fleetingly, Clara wondered how she'd gotten to the book room without going through this part of the complex.

No time to ask. They were now outside the main hall and the afternoon yoga session was about to begin. "Real quickly," Samantha whispered to Clara, "How's Dottie, I mean Arundati? Will she be alright without us checking on her?"

"She doesn't care if we use her full name or just go back to using Dottie, and yes, she seems to be hanging in there. Our fellow pilgrim, Ashok, is watching over her. Actually, I think he has a crush on her."

"Whatever..."

A soft gong sounded. "Ommmmm...three times.

The yoga session's beginning ended their conversation, to be continued later. Sundeep greeted the twenty-some yoga students with a gesture of *Namaste*, to which they all responded with their versions of the greeting. It was a relief, Clara thought to herself, to escape from worry about Arundati. She would totally immerse herself in this class and hope that answers bubbled up from her subconscious during meditation.

For forty-five minutes, led by Sundeep, they went through *asanas*, beginning with Downward Dog and Salutation to the Sun. They went on to Cat-Cow, done on all fours and a deep workout for the midriff. Next, the Cobra position and then the Plow. Clara kept herself from looking at others, people who she decided were doing the *asanas* more correctly, more thoroughly. After all, this was not a competitive sport.

Another sounding of the gong. Sundeep directed them to sit in the lotus position. Silence prevailed as the meditation began. Clara sat in a half-lotus position. She was working toward a full lotus but had not yet achieved it. She breathed deeply and let her mind float. Gratitude for her good health flowed through her; optimism about Arundati's situation filled her mind. She imagined her friend, under Ashok's care, getting better and stronger every day. She saw herself scrubbing the floor with Samantha alongside, then — after Samantha left to be with her extended family — she saw herself with another student. She'd never been very good at floor-cleaning, but she would perfect it. The floors would be spotless.

Her mind drifted on to what would happen next. When Arundati was better, she too would have a task. They'd do yoga together every day. But would they learn, as Sundeep suggested, who they really were? The future offered many options. By meditating and simplifying life, could they gain clarity?

A gong sounded before Clara could answer that question to herself.

Samantha caught up with her as the yoga students slowly emptied the cavernous room. She put her arm around Clara's shoulders. "That was awesome, don't you think? We need to check on Arundati, right? I've already checked with Meera, and it will be OK if we take food to her in the room until she gets better."

The two women headed to rooms on the upper level. When they reached Arundati's, they knocked gently. No answer, so they tiptoed in. "Oh hey, you two," said Arundati. "I was just waking up. I'm feeling a million times better. How was yoga?"

"We missed you," Clara said. "It was a wonderful class, but the best part was meditating. You're going to get better and before you know it, you'll be joining us."

"I have to leave the day after tomorrow," Samantha told them. "This morning I got a phone call from Rajeev and his parents have this huge extended family dinner planned. It's really kind of a big deal. I hate that I won't be able to pal around with you any longer. Even though we've only known each other for a few days, I feel like we've been friends for years. Don't forget that you and Dottie are invited to the wedding."

"That's so kind of you," exclaimed Arundati. "I can imagine that it will be a magnificent affair. I've heard about Indian weddings. Can't they last for days and have parades and processions? Elephants?"

"Well, yes. They are very elaborate. Mine will be fancy but not over the top. We will have a procession, I'm pretty sure."

Clara didn't want to remind her that they might be back in the states by then. Unlike Samantha, they weren't going to become expats. "That's so kind of you. If it were at all possible, we'd certainly be there. Who knows? There's still so much of India we haven't seen, the Taj Mahal, Agra, Fatepur Sikri. After Dottie gets well, we might have to make a return visit. Anything's possible."

Chatting about the day, Clara and Samantha went upstairs to Arundati's room. They entered quietly and found Ashok sitting by the bed as Arundati slept. It seemed that the Indian had appointed himself as the doctor in charge. "Ah yes, *Memsabs*, you are back just in time. Your friend is not getting better. She's been drinking lots of water but now has a fever and abdominal distress. I'm 99 percent convinced that she has amoebic dysentery. The only thing that will help her is an antibiotic called Cipro. Also, she must eat yogurt curds and rice. The diet I told you about was something I'd learned in medical school, but not so available here in India. Can one of you stay with our patient while I make contacts to get a prescription and go to a pharmacy to buy some Cipro. She needs to start taking this as soon as possible."

Samantha volunteered to do the evening floor-scrubbing for both herself and Clara. Ashok, refusing to let the women give him any money, went to obtain a prescription and get it filled. Clara took Ashok's place in the chair by Arundati's sick bed.

"Don't worry, Clara, I will do the work of two people. They'll never know that just one of us, not two, was taking care of floor duty. I'm taking a paper sack and I'll bring you back some rice and vegetables from the buffet. Stay strong."

As he left for a nearby medical clinic and the pharmacy, Ashok had a parting admonition for Clara: "Don't get too close. If this is the classic case of amoebic dysentery, it could be contagious. I reminded you and Samantha before, but I don't think anyone was listening."

Clara took Ashok's place at Arundati's bedside, pulling it a bit further away. "I'm really worried about you, Dottie. You don't mind if I go back to your old name, do you?"

"No, of course not. I'm still me, which ever version of my name you use. I think maybe it was the Arundati version that got me in this fix. If I hadn't gotten separated from you and Samantha, if I hadn't dipped into the river. That was stupid..."

"Quit beating yourself up. What's done is done and the important thing is that we didn't lose you. We got reunited and that's a miracle. With Ashok's help, we'll get you better." Clara didn't want to say anything, but her friend looked terrible. Deep circles under her eyes, her face pinched and drawn, and she looked as though she had a fever. Ashok was going to bring back a thermometer when he went to secure an antibiotic. "Have you eaten anything today?"

"Ashok brought me some rice and yogurt when you and Samantha were at yoga. He made sure I kept drinking water. He's so nice. He'll be a wonderful doctor. Do you think he's practicing on me?"

"I think he likes you and he's determined to help you get over this."

"I need to get over more than a stomach bug, Clara. I've spent my life thinking it would cure me of depression if I found my family tree, or even part of it. Before I got sick, I came to a realization that I would never locate Mother. Part of me felt guilty. After all, I'd been raised by a wonderful adoptive mom. Why wasn't that enough? Unlike your case, where there were some threads, some breadcrumbs to follow, here there is no way to trace anything."

Clara nodded her head in agreement and walked to the corner of the room where they'd stashed Dottie's gear. She got a bottle of water, opened it and brought it to her friend. "Here. You've got to keep drinking, even if you're not thirsty."

"You're taking such good care of me. I'm really lucky to have you as my friend. The sister I never had." She drank deeply from the water bottle. "You know what I've decided? It depends on what you mean by a mother. Is your mother the one who gives birth to you or the one who loves you the most? "

"After my New Mexico experience, getting close but being too late for Greta..."

"You mean because she had already passed away?"

"Yes, exactly. I decided that the one who raised me was my real mother. It gave me peace of mind and the psychic energy to do different things. To want different things. To aim for different things, if that makes sense."

"Yes! It makes perfect sense. But you'll have to excuse me, dear Clara. I'm having another attack." Arundati stumbled to the bathroom and turned on the faucet to drown out sounds of her loose bowels. Flushing, then long running the faucet as she scrubbed her hands. She emerged and collapsed back into bed. Clara had turned on a small table lamp and plumped up the pillows of Dottie's bed.

The light was growing dim, night falling. Clara did not want to mention Cipro again and Ashok's mission of mercy. She kept the conversation focused on adoption. "It seems to me that you're becoming more of a Hindu every day. First the *Kumbha Mela*, then dipping into Mother Ganges, as they call the river. Maybe India is your mother?"

"If you'd said that a month ago, I would have called you crazy. But now? It's what I'm coming to believe. You knew I was studying Hinduism at St. John's College all last year. It's the only religion I could embrace." She yawned deeply, winced, and shifted in bed. "I can't believe I've grown so weak. My stomach is queasy and I ache all over."

"This is a topic that makes us both weak. I can understand why you'd want to become Hindu. If I'd met my other mother, I would have happily embraced Native American spirituality. It seems like both of us lived between two shores — neither here, nor there. It's lonely. We both started life in a vast space that could not be filled. We have been free falling, confused by feelings difficult to share."

Dottie sighed. "I tried to hide from the feelings of guilt for not being content with my adoptive parents. But that early part would not go away. Abandonment was like a bully on the playground. It always found me."

"Yeah. I can relate. Those early feelings of abandonment. They hunt you with laser precision, reminding you that you're somehow disposable. OK, we both had decent adoptive parents.

216

They were good. They did their best. I don't know about you, but I always felt I had to be perfect. I had to make up for the daughter that my adoptive parents couldn't have. I was like a ghost, a substitute. I had to pretend to be the real daughter." Both women were silent, lost in thought.

A gentle knock interrupted the somber mood. Clara opened the door to Meera, who carried a cloth sack. "Samantha told me that Arundati was not well, so I brought yogurt and rice for her. For you, Clara, I have a curried vegetable stew." She wafted a greeting toward Dottie, whose eyes were closed. She'd slumped back into the pillow and appeared to be dozing. "The rice is for you both. Ashok, who's one of our most stalwart residents, said that Arundati should have yogurt and rice, but nothing else."

Clara was not surprised that Ashok had talked with Meera. He was probably a sort of doctor-in-residence for the *ashram*. No doubt there'd been others who came here and collapsed. India was a challenge to westerners, she'd come to realize. The overwhelmingness of the subcontinent could be brutal.

Meera brought the triple-layered metal lunch carrier to the room's one table and placed it, along with spoons and plates at the center. "Please bring these downstairs when you finish, or have your Samantha bring them to the kitchen." Clara didn't tell Meera that Samantha had floor scrubbing duty and wouldn't finish until the kitchen might be closed for the night. No point in pushing their luck; everyone here was unbelievably kind, but she couldn't let down her guard.

"I'm really starving," came a cry from the bed. "You don't have to wait on me. I can pull a chair over to the table." Dottie started to get up.

"Nothing doing, friend. I am going to wait on you. We'll have a bedside picnic and then continue the discussion we were having earlier." Clara turned on the overhead light, a bare bulb hanging from the ceiling. Austere, but perfectly adequate. Like everything else in the building. The vegetables were surprisingly delicious, sautéed in a mild curry sauce. The rice, was the best she'd ever tasted.

"I wish I could share this with you, but Dr. Ashok said nothing but very mild, bland food until we get you on antibiotics."

"You know, he's not a doctor yet," Dottie said. "He's taking a gap year before starting his internship. Or is it his residency? Anyway, he's such a gem. I can't believe he's taking such good care of me. I feel wretched, but his kindness is absolutely therapeutic."

They finished eating. Clara turned off the light and told Dottie to rest. She collected the dishes, then made her way down to the kitchen, which was still open. A few people were washing the last dishes of the evening. They were Indians dressed in white *salwar kameezes*. "*Namaskar*. Sorry to be bringing these to you so late. My friend is ill and cannot leave her room." She handed over the lunch pail, plates and utensils. "Please wash these in very hot water with lots of soap."

"Not speak English, *Memsab*," said the stout woman who seemed to be in charge. "Hot water. Yes. Soap." Obviously, though she did not speak English, she understood.

"Thank you, thank you." Clara folded her hands and bowed her head. She found interaction with the kitchen people oddly comforting. She wanted to find Samantha, who apparently was still doing floor scrubbing duty, maybe pitch in and help. However, she wasn't at all sure of which way to turn, and the last thing she needed was to lose her way. The whole place was quiet as the tomb, and she felt if she got lost, she'd never find her way back. No, best to retrace her steps back to Dottie.

Clara made her way down the corridor and climbed the narrow staircase up to the second floor. Even though every door looked the same, she knew by now that Dottie's was third from the end. The corridor was a bit dim, as lights were lowered at night to cut down on the electricity bill. Ah, there was Dottie's room. Or was it? Light streamed out from under the door. She clearly recalled turning the lights off. What was going on? Worried, she hastened her walk to a run.

As she neared the door, she heard voices. "Oh my gosh, it's you, Ashok. I forgot you were coming back from the clinic tonight. Did you get the Cipro?"

Ashok was sitting in the chair where Clara had been holding a vigil. Propped up by pillows, Dottie was still in her sick bed, but looking healthier than she had for days. Her cheeks were rosy, her dark eyes sparkled. "This man is my hero. Not only will he get me started on the antibiotic, he brought me some curd rice from a shop next to the clinic. Did you know that In India, yogurt is not called 'yogurt,' but 'curds'? Nothing against the *ashram*, but what he brought from the take-out place is a million times tastier. I just had a small taste. I have to wait an hour before having the curd rice. You're not supposed to take Cipro with dairy."

How had it come to this, Clara wondered? Certainly, she was relieved that Ashok had stepped in to help, but she was disappointed that their quest for Dottie's blood relations had turned sour. Maybe they, the adopted ones, weren't meant to trace back to their beginnings. Maybe they needed to adopt themselves. And just maybe they should start making plans to go back to Santa Fe.

"Don't you agree, Clara?" Arundati had been talking to her, but she hadn't heard. "Do you think Ashok is right?"

"Sorry, I was distracted. Right about what?"

"Maybe Mother India is enough. I could go on searching for days and weeks and never get any closer to finding my original mother, my birthparents. I could decide to adopt myself, to realize that if I accept that I had two mothers and that both, in their own ways, loved me."

"You're right. Ashok is right. That's a good thing for us both to acknowledge. Ashok, you're a wise man, and very helpful. May I pay you for the Cipro?"

"Nay. Because of my status as a medical student, the pharmacist, who is related to my father, gave me a special price. It is my way of welcoming you to India." Ashok opened a paper sack and removed a plastic bottle. "This works like magic. You'll need to take it for three days, twice a day." After washing his hands at the corner sink, he shook two capsules in his palm and took them to the patient. Dottie opened the water bottle next to her bed and gulped down the pills.

Clara felt a wave of relief, even though the illness was far from gone. Dottie would, with the help of modern pharmaceuticals, get better. That, and the special diet that Ashok was overseeing. Sadly, however, the illness was a clear sign that they needed to return home. She'd use her remaining days and Dottie's convalescence to work at the *ashram*, do yoga and meditate. There was one more thing she must do, however. She wanted to take gifts back to the Archuleta family and Estrellita, the *curandera* who'd helped her so much when her friend Annie died. At some point she'd sneak out for a quick shopping trip.

Ashok left for the men's quarters, Samantha returned from scrubbing duty, to check in on Arundati, who'd half fallen asleep sitting up. "I'm strong, and I'm not complaining," Samantha confessed, "but I'm not used to so much physical labor. Time for me to call it a day." She ran her fingers through her short blond hair. "First of all, I'm taking a long shower." She looked at Clara while walking to the door. "If you're going to join in the routine, remember that the morning meditation begins at five a.m." She blew kisses to Clara and Dottie and slipped out noiselessly.

Clara sat by the bed and closed her eyes. Even though her friend slept, she talked to her, first taking a hand and gently holding it. "Dear friend, I'm so sorry you feel rotten. I never should have let you slip out of my sight during the *Kumbha Mela* procession. If only I'd held your hand then. The last thing I remember you saying before we lost you was 'I want this to be a spiritual journey. I want us to say yes to everything.' I guess maybe that was saying yes to infections as well."

Dottie murmured something unintelligible. She was only partially awake. "Not sure," Clara continued. "I just remembered that you wanted to buy gifts before we headed back. Actually, I did as well. Does that sound familiar? We agreed that buying anything in the airport was a very bad idea. We'd pay top dollar. If you're enough better tomorrow, I'll slip out after the morning meal and shop for us both."

"Mmmmm...ok. *Dupattas...Gamchas...*"

Clara closed the door gently and walked to her room. She remembered an earlier conversation she and Dottie had about *Dupattas* and *Gamchas*. *Dupattas* were for women, the long shawls worn atop *saris*, brilliantly colored and usually worn over one shoulder. *Gamchas* were long scarves worn universally by men. They'd decided to buy a sampling of each, enough for everyone on their gift lists. She could do that tomorrow if Ashok could watch over Dottie. It was likely that he'd be all too happy to have bedside duty.

A long shower, slipping into her light cotton nightgown and nearly asleep before her head touched the pillow, Clara began a night of deep sleep. Something about the environment worked like magic for her. Usually a very light sleeper, at Sivananda Vrindavan she had no trouble sinking into the deepest slumber. However, this night's sleep was not without dreams...

*She was by an ocean. Or was it the river Ganges? She was barefooted and in the water up to her knees, a strong tide nearly knocking her over. The water changed from murky brown to a bluish translucency. She looked down and could see her feet. She walked out toward the horizon. Definitely, this was the ocean. Water as far as the eye could see. Her foot hit something hard. A piece of coral that resembled a small hand. She fished it up and turned back toward the shore. A strong wind knocked her over and she was underwater, then struggling to regain her footing. Gasping for air, she was going to die...*

Before that happened, the nightmare ended and she was awake. After savoring the relief of being alive, she realized that she'd lost the hand-shaped piece of coral. She also realized that there was something they had to do before leaving the subcontinent: return the hand of Ganesh to Indian waters. It was so long ago that they'd read the journals in Aunt Miriam's attic, she'd totally forgotten about that mission. It was far more important than shopping, but as Arundati was recovering, she hoped to accomplish both.

It meant leaving the *ashram* once again, leaving Arundati in the care of Ashok and Samantha. How could she? On the other hand, it would give her a sense of progress. They knew that the shopping wasn't as important as returning the ancient relic to India's rivers. She realized that they may have misplaced the hand and she would have to interrogate Dottie to try to locate it.

And she would have to do it without upsetting her friend. Pondering that, she carefully dressed in a new *salwar kameez* she'd purchased in Chennai. It was that beautiful shade of orange unique to India. She went to the kitchen, got curds and rice and brought them back up to Dottie's room. She'd brought enough for both of them, so she sat with her friend as they enjoyed breakfast together. It was hard to bring up the subject, but might as well get it over with.

"Do you remember the hand of Ganesh that we were going to throw into water when we got to India? With everything that's happened, we seem to have lost track of it. It has a curse that has gone through the ages. There is only one way the curse can be lifted, according to that manuscript we found in your aunt's archives. We must return it to an Indian body of water."

Dottie sighed. "My God, that seems like an eternity ago. Yes, of course I remember. That's the main reason we decided to come to India in the first place. It helped shape our mission. Along with clues to my lineage. Since we obviously haven't succeeded at that..."

"Sadly, it looks as though we aren't going to," interrupted Clara. "We might as well fulfill an old person's dying wish."

"That ancestor who's somehow distantly related to my family. Adoptive family, that is." Dottie always tried to make clear which family she was talking about. "Yes, that's something we can do. And we should." Next, Dottie asked the question Clara dreaded. "Do we even know where the hand is? Did we leave it in Chennai in storage at the hotel? Or do we have it here in one of our packs?"

Clara had to admit that she didn't know. She promised to look thoroughly through everything she had stuffed into her heavy-duty backpack. It was a small thing, the stone hand, and could easily be tucked inside a rolled-up pair of travel pants or tucked into the bottom of her toiletry bag. She'd hadn't remembered it until her dream last night. The nightmare. She opted against telling Dottie about the dream. She might be suffering a sort of Ganges PTSD, and it would not do to mention

222

her watery immersion in the Ganges, the probable cause of Dottie's current illness. Accident or not, it had been traumatic.

She made arrangements with Samantha and Ashok to look after Dottie. After getting detailed instructions from Meera, she embarked on a mission to buy the gifts they wanted to take back with them. In private, she told Dottie her plan to also look for a place to throw the hand of Ganesh into an Indian waterway. "It might not be offshore of Mahabalipuram, and it might not be the Ganges, but at least it will be a tributary of the Mother River."

"You won't believe this, Clara, but last night I actually found that forgotten artifact. It was actually in the middle of the night. I'd gotten up with another attack of Kali's revenge."

"You mean diarrhea? I thought you were over that. Aren't you taking the Cipro that Ashok brought you?"

"Yes, this wasn't a bad attack, and they're few and far between. Anyway, I was rummaging through my pack for my camping headlight. Not that I needed it, but for some reason I suddenly worried about being without electricity. I wanted a light source within reach, on the stand beside my bed."

"And you found the hand?"

"It was in the case that held the headlight, tucked away in the bottom of the drawstring bag. A weird place, I know, but there it was."

"That's perfect. Just leave it there, and we'll both remember how to find it. So here's my plan. I'll buy the *dupattas* and *gamchas* and I'll also try to find a bridge over the Yumana where we can toss the hand. You have to be there as well as me. It's important that we do it together." She paused for a long moment. "After you get completely better, of course."

Dottie agreed with the plan. Ashok would be coming to her room with her breakfast on a tray and Clara would wait with her until he arrived. Samantha breezed in while the two were talking quietly. "You look as though you're immersed in a conversational marathon." She was in high spirits, as this was the week she would be going to meet her fiancé's parents. "I'm really glad to see that Dottie's getting better. I guess the Cipro is getting the job done."

"It's Cipro, but it's also Ashok," murmured Dottie with a smile. "I can't believe how thoughtful that man is. If I recover completely, he'll be the one to take credit." As she said this, her cheeks flushed.

Clara, carefully noting that mentioning Ashok's name coincided with the flush, chimed in. "I feel guilty. Ashok has been doing everything, including staying on duty while I've gone to some meditation sessions. Dottie is so much better every day."

"I think it's more Ashok than Cipro," said Samantha. "Are you falling for your caregiver? Worse things could happen. These Indian men can be captivating. I'm proof of that."

"Don't be ridiculous, Sammy. I'm just very grateful. We've had a lot of time to talk. He's the only man I've ever met who doesn't glaze over when I bring up my adoption issues. With other guys, I have to quickly change the subject or they run the other direction. It turns out that Ashok's parent died in a boating accident when he was seven years old. His aunt and uncle raised him. He understands why I'm disappointed that I'll probably never get to meet my original mother. He's helping me come to terms with it....And speaking of Ashok, here he is."

The slender young man entered Dottie's room with a tray of curds and rice from the kitchen. "Hello *Memsabs*. Here I am, service with a smile. Dottie, I hope you took two capsules of Cipro at least an hour ago." He held up a bowl. "This freshly made yogurt will help you get stronger in no time. I've also got more bottles of water that should be enough for the morning."

Clara was about to depart. "What time will you be back?" Dottie sounded a bit anxious. "One of us getting lost was enough. Any idea?"

"According to Meera, the bazaar is nearby, maybe eight blocks. I can't imagine that shopping will take that long. Unless there's an English bookstore. I might go in to browse for a short time. Samantha, I'll do double duty for you tonight with the floor scrubbing. You've been covering for me for too long. I owe you."

"Just go," said Dottie. "We'll be fine here and my advisers—her term for Ashok and Samantha— may take me out walking on the grounds later this morning. Be safe and be sure to buy enough to have gifts for everyone at home." She blew Clara some air kisses and then turned her attention to the food tray Ashok placed on the table.

Clara picked up her backpack, slung it over her shoulder and prepared to go searching for *dupattas*, *gamchas* and a body of water. She went downstairs for a final consultation with Meera, who stood cheerfully at the main desk, on duty even though it looked as though there was absolutely nothing to do. She met Clara's *namaste* with a return greeting and a dazzling smile.

"*Memsab* Clara, I have written down the name and address of the *ashram* in English and in Hindi. Downtown it is easy to take a wrong turn. Please put it in a safe place in case you need to hire a taxi to get back here."

"That's so kind of you, Meera. If you could suggest some good places to shop. Dottie and I have promised to bring back some gifts to friends in the states. Also, I need to know if there are any bridges one can traverse for good overviews of the Yamuna or the Ganges rivers. Bridges with a safe place on the side for pedestrians."

As soon as she mentioned 'bridges,' Clara felt she needed to explain. Rather than telling Meera about the hand of Ganesh and the goal of returning it to a body of water, she made up a story about her uncle who loved to collect photos of rivers all over the world. It seemed better than going into the long story about the artifact. Mentioning a Hindu god might quickly get her into murky conversational territory.

Meera looked puzzled, but only for an instant, and then her dazzling smile returned. "Ah yes, some of our relatives can have very interesting hobbies. I have an aunt, Patricia Patel, who loves photos of walls. Stone walls, wooden walls, plastered walls...any walls. No matter where I go, I'm on the lookout to see if I can I take a photo for Aunt Patty. Oh, but your question. There are two possibilities for bridges over rivers."

"Could you write them down for me? You can use this same paper." Clara handed Meera the address note.

"Both are magnificent," Meera said as she added information to Clara's paper. "The Old Naini Bridge and the New Yamuna bridge both traverse the Yanuma. The New Yamuna was completed just last year and it has the best area for pedestrians. Did you know that Allahabad is the site of the Trivani Sangam, the confluence of the Yamuna, the Ganges and the Saraswati rivers. It is a very sacred confluence."

Hoping to leave soon rather than chatting the morning away, Clara abruptly cut in with a question. "That's fascinating, Meera, but I also need to get back to Arundati as soon as possible. So could you give me a couple ideas for places to buy gifts?"

"Ah yes, *Memsab*. You would find everything and more at Vivekananda Marg or Mahatma Gandhi Marg. I will write those places down. Everyone is very gracious, English speaking, and they take credit cards. They are very accustomed to dealing with Americans. Um, what I mean is that they are very friendly toward Americans."

"Any landmarks I should look for to find Vivekananda?"

"The shops are very near City Hotel. You don't want to go any further than Swaroop Rani Nehru Hospital. That will definitely take you out of the best shopping areas. I wish I could go with you, but we are expecting some young people from the Netherlands who have booked far ahead to stay at the *ashram*. I must be here to give them an orientation. Like you, they have been traveling in India for weeks."

Feeling a bit confused about where exactly she should be going, Clara thanked Meera. She realized that she had not packed enough water, just one bottle, but then told herself she could probably buy more at the Indian equivalent of America's Seven-Eleven shops.

She might have to save the bridge search for another time. This time, she would concentrate on shopping. Dottie might need another week, or even two, to completely recover. She would buy their gifts to get that out of the way and use Dottie's recovery time to soak in the atmosphere, to attend the meditations, do the morning and afternoon yoga, and yes, scrub floors. She donned a sun hat, hoisted her backpack straps around her shoulders, said goodbye to Meera, and stepped out into the blazing sun.

It was strangely exhilarating to be completely alone. Meera had sketched a line drawing of where to go. Just as instructed, she turned right and walked toward what she hoped was Vivekananda Marg. After the quiet and relative solitude of the *ashram*, the outside world made her a little dizzy. Like being back in the *Kumbha Mela*. However, this wasn't a religious pilgrimage. Just another day on the city streets of India.

She didn't want to appear lost, so she tucked the information paper in a fanny pack that she wore in addition to her backpack. Deliberately, she'd tossed a *dupatta* over her shoulders. It covered her backpack and also her fanny pack. The latter she wore with the pockets at the front. In it she had a credit card, some *rupees*, and — on the advice of Meera — her passport. All of this made her look a little lumpy, like a traveling tent, but she felt secure under the combination of coverings.

Taking a deep breath, she decided to quit worrying and look more closely at the surroundings. It would take her at least thirty minutes, she estimated, to reach Mahatma Gandhi Marg. Though the sidewalk was wide, she was shoulder to shoulder with women, teenagers, and men. Sweeping diversity and the same kind of bustling she'd discovered in any other big city she'd ever visited.

Shop after endless tiny shop. There was a Radio Shack, a custom *sari* shop ("Tailoring while you wait"), a candy store, a "battery emporium," tiny restaurants the width of a train car selling all kinds of dishes, none of which Clara could identify. That was all to her right. To the left, there was a dense river of mad, teeming traffic. Not just cars but motorcycles, bicycles, little vehicles that looked like golf carts, even an occasional lumbering elephant topped by a *mahoot*. With all of this, there were beggars weaving in and out of the melee. Amazingly, no one was getting mowed down.

## Chapter Forty-one
## Chennai

"*Memsab*, you want souvenirs?" asked a petite woman in what looked like sackcloth. Over the woman's shoulders were dozens of embroidered cloth purses, an array of *pashmina* shawls. They covered one side of the peddler. On the other side, she touted garlands of tiny stuffed elephants, fold-out packets of post cards and many other trinkets. "Very beautiful. Good to take home to your family. Price is cheap. What would you like to see?" Trinkets and shawls were unfurled and waved in front of Clara.

"No. No, thank you. Very nice, but no thank you. I'm looking for Mahatma Gandhi Marg. Is it nearby?" Maybe this woman would tell her if she was on the right track.

"Do not buy gifts there. You will pay too much. My crafts much nicer and half the price." She draped a sage green *pashmina* over Clara's shoulders. "This is perfect for you. Name your price. Many colors available."

Other street vendors were gathering around Clara. She should never have talked to the woman at all. Now her goal was to get away. The peddlers were buzzing around like flies. Every one with wares, all taking a mile a minute, waving purses, handicrafts, bells, trinkets in front of her. This wouldn't do. After a loud "No" and what she hoped were the correct words, "Nay, nay," she fought her way through the mob. She was practically running.

Just in time she saw a sign for the Saroop Rani Nehru Hospital, a landmark that Meera included in her directions. The turn to Mahatma Gandhi Marg was supposed to be right after that. To her relief, there it was: a street sign in English, one that she could read. It was the biggest department store in this part of Allahabad, a vast emporium.

Compared to the surrounding shops and stands, the Mahatma Gandhi was luxurious. A turbaned man— Clara thought he must be an official door *wallah*— greeted her with a friendly *namaste* as he held open the door for her. The array of goods was like what she'd seen in American stores. She spent twenty minutes just wandering around the racks of clothing, the cosmetic counter, a section of electronics, children's playwear, shoes, purses, luggage.

The shop men and women wore black suits with crisp white shirts or blouses, very trim and professional in their manner.

Finally, she was noticed. "Miss, may I help you?" asked a tall, slender Indian woman with chiseled features and her black hair pulled back into a bun. "Are you looking for anything in particular? We have several floors of fashions and housewares and I will be very happy to escort you to the right section. Our vast array can be overwhelming."

"Thank you. I'm looking for *dupattas* and *gamchas*. I need them for gifts to take back home."

"Oh, I see. We used to have an ethnic section, and we will once again, but that department is being renovated, so temporarily, we carry neither of those. You might find them at Grehasti Departmental Store. They have *saris*, *salwar kameezes*, *pashminas* and hand-embroidered jackets. I am sure they'd carry what you are searching for."

"Is it within walking distance? I am staying at the Sivanandra Vrindavan Ashram, about a mile from here, but I would like to buy these gifts today rather than coming back. You see, I'm on foot."

The shop lady frowned. "Walking? It is many blocks from here, near the Swaroop Rani Nehru Hospital and about four blocks from the Allahabad Museum. I would be happy to call a taxi for you. It's a service we like to offer our foreign guests."

Well, why not? Clara thought to herself. Thanks to Dottie's Aunt Miriam, their funds for the India trip were far from depleted. They'd been frugal, and the *ashram* was free except for donations. Feeling indulgent, she agreed to the shop lady's offer. In a short time, she was in a yellow and black sedan being whisked to the Grehasti Departmental Store. Why it was called "departmental" rather than "department" was a mystery, but if they carried the items she needed, they'd be fine.

Traffic was getting snarled up. Close to the noon hour. This was taking a long time. Had they been driving for an hour? Clara tried to ask if it was much further, but it soon became apparent that the driver did not speak much English. Her anxiety mounted, and she repeated the name of their destination: "Grehasti Departmental Store."

In that opposite Indian way of nodding "yes," the driver shook his head from side to side. "Yes, Grehasti. Soon there."

The New Swaroop Rani Nehru Hospital came into view. It dwarfed everything around it. Then, in five minutes, they were at the storefront of Grehasti. Not as big and modern as the Mohatma Gandhi, but still much finer than the humble store stalls

229

on either side. Clara breathed more easily. This was going to be do-able after all. "Thank you. *Isaka Mooly Kitana Hai*?" Meera had coached her on how to ask "How much does it cost," and also told her the cost should be less than five dollars, around 300 *rupees*.

The driver turned his head around and looked at his passenger. It wasn't at all clear that he'd understood her question, but he'd known what she was trying to ask. He pointed to the meter, which read 600. This was twice as much as it should have been, but Clara didn't know how to negotiate. At least not in Hindi.

"Too much," she said, as she sidled out of the cab onto the curb. For a minute she was afraid of being locked in. "How about 500?," she asked, as she put one foot outside the door onto the curb. The man behind the wheel shook his head, the Indian way of disagreeing. " Nay. Seex hunnard. Fair price."

Clara sighed, but did not immediately give in. "What about 550 *rupees*?" She held out the bills.

"No good." His tone was surly and his look dark. The head again shaking up and down. "Americans rich. No good." But even as he spoke these words, the driver reached out and snatched the bills. He nearly drove away with half of her still in the cab. She wobbled and regained her balance, took a deep breath, and tried to appear calm. A small group of people were standing around gawking. Probably not the first time they'd such a thing as a squabble between cab driver and passenger.

Clara's cheek burned, but she held herself erect and calmly walked into the glass doors of Grehasti Departmental Store. At least people would speak English here, and hopefully their wares would be labeled with fixed prices. She'd learned, however, that bargaining was expected in this country, so she mentally geared up to think prices. She didn't exactly feel that she'd be cheated, but she didn't want to seem like a gullible American who would just believe anything.

Just as in the Mahatma Gandhi Marg, the Grehasti Departmental was stuffed with merchandise. It was tastefully arranged and she was tempted to start looking at everything. But she had a mission and enough time had been wasted already.

A display of *saris* and *dupattas* occupied an entire corner of Grehasti's first floor. "Ah, here they are!" Clara said to nobody. She seemed to be talking to herself a lot today, maybe because no one around could understand her. Or maybe she needed help, she thought grimly.

Speaking of help, it appeared in the form of a young woman in a gold and white *sari* — apparently the "uniform" the female staff of Grehasti — appeared at her side. "What is *Memsab* hoping to find? My name is Avindra and I can help you find whatever you wish. Our store is full of many treasures and the finest quality. Would this be for you or for gifts? Would you like to look at locally created goods. We have many."

"Well, yes. I need *dupattas*, to take home to friends. *Dupattas* and *gamchas*, probably a couple dozen of each. And I might want to buy a *sari* for myself. I'm thinking about it, anyway."

Avindra thumbed through the stack of *dupattas* next to them. There were paisley designs, floral motifs, multicolored stripes, dotted, a rainbow of vibrant plain colors, *dupattis* with the animals of India around their borders: a vast array. "We have cotton, light weight woolens, silk. You will find hundreds to choose from. And *Memsab*, you must look at our *sari* possibilities. What better souvenir for yourself, and here at Grehasti we carry by far the finest selection anywhere and the best prices. While you choose which of the *dupattas* you would like I will find some *saris* that I think would suit you."

The saleslady brought out a gorgeous plum colored silk *sari*. It had a gold border with a lovely band of cobalt blue lining the gold and several cream-colored embroidered stripes on either side. The border alone was a work of art. If she didn't wear it, she could drape it over a bookcase and display it. But somehow, Clara could envision herself wearing it to a social event back home in New Mexico. As if she went to that many social events...Or maybe to a night at Santa Fe Opera. She shouldn't, but why not? When would she ever have this chance again? "Do I need to try it on?"

"No, *Memsab*. I picked out the right size for your slender body type, and since it is a wrap-around skirt, it fits most sizes. Come with me to the mirror and you can hold the *dupatta* — the shawl part — to see how well it suits you."

They walked to the three-paneled mirror and Clara saw that it did in fact suit her. Maybe she should buy one for Dottie as well. It would give her the incentive to get back on her feet sooner rather than later. "I have a best friend I'm traveling with who couldn't come with me today, but I think she would also love to

231

have a *sari*. Maybe something in red, with green and gold trim, She's a little shorter than I am, and I am a bit stockier. The *sari* is a great style. It flatters all types."

Even as she spoke, Avindra, holding the plum *sari* as if it were the crown jewels, walked over to an entire table of *saris*, all folded into cellophane-wrapped packets. "You can see that we have a great variety."

Clara pulled out a red packet from the center stack. "This is small, right?" she asked Avinda. "Is it OK to open it up?"

"By all means, open the package. You need to see more of the border and look at the blouse that goes under the *dupatta*. This combination — red, green and gold — is one of our most popular. I think your friend will thank you for having such good taste."

Clara unfolded the layers of silk. "Ah yes, these colors absolutely glow. I can see Dottie wearing this and looking so elegant. If I hadn't already chosen the plum, this would be my top choice."

"*Memsab* can buy more than one. You will find nothing like this when you go back home. And as we say in India, you cannot have too many *saris*."

"I would not want one exactly like my friend's. No, I'll stick with just one. Now let's see the *dupattas* and *gamchas* and then I might need your help with directions to get back to my *ashram*." They walked to another aisle in the sprawling first floor, where Clara picked out a dozen each of the gift. But instead of asking for directions to the *ashram*, she found herself asking how to find the nearest bridge. While she was out, it might be a good idea to find a good dropping off point. After all, a major part to their mission was to return the hand of Ganesh, that ancient relic, to Indian waters. Ideally, it would have been thrown into the Bay of Bengal. Or, they could have tossed it back to Mother India's waters during the *Kumbha Mela*. But, Dottie had tossed herself in at that point. So, a bridge over the Yumana would have to do.

Apparently, she'd been standing lost in thought for quite a while. Avindra asked a second time, "How would *Memsab* like to pay for these purchases?"

"Of course. I forgot that I hadn't given you my credit card. There's a sign on the door that announced that you take

Visa. I assume you also take Master Card?" She was maxing out on both cards, so she carefully juggled between the two. As Avindra ran the credit card, she tried to think of how she should couch her next question.

It was time to sign the sales tape. As she did, she decided to just come out and say it, except for the part about returning the hand of Ganesh. "You've been so helpful. I have just one more favor to ask."

"Happy to help, *Memsab*. What is it you would like?"

"Just directions to a view of the sacred river Yumana. I heard about a new bridge that has a pedestrian walkway and overlooks the water. My friend and I have to go back home soon, and I'd like to take some photos. We walked part of the *Kumbha Mela*, along the Ganges, but it was too hectic to do anything but just keep walking."

"Ah yes, of course," Avindra interrupted. "I understand. Unfortunately, the old Naini Bridge is not suitable for walking. There is talk of building a new bridge, but it is at least a decade off, maybe two. I would recommend taking an excursion. You will find various companies with guides who will take you on a day trip that includes the sacred rivers."

Clara sighed. If only it had been the relic that had been dropped into the Ganges rather than her roommate. They would have to figure something out before they left for home. But it was now mid-afternoon, and she'd meant to take just the morning for her excursion. She took her package from Avindra, thanked her again, and stepped out into the hot, crowded sidewalk. She realized that she had no idea whether to turn left or right. Or how to page a taxi.

# Chapter Forty-two

Surely, with the name of the *ashram*, Sivanandra Vrindavan, a knowledgeable cab driver could take her back. But how to flag one down? She stood on the curb as one, two, three yellow cabs sped by. They all were full of passengers. With sinking heart, Clara, still in front of the "departmental store," walked up and down the block trying in vain to flag down a taxi. She went back inside the store but Avindra had left on a lunch break. It was three p.m., Clara noted, but if stores here were like they were in the states, lunch breaks could come whenever. She'd never worked in retail but had friends who told her how they had to grab breaks when they could.

Maybe someone else could advise her about catching a taxi. Ah, here was a young man dressed in a black business suit. "Excuse me, I need to take a taxi to Sivanandram Vrindavan Ashram. I've been trying for half an hour with no luck. Could you advise me on a better place to flag down a cab?" She held out the slip of paper that Meera had filled out, with its name and address written in both English and Hindi.

"Is this the North Quadrant, *Membsab*? Allahabad is serviced by taxis who only go north/south or east/west? To advise you on where best to find your transportation, I need your quadrant."

Clara had no idea. She had not anticipated any trouble getting back, but now - between being directionally challenged and not speaking the native tongue, she felt alarmed. Taking a deep breath, then another, she said "Um, I think the North Quadrant, but I'm not sure. If you have a public phone, I could call the *ashram*." Even as she said this, she remembered that Meera had told her about having the afternoon off. A volunteer would be taking over the desk for her. And that volunteer — one of the residents like herself — might not speak English. No, it might be better to just go to the other side of the street in the hope of getting a driver who would understand her.

Thanking the black-suited young man, she walked on. It was clouding up and looked like the heavens would burst open at any moment. Thunder rumbled in the distance and the sky darkened. It was impossible to cross the street safely, cars zooming along amid motorcycles, bicyclists, pedestrians, an occasional camel or elephant. The smells of human squalor and car fumes, which she hadn't noticed on her way to the "departmental store," were suddenly overwhelming. She realized that she'd forgotten to eat lunch. As soon as she crossed the wildly busy street, she stopped to dig out an energy bar from her backpack. Once on the other side, she stepped inside a storefront to unwrap and eat it. How did anyone do anything in these masses?

"*Memsab*, you need help? My name is Charles, and I have often helped tourists here in Allahabad. You might say it is my hobby." The short mustachioed man in western clothes was at her side, ostensibly wanting to be of service. At least he wasn't selling anything. Or then again, wasn't he selling his services? At this point, even if she had to pay *baksheesh*, it would be worth it to find a way back. Arundati and Ashok must be worrying about her. She had promised to be back by lunchtime, and now it was close to evening.

She finished the last bites of her energy bar and rummaged in her backpack for Meera's note, which included the name and address of the *ashram*. However, it was not there. The note had vanished with its name, address, and phone number. She must have somehow lost it in the "departmental store," and she couldn't for the life of her remember it.

"I need to go to Vrindavan Ashram. The full name is Sivanandra Vindavan and I think it's on Yogita Lane. It's in the North Quadrant. Can you flag a taxi for me that will take me to the North Quadrant?"

"There is not an *ashram* in the North Quadrant, *Memsab*. Maybe you mean the Northwest? The taxis on this side of the boulevard go to both north and northwest. If you have a public phone, I could make a call. I can escort you to a pay telephone and help you with the dialing."

"Thank you, but I seem to have misplaced the phone number." This was feeling hopeless. How could she have let herself get lost? What was Arundati thinking, and who was taking care of her? She made a desperate effort to appear calm, and though he was a complete stranger, it was a comfort to have this so-called "Charles" by her side.

As the day darkened and the splattering of rain turned into a steady downpour, Charles pulled an umbrella from his satchel and put it over both of them. "*Memsab*, I have a solution. Let's go to a tea shop with a pay telephone, and I will use the phone to call an operator, who, we must hope, can give us the address of your Sivanandra Vrindavan. It may have another name, but we

235

will track down the information and get you in a taxi headed there."

"I'll buy you a glass of *chai*, and I'll pay you for your trouble." Though it was too premature to celebrate a rescue, Clara was cautiously optimistic.

"*Memsab* need not pay me. It is good *karma* for me to help a stranded foreigner." Charles led them to a tiny hole in the wall place that served *chai* and pastries. There was a pay phone on the back wall. "I will accept your offer of *chai*, and I recommend one for you as well. A glass of *chai* makes everything seem better."

Loud thundering sounded and a bolt of lightning lit the sky. It was now, though just late afternoon, more night than day. Clara ordered *chai* for two and gratefully sipped hers. Charles drank his glass down in one gulp. "Ah, very refreshing. And now I will call our information center so you can catch a taxicab that will take you home. Meanwhile, I encourage you to try one of the *samosas*. They are a most favored snack in India. Very nutritious."

That sounded wonderful. "May I order some for you as well?"

"No thank you, *Memsab*, as I had a very late lunch. The *chai* was more than enough. You should try both the potato and the cauliflower...would you like for me to order for you?"

"Yes, please." After which followed a rapid exchange in Hindi between Charles and the shop proprietor.

"One *rupee* for two. Is that OK?"

"Yes, I think so. Is that a fair price?"

"*Memsab*, it is standard, and not too much. Because I am with you, this shopkeeper will not overcharge you. You see, I bring him many customers, so he knows he must be fair."

The order was placed, Clara paid and moved with her *chai* and *samosas* from the counter to a tiny table on the other side of the shop. It was really no wider than a hallway, and she was glad they seemed to be the only customers. Small wonder, as outside, the heavens had burst open and the rain was falling in sheets. How strange to be sitting in the middle of downtown Allahabad, in a tea shop, at the mercy of a total stranger. Of all the surreal sights and events during this Indian sojourn, this had to be the most unimaginable. Despite all this, the *samosas* were delicious. She was just finishing her second one when Charles sat down across from her.

"Very good news, *Memsab*. I found out where your *ashram* is located, off the road that eventually leads to Ustapur Mahmudabad Village, just beyond St. Joseph College and Allahabad University. You are right, it is on Yogita Lane. And now we can go back out to the street and I will help you flag a taxicab and also make sure that the driver understands your destination." The tea shop proprietor had suddenly gotten busy with other customers coming for *chai* and pastries.

Clara was overwhelmed with relief. She finished the last bite of a cauliflower *samosa*, wiped her fingers on the paper napkin it was served on. She reached in her fanny pack for a ten *rupee* note. She wasn't sure if that was enough or too much, but her gratitude was intense. Even if it was too much, in a way it was not enough. Before they left the tea shop, she secured the bill in the outer pouch of her pack, to have it ready.

By the time they stepped out to the street, the rain had diminished to a light mist. Bare light bulbs, strung along looped wires, lined the streets announcing the small shops selling everything from textiles to vegetables to electronics. The sidewalk was filled with swarms of men, women, and children. This seemed to be a busy shopping time, at least for small businesses. The "departmental store" across the traffic-filled street was dark except for the large window displays.

"Here we are," said Charles, as a cab stopped right in front of them. He leaned over to the driver's side. Not a man, but a woman. Indian but wearing western clothes. "Uma knows the area you want, and she'll take you right there. She speaks English and will, I have no doubt, take you where you need to go." Clara slipped the *rupee* bill to him as he opened the back door of the taxi and ushered her in. "Thank you, or as we say in Hindi, *Isaka Mooly Kitana Hai*. Good luck, *Memsab*."

Before leaving, however, it seemed that Charles needed to have a final consultation. He spoke to Uma in Hindi. The word "*ashram*" was repeated several times. "*Haan, haan*," Uma replied, shaking her head from side to side. Clara knew that the head movement indicated "yes" rather than "no." She also knew that *haan* meant yes. So, it seemed that she would not spend the rest of the night wandering around Allahabad. Maybe driving around, but at least not outdoors and on foot.

Normally, she would have exchanged pleasantries with a driver, but she was simply too weary. Maybe just a few comments: "Thank you for driving me to Sivaanandra Vrindavan Ashram. Please drive me as directly as possible."

"That's my job, *Memsab*." came the reply.

At the mercy of strangers once again, Clara thought to herself. She was growing weary of this trip, of India, of being sick with worry about Dottie. Why had it seemed like a good idea to go to India? Why had she led Dottie on this aborted attempt to track down her parent? Maybe it was for the best; maybe birthmothers did not want to be found. Reunions did not always end happily. Some were not meant to be.

Uma at the wheel, the taxi was zooming through heavy traffic. Horns honked, the kaleidoscope of lights lining every street signaled shops that were open. Hordes of people still everywhere, walking with children, parcels, groceries. Motorcycles and bicycles. Clara wondered if there was ever a time when streets were quiet and deserted. Surely people had to sleep sometime. Then again, many had nowhere to sleep. The teeming homeless just rolled out mats or used cardboard boxes and no doubt filled the city parks.

Uma was weaving the taxi in and out of traffic. It seemed rude not to address her. "Your city is beautiful. I hope to see more of it before I leave India and my friend and I go back to the states." She made the first part up, as they really did not see the city before checking into Sivanandra Vrindavan. Who knew if it was beautiful? She would like to find out.

"You are traveling with a friend? He did not come with you today?"

"It's a *she*, not a *he*. Arundati, I usually call her Dottie. Unfortunately, she became ill a few days ago and is recovering. I'm sure she is worried about me. I was supposed to be back by afternoon, at least sometime before dinner. I lost my paper with the phone number or I would have called. Dottie is getting better, and then we plan to settle into the *ashram* routine." Clara didn't want to mention the possible source of Dottie's illness, the Ganges. For her, the so-called holy waters, had been toxic. Better steer clear of that topic. Her goal was to get home safely, and Uma was probably a devout Hindu. If Uma asked, she would just say it was something Dottie had eaten. Food poisoning.

Fortunately, Uma did not probe her on illness. Instead, she asked, "Who is taking care of your friend today? These places do not usually have a physician on the staff. My sister, who lives in your country, married to an American, came to visit me last year and then spent a month at an *ashram*. She said it changed her life."

Horns blasted away and several times their vehicle was almost side-swiped. It seemed that there were no real lanes and everything surged ahead helter-skelter. Clara admired anyone who could manage such wild traffic and still carry on a rational conversation. She wondered to herself how old Uma was, if she had a family, how much money she made, what led her to becoming a taxi driver.

Instead, she asked, "How, exactly was your sister changed by her spiritual retreat? Because of Dottie's illness I haven't had a chance to really experience much yet. But when she gets better, I will meditate, do yoga, and daily work. I'm really looking forward to it. Time ran out and her question went unanswered."

"Here we are at Yogita Lane," Uma said, slowing down the cab. "There are not street lights here. Will you recognize the building?"

Clara wasn't at all sure that she would. The street was lined with massive cement walls and ironwork gates that looked tightly locked. Fortunately, there were metal plaques on most of them announcing what was behind the walls. They drove by an area of tall palm trees, shrubs and gardens, and she remembered that the *ashram* was across from a park.

"I think we're close. This is looking very familiar."

Uma was leaning out of the window, reading wall plaques and translating their names. "Institute of Herbal Medicine, International Language School, Baba's Home Bakery. Ah, Sivanandra Vrindavan Ashram: Established 1970. Would that be your place?"

"Yes, the *ashram* is about 15 years old. This entrance looks familiar. Um...Would you mind going in with me, just in case it's not the right building?"

"Of course. We'll get you safely indoors. This neighborhood is a good one and quite safe, I think, but there are *goondas* everywhere, even in the best parts of town. And it is very dark, no streetlights or businesses. I will not even charge you extra for this special escorting."

But, a grateful Clara thought to herself, I will pay you extra, you dear, kind woman. She took the lead, opening the creaking wrought iron door for both of them. It was muggy after the recent rain, and very hot. They walked in silence over the moss-covered brick pathway, at last coming to a small wooden door. It did not look impressive enough to be the main entrance but Clara was too frazzled to recall what that door had looked like. But, happily, it entered into the reception area. Meera, who must never sleep, was still at the desk. Clara thanked Uma and paid her, adding a generous tip.

"*Memsab*, we were all very worried about you. Did you get lost? You were gone all day and half the night. Are you alright?"

"I'm fine. Really tired, but fine. I did get a little bit lost. But Dottie's the one to be worried about. I need to go upstairs to see her right away."

"You'll find *Sahib* Ashok with her. He brought her meals to her and has not left her side since you left. You'll see."

Clara ran upstairs, two steps at a time. Forgetting her exhaustion, she raced down the quiet hall to Dottie's room. She knocked...No answer. "Dottie! It's me, Clara. OK to come in?" Still no answer.

Unable to stand the suspense, she gently opened the door. The room was empty. No Dottie. No Ashok. Her friend must have taken a turn for the worse. Maybe Ashok had taken her to a clinic. Fighting off panic, Clara left Dottie's room and walked several doors down to her quarters. It was good to deposit the packages from the day's shopping on a chair. Finally! She collapsed on the narrow single bed and closed her eyes. She must have fallen asleep because the next thing she knew, Dottie was at her bedside.

"Oh my God, I've been so worried about you. Today was a turning point. Ashok tended me so well that I'm worlds better. I had such a good day that I decided to go to the evening lecture. You didn't see the note I left for you on the table?" Dottie's color had returned, her long black hair was pulled back into a sleek bun and her dark eyes sparkled.

We've changed places, Clara thought to herself. Now I'm the sick and feeble one. "That's such a relief. I think we owe a lot to Ashok. While I was busy getting lost and wandering about, he worked a miracle. You look like a new woman, and just wait until you see what I bought for us."

"You got more than our gifts to take home?" Dottie gave her friend a thank-you hug. "Well, I'm really too worn out to appreciate anything, and I think you need to take a hot shower and get a good night's sleep. We can reconnoiter tomorrow morning. You're the best, but now I'll slip away and retire for the night.

Wait until you hear about the lecture series I signed us up for, all about the four paths. We're going to dive deep into India's ancient teachings. We both have to scrub the kitchen and dining room tomorrow night, so the lecture will have to be after that."

It had been quite an endless day, one that Clara would never forget. After Dottie left, she disrobed and turned on the faucet for a shower. She stepped into the tiny corner-of-the-room bathroom and let water run until it grew warm. Eventually it would be hot. She noticed approvingly that despite all the rice and curry she'd been consuming that she hadn't gained weight, at least not very much. For once in her life, she was happy. She was without a boyfriend for the first time in years. For some reason, however, that made her feel liberated rather than sad.

Soaping herself thoroughly and letting the water, now almost too hot, massage her back, shoulders, arms and legs — every inch of her. She felt the day's tension melt away. The *ashram* had never seemed more like a haven. Dried, in a nightgown and stretched out in her single bed, Clara decided to count ten things for which she felt gratitude. It was an old practice, something she did a couple years ago when she taught at the American Indian Academy. Not aloud but silently.

Though she could barely keep awake, she managed to get to ten and they went as follows:

1. She wasn't still wandering Allahabad and had managed to return "home".

2. Arundati recovered and was back in action.

3. She and Dottie had accomplished their goal of walking in the *Kumbha Mela*.

4. They'd absorbed some of the spiritual guidance of the *Mela's* teaching gurus.

5. They would stay longer in India, enough time to absorb *ashram* life.

6. It was OK to change plans.

7. She had two beautiful *saris*.

8. She'd nearly let go of anxiety about the future.

9. Whatever happened, things were going to be fine.

10. Best of all, she and Dottie felt more accepting of their status as adoptees.

They had decided to "adopt themselves."

# Chapter Forty-three

The next morning dawned bright and sunny, all traces of monsoon rainfall, vanished. Dottie and Clara awakened in their separate dorm rooms, slipped into comfortable yoga clothes. The 5:30 a.m. meditation was just getting underway. Ashok, with whom they hoped to sit, was not there. He'd left to help an aunt and uncle who lived in a nearby village.

Outside the large main hall, used for both meditation and yoga, was a cart holding urns of *chai* and stacks of paper cups. This was all they'd eat until the late-morning vegetarian buffet. "I wish I knew their secret for making such an incredible beverage," Clara said as she downed a second cup.

"I think it's cardamon and other spices," Dottie said. "Maybe it's the tea they use or the milk. I think it's raw milk, but whatever — it's really delicious. Awesomely good. But we need to go inside and grab a mat." They lined up their shoes next to dozens of sandals, thongs and slippers and went inside the wide doorway.

It turned out that the mats were already in place and nearly everyone was occupied. Dottie led the way and they moved to the far right of the third row. Both women sat down cross-legged, closed their eyes and began breathing slowly and deeply.

Today's instructor was a woman who introduced herself as Ondra. The *ashram* often served as a training ground for people aspiring to become meditation or yoga leaders back in their hometowns or countries. It wasn't unusual to have a different man or woman at the head of the room.

"Please lower your eyes or close them entirely and take three deep breaths." After enough time for that, Ondra led the age-old chant...

"Om...

Om...

Om..."

"Today is a new day," Ondra continued. "We will greet it with the salutation to the sun, which we will perform three times. First, stand up. Plant your feet on the mat, shoulder width apart, weight evenly distributed. Both arms stretched overhead. reaching for the sky. Now slowly, back straight, go over to downward facing dog and breathe into the pose. Slowly move one leg back, then the other, and go into cobra."

The room was totally silent as a few dozen people sank into the snake-like posture, some more limber than others. One wasn't supposed to compare. But Clara found herself sneaking glances at various cobras all around her. Dottie was one of the most supple. In fact, Clara decided, she was the best. She gave herself a B+.

They completed the first salutation, followed by two more, and then settled in to meditate. "Find whatever position you can comfortably maintain, and we will meditate together. I will talk for a short time at the beginning, giving you thoughts to embrace, and a *mantra* to say silently to yourself. Do not be alarmed or frustrated if your mind does not obey; just keep coming back to the *mantra*..."

Clara sat with her legs crossed, her back very straight. Unlike Dottie, she could not stay in the lotus posture for long periods of time. Her friend was more supple. They tuned into Ondra, who was talking about being more open and accepting, about welcoming new thoughts and experiences "Your mind is your intimate friend and healer and when you attune your attention to your body, your mind welcomes joy and acceptance. Our *mantra* is 'Arul Kaunai Daya,' which means 'I open my awareness to loving kindness and empathy.' Now, close your eyes. Whenever your mind starts to wander repeat this *mantra* silently to yourself. I will sound the gong at the beginning and end of the meditation. Now, breathe deeply and repeat this mantra silently to yourself...

"*Arul Kaunai Daya...*

"*Arul Kaunai Daya...*

"*Arul Kaunai Daya...*"

After a deeply quiet time, everyone lost in separate worlds, the gong sounded. There would be an hour's break now, as they went into the dining area for a vegetarian buffet and more *chai*.

"I feel like I've had a vacation," Clara said. "I was so tired before we started. Now I'm completely refreshed. I don't know if I'm healed by turning inward, but I'm really refreshed."

"It's like being through the ringer, as in the old-fashioned washing machines. I love the feeling of washing off, clearing out the detritus of the conscious mind. Actually, I think I was sleeping through much of the meditation, a kind of wakeful sleeping. More and more, I think of my mother, that original mother, as someone on another planet. I'm slowly distancing myself from feeling that

243

she's anything more than a spirit, the original spirit who ushered me into the world. But as far as being someone real, a flesh and blood person, she's no longer really there. Does that make any sense?"

Fragrant aromas of curry, cardamon, and oregano wafted from the dining hall. Men and women in loose clothing lined up to go through the buffet line. Many dishes awaited them - *samosas*, chicken *tandoori*, saffron and green pea rice, *baingan bartha*, a dozen vegetable combinations, various breads (*naan*), puddings and *baklava*. "Mountains of food," said Clara. "I have to strictly control myself at these feasts. I don't want to go home weighing tons more. As great as yoga is, it doesn't burn calories the way running does."

"Somehow, the food here helps me eat less rather than more. Whatever they put with their *quinoa* is incredible, the carrots, tomatoes, and amazing spices."

Clara couldn't agree more. "Eating the right stuff makes a difference, that's for sure. Let's sit with some of our fellow dwellers. We haven't exactly been very sociable - what with your illness and my getting lost."

A 26 year-old student named Maria joined them soon after they took places at the end of one of the long white tables. They introduced themselves and were soon chatting away like longtime friends.

"We came to India as a sort of quest," Clara launched in. "We're both adoptees who never really knew our birthmothers. Arundati here...we call her Dottie...was originally from India."

"Somehow we hoped to magically find clues about my origins," Dottie said. "Of course, that was magical thinking. I got an inheritance from one of my aunts, part of my adoptive family, at the same time Clara and I were getting to be friends. Things just sort of fell in place for us to come to India. I thought that even if I could never find a birthparent, at least I'd get to know my country of origin."

"We'd tell you how we ended up at the *ashram*," Clara said, "but it's convoluted. Basically, we were inspired by a relic we found in Dottie's attic, actually in her aunt's attic."

"My favorite aunt died and left her house to me," Dottie broke in. "The condition was that I had to clear everything out and have her attorney sell it and give me all of the profits. While we were sifting through a lifetime of stuff..."

244

"Her aunt kept everything," Clara broke in, "including the journals and memorabilia of a relative who'd spent time in India. There were fascinating written accounts, but also fragments of this and that. One of them happened to be the hand of a statue..."

"Of Ganesh, the Hindu god who clears obstacles and paves the way for moving forward," said Dottie. "We found evidence in the journals that Aunt Miriam's cousin promised to return the hand to the Ganges, or at least to the waters of India. Since it had never been done, and since we both had our adoptions as sort of obstacles, we decided to do it for Aunt Miriam. We felt that the stone hand needed to be returned to the place it came from."

"Or as close to the place as we could," finished Clara.

"Wow! That's quite a story. And now, I can imagine that you'd like to know what brought me here. I'm originally from Spain, I grew up in France, but my studies brought me to the U.S. I studied geology at the University of New Mexico."

"Incredible!" Clara put down the fork she'd been using to shovel down large scoops of an eggplant curry. "We're both from New Mexico, Santa Fe to be specific. Sorry to interrupt, but I don't think it's an accident that we're all from the same place. No coincidences, but here I am interrupting again. Please. Continue."

"We want to know what you're hoping to find," Dottie said. "That is, if you came looking for something. I think Clara would agree that we came here in search of ourselves, the essence of who we really are."

"Getting in touch with our roots aside," Clara said. "You might say we've sort of adopted ourselves."

"I was always fascinated by India," Maria said. "I got a book on Hindu mythology when I was in fourth grade, from my favorite relative, Uncle Louie; I found it just as fascinating as the Bible stories my Lutheran parents told me.. I wouldn't describe myself as religious, but I know there's more to life than we think. I'm here for two weeks and I love that we'll be learning yoga as well as philosophy. I'm looking forward to all of it."

"What we've done so far," Dottie said, "has been wonderful. Despite everything that's happened — my illness, a thing of the past — and Clara's misadventures, getting lost in the city, we both feel more centered. Without distractions of the outside world, you really have time to explore inner spaces."

245

"I couldn't have put it better myself," Maria said. "Exploring inner spaces. The outside world has been made so orderly and quiet, one has time to do just that. I hope to get to know myself better."

A gong sounded to signal afternoon yoga class. No more talking, just stretching and breathing. For the next hours, Clara and Dottie were lost in their own worlds. Shadows lengthened in the great hall; it was time for *Savasana*, otherwise known as the Corpse pose.

The instructor, a trainee named Janet (it seemed there was a new person every day) talked to them slowly, her voice very soothing. "You've done a good job, refreshing the organs, gently relaxing your mind, asking your body to stretch the limits, to steady and balance your core. Now is your well-earned time to fully relax. Lie on your back, arms by your side, face upturned toward the ceiling. Close your eyes, clear your mind, and rest. I'll ring a soft bell when it's time to release the pose."

Long minutes passed. Clara felt herself falling asleep. In fact, she may well have drifted off. Pulling herself back into full consciousness, she focused on all the details involved in leaving India. But then she reminded herself that, before leaving, they had a mission to accomplish, the return of the Ganesh relic to the waters of India. If it couldn't be in the actual Ganges, maybe they could find a tributary that flowed into the Ganges. But how?

A soft bell released Clara from puzzling further. Apparently, Dottie's thoughts had followed along the same path. An interlude of "personal time" followed the yoga session. The two women, weary from hours of yoga but also energized, made their way upstairs. They decided to have tea time in Dottie's room, after changing into clothes for the evening. They would wear their new *saris*, as the evening buffet was a tribute to Swami Vishnudevananda.

They went to their separate rooms to shower and change, then met for tea. When Clara appeared in Dottie's room in her plum-colored *sari*, her friend applauded. "Is this the same woman I saw less than twenty minutes ago, worn down to a frazzle by hours of *asanas*? You look elegant! I'm heating up water for our tea. In the meantime, let me treat you to some beautiful dates and nuts that Ashok brought me this morning."

"Ashok!" Clara broke into laughter. "I thought we'd seen the last of him. Didn't he go visit relatives in some remote village?"

"Yes, he did. But he came back, bearing gifts and also what might be a solution. I know we have to do something with my ancestor's relic before we leave. Ashok actually had a brilliant idea."

"So now it's *your* ancestor? I thought Goldingham Dinegar was a relative of your late Aunt Miriam, the woman we have to thank for this whole Indian adventure."

"You know, I'm not too sure about our relationship, but it seems I'm distantly somehow related. Adoptively related, if there is such a thing. You know how it is with adoptees, I shouldn't have to tell you. Lacking a family tree, or maybe we have two family trees, we sort of invent our own. A family forest! Which leads to Ashok's suggestion. When I told him about our mission of returning the relic to the waterways of Mother India, he said there was a small river near his village that would be perfect. He said he could take us there."

"That's fantastic. Did he say when?" Clara had promised Meera that she and Dottie would do the after-dinner cleanup for the next four nights, and she didn't want to go back on her word. It would be all wrong to be the ugly Americans, unreliable and self-serving.

"As it turns out, he won't be free to take us to this special place for a week. That will give us a chance to redeem ourselves with the *ashram*. The floors will never have been cleaned so well."

# Chapter Forty-four

"I can't believe we're doing this!" Clara, who prided herself on being strong and fit, was longing to rest. She and Dottie had been scrubbing the cement floor for an hour and had barely cleaned half of it. It was late, about 9:30, as they'd helped the dish-washing and table-cleaning crew before starting on the floor. Now that daylight was long gone, the kitchen and dining area just off the great hall had taken on a surreal air. The walls, ceiling, cabinets and prep tables, all white, had taken on a ghostly air. The only light came from bare overhead bulbs, and the windows, now black rectangles, seemed to be spying on them.

"This work is endless. It's kind of creeping me out," Dottie moaned. "My legs hurt."

"We need kneepads, I'm using my folded-up *pashmina*, but it doesn't help very much."

It was hard to tell if their work was making a difference. Every few feet of the concrete floor that they'd finished scrubbing was then hosed down. The dirty water ran into drains throughout the kitchen/dining area. Maybe the difference would show up when the concrete dried, but they wouldn't be there to see that. It was nearly eleven when they finally finished and stumbled upstairs to their rooms.

"A hot shower'll be divine," Clara said. "I'm almost too tired for that, especially since we have to meditate so early tomorrow morning. Sleep fast, Dottie. I'll see you in my dreams."

The weary twosome exchanged a hug. This was, after all, a sisterhood. It was becoming increasingly clear that they had not gotten closer to their roots, either one of them, but it was also ceasing to matter as much. Resignation. Acceptance. More than a little sadness. They trudged wearily to their respective rooms.

Night passed all too quickly. Clara knocked gently on Dottie's door on the way to morning meditation. Even as she was knocking, the door opened. "Hey there, didn't I just see you minutes ago in the kitchen? Here's a motto for today: For every door that closes, another one opens."

"Speaking of a door closing," Clara said, "I think we both missed saying goodbye to Samantha. For awhile, she was our new best friend. She was all caught up in meeting her future mother and father in-law. I really liked her, and not just because she helped us so much. Hope she has a good life ahead of her."

"You knew she invited us to her wedding, didn't you? I'd go in a heartbeat if we were going to be here for it."

"Sure, me too. But isn't it about six months away? And isn't it in Chennai, way down in Southern India?"

"Yes, and yes. Still, I've heard that Indian weddings are incredible. They go on for days, include processions, sometimes with horses and elephants. Lavish partying. Apparently, guests are treated like royalty."

"That would be a way to experience the real India, for sure. But right now, on to humbler pursuits."

Dottie walked toward the door and opened it for Clara. "Morning meditation, here we come."

The hall was full of students sitting cross-legged or relaxing in *savasana* postures. Today their leader, taking a break from serving in the reception area, was Meera. As a *guru*, she turned out to be a natural.

The Hindu woman sat in a full lotus, dressed in a simple white *salwar kameez*, her long black hair flowing to her shoulders. "Good morning, dear fellow travelers," she began. "Before we start today's meditation, let's all stand up, stretch to the ceiling, and at whatever pace feels right for you, do three salutations to the sun. Then I will talk to you briefly, planting some seeds for thought. Whenever you're ready, begin your salutations, and when you have finished, make yourself comfortable in lotus or half lotus."

For fifteen minutes, there was silence except for slight rustle or an occasional expelled breath or sigh. Meera rang a gong softly and began. "Today, let us fill our hearts and minds with gratitude and gently drive away those negative thoughts that weigh us down. Today we will consciously shed the weight...

"We are endlessly renewed in the present moment. Our emotions flow freely; our lives are lightened. We are the source of our own inner healing. We find joy in healing and recovery. When we belong to ourselves, we belong to the whole human family."

The gong sounded once again and all twenty students sat with eyes closed. Thus began fifteen minutes of deep silence, contemplation and reflection. Dottie and Clara were grateful for each other. They had undertaken this meandering journey, their month in India, in search of they weren't sure what. They had bonded more than they could have imagined. Definitely a sisterhood. Were they becoming believers in reincarnation? They felt sure they'd been related in another lifetime.

Another sounding of Meera's gong, and they were dismissed with three recitations of *Om* and a final *Namaste*.

Then, in the gentle routine,, it was suppertime. A simple buffet of beans, lentils, and rice followed. As with most meals, Clara and Dottie ate in silence. Sitting at one of a dozen long white tables, they communicated with smiles or simple gestures. As they finished and had taken their dishes to the kitchen window to hand to the day workers, Clara pointed to the floor and nudged Dottie. She signaled an A-OK and Dottie answered with a thumbs up. They were silently applauding themselves for floors well-cleaned.

Back in the hall, they talked softly before going to their rooms for resting before an evening *Satsang*. "I'm getting accustomed to this way of being," Dottie confessed. "I'd love to live this simple, orderly routine forever. Reduced to necessities."

From the great hall and dining area, they made their way slowly upstairs. "Yes," Clara agreed. "But I know you're planning to see Ashok soon. We have to return the relic, the ancient artifact, to water, and you said he'd help us. As soon as you can talk with him, we need to form a plan. Did I tell you I've made a tentative plane reservation for us to leave for the states in two weeks?"

"Yes, I know. We don't have forever. I'll be talking with Ashok tonight or maybe tomorrow."

"The sooner we take care of the hand of the Ganesh mission, the better."

# Chapter Forty-five

After three days in the soothing rhythm of *ashram* life, Clara and Dottie both felt like new. On the afternoon of the third day, Ashok came back from his family errand. They were gathered in Dottie's room before afternoon yoga. Clara couldn't help but notice that while he gently hugged her, he embraced Dottie. Could there be more between them than just a friendship?

Hoping for more clues, Clara noticed that Ashok, as they claimed their yoga mats, stationed himself a couple rows away. Could it be fear of showing how he felt about Dottie, of not wanting Clara to know? She hadn't brought the topic up with her friend. And if she were to broach the subject, how would she word it? Wouldn't Dottie tell her if something was going on? Of course, Dottie was the one who got lost during the *Kumbha Mela*. Maybe they weren't as connected as she'd assumed.

Before she could speculate further, the gong was sounding. Meera again, starting with a *mantra* and then having them pose in Warrior. The *asanas* went on and Clara immersed herself in them. She could feel that she'd grown stronger and more limber. If only she could keep up this practice when they were back at home. "Quit future-izing," she told herself. "Be here now."

There was a Native American proverb that she loved: "Don't let yesterday use up too much of today." In her mind, it would just as well be "Don't let tomorrow use up too much of today." If India had taught her anything it was to expect the unexpected, to accept the flow of the universe. Maybe it was meant for Arundati, who apparently was not going to succeed in tracing her roots, to instead meet the love of her life. Rather than being alarmed at this turn of events, Clara was happy. Why not enjoy the possibility of romance, even if it wasn't her romance but Dottie's? And why not, she asked herself. Why not?

Meera was giving out thoughts for today's meditation, so Clara reigned in her wandering mind, closed her eyes and listened.

"Today we focus on miracles, on miraculous relationships. It begins with you. Now slowly inhale through your nose and exhale through your mouth three times...

"I am the unbounded changeless self. I am a wondrous miracle. As I love and honor myself, my relationships blossom...I cherish the beauty in myself and others...My loving light shines

251

for all to see..." Meera's voice was hypnotic. Clara tried to calm her racing mind. She wanted Dottie to be happy, and in a way it was more important than her own happiness. She'd not been lucky in love, but if her dear friend had found a soulmate, it would be deeply satisfying. Sad, no doubt about it, to fail in the Mother search. She should know about that. But to find a "significant other" might be a sweet consolation prize. Meera's last words played through her head and Clara, in her mind's eye, thought about blossoming...

Early the next day, Ashok joined in the morning meditation. After the session finished, he asked "Can you be ready to travel to Fatehpur tomorrow? It's about 117 kilometers from here and I want you to bring that relic you've told me about."

"You mean the hand that broke off a Ganesh statue?" asked Clara. "Don't tell me you found a body of water where we can bury it forever? Well, not exactly bury. Maybe I should have said where we can separate ourselves from it forever?"

"You mean pitch it?" Dottie walked out of the meditation hall to join her two friends. They headed outside to benches in the sunlit garden. "I can't believe we've carried this piece of rock around all month and never found anywhere to deposit it. We'd both be so happy to take care of that mission."

"I'm sure you remember the story," Clara said. "Dottie and I were cleaning out her Aunt Miriam's attic after the dear old lady died and left everything to her only living heir, Dot, and we found this account of a British traveler who picked up the relic in Mahabalipuram. It was a sort of distant relative of Dot's. The account was from decades ago."

"Goldingham was my relative's name. Distantly related and part of my adoptive family, but I count him as part of my family tree."

"We adoptees," Clara said, "have a family forest rather than just one tree."

Dottie continued "He didn't just pick it up from the beach," Dottie corrected, "he bought it from some young Indian boys. To make a longish story short, the relic brought bad luck. Apparently, throughout the decades and centuries, it was kept sort of carelessly. That's what we got from reading old journals and diaries.

"No one knew what to do with the stone 'Ganesh hand' from Mahabalipuram, but the families that possessed it, along with the original purchasers' journals and effects, always were stricken by tragedy. The thing was cursed."

"We are united in our mission to return it to the waters of India," Clara added. "Ganesh is the remover of obstacles, the Hindu god associated with good luck and overcoming obstacles."

"Well, *Memsahibs*, you will be glad to know, I've thought up a plan. We'll go to some historic ponds in the town of Fatehpur. There's a train that leaves at seven in the morning, going through the town of Kausambi, directly to the ponds. I think they are near the railroad station in Fatehpur, but if not, we can catch a bus. I went to them when I was just a child and I remember thinking they were magnificent."

"That sounds perfect," Dottie said. "Somewhere, I can't recall exactly when, I'd heard about these special ponds in Uttar Pradesh. Or maybe I read about them. There's one in particular, Rani Ka, that's supposed to be really beautiful."

"There are three Rani Ka ponds," said Ashok. "The biggest one has a stairwell going down to the water, graceful arches all around it, and beyond the bordering walls, a forest of lush trees. We could look at the others, but I've seen them all, and I feel confident that this one would be best."

"I'll trust you on that," Dottie said.

"What, exactly, is a stairwell?" Clara wanted to know. "Are they the same as "stepwells?"

"Pretty much the same thing," Ashok said. "They date back to 550 A.D., I've been told. The Rani Ka doesn't have as many steps as some of the other ponds, so it should be perfect for a 'water burial' for the Ganesh relic. Let's make sure we bring it with us. I'll put it in my backpack, or maybe Dottie should. Just so one of us does. Getting the relic disposed of properly is our mission, right?"

They had reached the upper level. Women's rooms were directly above the Great Hall. Ashok saw that the Ganesh statue's severed hand was securely stashed in Clara's backpack. "Prepare for early departure tomorrow morning."

## Chapter Forty-six

It seemed as though she'd just closed her eyes when Clara heard her travel clock's sharp beeping. The sound jerked her out of a disturbing dream. She was in one place but was supposed to be in another. No time to record this one in her journal. She clicked off the clock and jumped into practical travel clothes. Sturdy denim capris and a cotton Indian *kameez*. After brushing her teeth, gathering her hair in a ponytail, lacing her running shoes and checking her backpack for the third time, she went next-door to Dottie's room. It was only 6:30 and they were to meet Ashok in the reception area at 7. Still, she needed to make sure that her friend was totally prepared.

A good thing she checked. Dottie was still asleep. She sat next to the bed and shook her friend's shoulder. "Wake up, wake up! Hurry. Jump into your clothes. We'll miss the bus to the train station. Ashok is waiting in the reception room. We've gotta go. Now. Let me help."

Dottie, pushing hair out of her eyes, bolted to a sitting position. "Oh no, I thought I'd set my travel alarm. I'm so sorry. Don't shoot me. I can be ready in five minutes." She dashed to the bathroom and minutes later, was literally jumping into her clothes. Clara waited by the door. By 6:55, they ran downstairs and to the reception desk, where - sure enough - Ashok was nervously waiting, his backpack attached. "I was getting desperate. Come on, you two. The bus stop's a block away. If we're fast, we'll make it."

"Don't forget, I used to run marathons," Clara said.

"I'm in good shape," Dottie added. "Especially since I got all that extra sleep last night." The time for speaking over, the three raced through early morning crowds and catapulted themselves onto the creaky tan-colored bus.

Amazingly, even at this hour, shortly past seven, the bus was full of people. Ashok took care of their tickets and they found the last three vacant seats. "Not much time to sit. We get off in two more stops. Take in the sights and sounds. This is a typical Monday morning in Allahabad."

"Millions of people going about doing millions of things," Clara said. She stood up in advance of their imminent disembarking. Others got to their feet. The bus lurched to a stop next to a large tan building with ornate carvings around many-paned windows. "Here's our stop, move quickly, *Memsabs*."

"Are you saying these passengers can turn into a swarm of locusts?" Clara was stepping off the bus as she asked.

Ashok looked puzzled.

"Well, that's not exactly the right term. These people aren't going to cause a pestilence. Maybe a herd of cattle would be more apt."

Ashok neither agreed nor disagreed. Instead, he ran toward the train station, just a block away. He checked back frequently to make sure his charges were coming along. "We need to hurry or we'll have to wait two hours for the next departure," he called back to the two women.

Ashok, ten feet ahead of them, was already in line for tickets when Clara and Dottie, breathless from their dash, caught up. He insisted on paying for the tickets. Just as they reunited, the train came lurching into the station.

"Sorry, but I could only get second class. It should be fine and after all, it's only a short distance. It might seem long, as this is not a high-speed train. It's low-speed, and it stops often."

They climbed into a compartment and sat on straight-backed wooden benches. The train was nearly full, so they shared their bench with a middle-aged woman in a brilliant yellow *sari*. She greeted them with a gesture of *namaste* and a gracious smile. No sooner had they offered back the woman launched into surprisingly good English. "Hello, my name is Avi and I would love to practice my English by conversing with you. You *Memsabs* are American, yes?"

The train was leaving the station in jerks and starts. Avi peered at them with a smile, then pulled out a packet of her large basket. "Please have some. These are my favorite biscuits. My sister serves them at her restaurant in Fatephur. You are going there, no?"

Ashok was sitting next to Avi; Clara and Dottie were wedged into the seat across from them. The three friends introduced themselves to Avi. It soon became clear that their travel-mate was full of curiosity, and that she was not going to quit chattering. Clara took the lead in what promised to be a long, drawn-out conversation. "You are right. Arundati and I have been in your country for the past month. We hit a few bumps in the road and Ashok came to the rescue." She sent a look his way, hoping not to have to elaborate. Surely "bumps in the road" was enough to describe the Lane Masterson debacle, the *Kumbha Mela* separation, and Dottie's illness. She should have stopped

255

there but somehow felt a need to explain why they came to India in the first place.

Dottie broke in. "I'm part Indian, but I was adopted by an American couple when I was an infant. These parents either couldn't or wouldn't tell me anything about my origins. So, after they died, my ambition was to travel to India to find out everything I could about where I came from. Originally. I haven't been able to locate my mother. She may have already passed on, but I thought in some way I could become closer to her at least in spirit."

"Dottie," Clara interrupted. "I don't think Avi needs to know all that. The main thing is we both had a lot of curiosity about India and when we were able, we decided to make the journey." She did not mention the inheritance that made the trip possible. By now, the package of cookies - "biscuits" as Avi called them - had disappeared. "Sorry, but we've eaten every one of your crackers. Dottie forgot to bring our travel food."

"My fault. It was waiting to be picked up in the kitchen and in the mad rush, I spaced it out. It's my fault if we're all hungry. Maybe there's a tea *wallah* on the train and then when we arrive, we can find somewhere to eat."

Avi broke into laughter. "Oh, you are in luck. My sister in Fatehpur is married to a restaurant owner. Sonia's husband Raghubir has the Casual Canteen and the Scenic Lake Cafe. They would be wonderful places for you to go. Let me be your escort. They have the best *samosas* you will find in Uttar Pradesh. I will be happy to take you there and since you will be my guests, they will give you a very special price."

"That sounds very nice," said Clara. "But we have planned to go to the historic ponds and we have to get back to Allahabad by night." She turned to Ashok. "Do we have time to do everything? We'll definitely get too hungry if we try to fast all day." She did a double take, noticing that Ashok was holding Dottie's hand across the aisle between them. So, she thought to herself, there was something between them. And why not? Ashok had come to the rescue when Dottie was struggling with illness.

The train rumbled slowly through villages and countryside, occasionally lurching to a stop, then starting up again. Mobs of people were crowded alongside the tracks, some waving, a few with outstretched arms. Were they waiting to board, had they just disembarked, or did they have nothing else to do? Clara was so absorbed she didn't hear Avi, who was chattering away. In the meantime, Dottie and Ashok seemed to be engrossed in one another. She realized suddenly that she was being addressed.

"Yes, yes," Avi was saying. "The country people are always asking for *rupees*. Never open windows while you are on the train. They will reach right in and steal from you. If you've been traveling here for a time, you already know how important it is to be careful. You have your friend Ashok with you and this is good, but it is not good to go hungry. I will take you to my brother-in-law's restaurant for a very fine lunch. I think you will like the Casual Canteen. It has the city's best *samosas* and spinach *paneer* that people love."

"I think we should go there," Dottie said, "and I will buy our lunch. I'm the one who forgot and left our picnic in the kitchen this morning."

"That's kind of you," Ashok said, "but you certainly don't need to treat us. We can all pay our own way. We do need to eat. But also, we must not forget our errand."

"Errand?" Avi asked. "I know the city quite well and I can help you find where you need to go. Also, I will take you to the best places to shop."

The tossing of an ancient relic was more than just an "errand": it was a sacred mission. Clara wanted to steer the conversation away from the topic, as Avi was clearly very interested in taking them under her wing and also, truth be told, rather nosy. She invented a story to divert attention from the "errand."

"We cannot shop at all this visit. I promised a friend at home I would take photographs of the historic lakes near the city. She's writing a book on amazing travel destinations and I promised her I'd take pictures of the India that many tourists don't see. What we call off the beaten path. So, we'll have lunch at your friend's cafe but can't spend too much time. I promised the writer."

"I would be able to show you places for magnificent photograph," said Avi. "Really. I would be most happy to be your guide."

Clara pulled out a paperback book she'd been carrying around and reading only occasionally. She pretended to be engrossed, even as Avi chattered on. Let the others try to deflect their new best friend. The last thing in the world they needed was a snoopy hanger-on. Also, it might even be illegal to have the hand of Ganesh. The argument of its history — having been found in an attic and having been acquired many years ago by a member of Dottie's adoptive family— that might not make any difference to an Indian archeological society. But maybe her imagination was running away with her. Whatever the case, they would have to escape from this meddler right after lunch. She continued to read even as she thought about possible excuses.

Dottie and Ashok were putting up with Avi's incessant chatter. It wasn't exactly a conversation, as there was hardly a break. Avi was telling them all about her entire family, the Patels. She was from a family of ten children and she was right in the middle. Her next older sibling, a brother, was in the states, she said, with relatives in New Jersey. He was doing an apprenticeship with an uncle in the restaurant business. She, Avi, hoped to visit one day. Maybe she would move to New Jersey. Did they know anything about New Jersey? On and on went the monologue...

The train screeched to a stop, and here they were in the Fatehpur station. Ashok, Dottie and Clara stood up and shouldered their packs. Avi was charging toward the exit door. "Follow me," she urged. "I know which bus to catch directly to my brother's restaurant." People crushed into them from all sides, and it was an effort to stay together. They reached the exit door just in time to emerge, as it slammed closed right behind them and the train started moving forward.

"We don't have time for a very long lunch," Ashok said. "Is the service fast?"

They were following Avi as she hurried them toward a bus stop a city block from the railroad station. "Oh so speedy," said their self-appointed guide. "You will be in and out before you know it, and you will enjoy the rest of your Fatehpur visit more with being well-nourished."

"A mother hen and her chicks," Clara said to no one in particular.

"I'm grateful," Dottie said. "I don't mind being a chick. Between Ashok and Avi, we're in safe hands. No more of this getting lost."

A short bus ride took them to Casual Canteen, where the *samosas* were as good as Avi claimed they would be. Despite that, lunch couldn't be over soon enough. Avi's brother-in-law Raghubir insisted that they were his guests and that lunch was on the house. This generosity made it even harder to exclude Avi from their expedition to the historical ponds. Dottie suggested that they could at least tell her about their mission. Clara agreed. Avi didn't seem like a person who would have strong feelings about a relic from the ancient past.

As they were finishing their meal with *baklava* and mango pudding, Clara decided that there was nothing to lose by explaining their mission. "We came to India not just to see as much as possible of your fascinating country. We promised ourselves we'd try to find out about Dottie's birthparents."

"She was Indian," Dottie interrupted. "I think my father was as well, but my adoptive parents found me in an orphanage."

"Avi doesn't need to know our life stories," Clara said, feeling immediately embarrassed for sounding bossy. She dipped a *samosa* into a hot sauce. "I can't believe how delicious this cauliflower combination is. We just can't get Indian food like this in America. Compliments to the chef!"

"And this *Tandoori* Chicken," Ashok said between mouthfuls. "This is spicy in a way that I've hardly ever found in America. They love Indian restaurants there, and they're always trying. But they never quite get it right."

Avi smiled. "I will tell Raghubir. And I understand that you people have something important to do. You don't need to tell me about it. But I think I know someone who might be able to help Dottie find out about her ancestors. For another visit, another time perhaps." She left the table to get one of the restaurant's business cards.

When she returned, Ashok was trying to pay the waiter, who reminded him that their meal was a gift from the owner. Clara and Dottie had shrugged on their backpacks, impatient to leave. "Here," said Avi. She held a small white card with a photo of Casual Canteen on the front and the restaurant's address and phone number. On the back, she wrote "Swami Varun" in large print, followed by her name "Avi Bhattacharyya." She handed the card to Clara. "I do not have reliable telephone service, but my brother-in-law can always find me. I have written the name 'Swami Varun' after my name. He is a psychic who can tell you about past lives and he will be able to help with questions about ancestry. If you come this way again, I promise, he can help you."

Dottie was paying rapt attention, and she looked as though she wanted to hear more. Clara put her arm through hers and led her to the door. After profuse thank-yous, the were finally outside the restaurant. Clara hoped Avi wouldn't follow them,

259

and to her relief, she had gone back to the kitchen to talk with her relative.

"Free at last," she announced, "and now on to these famous historic ponds."

"This way to the bus," Ashok said, leading them two blocks away from the restaurant "They go back many centuries and are repositories of Indian history."

The trip seemed to be taking forever, the two women thought to themselves. Yet another bus ride, rumbling through crowded streets, people crowding around every window. Begging. Selling postcards and *pashminas*, *samosas*. Or just trying to cross the hectic streets.

The urban congestion around them turned into rural crowds. Carts overloaded with bundles and baskets, people walking with urns and buckets, bicycle-drawn taxis. The bus stopped at the entrance to Fatehpur's Historical Ponds. The large dark green billboard was, in Hindi. "Not many tourists come this way," Ashok offered, "but it is of great interest to those of us who like to ponder the past— no pun intended. The stairways leading down to the Rani Ka pond are also called *stepwells*, and the speculation is that there is an underground cistern that may be connected to Mother Ganges."

The three friends stepped out of the bus and followed signs to their particular pond. "There are twenty-five of these relics from the past, Ashok explained, and though the others are of interest, the one we're going to will be best for returning the statue fragment to a watery grave."

Dottie objected. "Not to a grave. I feel that in some way the relic will be reunited with Ganesh, a missing part returned to the whole. I know this may sound nutty to you two, but it can be a symbolic reconnecting, the broken made whole, the spiritual bonding that is needed for my adoptee soul..."

Clara broke into Dottie's soliloquy. "You know, it doesn't sound nutty. It makes sense that you are managing to find meaning in what we're about to do."

Foliage around them was now denser as they made their way along a wide asphalted path toward the Rani Ka Pond. The area was a national park, Ashok said, and many Indians loved to come here on holiday. "It's really popular with history buffs."

This wasn't a holiday or a weekend, so the historical ponds were practically deserted. Silence fell upon the threesome as they walked. After another five minutes, they reached a small wooden sign. Ashok said "Here's what we've been looking for. In Hindi, it says 'Rani Ka Pond, three tenths of a mile.' Clara, you might get the hand of Ganesh out of your backpack now so you don't have to look for it once we're there."

"Good idea," Dottie said. "We need to be subtle about this. Just in case there are people around, have it ready. Hopefully, we'll have the place to ourselves."

The day had been hot until they went to lunch, but with clouds moving in, it had grown cool. The terrain changed abruptly, from scruffy fields to forested gently contoured hills. Ahead of them loomed the massive walls around Rani Ka Pond. There were explanatory plaques along the way. Ashok interpreted a few of them, about this or that ruler, who reigned from 500 to 525 A.D. or who had twenty sons or daughters or armies.

Clara and Dottie walked along silently, each lost in her own thoughts. "But these tales from the past are too much to keep track of," said Ashok. "You're making your own history now. This may be the first time that a part of Ganesh has been thrown into the pond. Maybe it will set things right."

They passed through a massive arch to the terrace bordering Rani Ka Pond. A magnificent sight greeted them. The pond was a vast square of olive green water, silent and brooding. It was several feet below the area where they stood. There were arches and columns on all four sides, as well as wide steps leading to the water. For a long time, no one spoke. They slowly walked toward the first wide step leading to the pond.

Clara took the stone hand, fragment of the Hindu god Ganesh, out of her pocket and held it in her palm. She stood taller, her dark eyes directed beyond the terrace toward the pond's center. "Centuries late, we are returning this ancient artifact to Indian waters. May we be healed with this long overdue reuniting."

She passed the stone hand to Arundhati, who surprised Clara and Ashok by putting it deep into the pocket of her hiking pants and turning to them with a frown. "This isn't right. I should have said something before we came all the way out here." By now she was close to tears. "We have to take this relic back to the shore temple at Mahabalipuram, back to the Bay of Bengal. I've tried to talk myself into the historic ponds, the alternative ending to the saga, but it just hasn't worked."

"Somehow I was afraid of this," Clara said. "But I guess you're correct. The relic should be returned to the closest possible

261

waters near its source. Northern India was never appropriate. If we hadn't been caught up in the *Kumbha Mela*, if we hadn't met Samantha, if we hadn't gone to the *ashram*. So many if's." She trailed off.

They stood gazing into the pond. Afternoon clouds made the pond look dark. All other visitors seemed to have vanished. Silence surrounded them. Ashok was the first to speak.

"I think Dottie's right. If your relic came from the South, that's where it belongs. I wasn't going to interfere because, after all, it's not my relic. And here's some news you might find interesting. Our friend Samantha called me last night and told me that we must attend the wedding, no matter what. It's in Chennai and is going to be an all-out celebration. If you can change your travel plans, we can all go and join the festivities. It would be something you'd remember forever."

Instinctively, the three friends had turned away from the pond and started walking slowly in the opposite direction. Everything seemed to be going in reverse, but there was a certain rightness about this sudden switch. They were unusually silent, each lost in thought, as they absorbed the change in plans.

By now, they were nearing the railroad station. "Well, we can at least check on the luggage we left at the Chennai Hotel," Clara said.

" I'd kind of given up on ever seeing it again," Dottie added. "We can go to an Indian wedding, return the Ganesh relic to the place where it belongs, and then go back to Santa Fe."

They walked through the park surrounding pond after historical pond. Retracing their steps to the rail station, their journey in reverse. "You both look like you're in a trance," Ashok said. "But it is the right decision, absolutely right."

# Chapter Forty-seven

The Sivananda Vrindavan leave-taking, over three days, had been orchestrated by Ashok. Clara and Dottie let him make the arrangements to fly south to Chennai, with the understanding that he would accompany them. The night before they left, Dottie and Clara sat up late in Clara's room. The hand of Ganesh, the relic they'd carried with them throughout what had been a long, meandering journey, sat in the center of Clara's bedside table top. With great efficiency, the two women had packed up everything for tomorrow's journey to Chennai, the Tamil Nadu city where their month in India began. They'd said their farewells to yoga instructors and meditation leaders, plus fellow residents.

"I'm really going to miss life at the *ashram*," Clara said. "I could stay here for weeks. Maybe for years or even the rest of my life. It's easy when you know exactly what you're going to do every day. The structure is rigorous, but in a way, it's soothing."

"You know, I won't miss it as much as you," Dottie said. "I'll always associate it with my illness, that miserable stomach thing that hit me after I dipped into the Ganges."

"That was a disaster. But you did get better. And we got to know Ashok. Especially you got to know him. Your Indian boyfriend?" Clara quipped.

Dottie shook her head no, but she was smiling.

After a solid night's sleep, Clara and Dottie met Ashok in the foyer. Together, they began the long journey to Chennai. It was dark, before dawn, but Ashok took command, and all ran smoothly. By train and plane, they made their way south to Tamil Nadu.

At the end of a couple days, they were back where they'd started a month earlier. The big difference is that Ashok, their self-appointed guide, was with them. "Our personal escort," Dottie said more than once. Amazingly and much to their relief, Clara and Dottie found their luggage in the hotel's storeroom. Clara, the businesswoman of the two, paid for three weeks of storage and explained that they would be checking out after the weekend.

"We have just two days for an excursion to the Shore Temple at Mahabalipuram," Ashok told them. "Then it will be time for us all to attend Samantha's wedding."

"Next order of business," Clara said. "Ashok, we'll say Sayonara for now and get ready for tomorrow at the Shore Temple. This is going to be girls' night in."

Ashok looked baffled. "Girls night where?"

"That's another one of those crazy American sayings," she explained. "It means that as much as we love your company, my dear man, we need an evening alone. As you explained, we have to go to the Shore Temple tomorrow and right after that we'll all be celebrating Samantha's wedding, and after that..."

"We have to catch a plane to go back home," Clara finished. "I can't believe our Indian adventure is nearly at an end." She gave Ashok a sisterly hug. He walked toward the stairwell to the next floor. Dottie gave him an embrace that was a little beyond sisterly.

Ashok may have blushed at the signs of affection. "It is my pleasure and an honor to be an escort for such fine *memsabs*," he said with a small bow. "We must make the best of these last few days."

After he was out of earshot, Dottie confided to Clara. "Such a fine man. If only he were in America. I can hardly stand the thought of our never seeing him again."

"You never know," Clara said. "Anything can happen. For example, I think Ashok is falling for you. And I can tell that you like him more than a little."

Dottie protested, "He is fond of us both. Let's get organized. We'll order dinner brought to the room and be ready for our shore temple visit. You know how Ashok likes to start at the crack of dawn."

The two women chatted nonstop as they walked to their hotel room. Though not luxurious by American standards, the Chennai Somerset felt plush. After taking an hour to enjoy tea and *samosas* brought to their room, they looked through the luggage they'd stored at the hotel.

"Most of this stuff, I'm just dumping," Dottie said. "We took the essentials with us and bought quite a few Indian clothes along the way."

"It's amazing," Clara said. "I'm finding the same thing. Let's don't call it dumping. It will be donating. We can leave bags for the maid before we check out. At home, not very many people would want this stuff. Here, it's a different story."

A six a.m. wakeup call brought the three travelers to the hotel dining room by six-thirty. Breakfast was a pleasant buffet that included both rice and Indian vegetarian dishes, scrambled eggs, cereal, and muffins. Ashok, Clara and Dottie took advantage of the generous spread.

"Ah, my beautiful *memsabs*, it is good that we feast on ample breakfast. We will be traveling by several busses to the Shore Temple area and there will be neither time nor opportunity to eat anything. If you have them, put snacks in whatever you carry along."

"We're used to that," Dottie said.

"Yes," Clara agreed. "Don't forget that we've trekked all over India with beef jerky and power bars. And bottled water, which I'm happy to report I bought for me and Dottie last night." She handed her friend a couple bottles. She knew that Ashok would not want or need them. He was used to the local water. But for her and Dottie, bottled water was a must.

An hour of bus riding later, the three friends arrived at Mahabalipurim and the towering Shore Temple. After disembarking, they strolled through the sprawling grounds, along graveled paths and gardens filled with statuary. Finally, they neared the majestic temple, protected by a wire fence and seeming to gaze out upon the blue Indian Ocean. A wooden turnstile allowed them to walk out to the beach.

Clara passed the stone hand of Ganesh to Arundati, who held it reverently and stood before her two companions. "I believe that Ganesh," she proclaimed, "being the overcomer of obstacles, has helped me find a mother in India. I feel like I've met her in the faces of the Indian women of the *Kumbha Mela*, the pilgrims, of Avi and other women we've met along the way, of strangers on the street. It's hard to explain exactly how, but getting to spend time in the land of my ancestors...It's filled a place that was hollow." She tapped her heart.

The sea reflected a dazzling afternoon sky, white puffy clouds overhead reflected in the olive-green water. They stood silently, waiting, Ashok in the middle - between Dottie and Clara. He surprised them by laying a gentle hand on each nearby shoulder. It was a welcome gesture and made the moment even more intimate.

"It's been a wonderful journey for me," Clara said. "I will never find Greta. She slipped away before we could meet. But

India has helped me be at peace about that. It's hard to explain, but it's almost like I've been renewed."

Ashok said, "Dottie, you need to be the one to return Ganesh's hand to India's water. I have a feeling that it will remove any obstacles to our being able to continue our friendship. I didn't tell you this before, but I had been hoping you could come back for Samantha's wedding." Then, afraid of being rude, he added, "And Clara too."

Dottie removed her sandals and walked out into the water. "I'm going to send Ganesh's hand out with a quotation from my favorite poet, W. B. Yeats...

*In the deserts of the heart*
*Let the healing fountains start...*"

She tossed the small fragment into the sea. A small splash and then it disappeared, leaving a pattern of circular ripples. At that moment, an enormous white bird flew overhead and cawed, as if in approval.

# EPILOGUE

The splendor of an Indian evening added drama to "Le grand exit," as Clara called it. The sky was a tapestry of oranges, reds, and gold. The two women had checked into the Chennai Palace Hotel and reclaimed their suitcases. In their wanderings, they'd replaced their wardrobes with Indian garments. All the jeans, shoes, and jackets that had been in storage at the hotel now looked sad and useless. It seemed like years ago that they'd set out to learn about Dottie's heritage.

"I think I'll give these t-shirts away," Clara said, tossing more garments in the giveaway pile. "And I really don't need these slacks."

Dottie tossed a couple baseball hats on the heap. "It will cost a fortune if we go over our baggage limit, and I do need room for my *salwar kameezes*. Then there are presents for my college buddies. I got a little carried away, but at St. John's, they'll appreciate the incense and weavings, the tapestries and brass artifacts." She held up a statue of the Indian god Hanuman that she'd bought for Sanjay.

Ashok had checked into a separate room and was finalizing their travel arrangements, including a reservation for himself. It would be a surprise for his two friends; he had yet to divulge his plan to resume medical school not in India but in Albuquerque, New Mexico. As far as they knew, he would be their escort for the wedding and then they'd part company, maybe forever.

The next day, they invited bride-to-be Samantha for afternoon tea. Ashok said he'd see them at dinner, as this was a ladies-only event. Clara poured tea. Samantha looked radiant in a blue cotton *salwar kameez*. Marriage seemed to agree with her.

"I'm thrilled that we can be part of the nuptials," Clara said, "but I'm afraid we can't come to all it. I know that Hindu weddings last for days, but we can attend only days one and three."

"Whatever you can manage will be terrific." Samantha appeared to completely understand. "I've traveled back and forth enough to know that you might have to settle some passport business. Travel papers...they make you jump through the hoops."

Tea ended. After a hectic interlude of packing and preparing to return to America, the two adoptees threw themselves into the traditional Hindu celebration. Samantha was overjoyed that they could attend. The wedding of Samantha and Rajeev, as Clara and Dottie would later recall, started with the tinkling of a hundred tiny bells. The sun was going down as they rode in a special wedding guest van to a spacious reception hall. The trip was brief, not far from their Chennai hotel.

They were ushered into a huge open-air pavilion. One woman was on either arm of Ashok. Their party of three was shown to chairs on the bride's side of wedding guests. The bells, tinkling before, grew louder. Colored lights, festooning dozens of surrounding trees, were turned on. Heads turned as Rajeev, the groom, approached via elephant. Several hundred guests, applauded in delight as the decorated beast, with its human passenger atop, lumbered forward.

Just as the groom's entourage approached a raised stage, a spotlight illuminated the seated bride, their friend Samantha. Though she was still a blond with a pixie haircut, she was otherwise transformed. What followed, Clara and Dottie would remember, was a long ceremony with the bride and groom, Samantha and Rajeev, seated on a stage, the Hindu priest speaking and chanting. There was an exchange of marigold leis. Rajeev tenderly placed a lei around Samantha's neck and she, around his. The chanting went on; there was burning of oil and pouring of *ghee*. "I felt hypnotized," Clara would say afterwards. Dottie put her head on Ashok's shoulder, nearly asleep. Clara found herself lulled into a trance.

By midnight, they were back at the hotel. Despite the late hour, the two women repacked their bags, further gearing up for the journey. They would fly from Chennai to New York and on to Albuquerque, and finally to Santa Fe, New Mexico. "I don't remember it being so hard to get here," Clara said. "How did we get everything done?"

"Well," said Dottie, "we didn't do it in the middle of attending a wedding."

"Too much to do before tomorrow," Clara said. The formerly relaxing hotel room was now a scene of chaos. Suitcases out, piles of clothes, travel documents stacked on the corner table. Energized by thoughts of Samantha's wedding celebration, the two women charged through journey preparations.

There was twice as much as they could fit in their suitcases. After discarding, loading and sorting all day, they met with Ashok in the hotel coffee shop. It was 9 p.m., an hour before closing time. They were the only patrons, and their order of tea and *samosas* came quickly. The tan walls and shiny glass table tops lent an air of secrecy. "Here we are at trip and wedding attendance headquarters," Clara said.

"And here we are at the end of our journey and my quest," Dottie added. "I have to admit that I'm not unhappy about how this all turned out. No. I did not find anyone who could have been my birthmother, but I found something better."

"What?" asked Clara and Ashok, speaking at the same time.

"Promise me you won't think I've gone around the bend, that I've lost my marbles."

"Well, we knew you'd lost your marbles a long time ago," Clara said, "but we love you just the same. And actually, we've all sort of gone around the bend. I think that's why we're here." She laughed. "OK, bring it on. What did you find that's better than locating your birthmother?"

"I've had a recurring dream," Dottie said. "At different times in my life, it invades. A nightmare, really. I'm washed up to shore. I'm afraid. I'm all banged up and not even sure if I'll live."

"You've told me about this dream," Clara said. "When we were in your aunt's attic. The dream version of you was five years old, right?"

"You're correct. Five. But it wasn't a version. It was me." Dottie paused. "It was me in another lifetime."

Silence. Ashok and Clara stared at their friend "What do you mean by 'another lifetime'?" Clara asked. "You're saying that you're a reincarnation? You've been reborn into the current Arundhati? That's magical thinking."

Ashok finished swallowing the *samosa* he'd been eating. "It's not magical. It's Hindu. All of us have been here before, and we will return. That's what I was brought up to believe."

Clara looked at her best friend. "You mean that all our searching meant nothing to you? How can you believe that a dream is the same thing as finding your birthmother? Why are you telling this to me now?"

"I've been thinking about this ever since we got separated at the *Kumbha Mela*. You'll think it's weird, but the idea occurred to me after I fell into the Ganges. While I was wandering, trying to reconnect with you, it occurred to me that I belonged to India,

269

as though I'd been baptized, as though I was really in touch with my heritage, who I really am..."

"Ladies," Ashok broke in. "This discussion is getting far too weighty. I see both points of view. Clara is incredulous. Dottie is convinced. Think of me like a big brother who wants you both to be happy. I actually know that I'm a reincarnation, so I can't help but believe Dottie is right. It took your travel, wandering, and searching for her to come to this realization. Let's concentrate on having a beautiful evening and celebrating with Samantha tomorrow.

After what seemed like no sleep at all, the three friends taxied to the wedding pavilion. Trees around the property wore Christmas lights. White lights formed an arch around the grand entrance. The hall was filled with guests, seated at tables of six. Women were elegantly dressed in chiffon *saris*, the men in *salwar kameezes*, a few in western style suits. Clara, Dottie and Ashok arrived just in time for a performance.

A portly emcee was blaring to the crowd in Hindi, occasionally interjecting an English phrase. "What is he saying?" Dottie asked Ashok in a whisper.

"Mainly, it's something like this," Ashok whispered back. "Ladies and gentlemen, children, teenagers and babies, prepare for Bharatanatyam. He's telling us that this folk dance goes back to the seventh century and it started in the Hindu temples of Tamil Nadu."

"And now, the Kolattam Dancers," bellowed the huge announcer. Sitar music, which had been playing softly in the background, swelled. Six barefooted dancers pranced to the center of the hardwood floor. The dancing grew passionate, the music louder. The young women in their turquoise *saris* clacked together pairs of sticks. Each wore a white flower in her jet black hair and all smiled exuberantly. They waved their arms. They became birds.

The performance lasted for half an hour. As the finale drew near, the performers, two by two, wove in and out of an invisible circle. Their movements grew faster, the clacking sticks more frenetic, the music more intense. Finally, the turquoise "birds" fluttered to the floor in a human *mandala*.

Applause thundered from every table. The dancers took several graceful bows and exited. The music switched to DJ-operated disco. "And now, dear guests," boomed the announcer, "it is your turn. After Samantha and Rajeev have started us off, you are all invited to join us on the dance floor. Who can resist?"

The newly married couple, took center stage and danced to Etta James. They swept gracefully around the gleaming hardwood floor and were greeted with applause as the dance ended. After the slow number, the tone switched. Rock music filled the hall. No one could keep their feet from dancing. A handsome young Indian man wearing green and gold asked Clara to join him on the dance floor.

Ashok took Dottie into his arms and hoisted her in the air. "May I have this dance, my born-again, reincarnated lovely one? Before we go out there and shake a leg, I have a surprise for you. I'll be flying back to New Mexico with you and Clara. I'm transferring to the University of New Mexico Medical School."

"And why would you do that?"

"I think you know. To be near you."

# Glossary

**ALU GOBI.** Dish made with potatoes and cauliflower.

**ARAAM KE LIE PADAAV.** Rest stop.

**ARUL KAUNAI DAYA.** I open my awareness to loving kindness and empathy.

**ARUVEDIC.** Traditional Hindu system of medicine that seeks to treat and integrate body, mind, and spirit using a holistic approach.

**ASANA.** A posture adapted in hatha yoga.

**ASHRAM.** A hermitage, monastic community, or other place of religious retreat.

**BABA.** A word used to show respect to an elder.

**BAINGAN BARTHA.** Dish containing mixed grilled eggplant tomato, onion, herbs, and spices.

**BAKLAVA.** A dessert made of phyllo pastry filled with chopped nuts and soaked in honey.

**BAKSHEESH.** Small sum of money given as a tip, bribe, or charitable donation.

**BASHA.** Hut, typically made of bamboo and grass.

**CHAI.** Tea boiled with milk, sugar, and cardamon.

**CHAPATI.** A thin pancake of unleavened wholegrain bread cooked on a griddle.

**CURANDERA.** Spanish term for healer who uses folk remedies.

**DATIJI.** The addition of "ji" to a name denotes respect.

**DHAL.** Indian food made from cooked lentils.

**DHANYAVAD.** Thank You.

**DHARMA.** The principle of righteousness that sustains the universe, regarded as a cosmic law to be in harmony with by right behavior and fulfilling one's duty.

**DHOTI.** Garment worn by male Hindus, consisting of a piece of material tied around the waist and extending to cover most of the legs.

**DHULLA.** Archeological site known for inscriptions regarding the ancient history of India.

**DIVALI.** The Hindu Festival of Lights held in October through November. It marks the beginning of the fiscal year in India.

**DOSA.** Thin pancake made from rice flour, stuffed with vegetables, chicken or other ingredients, served with chutney.

**DUPATTA.** A shawl traditionally worn by women in the Indian subcontinent. The dupatta is used most commonly as part of the women's salwar kameez *(see definition below)* outfit.

**ENSHALLAH.** God willing, if Allah wills it.

**GAITER.** Cloth or leather leg coverings reaching from the instep to above the ankle or to midcalf or knee.

**GAMCHA.** A traditional thin, coarse cotton towel, frequently with a checkered design, used to dry the body after bathing or wiping sweat. It is often worn on one side of the shoulder.

**GANESH.** Elephant-headed Hindu god of beginnings. Traditionally worshiped as a remover of obstacles before undertaking any major enterprise, he is the patron of intellectuals, bankers, scribes, and authors.

**GHEE.** Clarified butter made from the milk of a buffalo or cow.

**GOONDA.** A violent person hired to hurt people or damage property.

**GUPTA.** Relating to a dynasty of Brahmin kings of northern India of the fourth to seventh centuries.

**GURU.** A spiritual teacher, especially one who imparts intuition.

**HINDI.** Official language of northern India, the fourth most widely spoken language in the world.

**HINDU.** Person who believes in the religion called Hinduism.

**ISAKA MOOLY KITANA HAI.** How much does it cost?

**KARMA.** The force produced by a person's actions in one life that influences what happens to them in future lives.

**KHEER.** Milk or sweet rice pudding.

**KUMBH MELA.** A Hindu religious festival celebrated four times each 12-year period, with the sites rotating between four pilgrimage places on four sacred rivers.

**KURTA.** A loose, collarless shirt or tunic worn by both men and women.

**LADDU.** Indian confection, typically made from flour, sugar and shortening, shaped into a ball.

**MAHOOT.** Keeper and driver of an elephant.

**MANDALA.** Symbol of the universe. Most have colorful, geometric patterns or designs.

**MANTRA.** A word or sound repeated to aid in attaining divine communion in meditation.

**MARGAZHI.** In the Tamil region of India, an auspicious month for spiritual growth. (November through December)

**MEMSAB.** Title for a woman of in a position of authority or the wife of a sahib.

**NAAN.** A type of leavened bread, typically teardrop shaped and cooked a clay oven.

**NAMASTE.** A customary, spoken greeting accompanied by placing one's palms together over the heart and slightly bowing the head. It's a respectful greeting that honors the other person or group and means "I bow to you." Sometimes spoken as "namaskar."

**NANDI.** A bull that serves as the mount of Shiva and symbolizes fertility.

**OM** or **AUM.** A sacred sound considered to be the greatest of all mantras, uttered at the beginning and end of Hindu prayers, chants, and meditations. The source of all other sounds, it symbolizes the three aspects of God: Brahma (A), Vishnu (U), and Shiva (M).

**PADDU.** Steamed batter made of black rice and lentils.

**PANEER.** Indian cottage cheese, made from cow or buffalo milk.

**PASHMINA.** A fine wool, similar to cashmere, made from the undercoat of domestic Himalayan sheep; a shawl made from this wool.

**PRANA.** Life force; the subtle energy that sustains the body.

**QUINOA.** Flowering plant in the amaranth family. The seeds are edible and rich in protein.

**RAGA.** In Indian music, a pattern of notes having characteristic intervals and rhythms, used as a basis for improvisation.

**RATHA.** A wooden chariot or carriage with four wheels. The ratha is pulled by horses, bullocks, or elephants and driven manually by rope. Rathas are used mostly by the Hindu temples of southern India for religious festivals.

**ROTI.** Flat, round bread cooked on a griddle.

**RUPEE.** The basic monetary unit of India. Depending on exchange rate, there are about 74 rupees to a dollar.

**SAAG PANEER.** Indian dish consisting of fresh cheese, combined with greens, in a creamy sauce.

**SADHVI.** A term that means "virtuous woman" in Sanskrit. A sadhvi renounces her possessions and focuses on spiritual pursuits away from the world at large.

**SADHU.** A man who has renounced possessions and lives as an ascetic, often wandering from place to place.

**SAHIB.** Polite title or form of address for a man.

**SAL.** A north Indian tree often used for timber.

**SALWAR KAMEEZ.** A pair of loose, pleated trousers (salwar) tapering to a cuff around the ankles, combined with a tunic (kameez).

**SAMADHI.** A state of intense concentration achieved through meditation.

**SAMOSA.** A triangular savory pastry fried in ghee or oil, containing spiced vegetables or meat.

**SARI.** Traditional Indian woman's garment comprising a length of cotton or silk elaborately draped around the body.

**SATSANG.** A spiritual discourse or sacred gathering.

**SAVASANA.** In yoga practice, a meditative posture in which one lies on the back, a pose of total relaxation.

**TANDOORI.** An Indian method of cooking meat or vegetables on a spit in a clay oven.

**TIKKA.** An Indian dishes of small pieces of meat or vegetables marinated in a spice mixture.

**VADA.** Savory fried snacks similar to fritters or dumplings.

**WALLAH.** A person who is associated with a particular work or who performs a specific duty.

**YOGI.** A person who is proficient in yoga.

**SOURCES:**

Collins Hindi to English Dictionary
The Free Dictionary
Merriam-Webster Dictionary
Swarajya Magazine
Rekhta Dictionary
Dictionary.com

# About the Author

Elaine Pinkerton, author and educator, avid hiker and grandmother of three, holds MA degrees in literature from the University of Virginia and from St. John's College in Santa Fe, New Mexico. Writing is her first love, but she's held many other jobs, including ski coach, technical writer, defensive driving instructor, and elementary school librarian.

Her publishing book credits include *Beast of Bengal, All the Wrong Places, The Goodbye Baby: Adoptee Diaries, Santa Fe on Foot,* and *From Calcutta with Love.*

She is also a freelance journalist, with articles published in *Runner's World, Family Circle, New Mexico Magazine,* and *Tumbleweeds Family Magazine.*

Made in the USA
Middletown, DE
04 July 2022

68373752R00166